Advance Praise for
The Sword of David

"*The Sword of David* is a breathtaking thriller. It has the best elements of *The Da Vinci Code* and a modern-day *Raiders of the Lost Ark* but trust me, Charles Lichtman has created a pulse-pounding novel that's entirely his own. I loved following the dramatic adventures of Chaim Klein as he travels the globe and confronts untold dangers in search of the physical Ten Commandments in order to fulfill a biblical promise. Lichtman based *The Sword of David* on his decades of research into the history and facts behind his story and they are just as compelling as the plot and characters. The ending is truly amazing. Read this book!"

—BRAD MELTZER, #1 *New York Times* bestselling author

"Loaded with action, history, secrets, and conspiracies. My kind of story."

—STEVE BERRY, *New York Times* bestselling author
of *The Kaiser's Web*

"*The Sword of David* is thrilling, compelling, and principled. It reminded me of *The Da Vinci Code* and will excite and educate all who read it. Exploring many fascinating destinations around the world, the novel never stops moving—and its stunning conclusion will give you hope about the future of the Middle East and the world."

—SENATOR JOSEPH LIEBERMAN

"*The Sword of David* is sure to keep readers tearing through the pages— and the surprise ending will reward them well. Highly recommended."

—JAMES GRIPPANDO, *New York Times* bestselling author
and Harper Lee Prize winner

"The past and present come together in this spellbinding novel, filled with revelations. A Jewish *Da Vinci Code* with an even better ending."

—ALAN DERSHOWITZ, *New York Times* bestselling author
of *The Case for Israel*

The
SWORD
of
DAVID

The
SWORD
of
DAVID

CHARLES LICHTMAN

BOMBARDIER
BOOKS

A BOMBARDIER BOOKS BOOK
An Imprint of Post Hill Press

The Sword of David
© 2021 by Charles Lichtman
All Rights Reserved

ISBN: 978-1-63758-006-6
ISBN (eBook): 978-1-63758-007-3

Cover design by Cody Corcoran
Interior design and composition by Greg Johnson, Textbook Perfect

Post Hill Press
New York • Nashville
posthillpress.com

Published in the United States of America
1 2 3 4 5 6 7 8 9 10

For Gayle,
my cheerleading best friend, my backbone,
and the love of my life for nearly four decades.
For Brooke and Jordan,
the apples of my eye and the best daughters
a father could ever wish for.

The
SWORD
of
DAVID

PROLOGUE

Jerusalem, September 8, 70 A.D.

The sun came over the Mount of Olives to the east of the Temple Mount, reflecting off the row of gold pillars rising high at the Second Temple's entrance. The High Priest squinted and said to Mordechai, his chief assistant priest, "General John has warned me that all of our people will be massacred by the Romans today—men, women, and children. The Temple, and probably all of Jerusalem, will be destroyed. There is nothing we can do to stop them."

"No, Your Holiness. Jerusalem is God's city. This is God's Temple. God will protect it. He will protect us," Mordechai replied.

The High Priest frowned and said, "Come now, you know better. The Temple can be destroyed, and it can be rebuilt. What we lose today we will regain tomorrow."

In the last month alone, the Romans had starved to death or crucified 55,000 Jews. Now the most powerful army on earth, led by General Titus, was ready to launch its final charge. The priests silently walked through the Temple into the Court of the Priests, and Mordechai slipped on his ceremonial, white linen robe. The High Priest

1

put on his royal blue robe, golden bells hanging from its fringes. He then donned a layered blue and gold headdress and a breastplate with twelve precious stones inscribed with the names of the tribes of Israel.

The men pushed aside a tall, thick curtain and entered the Devir, the Holy of the Holies. The golden-walled room was empty except for the Foundation Stone, upon which sat the Ark of the Holy Covenant. Exactly as described in the Torah, the Ark was a chest constructed of acacia wood and decorated with gold, silver, brass, onyx, linen, ram's hide, and goat's hair. Two-foot-tall gold cherubim angels with outstretched wings adorned each end of its lid.

The High Priest announced, "We must take the Ark to safety." The men picked up the Ark by its rails and carried it to the far wall, where the High Priest pushed a barely perceptible gold button, causing an equally undetectable door to swing open. The men disappeared with the Ark down a flight of steps, the door closing behind them.

At that moment, the Roman army began its final assault. The largest catapults ever built surrounded the Temple Mount and boulders bombarded the platform, crushing anyone in their path. Battering rams smashed the walls near the Royal Portico, wide enough for ten soldiers at a time to run into the complex. The Romans eliminated what resistance there was with little loss, and a steady stream of soldiers, many on horses, charged up the grand staircase.

Perched on top of the wall, Jewish warriors tilted a huge bronze cauldron pouring hundreds of gallons of boiling oil onto the soldiers below. Howls pierced the air as Roman warriors dropped to the ground in agony or ran away screaming, the hot fluid melting their flesh.

Scores of Roman archers fired arrows into the center of the Temple Mount platform, slicing through the flesh of Jewish soldiers awaiting battle. The front line of centurions charged ferociously into combat. At first the Romans appeared to be outnumbered, but as one centurion fell, another took his place. It didn't take long for the Romans to flood the Temple Mount.

The entire platform was a fighting ring with a continuous flow of boulders, arrows, and spears indiscriminately raining down on the combatants. Nonstop death screams accompanied the clash of metal on metal. It was a sword-and-knife, hand-to-hand fight for survival, with every soldier facing the same dilemma: kill or be killed.

With blood splattered across his armor, General John and his best soldiers rushed inside the empty Holy of the Holies to protect the High Priest and the Ark of the Covenant. Inside the Temple, helpless civilians huddled together. The Romans showed no mercy to any man, woman, or child.

Seconds later, a dozen centurions stormed into the Devir. General John barged past his men, swinging his gleaming silver sword at the enemy. To his surprise, the sword began to glow and hum. For an instant, everyone who could see it halted, stunned by the sight. With each slice of the blade, John's sword sounded like a windstorm growing in strength. Holding the sword above his head, the great general yelled, "This is the Sword of King David!" He charged the Romans, dispatching five in seconds, twirling around in a flow of movement. Although outnumbered, his soldiers seemed to find greater strength than they'd ever known, and they quickly massacred the remaining Romans.

General John ran across the Foundation Stone and pushed the button to open the hidden door. He and his men then raced down a narrow stone staircase that led to a tunnel; a golden glow lighting the passageway ahead. They quickly found the High Priest and Mordechai, who were carrying the heavy Ark of the Covenant.

Panic was evident in the High Priest's voice. "There is little time left. We must protect the Ark. It cannot fall to the Romans." He pointed at two soldiers and ordered, "Come! Take the Ark from us."

The High Priest focused on the tunnel wall. He placed each hand on separate stone blocks set at eye level and pushed against them. They slid inwards, and another group of blocks slowly swung outwards. Until that moment, anyone walking by that spot would not have seen a door to a hidden room.

Not far away, a commanding Roman voice exclaimed, "Over that way! The orange light—follow it!" Seconds later, a platoon of Romans charged the Jews. A new battle erupted, filling every inch of space in the narrow tunnel. General John and his men fought with the same strength and speed as they had minutes earlier. One slice of his glowing sword took off two Roman heads.

With the door to the hidden chamber fully open, the High Priest and Mordechai rushed inside. From thirty feet away, through the chaos of the fighting, a Roman threw a spear into the back of one of the Jews carrying the Ark. The Jew struggled to keep his balance while holding the Ark, fighting to stumble into the room. But his injury was too severe and he fell to his knees gasping for air, then collapsed, dead.

Thunder exploded as the Ark tumbled to the ground. Its contents spilled out, including Aaron's rod, the manna pot, a goblet, and two symmetrically shaped stone tablets engraved in Hebrew.

The High Priest and Mordechai pulled the Ark into the room. General John moved the Ark's lid into the chamber. Mordechai grabbed Aaron's staff, the manna pot, and the goblet and slid them across the ground into the chamber. The High Priest pushed against the dislodged stones and the chamber door began closing. Right before the door slammed shut, locking away the High Priest, Mordechai rushed out of the room, screaming, "The Ten Commandments! Get them!"

While fighting, General John and his soldiers scanned the ground for the holy tablets. The general spotted them first, dropping his sword and diving to the ground for them. But a Roman centurion was closer. Not even knowing what they were, he scooped them up and fled with his bounty. Another Roman spotted the unique sword, now losing its glow. He picked it up and followed his comrade. General John jumped to his feet to pursue them but was decapitated from behind. Soon thereafter, the other Jewish soldiers and Mordechai were killed.

At the same time, a Roman soldier placed a torch on the curtained entryway to the Devir, laughing as the flame raced up the fabric and reached the wooden ceiling, which instantly ignited. From there the blaze spread in all directions throughout the Temple, engulfing the entire structure along with its sacred contents and inhabitants.

Outside on the Temple Mount, the battle was winding down. The Jews were all but done; their soldiers could barely fight, tripping over piles of corpses. In places, the blood was two inches deep, a sea of death.

When the few surviving Jews saw their Temple ablaze, it sapped their will to fight. Many ran into the burning structure to die in the flames; others stood erect and closed their eyes, allowing themselves to be struck down. The destruction of all they held dear was overwhelming. Their apocalypse had come.

The Temple was gone. Almost 180,000 Jews died that day at the hands of the Romans. The few that were spared were sent as slaves to Egyptian mines or to Rome to build the Colosseum. Every building in Jerusalem was looted and destroyed.

After the Romans had laid waste to the city, there was no sighting of the Ark of the Covenant or the Ten Commandments. Only one item survived the siege on the Temple Mount. Buried under the rubble of the Temple was the Foundation Stone: a large rock upon which the Ark of the Covenant sat, where Abraham was prepared to sacrifice Isaac, and the place from where Muhammad began his Night Journey.

PART ONE

1

Jerusalem, Present Day

"Excuse me, Ms. Klein, I hate to impose, but may I please have your autograph?" asked a middle-aged woman who was holding out a piece of paper and a pen.

"Ma'am, I'm sorry. People come up to me all the time thinking I'm the woman who saved the president. I know I look like her, but it's not me," replied the younger woman.

"Oh, I'm sorry," the tourist said. "Please forgive me."

"Not a problem," Debra Klein replied. "It happens a lot."

The woman turned and walked away. When she was out of ear-shot, her cousin Chaim Klein turned to Debra and said, "I can't believe you just did that!"

Debra shrugged. "I know it was rude, but you have no idea what I've gone through. After all these years, I still can't go out anywhere without people recognizing me and wanting to talk about it. Why do you think I wear these big sunglasses?"

"Because it's a beautiful, sunny day in Jerusalem?" Klein replied. "And that woman recognized you anyway."

The cousins sat together sharing a meal at an outdoor pizza café in the modern Jewish Quarter of the Old City of Jerusalem. Debra observed that despite the heavy summer crowds, the pinkish-beige Jerusalem Stone sidewalks and the walls of all the buildings were spotlessly clean. Positivity radiated from everyone around them, with people laughing, dining together, couples holding hands, and kids everywhere.

"Seriously, I have no privacy," she said without smiling. "Even worse, on one hand, Congress recognized me as a hero; on the other, I get death threats for 'befriending' a terrorist. It's crazy!"

Fifteen years earlier, Debra had unknowingly made friends in a college class at George Washington University with a young under-cover Islamist terrorist who had slipped into Washington, D.C. His mission, set in place by the infamous Carlos the Jackal, was to kill U.S. President Tate and every dignitary present at a presidential inaugural ball at the Kennedy Center. With seconds to spare, Debra and CIA agent Norman Richards saved the day by preventing poisonous gas from filtering through the building's vents, which would have exterminated all the VIPs. To her dismay, Debra became an instant celebrity, simultaneously praised by most for preventing the catastrophe while being condemned by some for her friendship with the terrorist, even though she didn't know about his terror connections until it was almost too late.

Klein pulled her in for a hug as his stomach twisted into a knot. "Well, the family here is very proud of what you did on that Inauguration Day. Come, let's take a walk," he said as he led Debra away. Twenty-five years ago, when they were both ten, Debra's family had visited Israel from Chicago, their hometown. Debra and Klein instantly became playmates and stayed in touch from that time on. They had grown close, and over the years they agreed they were more like a brother and sister than just cousins. Here they were now, celebrating twenty-five years of being sort-of siblings.

"That's nice of you to say, but to me, it's your grandparents, Uncle Ehud, and the rest of your family who are the heroes. Your stories about them are amazing. Auschwitz, the hospital, the wars, politics. I can't wait to see everyone tonight! What's it been, three years since all of us have gotten together?"

Klein thought with pride about his family. After surviving Auschwitz, his grandparents had made their way as teenagers to the Promised Land, then called Palestine, now called Israel. They met while fighting for their nation's survival in May 1948 and married after knowing each other only a month. Their three children—including Ehud, Klein's father—were part of the first generation of post-World War II Sabras born in Israel.

Klein's father, Ehud, met his future wife, Aliza, at Israel's renowned Hadassah Hospital, where she had nursed Ehud back from near death caused by serious wounds suffered in the 1973 Yom Kippur war. Even though they were quickly smitten with each other, Aliza turned down Ehud's marriage proposal twice before finally accepting—her demurrals intended to show her future husband that despite his dominating personality, they would always be equals. And they were.

As a career soldier, Ehud rose quickly up the ranks of the army, becoming one of the youngest generals in Israel's history. Aliza forged her own path as Director of Nursing at Hadassah Hospital. The couple somehow found time to have four children, including Chaim.

Klein's older brother was a lawyer and member of the Knesset. One older sister was a doctor and the other was a respected activist and journalist. Chaim followed his father's path into the military.

His expression turning serious, Klein said, "My grandfather and every other refugee and Sabra did what they had to after World War II by coming to Israel to make it a nation. We're not unique. You know that everyone here in Israel serves in the military when they turn eighteen. Israel is filled with heroes from all generations who built this country, fighting for it with their blood. Over and over."

"And what about you?" Debra asked. "How many terrorists did you capture or kill when you were in the army? Last night at the dinner party with your army unit, your friend Bennie said you saved a lot of lives and were the bravest of them all, and the rest of your friends agreed."

"Maybe I was just the craziest. But you know I can't talk about that."

"Can't or won't?"

"Both. I've told you that a million times," he said emphatically. Pointing ahead, Klein added, "But how about this view of the Temple Mount? Does it get any better than this?"

The cousins now stood between two buildings on a narrow sidewalk, gazing out at a full vista of the Western Wall Plaza and the Temple Mount. "I come here every day for work. I've seen this view literally thousands of times and I'm still in awe of it," Klein said. "The history of the Temple Mount is remarkable. There is no place like it anywhere in the world. The Second Temple sat exactly where the Dome of the Rock is now and the Wall just underneath it is Judaism's most holy site. According to the Bible, the earth and Adam were created from the Foundation Stone, the big rock that's inside the Dome. It's also where the Ark of the Covenant sat. Christians also revere this place—think about how many events in Jesus's life happened here, especially toward the end of it. And the Dome of the Rock is Islam's third holiest site because Muhammed rode his winged horse Buraq on his Night Flight to heaven from the Foundation Stone. I actually think the Dome rightfully belongs to all three religions since the Foundation Stone sits within it."

"Maybe so, but the Temple Mount is also the center of many of the world's troubles," Debra said.

Klein stayed silent, knowing she was right.

"Since you work inside, can we go onto the Temple Mount and visit the Dome? It's so beautiful," Debra asked. About eighty yards away, the blue-tiled, golden dome shrine glistened, dominating the Jerusalem skyline.

Klein shook his head. "Nope. Impossible. We can only walk around the Temple Mount on Sunday mornings, and since the second intifada, only Muslims are allowed inside the Dome and the Al-Aqsa mosque. But let's go down to the plaza so you can visit the Wall."

A couple of minutes later, when they had reached the security entrance to the Western Wall Plaza, Klein said, "I know you want to see other parts of Jerusalem this trip, and not just the Jewish sites, but you can't go into the West Bank or Gaza. You can go into East Jerusalem and of course the Old City, but I want to make sure you understand its layout so that you can go exploring by yourself and not get lost."

"I actually want to do it myself so I can go at my own pace. I remember it's easy to get around the Muslim Quarter, and I understand it's still really safe, right?"

"Yes. Totally. Same with East Jerusalem, but stay on the commercial streets. The Palestinians who live and work in Jerusalem are nice, good people. Go into their cafés and shops and you'll see they're very hospitable. Especially Baidun, the antiquities dealer on Via Dolorosa. I have a lifelong Palestinian friend, Malik, who lives in the Muslim Quarter too. Great guy. Maybe one day you'll meet him. But remember, if you shop in the market, everything is negotiable. Buying anything there is a game."

As they entered the security checkpoint, the three soldiers on duty warmly greeted Klein as he and Debra entered the security checkpoint. While walking through the metal detector, pointing behind him with his thumb, he said, "That's my cousin Debra. Tell everyone she's trouble and to watch her carefully. You never know what to expect from her."

Debra made a silly face at the soldiers, who laughed.

After she cleared security, the cousins stopped a few feet away at the top of a long flight of steps leading down into the Western Wall

Plaza. A new prayer building had just been completed adjacent to the steps, facing the Wall. Klein draped his left arm around his cousin, as he had done by habit since they had met as children. Pointing straight ahead at the Western Wall with his right arm, Klein said, "Isn't it crazy? That's my office!"

"So how come you won't tell me what you actually do in there?"

"Because I can't. Just like I'm not telling you what I did in the army." He laughed and added, "You never quit, do you?"

"Well, your friends did tell me some amazing stories about you at dinner."

Klein shook his head. "They shouldn't have. I signed pledges to keep secret what I do here, and what I did in the army."

Debra grabbed his big bicep, looked into his warm brown eyes and replied, "No, it's good. Your word should count for something. Your integrity is one of the reasons you're my favorite cousin. It's certainly not your good looks or charm. Anyway, I'll let you redeem yourself, but only if you answer a serious question. In your visits to America and on our phone and FaceTime calls, you've never told me how you got interested in archeology to begin with."

Klein tilted his head and smiled. "On my eighth birthday, my father put me in the car and drove me to this big field out in the middle of nowhere, a place called the Elah Valley. We walked into the middle of the field and he said, 'Chaim, do you know what happened here?' When I said no, he pointed at me and said in the most serious tone you can imagine, 'Three thousand years ago, this is where David slew Goliath.' When he told that story, he said my eyes opened up to the size of plums. We walked around for a while, then he leaned over and picked up a rock. He handed it to me and said, 'This is the rock David used in his slingshot. It's yours now.'" Klein paused and looked away wistfully. "I was hooked on archeology and history from that moment on. You know what? I still have that rock. And to me, it will always be the rock that killed Goliath."

Debra said, "I love that story."

"Okay, so let's go now to the Wall."

More than a thousand people were milling about the plaza, the spiritual and religious focal point for Jews in Jerusalem and worldwide. Debra and Klein took a few minutes to take in everything going on around the Wall.

A family from America who had come to celebrate their son's bar mitzvah at the Wall was posing for family pictures. Theirs was one of about a dozen bar mitzvahs taking place at the Wall this morning. Numerous Christian tourist groups huddled around their tour guides, listening to lectures about the Temple Mount, where Jesus had driven out the moneychangers only days before his arrest and crucifixion by the Romans.

Klein and Debra laughed as a Hasidic rabbi rushed by them with his prayer book under his arm while screaming into his cell phone. Nearby on the steps, a family of six shared a picnic meal. In another direction, a number of Hasidic boys played some kind of handball game against a building adjacent to the Wall. Not far from them were two men sitting on a ledge, playing chess. A steady flow of young Israeli soldiers with assault rifles slung around their shoulders patrolled the plaza in groups, scouring the crowd for unusual activity.

After about ten minutes, Klein asked, "Did you bring a note for the Wall, or do you want to write one now?"

"Oh no, I put a lot of thought into it." Debra retrieved a postcard-sized paper from her purse and flashed it to Klein, showing that it was covered front and back with tiny print. Debra said, "See. God and I have a lot to talk about today."

"You think God has all day to read that? Do you think He even *can* read those tiny scribbles?"

"Yes, as long as *She* wears her glasses, *She'll* be able to read the note."

They laughed, then Klein asked, "So, do you want to go say hello to your friend God?"

"Aren't you coming with me?"

He shook his head. "I'm here every day, and besides, I'm not allowed in the women's prayer section. If I really want to speak with Him...*or Her*, I have a private spot inside the Temple Mount where we have conversations. Now, you He'll be happy to hear from because it's been a while since you were here last. Take as much time as you want. I'll be over by the entrance to the tunnel tours," he said, pointing to double glass doors.

The Western Wall Tunnel was one of the most significant archeological expeditions in Israel, comprising an excavated walkway running under the Western Wall and Temple Mount, just as it had existed 2,000 years earlier. The digging caused widespread Palestinian riots that had led to the first intifada, which began in late 1987 and continued for nearly six years. After that, it was rumored but denied by the Israeli government that further excavations continued underneath where the Second Temple sat. Klein was now part of a small team whose job was to explore every inch of that space with a rubber hammer, chisel, and bucket—and to keep his mouth shut about it.

Debra entered the women's prayer section at the Wall, double-checking that she was dressed respectfully. Wearing an ankle-length white skirt, a long-sleeved white top, and a straw hat, with her brown ponytail dangling down her back, she realized that she was not only dressed appropriately but that she also looked very American.

Debra slowly approached the Wall, focusing on its casket-sized beige stones. Moving with small steps, as she drew nearer, the Wall seemed to magnetically pull her in close. When she was finally face to face with it, she rested her palm lightly on its surface.

Debra folded her note as small as possible, then examined the cracks in the Wall, amazed at the innumerable personal messages to God. She then found a perfect spot to place her note, put it in, and closed her eyes. She rested her forehead against the Wall, took a deep breath, and slowly recited her prayer.

A few minutes later when she finished, her eyes still closed, she took a few measured breaths and started over, this time emphasizing every special request with a "please." Tears streaming out of her eyes, she looked to the heavens and whispered, "Please God, please listen. Please help this world find peace where all people and all races and religions simply accept each other." She closed her eyes again, took a few breaths, and began her prayers a third time. She drifted into a meditative trance as if she were floating away, not opening her eyes until minutes later. What had just happened to her was mystical and wonderful—beyond anything she'd ever experienced or even thought possible. She had just achieved true inner peace while communicating with God.

While turning away from the Wall, Debra noticed an elderly, frail woman in a wheelchair about ten feet away. Tears were pouring down the old woman's face. Debra could feel the woman's pain as if it were her own. She walked up to the woman and knelt before her on one knee, gently taking the woman's hands in hers and looking deep into the old woman's eyes. Debra gave her a gentle, reassuring smile and a compassionate nod.

Neither said a word for over a minute. The old woman then reached over, pulled Debra in close, and hugged her tight while she resumed her crying, her head resting on Debra's shoulder. Debra held on, patting her head and neck, comforting the woman with kind words. When they let go, Debra slowly rose to her feet, bent over, and kissed the woman lightly on the forehead. The woman grabbed and squeezed Debra's hands and through a weak smile said, "God bless you, my child. *Shalom*."

Debra walked back into the center of the plaza, heading toward the entrance to the tunnels where Klein was leaning against a wall, one hand in his pants pocket, the other pressing a cell phone against his ear. From about fifty feet away they saw each other at the same time. Klein saluted her with a sweeping gesture.

Just then, an Israeli soldier hurried by, smashing into Debra. Their eyes locked. She thought it odd that he didn't apologize for almost running her over, especially since he was an Israel Defense Forces

(IDF) soldier. He backed away from her as Debra frowned and said in Hebrew, "You could say *Excuse me*!"

He responded with a contemptuous stare. An instant later, he yelled, "*Allahu Akbar*! God is great!" Before anyone could react, the man reached inside his shirt, pulled out a hand grenade, removed the pin, and threw it into the men's prayer section of the Wall. He again yelled out "Allahu Akbar," sneered at Debra, placed his hand over his heart, pushed down on his shirt pocket and blew himself up.

The two explosions happened within seconds of each other, reverberating off the Wall with such magnitude that the noise echoed throughout the Old City. The disguised terrorist had so much explosive material packed into his vest that his limbs and head were severed, his midsection was ripped open, and body parts were blown everywhere. Hundreds of nails and metal pellets that had been wrapped around his vest became deadly projectiles flying in every direction.

Pandemonium broke out on the Western Wall Plaza. Some people stood still in shock, but most fled the scene, wildly screaming—some in fear, some in pain. Many frantically called out in search of their children, who'd had free rein to play about the plaza.

A number of Hasidim protectively hugged Torahs, carrying them to safety. An older rabbi held a Torah in one arm while bleeding profusely from the chest. He fell to one knee, gasping for air, trying to prevent the sacred scrolls from touching the ground. A teenage boy there to celebrate his bar mitzvah ran up and took the Torah from the rabbi's arms. As he did, the rabbi fell dead to the ground.

Israel was accustomed to terrorist attacks, but it seemed inconceivable that even the most radical of terrorists would go so far as to attack the Wall. Air raid sirens wailed, and within only a couple of minutes, fully armed Israeli soldiers poured into the plaza. Ambulance sirens approaching the Jewish Quarter became louder and louder.

Klein had witnessed the attack from across the plaza. He remained unscathed from the shrapnel that left over eighty wounded or dead, including three people who had been standing near him. Klein sprinted through the chaos to find Debra lying flat on her back. Blood oozed from her neck and chest, in which two nails were deeply lodged.

Debra's bright blue eyes had turned gray, and she stared blankly ahead. Her breathing was erratic and labored. Klein yanked out the two nails and pressed a hand on each wound, trying to stop the bleeding, but to no avail. Her blood seeped through his fingers and he watched helplessly as her white top turned red.

"Debra, hold on! Debra, breathe! Look at me! Stay with me!" Tears welled up in Klein's eyes, and over and over he yelled, "*Breathe!*" He looked up to the skies and cried out, "Please God, save her!"

Debra lightly squeezed Chaim's hand and whispered, "Don't worry, cousin. Everything will be okay." As the color drained from her face, she let go of his hand and closed her eyes, leaving behind a peaceful smile.

2

The next day, his hands deep inside his pants pockets, Chaim Klein trudged across the Western Wall Plaza. His mind was numb and in shock. His feet moved forward on automatic pilot. He kept asking himself, *How can these people act as if nothing happened here yesterday?*

Klein stopped at the very spot of the terrorist attack. He closed his eyes and relived the horror. Two explosions. Death, from the very young to the very old. Body parts and pools of blood everywhere. Screaming, moaning, and sobbing. People running frantically. Sirens. Soldiers. Emergency vehicles. Holding Debra in his arms, helplessly watching her fade away.

He snapped the vision out of his head to see today's reality. The blood was already scrubbed away. The Wall was again filled with Jews praying. Mothers pushed strollers and kids played ball. A tour group was learning biblical history, taking pictures. The Hasidim were on their cell phones, interrupting prayer for business. Today proved that in the wake of a terrorist attack, every Israeli understood that the only thing to do was go right back to their everyday routines. Otherwise, the criminals would achieve their goal of terrorizing Israelis, and the citizens and government of Israel would not allow that.

Klein walked under the arched entrance to the tunnel's public tour, from where he had witnessed the attack. Standing guard was Ori Levin, a former IDF colonel and Shin Bet agent, now head of security for the Western Wall Plaza. Levin's and Klein's fathers were best friends; for forty years they had been colleagues on Israeli security and defense matters exposing terrorist rings and handling counter-terrorism operations in Gaza and the West Bank. At work, Klein called him Ori. On holidays, on weekends, and in the evenings, he was Uncle Ori.

Bald and beefy, Levin was often underestimated by those who didn't know him, given the dopey smile usually glued to his face. In reality, though, no one ever outsmarted Levin, and few could physically get the best of him. Klein tried to scoot past him, but a tree trunk of an arm grabbed Klein's shoulder, locking him in place. Levin read the sadness in Klein's eyes, then pulled him in for a suffocating bear hug. Klein gulped back tears, not wanting to break down in front of his longtime friend. He hugged Levin back, then said, "Please, I need some space, Ori," and he turned away thinking, *Why can't people leave me alone? I don't need anyone's help now any more than I have whenever I've lost anyone else.*

Klein walked past newly inducted male and female Israeli soldiers standing around a model of the Temple Mount, being taught their Jewish history to drive home why they had to fight so hard. They'd learn about the destruction of the Second Temple and later they would climb Masada, where 967 Jews held off the Roman army on top of a mountain for seven years until 73 A.D., before the Jews committed mass suicide—death being preferable to becoming slaves or being slaughtered by the Romans. The new soldiers would also study the Spanish Inquisition, the Russian pogroms, the Holocaust, and the all-out attack from all borders on Israel by its Arab neighbors on May 15, 1948, the day after Israel declared its statehood. Two millennia of persecution against the Jewish people could not be forgotten.

Klein passed through a dark stone hallway that led him to the beginning of the tunnel. Leaning against the massive rectangular stone known as the Master Course was his boss, Dan Beer. Klein assumed that Ori had texted Beer to tell him that he'd come to work, and now he'd receive a lecture. He grimaced, knowing his only choice was to face his mentor and get it over with.

"What are you doing here?" asked Beer, his arms crossed over his chest while staring up at his much taller protégé.

"Last I heard, this is where I work."

"Listen, Chaim, I feel horrible about Debra. You should be home with your family. Take a few days." Beer pointed at the exit.

Klein replied, "No. This is where I need to be."

Beer pointed at the wall. "What is that?"

"The Master Course."

"How big is it?"

"Length, forty-four feet. Height, eleven feet. Width, twelve feet. Weight, five hundred seventy tons." The stats were embedded in Klein's memory, having led countless tunnel tours.

"How long has it been there?" Beer continued.

Klein wondered where he was going with this. "More than two thousand years."

"And how long will it be here?"

"Forever."

"Exactly. Now go home. Whatever you think you have to do here can wait." Beer rested his hand on Klein's shoulder and patted it reassuringly.

After a long silence, Klein turned around and said, "You saw the plaza this morning. It's as if the bombing didn't occur. We move on. It's how we survive. Being here will get me through this mess. I know that Debra would want me to keep working."

Realizing any further discussion was useless, Beer looked at his watch and said with a smirk, "You know you're forty minutes late for work?"

"I'll stay late and make up the time," Klein replied, rolling his eyes.

"Okay, but call me if you need anything."

"Thanks." Klein headed up the tunnel, which shrank to less than a yard wide, its granite walls bathed in orange light. After he passed Warren's Gate, one of the ancient entrances to the Temple Mount, he climbed four steps to an arch marked by an illuminated, etched glass sign that read, "This point is located opposite the Foundation Stone, which is the site of the Holy of the Holies." A young woman prayed inches from the Wall. Inside an alcove, a dozen Hasidim men prayed silently, rocking back and forth in a collective rhythm. This scene near the Foundation Stone takes place every day and night.

Klein stared at the sign, pondering its significance. Despite growing up in Israel, having been a student of Jewish history and working in the Temple Mount, Klein doubted that God even existed. Further, he didn't believe that even if God *did* exist that he'd listen to his prayers. That God allowed all of the world's senseless hatred and killing made no sense. Despite Klein's skepticism, he knew that he had something to say, and he wanted God (if there was a God) to hear him in a quiet, private setting.

To his left was a one-room synagogue. But Klein climbed to the top of a nearby stairway that ended at a metal door with a sign that read: Danger-Electrical." He pulled out a key, unlocked the door, and walked through it a few feet to another metal door. After he punched in a twelve-digit number, it swung open. He picked up an LED lantern off the ground, turned it on, and walked straight ahead until the chamber ended in a left turn, which he followed to a walkway that placed him deep inside the Temple Mount.

Digging inside the Temple Mount was prohibited by an agreement that the Supreme Muslim Council and the Israelis had reached in 1996 after the first intifada. But Israel had secretly disregarded the agreement. Whatever could be uncovered was too important to be ignored. No more than a dozen people in all of Israel knew of the secret excavations directed by the Israel Antiquities Authority and Shin Bet. And only two highly trusted men who had the right military and educational pedigrees worked inside the Temple Mount: Klein and Beer, with Levin as their security chief. Every day they probed the vast 2,000-year-old network of Temple Mount rooms and tunnels that the public never saw, much less knew existed.

Klein stood in a passageway built by Herod. For most of the past 1,400 years, this basketball court-sized space was used by the Muslims as a water cistern, although it had been closed off and unused since the mid-1800s. Klein walked through it until he came upon another recently uncovered long tunnel and staircase that they'd discovered two years earlier. It had been painstaking and slow work to quietly remove tons of small rocks and debris from the tunnel and inch their way forward to the staircase. Klein and Beer concluded that in ancient times the stairway had led up into the Temple—now the Dome of the Rock—and that it had been blocked off by the Muslims for just that reason.

Klein put down the lantern and sat cross-legged on the stone floor, resting his back against the cold stone wall. He stared down the long, pitch-black hall, feeling that this was exactly where he belonged. In the darkness. No sound. No light. No people. He had been here often, only fifty feet or so from the Foundation Stone, but never to pray, only to think or escape. Now he was here to mourn. Klein sat silently for a few minutes before pleading aloud, "Why Debra? How could you let her die? You know what she meant to me!" He pulled his knees to his chest and dropped his head as tears ran down his face. With both anger and grief, he screamed, "Why do you let so many innocent people die? Why are we so hated? Why can't there be peace?" Publicly, Klein always tried to be strong, unwilling to show emotion to other people. But now, in private, he felt the need to let go of all the bottled-up pain. He thought of his grandfather and father, both of whom had seen more than their share of death and who never showed emotion in front of him, regardless of who died or how. He didn't know how they did it, yet here he was right now, just like them. Mourning was to be kept private. And he felt like a fraud to publicly hide the emotions that ate up his insides.

Three years ago, Klein had lost his two closest friends, Shlomo and Micah, men who had been like brothers to him. Lieutenant Klein had commanded the premier IDF special forces Unit 217, frequently called Sayeret Duvdevan—one of Israel's crack anti-terrorist squads— that was sent on yet another raid into the West Bank to kill a would-be Hamas bomber and his handler; a surgical operation like the others that Klein had performed countless times. Klein was *the* pro at slipping into hostile territory, eliminating a threat, and getting everyone out safely. But not that time.

Working in the shadows and darkness of night, Klein's unit surrounded a small house at the end of a quiet street in Jenin. Klein picked the front door lock and silently led eight men through the door. Three terrorists were quickly eliminated, and an explosive vest was recovered. But the moment Klein and another soldier stepped outside, a barrage of AK-47 bullets flew at them from all directions. Klein's man fell instantly. Somehow Klein was untouched, and he ran low through a rocky field next to the house, finally reaching cover. He quickly learned that hidden inside the house were five other Hamas fighters, who captured the other six members of Klein's team.

Hamas' goal was to set up and massacre its nemesis, Sayeret Duvdevan, planting the fake tip about an explosive vest with Mossad as a trap. In the past two years, Klein's unit had stopped seven suicide bomber attacks, assassinated nine key Hamas leaders, and arrested over 200 terrorist accomplices. To Hamas, killing a team of Israel's best commandos was far better than attacking yet another disco. Having surrounded the house and holding six Israeli soldiers hostage, Hamas sent a message to Israel through a respected Palestinian journalist that it would kill the rest of Klein's unit in two hours, unless Israel released fifty-six of Hamas' most dangerous men from prison.

Longstanding Israeli policy mandated that there would be no negotiation with the terrorists. Consistent with Sayeret Duvdevan's motto "Leave no man behind," a rescue mission was quickly planned by IDF specialists in Tel Aviv, to be led by Klein. Nothing was going to stop him from saving his unit, which included Shlomo and Micah.

Two other Duvdevan teams on standby were dropped by helicopter a half mile away from Klein. Using GPS, they quickly navigated on foot to him. Despite the external perimeter of the house being heavily guarded by twenty-five Hamas fighters, plus the five inside, the Israelis still had the upper hand with their superior training and weaponry. The hunters became the hunted. Over the course of an hour, with the benefit of experience, infrared sensors, and night vision goggles, the Israelis methodically killed every one of the Hamas guards outside.

The moment Klein burst through the front door with three others behind him, Shlomo and Micah were murdered. Klein snapped and went on a rampage. Bullets fired right at him miraculously missed. With his Sig Sauer P226 and gymnastic Krav Maga moves, he quickly killed three Hamas guards. The invading Duvdevan soldiers took out the remaining two terrorist fighters in the house. Although the rescue mission had saved five Israelis; Shlomo, Micah, and one other were lost. Klein could never accept that he had failed to save his brothers.

At the time, Klein was already the youngest Duvdevan lieutenant in Israel's history. That night he had done the work of ten men, cementing his hero status and following in the footsteps of his father and grandfather, who had also fought for Israel and were heroes in their own right. But Klein felt that he had failed. His heart had been broken. Just as bad, he had lost his calculated and daring edge. Afterwards, his superiors found a perfect new job for him: working in secret inside the Temple Mount.

Still sitting with his back resting against the wall, Klein blamed himself for not protecting Debra. He should have escorted her at every step. The image of holding his blood-soaked, favorite cousin in his arms was indelibly hardwired in Klein's head. He began to sob, his chest pounding from the pain as he screamed and cursed at a God he didn't believe in, for His apparent willingness to let innocents die.

When he could cry no more, he wiped his tears away with his shirt, turned off his lantern, and sat in the darkness for another hour.

Klein finally turned the lantern back on and stood. To stretch out, he faced the wall and rested his head against the surface, extending his arms sideways. He lowered his arms slowly, letting his fingertips brush against the wall. Something about the stone felt different, so he did it again. This time, he realized that when his arms were evenly out-stretched at shoulder level, there were two equidistant vertical cracks in the stones.

He raised the lantern to eye level and stood directly in front of the crack to his left. It ran vertically straight up from the floor for six feet, then horizontally four feet to his right side, and then back down to the floor. *Was this another tunnel?* He pictured the map of the tunnels that he and Beer had painstakingly drawn and revised many times, trying to figure out what was hidden behind the passage wall. Klein knew two things: whatever was behind the wall had to date back to the time of Herod, and it had been constructed as a subterfuge.

There had to be a door, and if so, where was it and how did it open? Holding the lantern against the wall, he scoured every inch of the surrounding stone blocks, looking for clues. Most of the blocks in this section of the wall were the same size, except for two slightly longer rectangular stones set next to the cutout section at eye level. He tapped on the blocks to see if they were hollow, but they weren't. Scratching his head, he tried to think through the possibilities. "I give up," he finally grunted, placing one hand on each of the two longer stones and pushing them in frustration.

Suddenly the two larger blocks shifted backwards into the wall. As he watched in amazement, the cutout proved to be a stone doorway that slowly began to grind open. Thirty seconds later, the door was fully open. Holding his breath, Klein peeked behind the door, then gasped. "Oh, my God!" he said aloud.

Facing him, sitting erect in a silver chair, was a skeleton clothed in an ankle-length, royal blue robe, with golden bells hanging from its fringes. The magnificent layered blue and gold headdress and the colorful breastplate adorned with twelve precious stones and inscribed with the names of the tribes of Israel confirmed that Klein had come face-to-face with ancient Israel's High Priest.

Klein stared at the skeleton and cautiously inched forward. It seemed surreal and illogical that the corpse was regally sitting up, its robe clean and unwrinkled, untouched by time. Klein crouched down to more intensively study this extraordinary find. He focused on the High Priest's skull and realized that the priest seemed to be looking at something by the opposite wall.

Klein turned slowly turned to look behind him. He fell to his knees in utter shock. Sitting next to the wall was a rectangular, four-foot-long golden box with two winged angels on its lid. Klein could neither move nor cry out. Resting six feet away from him was the Ark of the Covenant.

3

Ramallah, Israel, the West Bank

"You must be so proud of Mahmoud. To not only die a *shahid*—but to do so in such spectacular fashion! Your son will forever be a hero to our people," the Palestinian woman said to Mahmoud's mother, the famous Al-Haqq reporter Suha Kassem, while giving her a long hug in the Kassem family parlor. "If only one of my children could die a martyr."

"Wafa, one day it will happen," Suha replied, squeezing her friend's hands. "Hamas and Al-Aqsa are always looking for good candidates. You'll have your turn."

Four other friends, nodding, circled around Suha.

"How is Amir taking this?" asked another woman. "Your husband was so close to Mahmoud. Didn't Amir want Mahmoud to join his practice after he finished medical school?"

Looking at her husband, Suha crossed her arms over her chest and said, "Amir is a good husband and father, but he's an idealist like his father, Ghassan. Amir doesn't understand that Mahmoud's sacrifice has done more for the Palestinian cause in one day than in his lifetime of treating people at his clinic. And Mahmoud was only twenty-three years old!" As she watched her husband Amir being comforted by his father, she sighed and added, "Amir really loved that boy. He hasn't stopped crying since we received the news."

Since Mahmoud's death, Suha had been playing the role of the strong, proud mother of the martyred son. Suddenly she too had to fight back tears. Even though she had three other sons, including two young twin boys, she had not allowed herself a moment to mourn her oldest son's loss. Mahmoud, her brilliant, charming boy, may have been a hero, but now he was dead.

"And Ghassan?" asked Wafa.

"My father-in-law blames me for this, even though Mahmoud always had a mind of his own." Looking away, Suha added, "I admit it bothers me that my other boys won't have their big brother around. They idolized him."

Across the living room, a group of young men in their late teens surrounded Khaled, Mahmoud's twenty-year-old brother. "Do you realize that your brother sleeps with seventy-two virgins tonight?" asked one of Mahmoud's friends.

"And Khaled has none," added another friend. "If Mahmoud was a good brother, he'd send you at least one virgin down from heaven."

"This is no time for jokes!" Khaled barked. "My brother performed his duty to Allah, dying a shahid for the Palestinian cause, so that one day we will have our own homeland."

"You know that we honor Mahmoud today," the friend replied defensively. "We all wish we could be martyrs."

"I *will* go," Khaled's close friend Eyad Hamoud insisted, his eyes glaring. "I will get my family's revenge. If I kill only one Jew or infidel, my death will be worthwhile."

Eyad's friends understood. When he was seven, Israeli commandos had killed his PLO assassin father in a firefight while resisting arrest. The burning desire for revenge had run through Eyad's veins ever since then. As a child, he pledged to die a martyr for Hamas or Al-Aqsa Martyrs Brigade, the largest faction of the PLO, and he still passionately believed in their cause.

"We must fight the Jews any way we can! Only violence moves them," Eyad declared. "Our people can never have a life while they occupy our land."

Khaled interjected, "Last week my mother was with her Al-Haqq television crew filming a story in Jenin about two high school graduates going to Paris for college on a full scholarship. The Israelis stopped her truck, smashed all the equipment, then left without saying a word."

Eyad added, "The Jews know your mother is Al-Haqq's top correspondent in the West Bank. Her stories reach one hundred million people around the world. She told me that the story she aired about that incident went viral. Perhaps that makes it all worthwhile, but still, I know how that makes you feel." Eyad had eaten countless meals in the Kassem home, and Suha was like a second mother to him.

Another friend looked straight into Khaled's eyes and asked, "So Khaled, will you follow Mahmoud and become a shahid?"

Although he had sworn secrecy to his recruiter, Khaled replied confidently, "Hamas told me that I will get to pick when and how I will die. You know, normally shahid simply go where they're told. I think Hamas will let me do something as special as Mahmoud."

Eyad said, "I've also been speaking with Hamas."

"Who is your contact?" Khaled asked.

Eyad's eyes darted around the room. He quietly answered, "Jamal."

"Mine too! It would be great if we could do this together."

Jamal was a Hamas commander known only by his alias, a first name. His job was to recruit and filter out candidates from a seemingly endless list of volunteers, determining who would pass the rigorous selection process for martyrdom.

Khaled turned to his friends and announced, "When the time is right, Eyad and I will tell Jamal about you." He put his hand into the middle of the group and said, "To dying for Allah and our jihad cause of killing our enemy, the Jews. We shall all be shahid together!"

One hand on top of the other, in unison, they said, "Dying as shahid together!"

Across the room, his eyes bloodshot and drooping, Amir sat with his father, watching his middle son make a pact with his friends to die together as martyrs. He didn't have to hear what they said to know it wasn't good. In a broken voice, he said to his father, "Look at Khaled with his friends. He's only twenty and has such promise—but you can see they are looking for trouble. I've lost control of my family, and Mahmoud's actions discredited your lifetime of work. I'm so sorry." Amir buried his head in his hands.

Ghassan replied, "You've done nothing that needs forgiveness. Both of us had many talks with Mahmoud about the horrors of violence and the potential benefits of peace. Unfortunately, this is how he has reacted to our people's suffering. With the two of us talking of tolerance and peace, while his mother lectured him on how revolutionary violence brings freedom and change, Mahmoud was pulled in two directions. Frankly, history is on Suha's side; the Americans used violence to gain their independence from England, as did the Israelis in 1948. And she is superb at twisting historical facts to make a point."

Amir watched Suha holding court with her friends. His wife looked regal: tall, slender, with flowing black hair. She wore a simple white blouse, a black knee-length skirt, and elegant gray heels. He knew his father was right about how Suha had captured both Mahmoud and Khaled's attention. "I understand your point, Father, but still, Mahmoud dishonored and discredited you."

"No!" Ghassan said. "Mahmoud was recruited by Hamas specifically because of Suha *and* me. It was about *us*. Mahmoud didn't discredit me; Hamas did. Using my grandson to attack the Wall minimized me, and it proved they are willing to kill Jews anywhere. But the peace process with Israel is cyclical, and the flame of this intifada will burn out. My message will be heard again. Remember, most Palestinians and Israelis want peace and for the violence to stop."

"I think it's too late," Amir said sadly. "This last round of violence has already infected the young. Another generation may be lost."

As Ghassan took off his wire-framed glasses to clean them, his twelve-year-old twin grandsons ran up to him. One of the boys, Bashar, said, "Father, grandfather, we want to be heroes like Mahmoud! We also want to be shahid!"

Ghassan and Amir exchanged grim looks and were struck silent.

Ghassan's eyes shifted to the front door as two men entered the house. One wore a print shirt with sunglasses, a full beard, and an AK-47 around his shoulder, complementing his shaved head and muscular physique. The other—slender with dark curly hair and a scruffy beard—wore a black t-shirt and blue jeans. The man walked with a noticeable limp, but it was the patch over his left eye that was his telltale introduction to those in the room. He walked up to Suha and said, "Mrs. Kassem, my name is Jamal. I came to—"

"I know who you are," she interrupted.

He nodded and continued, "On behalf of the Palestinian people, I congratulate your family on the heroism of your brave son, Mahmoud, who died a shahid for Allah. But also, my sympathies for your loss. Death, even when by honor, is never easy."

Amir and Ghassan pushed through the guests toward Jamal. Amir shouted, "You do not represent the Palestinian people! You are not welcome here!" He pointed at the door. "Leave my home!"

The room fell silent. Ignoring Amir's order, Jamal replied, "As-salaam alaykum—may peace be upon you, Mr. Amir and Mr. Ghassan. Please accept my congratulations and condolences. I hope you accept that Mahmoud is truly a hero."

"What I accept is that you killed my son and pervert Allah's words!" Amir yelled. Although he knew a home visit by a Hamas representative was standard Hamas procedure to honor and reward every martyr's family, Amir was angry.

Suha stepped between them. "Jamal, perhaps this is not the time for a visit." The plea in her eyes said more than her words.

"Yes, you are right. I mean no disrespect to anyone, so I'll be quick." He reached into a worn backpack, removed a DVD, and handed it to Suha. "Mahmoud recorded this message to your family, explaining his martyrdom, saying goodbye, and pledging to watch over you from heaven." Glancing at the twins who had crept toward him, he added, "Your brother spoke of you often. He knows one day you will make him proud."

Amir leaped toward Jamal and shoved him hard in the chest. Ghassan grabbed his son and pulled him back. "Amir, stop now or you'll regret it later!" Amir's posture remained tense, but he stepped back and turned around, his chest heaving.

Jamal remained calm and seized the moment. "I came here today only to extend good wishes to your family. One last item and I'll be on my way. Since your family is financially comfortable, Mahmoud asked that the monthly monetary stipend you would normally receive for his sacrifice go to the orphanage in Ramallah, founded long ago by Chairman Arafat. We know you are generous people."

Ghassan stepped forward and replied, "Thank you. Now go back and tell Hamas that attacking the Jews at the Western Wall can only provoke severe retaliation that will result in more and more children becoming orphans." He turned and addressed the room. "Is that what you want? Parents without children? Children without parents? Violence begets violence. Every attack hardens the other side's position. We live within a vicious circle of spilled blood, with no winners." He slowly enunciated each word. "We cannot teach this to our children. They must not grow up in this culture."

Jamal pointed at Ghassan and said coldly, "You have spoken of peace with the Jews for forty years and it has gone nowhere. You have failed! Hamas is closer than you ever were to creating a Palestinian homeland." He turned to the room and added, "You should all think about *that*!"

Jamal made eye contact with Khaled and Eyad, acknowledging them with a smile. Khaled realized that Jamal had planned all along for him and Eyad to be recruited together.

Amir said, "Khaled, you're only twenty. Remember, peace will come from you—your generation. You can choose death and hate or life and peace."

A second later, the front door crashed open. Four Israeli Special Forces soldiers burst into the house: the first diving onto his stomach, the next dropping to one knee, and the other two standing as bookends, their Uzis trained on different spots in the room. Jamal's bodyguard started to raise his AK-47 but was shot in the chest by a riptide of bullets that smashed him backward into a wall. Some women and children screamed, but otherwise no one dared move.

The soldier on his stomach rose and whispered into a microphone clipped to his shirt. Eight more commandos instantly poured into the house through the front and back doors. They spread out, indiscriminately ripping apart and searching every drawer, cabinet, closet, and inch of the home.

The sergeant approached Jamal and declared in Arabic, "Jamal, you are under arrest. You will come with us."

"My name is not Jamal."

"That is true. You are Muhammad al-Salwi from Jenin. You have a wife, three children, and an engineering degree from the University of Cairo. You were in Ramallah yesterday and before that, you were in Hebron. You have a red Nokia phone in your pants pocket and your driver Ibrahim was just arrested one block from here. You recruit homicide bombers for Hamas. Shall I continue?"

Jamal's eyes shot venom at the Israeli, who stared him back down. Jamal replied, "I will not come with you. Look what your people have already done to my eye, my leg. You'll have to drag me out of here by force or kill me."

"Have it your way," replied the sergeant. Another soldier standing behind Jamal put him into a headlock and jammed a needle in his neck. Jamal jolted forward, his eyes rolled back, and he collapsed to the floor.

The sergeant announced, "Jamal is not dead. He is under arrest for causing the deaths of over three hundred forty Israeli citizens. He will be given a lawyer and a trial with full civil rights, which is more than any Arab country gives, and more than he gave his victims." Israel's courts were indeed available to all, even to Arab terrorists.

The sergeant again spoke into his transmitter, and two more Israeli soldiers entered the house, carrying a stretcher. They rolled Jamal over and handcuffed his hands behind his back, shackled his feet, dragged him onto the stretcher, and carried him out of the house. They returned soon after to remove the corpse of Jamal's bodyguard.

Finally, the soldiers concluded their search of the house. One soldier carried out five laptops and a briefcase. Three others struggled with a file cabinet.

"You can't take those computers!" Suha yelled, throwing her arms in the air. "My sons need their laptops for school! One of them is mine. I'm a journalist, and those files are privileged. My husband is a doctor. His computer has patient records on it!"

The sergeant spit back, "Yesterday your terrorist son killed forty-three Israelis and wounded thirty-eight more at our holiest site. Israel has *never* desecrated your shrines. Your reports on Al-Haqq prove you're a terrorist sympathizer. Mrs. Kassem, we should be arresting you as well." He snatched the DVD from her hand and glared at Ghassan. "Kassem, you claim to support peace and oppose violence? Now the world will know you're a fraud!" He grabbed a picture of Ghassan receiving the honorarium for his Nobel Peace Prize nomination and threw it against the wall. Father and son looked at each other, knowing there was nothing they could say in their own defense, even though the Israeli was wrong.

As the soldiers carted away the confiscated property, the sergeant announced in a booming voice, "You have thirty seconds to leave this house. If you stay, we are not responsible for what happens to you."

Amir understood what was happening. He grabbed the sergeant's arm and pleaded, "No please, this is my family home. You can't—"

"Leave now or stay. It doesn't matter to me." The sergeant yanked his arm free and stalked off.

Ghassan and Amir started herding family and friends out the front door, finding three platoons of Israeli soldiers, two M113 field tanks, four armored cavalry trucks, and a bulldozer. Roadblocks had been set up on both ends of the street, guarded by more tanks whose drivers ignored the mob of Palestinians pelting them with rocks and bottles. Once the house was emptied of civilians, two commandos reentered the home, each carrying C-4 plastic explosive devices. They exited a minute later.

The Kassem's family, friends, and neighbors huddled together on the street, crying and screaming hateful names at the Israelis, punctuated with vows of revenge. The soldiers were tensely positioned with weapons drawn, ready to exercise crowd control.

Thunderous blasts erupted, imploding the building. The roof and second floor collapsed with a deafening crash. A thick cloud of white dust and smoke blanketed the air. Just two minutes later, with plumes of smoke and flames still peppering the remains, a bulldozer plowed into the wreckage, crushing it. When the task was completed, the Israelis backed their equipment and soldiers away from the rubble, then moved slowly to the outskirts of Ramallah, facing barrages of rocks, bottles, and sniper fire along the way.

Surrounded by their sobbing neighbors, the Kassem family stared at the smoldering remains of what had been the residential jewel of Ramallah's most prestigious family. The twins were crying, their heads buried in Suha's side. She showed no emotion. Amir fell to his knees. Looking up, he said to his father, "In the name of Allah, what could be worse?"

Ghassan mumbled, "Nothing," as tears streamed down his face.

Glaring at the Israelis, Khaled stood next to Eyad, his chest heaving. But he was not crying. He turned to his friend and in a harsh tone, he said, "We used to have everything. Now we have nothing. The Jews will pay for this. More than they can ever imagine."

4

Jerusalem

Israeli Prime Minister Eli Zamir pointed at the Ark of the Covenant and the eerie remains of the High Priest. "So, Rabbi, do we move them or leave them here?" he asked the Chief Rabbi of Israel, David Schteinhardt.

"We absolutely cannot move the Ark," said the Chief Rabbi. "Its home is on the Temple Mount. It must remain here, as it has for the past two thousand years." Stroking his long white beard, he peered at Zamir through his thick glasses.

Dan Beer blurted out, "Rabbi, I'm sorry to disagree, but the Waqf still controls this space, and we know they come down into this hallway every so often. We can't guarantee the Ark's safety." The Waqf is an Islamic religious organization responsible for the maintenance and especially the security of the Al-Aqsa Mosque and the Dome of the Rock on the Temple Mount.

Ori Levin, turned to his long-time friend Zamir and quickly added, "Eli, we're not even supposed to be down here, much less digging around the Dome of the Rock. The first intifada began because we dug out the tunnels. The second intifada started because your predecessor walked up onto the Temple Mount unannounced— and over twelve hundred people died. If they find out about the Ark and our digging around here, it will ignite another battle. And we would never get the Ark back!"

Schteinhardt crossed his arms and said, "I will meet today with the High Rabbinical Council to determine whether or not we can move the High Priest and the Ark. But at least for now, I assume we have every confidence that Chaim especially will do what's required of him."

"What do you mean *required*? How do I figure into this?" Klein asked.

The Chief Rabbi stared at Klein, surprised by his question. "No one told you about the High Priest's parchment?"

"No," Klein said, drawing out his response. "I don't even know what parchment you're talking about."

Klein looked at Beer for an explanation. Beer said, "I was looking for the right moment to discuss this with you, but everything's been happening so fast—"

Rabbi Schteinhardt interrupted by raising his hands above Klein's head and chanting a blessing. Klein nervously asked, "What does everybody else know that I don't? Am I going to be a sacrifice or something?"

The others burst into laughter. Beer said, "We found a parchment that the High Priest wrote. It stated that he brought the Ark here in 70 A.D. to keep it safe on the day the Romans destroyed the Temple. But there was a battle right outside the door, and although the Ark was pulled to safety, the Ten Commandments disappeared. He thought the Roman soldiers took them. The High Priest also wrote that the Ark could not sit on the Temple Mount *unless* the tablets were inside of it."

"Well, that should take another two thousand years, because finding the Ten Commandments is impossible—not to mention that we don't control either the Foundation Stone or the Temple Mount," Klein said. "Besides, what makes anyone think the tablets still exist after all this time? This all sounds preposterous."

Schteinhardt said, "They exist somewhere. It may take a while, but you'll find them."

Klein glanced at the Ark, then looked up abruptly. "Time out! *I'll* find them?"

"The High Priest's parchment mandates that whoever finds the Ark is responsible for reuniting the tablets with it," replied the Chief Rabbi. "You have set the wheels of history in motion, Chaim. This is now your responsibility. You need to find them."

Klein replied, "Rabbi, I've known you most of my life. You've always had a pretty good sense of humor, especially for a rabbi, but you've outdone yourself this time." Klein was smiling, but when he noticed no one else was, he added, "Honestly, and with due respect, you can't be serious. This is ridiculous."

Prime Minister Zamir replied, "You're right, Chaim. It sounds ridiculous. I can't argue with you about that." Pointing at the Ark, he added, "But then look what you found! Who would believe *this*?"

"Chaim, there's something else you should know about the High Priest's parchment," Rabbi Schteinhardt added. "According to the War Scroll of the Dead Sea Scrolls, finding the Ark makes you the General of the Sons of Light."

Although Klein understood where the conversation was heading, he rolled his eyes and shook his head. Of course he knew that the War Scroll was one of the Dead Sea Scrolls, mostly written before the time of Christ and hidden away for centuries in the Qumran caves near the Dead Sea. Klein had always been dismissive of the War Scroll because it effectively forecast an Armageddon-like final battle between the forces of good and evil. Rabbi Schteinhardt's statement that he was now the War Scroll's General of the Sons of Light struck him as absurd. But Klein decided a more diplomatic approach would be more helpful.

Klein crossed his arms and replied, "I'm just an archeologist. I'm not in the army anymore, and I was only the leader of a Sayeret commando unit. I'm not a general."

Klein read the dismissive expressions on everyone's faces. "It makes no sense that just because I accidentally stumbled upon this room, I must then find the Ten Commandments and engage the Sons of Darkness, whoever they are, in a final battle. Isn't that the gist of the War Scroll?"

"Yes, basically," Schteinhardt replied. "But Chaim, you know who the enemy is. Haven't you been fighting the terrorists for much of your life?"

Klein nodded.

"Chaim, we've been working inside the Temple Mount all this time, hoping that one day we'd find the Ark, right?" Beer asked.

"That's true, but I didn't ever really believe that we would. And neither did you."

"Fair enough, but you did find it. So let me ask you this…do you think the Israelites wandered the desert for forty years, being fed manna by God every day?"

Rather than answer, Klein instead gave his friend an exasperated *Are you serious?* look.

Zamir said, "Look in the Ark."

Klein lifted the lid and peered inside.

"See that small round vase? Do you know what it is?"

"Holy oil used in the Temple?" Klein replied.

"The High Priest's parchment says that's the pot that produced the manna that fed the people in the desert all those years," Beer said.

"See the stick in there?" Levin said. "It looks like a broken tree branch, right? That's Aaron's staff. The Torah says these items were in the Ark with the Ten Commandments, so it's not just the parchment identifying them."

"This is a lot to take in." Klein exhaled deeply and folded his arms.

"Yes, it is, but finding the Ten Commandments and reuniting them with the Ark could change the world," said Rabbi Schteinhardt. "Since Christianity, Islam, and Judaism all revere the Old Testament and the Ten Commandments, perhaps the tablets could bring people together. So listen, Chaim, God will be with you as you travel down this difficult path."

Klein said quietly, "I don't know if I even believe in God."

"But of course you do. More importantly, God obviously believes in you," the Chief Rabbi replied. "In fact, how can you afford not to believe?"

"I don't have the strength," Klein said.

"No, you do! We know you!" Levin retorted in his well-known booming voice. "The parchment says that whoever found the Ark was chosen for his strength. What does that tell you?"

Klein leaned his head back against the wall and closed his eyes. He knew that one way or another, he had no choice. There was no chance he could say no and that would be the end of it. He realized that having made a lifetime commitment to Israel, if his actions could help his country, he would do it. He opened his eyes, exhaled deeply and calmly said, "This all seems incredible to me, but I understand. This is my responsibility. I'll do the best I can, but I have one condition."

"What's that?" Zamir asked.

"I don't want anyone calling me the General of the Sons of Light. That name sounds like it came out of *Star Wars* or some superhero comic book."

The Chief Rabbi threw his arms in the air and exclaimed, "But that's the biblical term! That's God's title for you!"

"I don't care."

"Okay, we'll try," Zamir said. "But no promises."

As Klein shook his head in frustration, Levin cupped the back of his neck and said, "I've known you from the day you were born. You've always been special. A brilliant natural leader, a fierce and fearless warrior. A man who knows right from wrong. You were made to take on this enormous responsibility."

Klein said to Levin, "That's good to hear, because whatever I have to do, you're going to be right next to me." Looking at Beer, he added, "That goes for you too."

Prime Minister Zamir nodded. "Whatever you need, Chaim. You will have the full support and resources of the State of Israel."

Klein responded, "But if I miraculously find the Ten Commandments, you know the Waqf and Palestinians won't want the Ark and the tablets to be reunited. They are extremely protective of the Temple Mount. We've had two intifadas over incidents that occurred here. This would be a highly sensitive and complicated situation with them."

"We'll worry about that when the time comes," Zamir said. "And Chaim, thank you. I know you'll give it your all."

Klein looked away, contemplating the history of his grandparents and entire extended family defending Israel in many wars brought by its many enemies, fighting solely to assure that the country and people he loved could survive and prosper. He nodded repeatedly and firmly said, "Of course I should do this." He realized that he'd been fighting this battle against terrorism for a long time, so finding the Ark and following the War Scroll's message, in a way, renewed his military tour of duty. "This is in my blood, so let's see where it goes." Klein turned back to the Ark and pointed to another artifact. "What's that?"

The room stayed uncomfortably silent until Rabbi Schteinhardt finally said, "We aren't sure. But the High Priest's parchment states that piece will help authenticate for the world who you are and prove the legitimacy of your mission." He reached into the Ark and withdrew a white porcelain cup with a blue Star of David painted on it. Carefully, he handed the ancient object to Klein. Everyone stared at Klein's outstretched hand.

Klein was startled by the cup's weight and he was fascinated by its instant magnetism in his hand.

"We don't know quite what to make of it being there, but we're not in a position to question the High Priest," said the Chief Rabbi. "All we know is that it belonged to a famous rabbi who died before the Temple was destroyed."

5

Mecca, Saudi Arabia

Sitting on their heels with their knees bent, over 800,000 pilgrims attending the Hajj in the Grand Mosque chanted, "*Ashhadu an la ilaha illa Llah, wa ashadu annu Muhammad rasulu Llah.*" I testify that there is no God except for Allah, and I testify that Muhammad is his messenger.

Having finished reciting the *shahada*, the first of five ritual Islamic prayers, the largest religious congregation in the world rose from their carpets. Each person greeted the person on his right, then his left, with "*As-salan alaikum wa rahmutu Llah.*" Peace and the mercy of God be with you.

A special group of fourteen worshipers was honored with seats merely feet from the 1,400-year-old Ka'aba, the irregularly cube-shaped central shrine of Islam. Rising forty-three feet high, the windowless black cube sat in the middle of the enormous Grand Mosque courtyard, its sides ranging from thirty-six feet to forty-two feet. The roof and outer walls of the Ka'aba were covered by a black brocade blanket, the *kiswah*, hand-embroidered with gold thread incorporating the *sh*ahada and verses from the Koran. One of the special worshipers rose to survey the enormous courtyard. He stood out in the crowd with his chiseled frame and towering height. Scanning the crowd, nothing seemed unusual and if it were, he would have noticed. In his line of work, his obsessive-compulsive nature, perceptions, and instincts had kept him alive over the years.

Security escorted the special group to the revered Black Stone, the Islamic symbol for eternity, embedded into the east wall of the Ka'aba. Said to be a meteorite, the Black Stone was set into an oval sterling silver casing that resembled a large silver eye. The Ka'aba and the Black Stone are what lead Muslims to symbolically face Mecca when praying.

Each special guest was allowed to kiss the Black Stone; merely touching it was the greatest of honors. To the commoner observing such special treatment, these appeared to be very important and honorable men. People bowed their heads in respect, not knowing who these fourteen men were.

Having finished their pilgrimage prayers, the special group exited the Grand Mosque through an arched triple gate into the increasingly modern city of Mecca. The entourage turned up the first street and entered a modern skyscraper. Its two-story lobby was like something in Manhattan, with polished green marble floors accented by brushed nickel that trimmed the light birch walls. A stocky male receptionist in an impeccably tailored suit was flanked by three uniformed guards. An elevator brought the group to the thirty-eighth floor penthouse and into another resplendent lobby, marked by an Arabic sign that said Muslim World Foundation.

The men were directed to a room where they changed out of their religious white *ihram* clothing, simple white sheets, back to their street clothes. Fifteen minutes later, given time to deal with emails and phone calls, they were directed into a conference room.

Abdullah Al-Talib, a tall, lanky man in a flowing white *kaffiyah* and matching *gutra*, was waiting for them at the head of the table. His leathery face and long white beard made him look two decades older than his fifty-eight years. The other guests quickly took their seats, designated by place cards. Waiting for each man was also a steaming plate of lamb and rice, with hot tea and a bowl of fruit.

The leader stood and chanted a prayer over their meal. Opening his arms wide, he said, "As Secretary General of the Muslim World Federation and on behalf of the Kingdom of Saudi Arabia, I welcome you to Mecca. We are honored that your distinguished countries and organizations join us today." Recognized were representatives from Iran, Iraq, Syria, Hezbollah, Hamas, and Islamic Jihad—an odd mix given the tensions between Saudi Arabia and Iran.

The Muslim World Foundation was a Saudi governmental entity that had provided hundreds of millions of dollars to terrorist groups worldwide. Since the 1980s, a $70 billion Islamic fundamentalism campaign built at least 1,500 mosques, 200 schools, 202 colleges, and 210 Islamic centers in non-Islamic countries, including the United States. This had created an international feeder system of radical recruits. The Saudis had mounted perhaps the largest and most effective global propaganda campaign in history, paid for by the sale of oil, largely to the West.

Al-Talib moved behind the man who stood out by his massive size and rested his hands on his broad shoulders. "Omar Rafsani needs no introduction. Before the illegal invasion of Iraq by America, Omar was handpicked by Saddam Hussein to be trained in guerilla military warfare by the legendary freedom fighter Carlos the Jackal. We all know that Rafsani served as General of Iraq's Mukhabarat and after Saddam's departure, he migrated former Iraqi army officials into al-Qaeda Iraq. He has personally handled sensitive projects for most of us in this room. Rafsani will direct the project we are here to discuss today."

The world's top intelligence agencies had long considered Omar Rafsani one of the most dangerous men on earth. Fearless and brilliant, he had a wealth of experience in hands-on terrorist strategic planning and execution, personal defense skills, and an encyclopedic knowledge of weapons and explosives. Since the 2003 invasion of Iraq, the United States had a $10 million bounty on the man it had labeled the "Ace of Diamonds."

As Rafsani was about to speak, the Iranian, Qassemi, blurted out, "Rafsani, we know you had a relationship with bin Laden and have one now with ISIS. Saddam and Osama were political enemies and Iraq *never* supported al-Qaeda. Where do you stand?"

"That is a fair question," Rafsani said. "Before Osama went to Afghanistan, he was in Sudan funding terrorist training camps conducted by my mentor, Carlos. I became friendly with Osama and al-Zawahiri, training both Taliban and al-Qaeda recruits. After Saddam was gone, al-Qaeda provided support to the freedom fighters who became al-Qaeda Iraq, and then later, ISIS. I've worked with ISIS since then. Although some of you consider ISIS as contrary to your interests, our anti-Zionist, anti-Western infidel interest is not. And yes, I speak for al-Qaeda. I also thank the Muslim World Foundation for its support."

Rafsani scanned the table to make sure he had everyone's attention. "Going back decades, the infidels have interfered with our affairs, having brought war against us while continuing to support the Zionist state. They have illegally occupied our lands, tried to control our oil, and demeaned our religious beliefs. Praise Allah, despite some of our differences, we have all helped jihad become an international resistance movement. We have learned that every time any of us commits jihad against the infidels, this advances our cause. We shall now commit jihad against them on a scale the world has never before seen. We may not have jets and tanks like the West, but our army of tens of thousands of shahid is more powerful than any expensive machinery. Just one of our men alone can be as dangerous as any jet bomber." Rafsani pounded his fist on the table and yelled, "With your support, by lending us some of your best soldiers, our jihad will be unstoppable."

Hezbollah's Sheik Hassan Nasrallah shouted, "We will fight forever! The Koran at 4:74 to 76 commands, 'Let those fight in the Cause of God who sells the life of this world for the next life. To the one who fights in the Cause of God, whether he is killed or achieves victory, we shall soon give him a great reward. Our Lord! Save us from this land whose people are oppressors.' Praise be Allah!"

"Praised be Allah!" the group responded.

"Rafsani, we are already engaged in Holy War," said Ahmed Qurei of Hamas. "Every single day we fight the struggle."

"Yes, but we all fight separately. Both Hamas and Al-Aqsa are located in Palestine, engaged in the same war, but do you coordinate in battle? No, you compete."

"We have different interests," replied the frowning Al-Aqsa representative.

"No! Your interests are the same! You both wish to drive the Zionists into the sea. Correct?"

The men nodded in concurrence.

"Imagine what could be accomplished if we all moved in the same direction?" Rafsani said.

"So Rafsani, exactly what is the plan? What do you need from us?" asked the representative of Islamic Jihad.

"I'm sorry, but right now I cannot share the details with you," Rafsani answered. "Don't be offended. But I promise you, the plan will bankrupt the United States and Europe, extinguish the Zionist state, and empower Muslims worldwide."

"Omar, at least tell our friends how you come to that conclusion," prodded Al-Talib.

"Of course. We will execute attacks of a magnitude never before attempted. These acts will create worldwide chaos. No infidel country will feel safe. After that, the U.S. will need trillions of new dollars to protect their infrastructure. The United States is already bankrupt with an all-time high deficit and an insufficient tax base to pay for what they call their 'war on terrorism.' Our friends in Saudi Arabia and Iran will then manipulate oil prices. This will create runaway inflation. It will be the financial end of the United States and the European bloc as the world now knows it. By participating here, you will get your revenge on the infidels."

Al-Talib looked around the table. "Please know the Muslim World Foundation has spent significant time with Omar, reviewing his plans to make sure that our goals are attainable. We are proceeding with this project and providing our full financial support to ensure its success. Taking a vote on this matter seems unnecessary. If any of you do not wish to participate, speak up now."

The room remained silent.

"Then we will proceed!" Rafsani said. "I will contact each of you as I need to. In order to protect our plan, you will know only what I think you need to hear."

"One question!" called out the Iranian representative. "How many infidels will you kill?"

Rafsani replied, "Easily hundreds of thousands. Hopefully over a million. Of course, excluding what we do to the Zionists."

"In one day?"

"Of course!"

The room broke out into applause and cheers.

6

The Massawa Channel, Red Sea

Confirming that Klein and Levin were set and ready to go, Dan Beer flicked on the engine to the Nautilus motorized rubber raft, and it lurched forward. They had just been planted in the Red Sea by an Israeli submarine two miles off the coast of Eritrea in the Massawa Channel, on their way to Ethiopia, surrounded by about one hundred tiny islands comprising the Dahlak Archipelago. The rough waters and currents made it difficult to slip into Eritrea, but the starless black night provided a cloak of security. Following a border war with Ethiopia, Eritrea held the patch of land that segregated Ethiopia from the sea, and the Israelis had calculated that the safest and shortest route into the heart of Ethiopia was through Eritrea.

The boat bounced across the heavy chop toward a pinpoint location on a desolate rocky shore. Beer captained Nautilus boats while serving in Israel's elite S-13 navy corps years ago, including clandestine trips into Ethiopia on this same course. Back in 1990, Beer's intelligence helped make possible Operation Solomon, the rescue mission that spirited away 14,325 Ethiopian Jews to Israel in thirty-four C-130s in only thirty-six hours.

Beer moved to the front of the boat, leaving Klein to steer the rudder. Beer noticed that Levin looked miserable. Levin hated boats and deep water and the combination of his sixty-two years and portly body were hardly conducive to the rigors of this ride. Beer knew that Levin would probably be even more irascible than usual.

Beer glanced back at Klein. In contrast to Levin, Klein sat erect with a focused stare, simply squinting ahead, seemingly oblivious to the boat's volatile movements and the hard spray of the sea pelting him.

Their GPS confirmed they were now about 200 yards off the selected landing area, an uninhabited beach. The men changed to night vision goggles to pick out and dodge the many large boulders jutting out of the sea. When the boat was fifty yards from shore, Beer signaled Klein to cut the engine, leaving just enough power to inaudibly push them onto dry ground.

The moment the boat glided softly onto the beach, the men jumped out and pulled the craft up onto the sand. They stripped off their black head-to-toe waterproof gear, stuffed it all into a weighted canvas bag that they zipped shut, and tossed the bag into the boat.

They turned the boat around, Beer flipped on the motor, and they pushed it into the water. When the craft was forty yards out, with the aid of his night vision goggles, Klein emptied five bullets into its side. Even though the beach was desolate, Klein had attached a silencer to his weapon. The procedure worked as well as it had in the practice run yesterday off the Mediterranean coast, and the dark water quickly swallowed the boat.

Given that they'd be traveling through Ethiopia, the men dressed as backpackers, and having not shaved for three days they looked the part. They held American passports with visas and a fortune in Ethiopian birr that they knew was far more likely to get them out of a sticky situation than anything else would. Each man carried a knife and a Glock 18 machine pistol with extra clips. Their iPhones were linked to an Israeli satellite, assuring worldwide secure e-mail and phone communications. If they sent a distress signal, Israeli commandos in the submarine that brought them were on twenty-four-hour standby, ready to pluck them out of whatever predicament they faced.

Beer surveyed the hilly coast that rose only yards off the beach, gradually expanding into a mountainous region. "The path starts at the base of that taller hill over there to the left. Let's go." Beer turned to the grimacing Levin and said with a grin, "Ori, fun boat ride, huh?"

Levin replied, "Yeah, and just wait, when we get back I'm going to use your nose as a ping pong ball, you schmuck." They all laughed.

With the guidance of high-beam flashlights, Klein, as the most experienced hiker, led his colleagues up a steep, rocky path that required cautious movement—one sprained ankle would put everything at risk. Only his staccato warnings of obstacles in the trail broke their silence. After half an hour, they reached a dirt road and Klein pulled a Midland long-range radio from his backpack. He turned it on to a preset frequency. "Rock One, at the top. Repeat, Rock One at the top."

Seconds later a deep voice replied, "Rock Two, a kilometer away. Hold tight."

Within minutes, a vehicle rumbled toward the Israelis hidden in the brush, with the men's flashlight beams pointed into the road. A beat-up black van stopped and a tall, powerfully built African man with a shaved head jumped out and embraced Klein in a full bear hug. "Chaim, look at you! All grown up!" said Ezana Meroe.

"What are you talking about? You just saw me two years ago."

"No, then you were a boy. Now you are a man, and you look just like your father!

With a booming voice, Meroe cried out "Daniel!" and grabbed Beer, practically squeezing the life out of him. He took a step backwards and said in a serious tone, "My brother, you are still my hero!"

Beer reached up and rubbed Meroe's head. "No, Ezana, you are *my* hero!"

The men stood toe to toe laughing. Meroe had been Beer's Ethiopian counterpart during Israel's Operation Solomon. Beer and others had planned the massive escape of 14,325 Ethiopian Jews in thirty-six hours while Meroe did the groundwork, rounding up the refugees and transporting them from Gonder and Lake Tana to Addis Ababa, from which their flights left for Israel.

His arm around Meroe's shoulder, Beer nudged his friend over to Ori Levin. Before Beer could say anything, Meroe extended his hand, his huge grin displaying a gold front tooth. "You must be the *benzonah!*"

Levin looked stoic for a second before forcing a smile. "So, Dan calls me a son of a bitch? He's right and this benzonah wants to get moving—now." Levin climbed into the van, indicating that the others should follow.

"Ori is right," Meroe responded. "We need to drive in the darkness as much as possible to reach Ethiopia. We have only a few hours till daylight, and if we do not speed or draw attention to ourselves, we should hit the border near dawn."

"And then it's about eighty kilometers to Aksum, right?" asked Beer as the van took off.

"You have a good memory, my friend, but remember, much of the road past the Ethiopian border is unpaved, and it is especially treacherous through the Simen Mountains."

"Then slow down there. I don't want to fly off some cliff."

"Yes, of course. Why are you going to Aksum?" asked Meroe. "For another airlift? If so, the government should be receptive now, especially if there is a trade of weapons for Jews, like last time."

"No, Ezana, we're going to the St. Mary of Zion Church," Beer replied.

Meroe asked, "Daniel, why are three former Israeli Special Forces soldiers who all work at the Wall slipping into Ethiopia and planning to visit the monastery that legend says is home to the Ark of the Covenant?"

"Do I really need to spell it out?" Klein said.

"It's going to be a waste of time," Meroe bellowed. "No one has *ever* gotten inside to see their secret."

"Probably right, but we're here, so we're going to take a shot."

The exhausted Israelis needed to take advantage of every opportunity to sleep and were already nodding off.

ABOUT AN HOUR LATER, the chatter between Meroe and Ethiopian border guards woke the Israelis simultaneously, and they didn't need to speak Tigrinya to understand that the conversation was going poorly. Meroe announced, "They not only want a crazy sum of money to let us enter the country now, but they want to hold your passports as well—meaning they'll want as much when you *leave* through here, which is not in our plans."

"How much do they want?" asked Klein.

"Doesn't matter. Just give it to them," directed Levin.

"It does matter," answered Meroe. "They want 400,000 birr."

The Israelis realized that this was not a routine shakedown. They knew through intel that the typical Ethiopian border bribe was 5,000 birr per person.

"Maybe they think we're drug dealers or criminals?" asked Klein.

"No, worse. They believe you're rich Americans," replied Meroe.

Taking direction from their commander who was standing at Meroe's window, four armed guards started moving toward the van. Another four went to pick up rifles leaning against the wall of the one-room checkpoint building thirty feet away. Meanwhile, the conversation between the commander and Meroe was turning more hostile.

Levin blurted out, "Ezana, tell them we'll pay forty thousand. That's double what they should get for all of us, and it's half of what we have."

Meroe softly replied, "We are past that point, Ori. Now we are all under arrest. They are going to search us and take *all* your money.

Then they will let Dan and Chaim through the border to get to Addis Ababa and a bank where you can get the balance wired to you. You'll be held in custody until they return with the money. It'll have to all happen in twenty-four hours—or you're dead."

"I don't respond well to threats," Klein said coldly, staring out the window at the soldiers.

"And besides, what they're suggesting is not even physically possible," Beer added.

"The negotiation is over," answered Meroe, the resignation in his voice evident.

"I know that's what they think. But it's not over for us," Klein replied, matter-of-factly.

The van was surrounded by the soldiers, all menacingly pointing their weapons at them. Klein assessed the situation and said, "There are nine of them, and they are mostly kids. I like our odds. I'll take the five on this side. Dan and Ori, you split up the four on yours." Shielded by the van's tinted windows, Klein pulled out his Glock and slipped it into the front of his pants.

Meroe whispered, "Is this necessary?"

"Unless you can strike a deal in the next few seconds," Klein answered calmly.

At the same time, a guard smacked a window with his machine gun, signaling them to get out of the vehicle. Klein discreetly loosened the knife from his ankle sheath, hiding it in his palm. He saw from their subtle body movements that Beer and Levin were making similar preparations.

"Ready?" said Klein. Upon receiving confirmation, he ordered, "Go! Now!"

Klein opened the door and instantly jammed the knife into the stomach of the guard standing there. As the man screamed and dropped his weapon, Klein ripped the blade upward and yanked it out of the Ethiopian's body. With catlike quickness, Klein leapt sideways, spun around and high-kicked the commander in the throat, knocking him to the ground and leaving him gasping for air. In a continuous movement, Klein threw the knife into the throat of the guard farthest from him. He turned to the next guard, grabbing him firmly by the head with both hands, and in one jerk of his powerful biceps instantly snapped the guard's neck. He spun to his left while pulling his gun from his shirt, landing in front of another soldier, whom he shot point-blank in the chest. Klein dove to the ground, rolled, and landed shots in the foreheads of two other guards. As the fallen commander struggled to move for his weapon, Klein peeled off three shots into his chest.

Simultaneously, both Levin and Beer had jumped out of the other side of the van and opened fire on the four other guards with a barrage of bullets from their automatic Glocks, killing them all before a single defensive shot could be fired. When it was done, they stood together in silence, surveying the slaughter they'd perpetrated in only a few seconds. Klein walked over to the dead guard; Klein's knife was still stuck in the guard's throat. "Sorry, I need this back." He yanked it out, wiped the blood on the soldier's pants, and put the blade away. He announced to the others, "Time to go."

Levin replied, "Right, but we need to decoy this mess so the Ethiopians will think it was rebels or Eritreans." Pointing at two victims, he added, "Let's put them in the back of the van. If they're missing, the military might think they're traitors. We should also take their weapons."

Beer added, "And let's line up these guys along the guardhouse wall so it looks like an execution."

Meroe looked down, kicked the dirt, and growled, "This violence is very bad. *Very bad.* Do what you must, and then let's leave. If we get caught, the torture we will face will be far worse than the death you will wish for."

No one cared to comment. They quickly destroyed the inside of the guardhouse and all electronics. Levin then emptied a machine gun clip into the neatly lined-up bodies propped against the outer wall and picked up a walkie-talkie lying nearby. The van door wasn't even closed before Meroe began speeding away.

What they didn't know was that the tenth man of the border squad had gone into the woods nearby to relieve himself just as the Israelis arrived at the border crossing. Hiding in the brush, the soldier stayed out of sight and witnessed the execution of his compatriots, making mental notes of the entire event and the attackers.

Their van charged up a winding, narrow road into the rugged Simen Mountains. Except for the buzz from monitoring the Ethiopians' walkie-talkie, silence filled the vehicle. Everyone was displeased about the unexpected rough start to their mission. Klein emailed a report to Mossad Chief Dudi Bareket, who responded at once that the submarine rescue team remained positioned in the Red Sea. Klein replied that since they had made it into Ethiopia and there were no witnesses, they would proceed with the mission.

Forty minutes later, the sun peeked out from the night sky. The van had climbed 4,200 feet into the mountains. Levin instructed Meroe to stop in an uninhabited area surrounded by dense trees. The men exited the van and looked down to see a sharp drop down the mountain. Beer grabbed the confiscated guns and tossed them down, watching them bounce until they disappeared. The border guards' corpses were disposed of next, probably never to be found.

Beer said to Meroe, "Make no mistake, Ezana. I take no pleasure in killing. But these things happen. During Solomon, if I had to do something like what we had to do today—to save the mission, or myself, or thousands of lives—I would have also done it then. There is always a bigger picture to consider."

"What's done is done," Klein added. "The good news is that we escaped without injury and without threat to the mission. Let's move on."

7

Aksum, Ethiopia

Only Klein fell back asleep. Beer and Levin closed their eyes trying to nod off but never did, silently fretting about their unfortunate deadly encounter at the border. Meroe made excellent time driving, reaching the outskirts of Aksum over an hour earlier than expected. He pulled onto a side road outside the small, impoverished city, which stuffed 65,000 people into only about seven square miles. At 9:00 a.m. he navigated to their destination, St. Mary of Zion Church.

The Israelis and Meroe stared at Ethiopia's most renowned Christian Orthodox Church, as a teenage boy passed them pushing along his herd of goats. The church was a small and simple one-story tan building with a short courtyard walkway lined with tall weeds and grass. The façade's cross-shaped white window frames were filled in with blue wrought iron windows, and a red curtain covered the front door. Early sunlight was lighting up the church.

"This is it?" Klein said, frowning with incredulity. "Are you sure?"

"What did you expect, the Vatican?" said Beer. "We're in Ethiopia."

Klein nodded. "If this chapel houses the Ark of the Covenant, then yes, I thought it would look more impressive than this." Despite 2,800 years of consistent historical reports that the Ark of the Covenant had been moved to Ethiopia by Menelik, son of King Solomon and the Queen of Sheba, Klein was having a difficult time accepting that story as true. After all, he had found the Ark in Jerusalem. Nonetheless, this seemed like the best place to start his search for the Ten Commandments.

As he studied the building, it struck Klein as odd that St. Mary's had no security given the large number of people who unsuccessfully visit the church in an attempt to see the Ark. He also knew that the Nazis had showed up here during World War II seeking the Ark and left empty-handed, and they weren't the kind of people who just took no for an answer. Klein remembered how that Nazi story had given rise to the movie *Raiders of the Lost Ark*.

Women were prohibited from entering the chapel, but its courtyard was filled with about two dozen female parishioners who were all covered from head to toe in white, sheet-like robes and huddled in prayer. Two old beggars, dressed in rags, sat on the pavement outside the gate, animatedly talking with each other. Just up the road, a small group of young boys played street soccer while three dogs yelped wildly and ran with them.

Beer finally broke the group's uncomfortable silence, "Who knows? Maybe the Ten Commandments are here. For a very long time the St. Mary's priests have acted like they're holding something important."

Meroe insisted, "Chaim's story about finding the Ark on the Temple Mount is interesting, but the real Ark is in there."

"Then I look forward to the priests proving it," replied Klein, as the men headed up the walkway. Everyone was still dressed in their hiking clothes with their weapons hidden away, as they would never leave them behind, no matter where they were going.

Meroe shook his head. "Chaim, as I told you, nobody gets in to see the Ark."

Klein shrugged. "I'll be the exception."

Just as they reached the front of the chapel, the red curtain opened. Standing there with unfriendly stares were two ancient, rail-thin monks with white, foot-long sculpted beards, clothed in long black robes, and white, turban-like hats.

Klein bowed slightly to show respect, then spoke in Hebrew, with Meroe translating, "My name is Chaim Klein. I am a representative of the State of Israel and—"

"No, you cannot see the Ark," one of the monks said sternly. "Goodbye."

"May I at least please speak to the Atang?" pleaded Klein, referring to the priest vested with responsibility as the Keeper of the Ark. "It is critical."

"It always is," replied the monk as he started to close the door.

Klein stepped into the doorway and handed the monk an envelope. "The Atang will want to see this! I promise you."

The monk opened the envelope and pulled out some pictures; the two monks studied each photo. The monk looked curiously at Klein and said, "Wait here."

Five minutes later, a diminutive, very skinny man who looked to be in his nineties opened the door, clutching a nine-inch, solid gold cross inlaid with colored gemstones. He wore a floor-length burgundy satin robe embroidered with tiny crosses and doves and with a white and gold collar, along with a tall, multi-colored headpiece. The priest sized up the Israelis and Meroe and his friendly smile put them at ease. "I am Abba Mekonen, the Atang, the Keeper of the Ark of the Covenant. I have seen your photographs. Why are you here?"

"My name is Chaim Klein. I am an Israeli archeologist, and I found the Ark behind a wall in the Temple Mount. Those pictures are proof." He stuck out his hand to show good manners, but Abba Mekonen ignored the gesture.

"Your pictures are interesting, but not proof. I have the Ark. *I am the Keeper.*"

"Very respectfully, sir, the pictures show me with the Ark and the High Priest! The Ark is in Jerusalem," he said firmly.

"Really? Anyone can fabricate a photograph," said the Atang. "We keep the original Ark of the Covenant that came from Solomon's Temple safe here. Even if you are telling me the truth, and you did find *an* Ark in the walls of the Temple Mount, you must realize it had to have been constructed after Menelik brought ours to Ethiopia."

Klein turned to Beer and Levin and raised his eyebrows.

Reading Klein's expression, the Atang declared, "It seems to me that you never seriously considered that we have the original Ark."

"I wouldn't know, because you haven't shown it to me," Klein replied.

The Atang stared hard at Klein for a few seconds, then calmly replied, "So just tell me: why are you really here?"

"Because a scroll written by the High Priest instructed that I must find the Ten Commandments and restore them to the Ark."

Mekonen replied firmly, "I know what I protect. Many have come before you, and many will follow. You won't see the Ark." He started to close the door and at the last second, Klein wedged his foot inside it and pulled out a bubble-wrapped package from his backpack. "Wait! One more moment!" Mekonen opened the door a few inches and the monks watched with curiosity while Klein undid the wrapping. Klein held out a small, ancient white ceramic goblet with a faded blue Star of David painted across the middle. "Does this mean anything to you?"

The Atang's eyes opened wide and locked onto the porcelain cup. Stunned, he said, "It has been passed down through countless generations of Atangs that one day a man would appear here with this cup, and that would validate his right to see the Ark. Please come in."

Once Klein and his group entered the chapel, the beggars who had been watching from a distance took note of what happened, then scattered up the street.

The Israelis and Meroe took seats at a rickety wooden table in a back room, and the now-friendly monks served their visitors fruit and juice. The Atang stared first at Klein, then the chalice. "Mr. Klein, we are constantly visited by journalists, archeologists, governments, even men of God from all religions. Everyone has a reason to see the Ark. We've never let anyone in, but now I have a responsibility to do as you ask."

"Thank you. Obviously, I need to see the Ark." Klein pointed at the goblet and added, "What do you mean by responsibility? And how did you know what this is?"

Through a smile showing crooked yellow teeth, Abba Mekonen replied, "An interesting point you make. When you visit the Ark, you will know the importance of this cup."

"Can you take us to it now?"

"The other men cannot see the Ark. It is only for your eyes."

"But you just said you're supposed to do as I ask."

"I will do what I can to assist you and your friends. They can accompany us to the sanctuary, but only you can set eyes upon the Ark."

The Atang shuffled across the room with a younger monk, who was introduced as Brother Hepartie. Together they escorted Klein and his group down a long, rickety staircase. When they reached the bottom, Mekonen retrieved cloth and straw torches from a bin, handing one to each man. "Soak them in there," he instructed, pointing at a metal drum filled with kerosene. The young monk then lit each man's torch from his own.

"You could easily get lost down here and never find your way out, so don't wander away," said Mekonen. A few minutes later, while walking down a twisting, gravelly path, Klein tripped and fell to one knee. He yelled, freezing everyone mid-step. Propped against the wall was a skeleton covered by a dusty Nazi uniform with a red and black swastika armband, wearing a storm trooper's helmet. Klein glared at the corpse, which still reeked of evil.

The Atang said, "I still remember the day in 1944 when this Nazi soldier and a dozen others showed up, demanding the Ark. I was fourteen and just arrived here to start my training as a monk. They threatened the Atang's life if he didn't lead them to the Ark, so he told them it was downstairs, and they were welcome to go look for it. They stampeded down the steps. None came back—probably because these tunnels are seemingly endless. There is also some quicksand and many unexpected drops of fifty feet or more. The next day, another truck arrived wanting to know where the other soldiers were, and again, demanding the Ark. The Atang sent them down here—and they met the same fate. The third day, the Nazis returned and picked up their trucks, and we never saw them again. This corpse is the only one we ever found."

Another ten minutes and many turns later, they stood before a cave. The Atang and Brother Hepartie pulled open a thick royal blue velvet curtain and the Keeper said, "Please Mr. Klein, enter the Holy of the Holies. Your friends must wait here."

Mekonen lit torches on both sides of the entrance, illuminating a narrow, oval-shaped cave about forty feet long. Klein was stunned to see the Ark of the Covenant sitting on a platform, identical to the Ark he had found in Jerusalem. Balanced on each end of the Ark's lid sat two golden cherubim that emitted a glowing white light, while sparks continuously flashed between the winged angels. Even more remarkably to Klein, the room was filled with a gentle low-pitched hum, emanating from the Ark.

Klein knew now that he was unmistakably in the presence of some kind of spiritual force, but he couldn't grasp exactly what it was except that the Ark was clearly more than a mere historical artifact. He approached the Ark cautiously, unsure of what to do. He finally spoke. "Abba Mekonen, there are two Arks. I don't understand. The Ark I found in Jerusalem looks exactly like this Ark."

"Did your Ark give off that light and sing to you as this one does?"
Klein shook his head.

"Chaim, the Book of Exodus describes exactly how to build an Ark. There could be five Arks. Who knows? God is everywhere, yet he shows himself only where he chooses to do so, which, as you can see, is here. Perhaps one day, the Ark in Jerusalem will come to life as well."

"How would that happen?"

"Perhaps upon your finding the Ten Commandments. Of course, my predecessors also taught me about the War Scroll and the battle you will face against the Sons of Darkness."

"How could you possibly know that? I just found the Ark not long ago and there are not even ten people in Israel who know about it."

"I have always understood you could someday come."

"What do you mean by that? What will I find here?"

"Knowledge. What could be more important than knowledge?" Abba Mekonen rested a reassuring hand on Klein's shoulder. "Look around. My predecessor Atang said that roughly five hundred years ago European knights came and decorated this cave for the Ark. Those men told the Atang about the porcelain cup and the War Scroll, and they proclaimed that one day a great warrior would arrive here and that only he should be allowed to see the Ark. We were told to protect the Ark at all costs, and that this powerful man would lead a battle against those who do evil. Since then, this instruction has been passed down from one Atang to the next. Now you are here, and in this chapel are the answers you seek."

Klein looked at the walls around him. Although the chapel was constructed around a small, enclosed cave, it was impressively decorated with a series of statues and other art. To the right of the Ark stood an eight-foot-tall marble sculpture of Moses holding the Ten Commandments in his left arm, with his right arm fully extended, holding a staff in his clenched fist. The Hebrew-engraved base read, "Who am I that I should go to Pharaoh and lead the Israelites out of Egypt?" Klein recognized the quote from a reluctant Moses to God, questioning his role as the Israelites' leader, having five times refused God's mission before finally accepting it. The message felt personal to Klein.

The statue to the left of the Ark caught his attention next: King David held a sling in one hand and a rock in the other, with a long sword resting at his feet. Klein turned in a circle, taking in the rest of the glorious room, his eyes bouncing from the Ark to the various statues and to the back wall with two painted pictures. He glanced at the Atang and Brother Hepartie, who were now sitting cross-legged on the deep blue rug that covered most of the rock floor.

Klein walked to the back of the chapel, where he was drawn to a white marble statue of Jesus. He stared at its right hand holding a cup, then he focused on a white cup stitched into the center of the blue rug, next to where the priests were sitting. His eyes darted back and forth between the statue of Jesus and the rug. Klein pulled the porcelain cup out of his backpack and studied it next to the cup on the statue. "This cup, the statue, the rug! They all bear the Star of David—all three cups are the same, even the color!"

Abba Mekonen grinned broadly. "Now you understand! Your possession of the cup, which I have seen a thousand times in this room, validated your singular right to see this chapel. Did you also notice that the sword at the base of King David and the sword that the soldier on the horse statue is holding are identical?"

Klein shook his head, then walked back and forth between the two statues, comparing the weapons before returning to Abba Mekonen. Klein said, "I don't understand. The soldier on the horse is England's King Richard the Lionheart." Klein had been to London twice before and remembered the statue well—it sat right outside Parliament. Here was a smaller version of the identical statue.

"I know of King Richard. That statue was brought here only about one hundred years ago by a man claiming to be a knight. His foreknowledge and description of this chapel convinced the Atang that he was part of the original group that had built the chapel long ago. The knight said this statue was a new gift, and that it related to the statue of Jesus with the cup."

"There is a much larger version of this same statue in London at Westminster Abbey. Why on earth would it also be here? Maybe I should visit there...."

"That is for you to figure out."

Klein took cell-phone pictures of all the sculptures, frescoes, and paintings in the chapel—including a mural on the ceiling centered above the white cup on the rug—excepting the Ark, which Abba Mekonen prohibited.

Klein then sat on the rug with the priests and stared transfixed on the Ark for five minutes. He walked up to it, slowly put his hand on its lid, dropped his head, and prayed. Then he slowly turned to the Atang and asked, "The Ten Commandments were never here, were they?"

"No, but perhaps now you are equipped to find them."

"We'll see. I *think* I have what I need."

They left the chapel to find Klein's crew and an older monk anxiously waiting for them. "Abba, three truckloads of soldiers are upstairs in the chapel, demanding that we turn over these men. They say they killed patrol guards at the border."

"We did. It was necessary to protect ourselves," Klein said unapologetically.

Abba Mekonen replied, "Mr. Klein, there are evil people in this world. You will fight to protect the rest of us. Many will die and some will be innocent, but in the end, many more will be saved. In your journey, you will do what you must, regardless of your methods. You have been chosen by God for a wondrous future, and much responsibility lies in your hands."

Turning to the older monk, the Atang said, "Brother, walk slowly back upstairs, then allow the soldiers to come down here to try to find these men." He turned back to Klein, raised his eyebrows and grinned.

Unable to hold back, Levin said, "Chaim, did you get the tablets?"

"No, but the Ark was there, along with clues on how to find the tablets."

Stunned, Beer asked, "*The Ark was there?*"

Abba Mekonen replied, "The Ark has always been here. Hasn't it, Mr. Klein?"

"It would seem so," Klein replied, nodding to his team.

"Did you find anything else?" Beer asked.

"Yes, Dan. Knowledge. What could be more important than knowledge?" Klein looked over at the Atang, raised his eyebrows, and smiled.

Beer and Levin returned a blank stare. "I have some ideas about where else we might be headed," Klein added.

The Atang said, "Now Mr. Klein, you and your friends must leave, as it seems you cannot go back upstairs. There is a path—two right turns from here—that will take you into the mountains two kilometers away. I am confident that you will find your way. Go now! God be with you."

Abba Hepartie passed out fresh torches to Klein's men.

Klein gently reached out for Abba Mekonen's small hand, bending down to look the Atang squarely in the eyes. "Abba Mekonen, I've known you for only two hours, but I'll never forget you. I will see this through to the end. Thank you for your help, kindness, and wisdom."

The Keeper smiled faintly. "I should thank you. I was never sure that the glorious prophecy that has been part of this church for hundreds of years was real, and yet it is, and I am now part of it." The cave echoed with the sound of men screaming for help until there was silence. He shrugged and said, "Quicksand."

Klein and his group turned and disappeared into the darkness of the underground.

Forty-five minutes later, Klein's group emerged out of a mountainside crevice. Under cover of night, they stole a small, windowless, beat-up car, which ran out of gas five miles before reaching the Eritrean border. They hiked an off-road path into and through Eritrea, avoiding all human contact.

The following night, they stole a truck, which deposited them on the road near the beach where they initially landed. When they made it to the sand, two black rubber Nautilus rafts belonging to Shayetet 13, the Israeli Navy's Special Forces, were waiting in the shadows. The rafts whisked them away to the safety of the submarine sitting in the Red Sea, then back to Israel. Once Klein was on board, having eaten and cleaned up, he lay down on a bunk. He pulled out his phone and studied the many photos he took in the cave, trying to piece together what had to be clues meant only for him. He didn't even know where to start. *This whole thing is crazy,* he thought. He then started to doubt whether he was actually in the presence of God. *There had to be some bizarre underground electrical force causing the sparks and the hum to emit from the Ark.*

There sure was no Burning Bush telling him what to do, though he was sure he wasn't Moses. Finally, he muttered softly to himself, "I'm clueless. All I know is the statue of King Richard in London. Fuck it. That's it. London." He closed his eyes and was out within seconds.

8

Ramallah, Israel

Mahmoud Kassem's suicide attack had drawn unparalleled worldwide attention because it occurred at the Wall. After that, it wasn't Israel's arrest of 165 militants or the air strike assassination of a Hamas bomb maker that received worldwide news coverage, but rather, the bulldozing of the Kassem family home, displacing the martyr's mother Suha, a prominent Al-Haqq newscaster, and Mahmoud's grandfather Ghassan, the legendary moderate Palestinian peacemaker.

Muslims around the world supported the Kassem family by providing clothes, food, household goods, furniture, and construction materials. Now, six months later, they were living in a newly constructed home on the site of the old one.

"You have humiliated our family in front of all of Palestine!" Khaled Kassem shouted at his parents and grandfather, his arms flailing. He collapsed onto a kitchen chair and yelled, "Now what do I do?"

Amir took a deep breath, then sternly replied, "Go back to school where you belong." Amir turned to his wife and pleaded, "I could use your support, Suha."

"Seriously? You left school to find yourself. Why should Khaled be different?" She exhaled hard, crossed her arms over her chest, and shook her head.

Pounding his fist on the table, Amir exploded, "I went on an archaeological dig to the pyramids and received college credit! You can't possibly think that is the same as Khaled going off to die with Hamas? In Allah's name, what are you thinking?"

Suha glared back at her husband. "Neither of us knows that's what he wants." She turned to Khaled. "Is that what you're thinking? To be a shahid?"

"Absolutely not."

"See, I told you so," Suha said.

"I know you're lying, Khaled," Amir replied. "Jamal came to our house to recruit you, not to express condolences for Mahmoud."

"Was that necessary?" Suha glared at her husband. "Khaled has *never* given you reason to distrust him."

Amir muttered, "Unbelievable." He looked back at Khaled. "So, you told us we've embarrassed you because our house was rebuilt? *We're* humiliated? I can't wait to hear how."

Khaled was tired of the lectures he'd received from his grandfather and father about peace and civility with the Israelis leading to a better life for the Palestinian people. He was also

suspicious of his mother, who had not once since Mahmoud's death spoken to him about how proud she was of his brother for dying a shahid. Khaled thought that made no sense. After all, for most of his life, his mother had taught him about Western oppression against Islam and using extreme measures to fight back, and now she stays silent? He said to his father, "After the Zionists bulldozed our home, we should have left it as rubble and gone to live with Uncle

Abu in Gaza. That's what *all* Palestinians do when the enemy destroys their homes. They go live with relatives."

"You really think the answer is to have eleven people living in a two-bedroom house built for four?" Amir shouted, with Ghassan nodding in agreement. "What's wrong with you? You should be grateful to have a place to live. You should be proud of this family!"

"I'm proud of Mahmoud," Khaled replied. "That's who I'm proud of. No one else. Mahmoud made the Jews suffer. They have made our people suffer forever. There cannot be peace with those animals. There can only be revenge for what they have done to us."

Mortified by the special treatment his prominent family had received, Khaled stared coldly at Amir and said, "I'm old enough now that I don't need your permission to do what I want with my life. You can't stop me."

Amir sank in his chair. "Khaled, I cannot lose another son. I love you, and I've always believed you have greatness within. Even if your politics and views on Israel are different from mine and your grandfather's, you can use your voice to lead those who will listen. Please, you don't have to die wearing a suicide belt."

Suha looked at Khaled and added, "I admit that it was easier to report about and support shahid until it was my own son who became a martyr. I question what Mahmoud's violence achieved. I don't know that Allah intended that jihad should destroy families. But Khaled, I know you've always made good decisions, while your brother was simply drawn to destroying the Israelis."

Khaled stared blankly at his mother, stunned at her pronouncement, then turned away.

Ghassan peered at his grandson through his black horn-rimmed glasses. When he really wanted to be heard, he spoke in little more than a whisper, as he did now. "We are going through a crisis, Khaled. We need leaders to help our people get good jobs, put food on our tables, and place modern textbooks in our schools. How do we change despair to hope? How do we improve our standing in the world community? Wouldn't you rather be remembered for helping *all* of our people instead of being forgotten a month after dying as a martyr? Anyone can choose to die. Can you choose to live?"

Khaled shouted, "Allah commands that we kill our enemies, the non-believers. It's the law of Islam."

"No, that is *not* a law of Islam. That is an interpretation that most imams disagree with," replied Ghassan. "Do you agree with what the Koran says? 'The righteous shall surely dwell in bliss' on Judgment Day."

"Yes," Khaled replied begrudgingly.

"Which do you think Allah would approve more: killing twenty Jews and yourself or helping our people?"

Khaled simply shrugged.

"And what is the root word of both Islam and Muslim?"

Khaled said softly, "*Salaam.*"

"And what does salaam mean?"

"Peace," Khaled said, his voice falling off. He didn't want to argue with his grandfather, but he'd heard this salaam speech at least fifty times.

At that moment, the front door opened and Eyad's voice could be heard as he entered the house. "Khaled! You ready?"

"I'm in the kitchen."

Eyad walked in and executed a four-part hand grasp with Khaled. He acknowledged the others, reached around Amir for a falafel, and shoved the whole thing in his mouth. He mumbled through a mouthful, "Family meeting? Need an opinion?"

There was an awkward silence before Amir answered, "No."

Eyad grabbed another falafel and said, "Got it."

Khaled rose from the table. "We're going out for a while."

"Where to?" asked Amir.

"Big football game."

"Okay, have fun," Suha replied.

As the door closed behind them, Amir said, "They are not going to play football."

"Why do you say that?" Suha asked.

"First, because they were not wearing sneakers. Second, it's midday. Third, they never play now, because of the heat. Did you see them take water?"

Suha looked away. "No."

Amir pointed at his wife. "Losing one son wasn't enough? You know he's always listened to you, not to me. You just had a chance to tell him what you've told me the past few weeks—that you hope he stays in school and doesn't become a jihadist, or worse, a shahid. Suha, I pray in the name of Allah that your choice of words doesn't come back to haunt us all."

Suha stayed silent, realizing that her husband was right.

TEN MINUTES LATER, Khaled and Eyad stood in front of a grocery store a few blocks away. Just as Khaled checked his watch, a small transport truck with its side and back windows covered in gray canvas pulled up and stopped. The driver, hidden behind dark sunglasses and a black cap, instructed, "Climb in the back."

Without showing themselves, two men stuck their arms from the back of the truck to pull them in. The boys were thoroughly searched while seated on a wooden bench that ran the length of the truck. They then drove in suffocating heat and near darkness for about forty minutes. When the vehicle stopped, Khaled and Eyad were blindfolded, escorted out, and led into a building. Soon they heard footsteps entering the room where they waited silently, standing erect and following firmly stated instructions, still wearing their blindfolds and unaware they were being watched the whole time.

"We understand you wish to die as martyrs," said a commanding voice.

Eyad answered without hesitation. "I am ready for jihad and to die for Allah."

Khaled replied, "I will too, but only under special circumstances."

CHARLES LICHTMAN

"Eyad Hamoud, you are fearless, clever and quick witted, but rash in your judgments—sometimes thinking with your heart, not your head," the man said. "Not unlike your father."

"You knew my father?"

"I do the questioning," the man curtly responded. "And you, Khaled Kassem, are very bright and a deep and creative thinker. But sometimes you're too cautious, like your father and grandfather."

"Most people say I'm like my mother," Khaled retorted.

"Only when you react with your temper, not your mind. Your mother is very smart, but it is her *emotional* reporting that has made her so popular on Al-Haqq." After a pause, he continued, "So tell me why you want to die for Allah."

"Because it is what the Koran teaches," Eyad said. "And I am ready to do whatever you ask from me, so being *cautious* is no longer relevant."

The man brusquely said, "Come now. Don't play games with me. I know you have each had religious training, but neither of you is a zealot. Tell me the truth now or this discussion is over, and I'll send you home."

Eyad spoke up. "I *do* believe in jihad. I *am* a zealot. I want revenge for my father. I want to kill Jews. You understand? *I want to kill Jews.*"

"Hmmm. You have a lot of anger in you, Eyad. But that's not necessarily a bad thing. And what about you, Khaled? Why do you really wish to follow in your brother's footsteps? Is it to lash out against your father and grandfather, who disapprove of our methods?"

"My death can make a greater statement than Mahmoud's."

"You speak nonsense! What makes you think that *you're* special when we have an unlimited supply of young jihadis waiting for their call to serve Allah?"

Khaled snapped back, "Because none of them are named Kassem. You know as well as I do that being Ghassan Kassem's grandson and Suha Kassem's son carries weight. You understood that when you used Mahmoud and if anything, I can do more for you."

76

"And why do you think that?"

"Because I'm smarter than my brother."

"Intelligence had nothing to do with your brother being a shahid and killing Jews."

"You used him for his name. Maybe I can be of more use to you alive than dead. At least for now."

The man grunted. "How? Explain that to me."

"Train me to help lead this organization. One day, if Allah wills it, I will die for our cause, but until then, I want to learn everything possible about recruiting shahid. About training freedom fighters. About bringing the Zionists and infidel pigs to their knees. I will do whatever you ask, even blowing myself up for the cause. I can help you. I know that you've checked me out. You know that for two years I led my student government in college. That I've written editorials for Al-Haqq about how our people must come together to fight the Zionists."

The interrogator was quiet for a moment, then said, "That is a unique proposition and you do have an interesting background."

"Suicide bombings are a form of propaganda," Khaled replied. "Whether you send Mahmoud to the Wall or someone else to destroy a bus or a café, it is meant to send a strong message. We don't just kill Jews; we infuriate them. We make them insecure and instigate their revenge, which keeps the battle going—a battle in which time and numbers are on our side. It also shows the world we will die for our cause, no matter how long it takes, and that we are an impossible enemy to defeat. I want to help you build our platform."

"Are you willing to discredit your father and grandfather?"

"They have already discredited themselves."

"And your journalist mother?"

"She was proud of Mahmoud. She will be even prouder of me." Khaled hadn't forgotten about his argument only about an hour ago with his mother, but he believed that her statements were momentary lapses of reason.

"And what do you think of your friend's idea, Eyad?"

"I don't know what to think. He never told me this before. But we're a team."

"Does this make sense to you?" Khaled asked the interrogator.

"Actually, it does," he replied. He motioned to one of his soldiers to remove Khaled and Eyad's blindfolds. He then squeezed Khaled's hand hard but said through a warm smile, "My name is Omar Rafsani. We are now brothers."

PART TWO

9

Tel Aviv

Klein dragged his feet entering the conference room on the seventeenth floor of the Matcal Tower, home to the Israel Ministry of Defense and the IDF. Peering over his readers, Dudi Bareket said, "You look like hell, Chaim! Are you sick?"

"No, worse than that," Klein muttered, rubbing his temples. "I had a bad date last night."

"*You* had a date? No way!" Dan Beer exclaimed. "So, you didn't get any sleep?"

"I did. I got drunk and passed out at her place and yes, before anything happened."

"*You* got drunk?" replied a mystified Ori Levin. "I think that's a first."

Klein concluded his best exit strategy on the topic was to tell it straight and move on. "Well, it's no secret I don't have great luck with women—and I don't know why. So I got fixed up with this woman

81

whom I took to dinner, and she started drinking right away. I thought I'd try matching her drink for drink—something I never do—and we had three big dirty martinis and….." At that moment, Klein realized that sitting at the end of the conference table was Chief Rabbi Schteinhardt, giving him a look he had never seen before. He then noticed that Bareket, Beer, and Levin were holding back laughter. Looking away, he said, "I'm sorry, Rabbi. I don't even know what to say."

Deep down, Klein knew that the fact he had seldom had romantic relationships with women was tied to his overwhelming sense of duty, whether it was in his military service, his job, or helping out anyone else. The responsibility of performing his duty was drummed into Klein's head by his father from the time he was a young boy. Klein liked women and was attracted to them, but never felt comfortable communicating with them. He'd only ever had three serious girlfriends, and none lasted more than six months because his Sayaret unit, friends, and family were always more important to him. Klein never fell in love and he was never broken-hearted when he was dumped. He discounted the prospect of having a long-term relationship with any woman.

Rabbi Schteinhardt stroked his long beard. "Say three Hail Moses and that should do it, Chaim. That will carry you to Yom Kippur."

Everybody laughed as the door opened and Prime Minister Eli Zamir entered. "Sorry I'm late." Everyone knew the Prime Minister was always late, especially if he was flying by helicopter from Jerusalem to Tel Aviv.

"You didn't miss anything, sir," Klein replied.

"I assume not," Zamir replied, but upon a mere glance at Klein, he added, "Chaim, are you okay? You don't look so good." Zamir knew Klein well, given that he was one of his father's longest and closest friends. Zamir knew Klein as well as Levin and Beer did.

Klein instantly responded, "Yes sir, I'm fine. "If possible, can we get started?—Ori, Dan, and I have a lot to do to prepare for our trip to London this week."

"Agreed, and as always, I have an overbooked schedule," Zamir said, taking a seat. "I understand you consider your trip to Ethiopia a few weeks ago a success."

"Yes, sir."

"I assume you heard I had a major problem with it? I don't know how your definition of success can include nearly starting an international incident by killing border guards in a country we wish to have good relations with, since something like 130,000 of our citizens come from there?"

"We didn't have a choice. You know that from our debriefing, but my understanding is the Ethiopians still haven't learned who did it."

"Whatever. But you also came back empty handed. No Ten Commandments, right? Just *knowledge*, which I understand *might* be clues to suggest that the Ten Commandments *might* be in London?"

"Yes, sir," Klein said softly.

"Mr. Prime Minister, may I speak?" said Rabbi Schteinhardt.

"Of course."

"It may take Chaim quite some time before he has success. The tablets have been missing for two thousand years."

If it was anyone else who came to Klein's aid, Zamir would have been intolerant. But since it was the Chief Rabbi, he took a deep breath and smiled. "Of course. You're right. So, gentlemen, let's talk about London."

"Chaim is still doing research, while Dan and I are working on logistics," Levin said.

Zamir shook his head. "Well, you need new logistics because of the Heathrow incident last weekend. No one can believe that three highly educated kids from good Muslim homes spent two years planning the single largest terrorist attack in history. They destroyed nine jets and an entire international terminal, which as you saw, became a fireball. Right now, the death count is over eleven thousand. It's horrible."

"It's beyond comprehension, but what does that have to do with us?" Beer asked.

"Mullah Riyadh Sawalha," said Bareket. "Ever hear of him?"

Klein, Beer, and Levin shook their heads.

"Didn't expect that you would," Bareket said, as he opened an inch-thick, red folder stamped Top Secret. Glancing at a summary sheet, he lectured, "Mullah Riyadh Sawalha is the mullah at the Mujahid Mosque in London and spiritual leader of the Deobandi sect of Islamic fundamentalism in England. The Deobandi make the Wahhabi look tame. As you know, Wahhabism is an ultraconservative, fundamentalist Sunni Islamic movement. The U.S. State Department has estimated that for the last forty years, the House of Saud has directed at least $10 billion to select 'charities' focused on subverting mainstream Sunni Islam via Wahhabism. The Deobandi control about eight hundred of Britain's seventeen hundred mosques and are trying to radicalize about two million British Muslims. In practically every sermon, Sawalha preaches armed jihad against the West, including us. Last week he posted a video of his Friday *khutba* on the Mujahid website that said, 'I command you to shed blood for Allah and you shall do it here. You shall do it against the Zionist state. You shall do it everywhere.'" Pointing at Klein, he continued, "Abu Hamza came from the Finsbury Park Mosque just a few blocks away, and now all of the serious jihadists who have followed in Hamza's shoes have moved over to the Mujahid Mosque. Sawalha is even more dangerous than Hamza."

Abu Hamza was a one-eyed, Egyptian cleric who had become Imam at the Finsbury Park Mosque in 1997. He literally had hooks for hands and was sentenced to seven years by a British court for inciting violence and racial hatred. He was then extradited to the United States, where he was convicted of terrorism charges, and in 2015, he received a life sentence from a federal judge in Manhattan for committing terrorist acts worldwide.

"Sir, *every* fundamentalist mullah preaches violence and death to the infidels, the destruction of Israel and the death of every Jew," Klein said. "So why is Sawalha more dangerous?"

Zamir blurted out, "Because the three young men who blew up Heathrow regularly attended the Mujahid Mosque Friday prayers just to hear Sawalha's khutba. They left a video that credits Sawalha as the inspiration for their attack. Sawalha's sermons and all of the mullahs from that mosque going back to Abu Hamza have spawned dozens of terrorist attacks in London and elsewhere. The British want to close the mosque but don't want a civil war in the streets. Some of these mosques have become terrorist recruiting stations."

"I'm guessing the Brits now want Sawalha dead," Klein said.

"And so do we," Bareket said. "We have stopped seventeen of Sawalha's recruits trying to get into Israel from jets arriving from London. We know he has sent hundreds of recruits through Syria and Iran to Hamas and Hezbollah."

"You're right, sir," Klein said. "Sawalha must be taken out."

"Glad to hear you say it, because you're going to do it, Chaim," the Prime Minister said firmly.

"Seriously, you want *me* to kill him? Don't I have enough to do in London?"

"Was there something unclear in what I just said?"

"What about the Brits? This should be their job. Or our agents on the ground there."

"Israel and the U.K. have the same problem," Bareket replied. "We've both spent years infiltrating that mosque. We can't lose those agents and start over again. The information they collect is invaluable. We need an experienced, fresh face to get into the mosque, do the job, and get out. Not someone they've ever seen before. Chaim, you've infiltrated the West Bank and Gaza dressed as a Palestinian and speaking Arabic something like thirty times?"

"At least."

"And not once have you had your cover blown."

Klein frowned. "Sir, you realize if we kill Sawalha, another Abu Hamza or Sawalha type will just take his place."

"You're right. And if he preaches the same way, we'll kill him too," Zamir said. "And as always, the Brits will provide support. Our war against terrorism has been a partnership with the free countries of this world even before the Munich Olympics. This time, though, getting Sawalha is personal to them, which makes it worthwhile for us to take care of their problem."

Recognizing that he really didn't have a choice in the matter, Klein said, "Fine, we'll do it. At some point, it's him or us. If Sawalha lived in the occupied territories, I wouldn't hesitate to take the assignment. But since he's in London, we'll have to be doubly prepared, especially about knowing the neighborhood."

Zamir nodded. "You'll have every resource backing you up, both from the U.K. and us."

"I wouldn't have said yes if I had any doubt about that."

"Chaim, you need to know that for the past year, we've been working on adapting a plan that originated with the Indonesian Muslim community focusing on educating and empowering moderate Muslims to stand up to the fundamentalists. We're rolling this plan out while you're in London. We can fight the Islamist fundamentalists alongside our allies, but only other Muslims can defeat them."

"I like it!" Klein said with a smile. "We've been fighting terrorists and killing the bad guys since before the founding of Israel. I don't quite know how, but I agree that long term, only other Muslims can fix this problem."

Prime Minister Zamir nodded at Klein. "Chaim, we need your help on one last thing. Our source in Mecca tells us that Abdullah al-Talib, the Secretary General of the Muslim World Foundation, will be in London next week. To be direct about it, we need you to kidnap him. And nobody has kidnapped more terrorists than you."

Klein didn't blink. "Whatever. As the British say, in for a penny, in for a pound. I know all about al-Talib. One of the most powerful men in Saudi Arabia. Deep ties to the royal family. Controls the so-called charity money that funds terrorism. But kidnapping al-Talib will be even harder than killing Sawalha. And is that all? Sure you don't need me to pick up some tea and biscuits for you from the Queen?"

"Not funny," Zamir growled.

Levin quickly added, "And I can't imagine that the Saudis will react well when they find out we kidnapped that guy—"

"We are not going to kill him," Bareket answered. "We just need al-Talib to give us data about the financial structure of the Foundation. Such information could seriously embarrass the Saudis and shut down the organization."

"This is a big picture issue," said the Prime Minister. "Once we get what we need, we'll let him go, unhurt. And assuming we do it right, neither he nor the Saudis will ever know who took him. They'll think it was the Iranians."

"Do the British know about this?" Levin asked.

"Let's just say we do favors for each other. Sometimes that means looking the other way. You know we won't leave you blind."

"And Chaim, al-Talib is also out to destroy our people," said Rabbi Schteinhardt.

"Thank you, Rabbi," Klein said dryly.

"I never suggested being General of the Sons of Light was going to be easy," the Rabbi replied.

His voice dripping with irony, Klein said, "All in a day's work. No problem. I get to go to London and find the Ten Commandments, kill a notorious terrorist, and kidnap another one. So, I assume the three of us will all get special pay for this and maybe not fly coach?"

Zamir laughed. "No combat pay, but you're flying up there on a diplomatic visa. And you know Chaim, when you're all done with this Sons of Light mission, we might even rename Ben Gurion Airport after you," Zamir said.

"Perfect. My mother will be so proud."

10

London

The Israeli operatives stepped out of the Finsbury Park tube station into the open air, greeted by a brisk wind mixed with cold drizzle that slapped them in the face. They ignored the elements, focused on their next few complicated hours.

"Can you hear me?" Klein said, testing the undetectable sound transmitter built into his non-prescription oval lens glasses, comprising part of his disguise.

"Loud and clear," replied the London-based Mossad handler.

Beer and Levin tested their equipment; Beer's audio was built into horned rimmed glasses and Levin's was in a hearing aid.

"And the video?" asked Klein.

"Perfect."

"How about now?" Klein put his finger over his camera, which was a fake button on the lapel of his worn brown leather jacket.

The handler's laugh was interrupted by Bareket. "Remember, Chaim, if everything isn't perfect, then abort. *Understood?*"

"Yes sir," Klein replied indifferently. He knew from experience when to shut down an operation rather than risk injury or death. Nevertheless, missions were seldom aborted—circumstances are *never* perfect; they always require improvisation and additional risk.

Klein thought back twelve years when he had learned from a trusted informant that a high-ranking Hamas officer was attending religious services at a mosque in Hebron. Time was short and without seeking permission, he and his Sayaret Duvdevan unit disguised themselves as Palestinians. Ninety minutes later, they kidnapped the terrorist outside the mosque and whisked him away. Instead of a court martial, Klein's reputation only grew for pulling off an impossibly daring mission, and his unit was thereafter regularly sent into the occupied territories to kill or capture terrorists. But sending Klein and his unit into the West Bank or Gaza where he knew the lay of the land was one thing. Dropping him into the middle of unfamiliar London was another.

Klein, Beer, and Levin all wore convincing facial disguises and were dressed in clothing consistent with this heavily Muslim section of North London: an odd mix of colorful jackets, shirts, and pants that didn't match.

Having memorized the map of Finsbury Park, they proceeded toward Seven Sisters Road, casually strolling along the crowded sidewalk. Halfway up the street, which was dotted with restaurants, boutiques, a Middle Eastern café, and a smoke shop, they entered a tiny Islamic bookstore. Even though Klein had slipped into the West Bank and Gaza countless times speaking Arabic and dressed undercover as a Palestinian, they had to determine immediately whether or not Beer and Levin could also pull it off.

Standing near the door was a tall, thin man with leathery skin and yellowish eyes wearing a keffiyah and white thobe, which fell just short of his worn brown sandals that allowed his mangled left foot room to breathe. Well into his seventies, the man fingered his long scraggly grey beard and greeted them. "*A salaam alaikum.*"

"*Alaikum a salaam*; peace be upon you," responded the Israelis. Klein sized up the man up as being Afghan, surmising his foot had been injured fighting the Soviets. Scanning the bookstore, he observed that the warped wooden shelves lining the walls were at best half-filled and that almost all of the titles were printed in Arabic.

Klein asked for an Arabic version of the *Protocols of the Elders of Zion,* the notorious anti-Semitic propaganda rant first published in Russia in 1905, which has been cited as gospel against the Jews and Israel ever since. Henry Ford distributed 500,000 copies in the 1920s, the Nazis followed suit in the '30s and '40s, and today by Hamas, Hezbollah, and many Arab countries. After introducing himself as the proud owner of the shop, Abdul Qahhar, which means Servant of Allah, emphasized his belief in the truth of *The Protocols* and its importance in educating the world against the evil Jews. In impeccable Arabic, Klein animatedly agreed with him, engaging in an extended anti-Semitic rant. As Klein paid for the book, Levin pulled an orange sheet of paper out of a leather valise.

"My brother, may I put this flyer on your message board up front?" Levin asked in Arabic.

Abdul Qahhar read the paper, then looked mystified his customers. "Muslims for Peace? Who is that?"

In a scripted response, Klein replied, "We're a Muslim group founded in Indonesia that believes that extremists distort the Koran and have given Islam a bad name. We love Allah, but do not believe in jihad. We should never kill innocent people. Our women should be treated with respect and our children educated. Islam should build bridges with other cultures, not label them infidels. We believe it is for the ninety-five percent of the world's moderate Muslims like us to work with our fundamentalist brothers to improve our image and lives worldwide—especially in the Middle East."

Abdul Qahhar exploded, "Get out! You're insane! You have blasphemed Allah! Leave my store now!" He pointed to the door, furious.

The Israelis didn't budge, and Beer responded calmly, "Abdul Qahhar, we would never insult Allah or you. We think alike on many issues, and you know the Koran teaches that one should respect others. We respect you and please, we ask that you respect us. All we seek is a peaceful dialogue among *all* Muslims. How powerful would Islam be if we were united and if non-Muslims did not see us as a threat because of terrorism?"

"You are in the wrong neighborhood to send that message."

"No. The Mujahid Mosque here in Finsbury Park is where we should start the dialogue," said Klein. "Most Muslims in London think as we do and are angry and sad by the bombing at Heathrow. We hate being depicted as murderers."

Abdul Qahhar sharply answered, "It was jihad. It was God's will." He stopped and pointed at Klein. "And you will never see heaven."

"So, you won't let us put up our flyer?" Levin asked, solely to goad Abdul Qahhar.

"Absolutely not. It's time for you to leave."

Once the Israelis left the shop, Bareket yelled through the transmitter, "What was that about? I told you to avoid risk, so what's the first thing you do—"

"Dudi, be quiet!" Klein shot back. "That was a dress rehearsal to see if our disguises would pass a local test."

"Which went perfectly," added Beer.

A few streets up, in a traffic-clogged corner near the Highborn Soccer Stadium, the Israelis walked past the Finsbury Park Mosque. Excepting its towering white minaret and gold-painted dome, the mosque was a five-story, modern, red brick building, with blue-green reflective glass windows. It was built in 1990 with Saudi "charity" money, and Prince Charles attended its opening ceremony. In addition to Abu Hamza, Richard Reid, the "airline shoe bomber," and Zacarias Moussaoui, a 9/11 co-conspirator, had also been indoctrinated at this mosque, which had ties to al-Qaeda and the Muslim Brotherhood. Years later, the Finsbury Mosque moderated its views.

"This mosque seems to have turned things around now," Klein said. "I sure hope their members show up to support our Muslims for Peace rally.

Five minutes later and a few blocks up, the Israelis entered the Mujahid Mosque, a converted commercial building across the street from Finsbury Park. Inside the building, the Israelis sat on the first-floor red carpet, close to where Sawalha would speak to nearly one thousand of his followers. The Israelis followed strict Islamic custom by wearing *thanikas*, Islamic prayer caps, and by removing their shoes, leaving them in wooden bins near the entrance. They even participated in the rituals and chanting of prayers during the religious service led by Sawalha. Finally, when the mullah presented his Friday khutba, they sat quietly through the thirty-minute, hate-filled, anti-West, anti-Semitic invective that praised the attack at Heathrow, calling the young martyrs heroes to all Muslims.

After the service concluded and traditional Islamic greetings were exchanged, a mix of young and old men crowded around Sawalha. Finally, Klein stood next to the stocky man with a round face and thick black beard. "Imam, that was a powerful sermon. It is clear you have many believers here with you."

"I am blessed that Allah has graced me with the privilege of speaking on his behalf."

"We agree. And that is why we invite you to speak to our group."

"I welcome the opportunity to speak to all believers."

Levin handed an envelope to Sawalha, his name printed on the front in perfect Arabic calligraphy. While Sawalha eyed Levin, Klein imperceptibly dropped a tiny white plastic dot into the open waist pocket of Sawalha's white robe. Sawalha opened the envelope, removed an orange sheet of paper, and read it quickly. His black beady eyes peered at Klein and Levin. "I've never heard of the Muslims for Peace."

Making sure everyone could hear him, Klein passionately recited back to Sawalha the exact description of the MFP that he provided Abdullah two hours earlier.

"You are worse than the infidels!" Sawalha screamed. "You speak blasphemy about Allah, and you insult me in our house of God! You should all die!"

Klein answered calmly, "Mullah Sawalha, you do not speak for Islam. Most Muslims honor the Koran without distorting it, as you do. We will work around the world so Muslims can be accepted by all." He dropped his voice and added, "So maybe *you* should die?"

Two bodyguards stepped forward and the larger of them gripped Klein's right shoulder and gruffly said, "You cannot speak to the Mullah like that."

Klein pivoted his left foot forward and with his left hand, he grabbed the top of the man's wrist. He brought his right hand up, latched onto the guard's thumb, and snapped it backwards, sending him into shrieks of agony. Beer and Levin already assumed subtle defensive fighting positions. Silencing the mosque, Klein announced, "Against the laws of Allah, this man struck me. We came in peace, and we are leaving in peace!"

The crowd parted out of their way as the Israelis marched out of the *Musillah*, feeling the stares of a thousand eyes. They quickly found their shoes in the bin, put them on, and walked outside, where, to their good fortune, a big black London taxi was waiting. They got in and were taken aback when the driver said, "Chaim, you know, it's lucky you're not dead."

Klein leaned forward, smacked the driver on the shoulder and laughed. "Unbelievable! Ezana, how come no one told us you were here?"

"After your visit to Ethiopia, Bareket moved my family here for safety reasons. I'm still on the Mossad payroll. I was listening to your encounter with Sawalha. You are *crazy!*"

Bareket chimed in with his own praise, amazed that the plan played out exactly as Klein had predicted. Klein replied, "We still have the fun part ahead of us. Have we picked up Sawalha's signal?"

"Yes, he is still in the mosque," replied the handler.

An hour later, the Israelis stood at the front door surveying the layout and crowd in The Homeland, a small neighborhood restaurant specializing in Afghan cuisine. Even through the dense cigarette smoke, the aroma of cooked lamb filled the air. They quickly spotted Sawalha sitting in the back corner at a table of six.

The Israelis dropped copies of the orange flyer on every table. They worked their way to the back corner where Sawalha was glaring at them. "Why are you here?"

"You were rude to me earlier," Klein replied, "I came for an apology."

Sawalha's nostrils flared. "An apology? You broke my guard's thumb—in a mosque!"

"He attacked me. Everyone saw that. I simply tried to have a conversation with you."

"You insulted Allah. You speak blasphemy against jihad. You disrespected me."

Klein responded, "It's you who disrespects Muslims who refuse to accept your message of hate and violence." The room fell silent.

"So you came here looking for trouble. If that is it, I can accommodate you." Sawalha snapped his fingers twice. The guard at the table rose, as did two other large men sitting by the front door.

"Now you threaten violence against me and my friends? Against brother Muslims!" Klein yelled.

"You are misguided fools! You must show me respect."

"You talk to me as if I am a shoe! Well, then Sawalha, you are a filthy pig!"

Those at the Mullah's table were visibly shocked and Klein grinned, knowing he had hurled one of the lowest insults imaginable to a Muslim.

Sawalha rose from his chair and yelled at his bodyguard, "Kamel, show this man to the door."

Klein faced the restaurant crowd. "I did not come here for trouble. Please look at our flyers. I am from the Muslims for Peace. I represent the vast majority of Muslims who disapprove of Mullah Sawalha, who preaches only hate and incites violence. Today at the Mujahid Mosque, he spoke about the attack at Heathrow and said, 'Every non-Muslim that died that day deserved a death of fire.' He also said, 'Suicide attacks in Britain must continue.' You and I both know he's not right! We are peace-loving people, but now we're victims of prejudice because of radicals like Sawalha. Come to our rally Sunday morning in the park across from the Mujahid Mosque, as we take back our religion from criminals like him."

Klein saw that he had struck a chord with some of the restaurant patrons. He walked up to Sawalha, pointed his finger an inch from his nose and said, "When you send others out to kill falsely in the name of Allah, you become a murderer yourself. The Muslims for Peace will stop you and save Islam."

Sawalha threw his arms into the air. "You subvert our religion! You deserve to die!"

"Our people know right from wrong and will step forward," Klein answered. "Today is a new beginning. Your reign of terror has come to an end."

Incensed, Sawalha commanded his guard, "Kill the infidel!" The guard pulled a gun from his jacket and aimed it at Klein, only two feet away.

Klein jerked his right arm straight up, deflecting the guard's arm, and a stray gunshot flew into a wall. He then stepped behind the guard and locked his throat into a chokehold while chopping his right fist on top of the gun to gain control of the weapon. Patrons screamed and scattered from their tables as dishes crashed to the floor. Klein dug his thumb into the soft, fleshy spot between the guard's thumb and index finger, loosening his grip on the weapon. He then yanked the guard's arm upwards, so his gun was pointed at Sawalha. With his finger on the trigger along with the guard's, Klein pulled off two shots.

The first exploded into Sawalha's chest, and the strong kick upward from the gun sent a second bullet square into his forehead. Blood and brain matter splattered everywhere. Sawalha fell straight back on the floor dead, his eyes wide open.

Pandemonium erupted as some patrons rushed for the door; others dove to the floor or scampered beneath tables for cover. The stunned guard gave up his struggle for an instant, allowing Klein to bring his right hand up to crack the man's neck in a twisting motion, rendering him unconscious. He crumbled to the floor.

Both guards at the front door charged Klein, guns drawn. One fired a shot and Levin fell to his knees, blood spurting from his chest. Beer reached Levin just as the other guard pointed his gun directly at Beer, who dove forward, barreling into the guard, knocking him backwards. But the guard's shot hit Levin again. He lurched erect, then a moment later collapsed to the floor. Beer grabbed a fork off the floor, roundhouse-kicked the guard in the chest, then repeatedly jammed the fork into his neck.

The other guard pointed his gun at Klein, who leaped towards the guard as a bullet whizzed by his ear. They smashed into each other and fell to the floor, but Klein bounced up and spun around with a back kick, catching the guard in the face and knocking him into a table, sending plates, food, and glassware flying. The guard slowly rose to his feet and again raised his arm to shoot Klein. As he was about to pull the trigger, Beer smashed a chair on the guard's neck and head, killing him.

The restaurant was in shambles. The few remaining patrons were huddled together in fear. Klein looked at Levin, who remained motionless. He searched for a pulse and shook his head sadly at Beer. Klein silenced the restaurant and declared in a hoarse voice, "You saw what happened. They started the fight. They had the guns. Not us. We must get our friend to a hospital immediately. Can anyone help us?"

A large black man moved toward them from the back of the restaurant. "I saw that you defended yourselves and I will help you."

They knew it was too late for Levin, but as is always the case with Israelis, they never leave their men behind. Meroe said, "I think we can get him to the emergency room faster in my car than if we wait for an ambulance."

Klein, Beer, and Meroe carried Levin's corpse out of the restaurant. As they reached the sidewalk, a van pulled up and two men jumped out to help load Levin and the others inside. It then sped away.

During the melee, only one person had remained calm; a large, physically imposing man with short-cropped black hair and dark, piercing eyes who had been seated at Sawalha's table.

Only Omar Rafsani had heard that when Levin was shot, his friend cried out in Hebrew.

Only Rafsani had observed that when Klein was wrestling with the guard, his hair moved out of place because it was a wig, and that the man was an expert in self-defense.

Only Rafsani had understood that the black man volunteered his help too quickly, and that a van conveniently pulled up outside the restaurant for a timely getaway.

As police sirens neared the restaurant, Rafsani looked under the table, grabbed Khaled Kassem by the shirt collar, and yanked him to his feet, dragging him out of the restaurant.

11

Thousands of orange flyers were passed out and posted throughout London, advertising the Muslims for Peace rally in Finsbury Park in front of the Mujahid Mosque. Full-page ads for the event appeared in London newspapers and local Islamic periodicals. The BBC provided substantial coverage on Friday and Saturday. Conversely, there was sparse reporting of the killing of the notorious radical, Mullah Sawalha.

On Sunday, a peaceful crowd of over 25,000 Muslims flooded the park and streets around the mosque, far in excess of predictions. The program featured three local imams addressing the need for moderate Muslims to take back their religion from the radical fundamentalists, by supporting the MFP becoming a worldwide movement. A who's who of Britain's prominent Muslim business and cultural leaders, including London Mayor Sadiq Khan, ratified the message of the imams. Representatives of the Anglican Church and the Jewish community also expressed their support. Enthusiastic applause and cheers greeted every speaker.

A new MFP web site was announced. Volunteers were enlisted to work on growing the organization. The 10,000 red, green, and white

MFP buttons were snapped up quickly. When the rally ended and the crowd peacefully dispersed, the news accounts that followed world-wide—except those in the Middle East—praised the event, calling it a historic and optimistic option to a problem that seemed unsolvable.

At the same time that the MFP rally was concluding, a black stretch limousine pulled up to Door 10 at the Hans Road entrance to Harrods. Behind it, a white Mercedes CLS was parked at the curb. Klein and Beer climbed out of the limo, wearing the same facial disguise as on Friday night, except today they were dressed in dark suits with white shirts and ties. They walked straight into the Fine Jewelry and Watch Room, the largest room on the first floor of England's legendary store.

They stopped in the modern light wood and glass-cased room to scope out the situation, soon spotting their target: a man wearing a white linen kaffiyah and gutra. The middle-aged Arab was conversing about a Rolex with an elegant fortyish Indian saleswoman in a black pantsuit with long black hair. Standing next to the Arab was his stocky bodyguard in a brown-striped suit. Klein and Beer approached them.

"Abdullah al-Talib," Klein said as a statement, not a question.

The tall, leathery-faced man with a long white beard was startled. He replied with a simple "yes" that was more a question than a statement.

The suspicious bodyguard focused on the strangers. Klein and Beer took out their wallets and showed them official U.K. security badges and hologram picture IDs. In Arabic, Klein said, "Sir, we work for the British government, Special Consular Services. I am Agent Habib, and this is Agent Kasmir."

"Does this pertain to my meeting with Ambassador bin Nawaf this afternoon?"

"No, sir." Klein frowned and spoke softly. "Unfortunately, we just received a call from the ambassador, advising that your daughter Fahda and grandson Mutaib were in an auto accident in Riyadh with their cousin Kamal earlier today. Your family tried to reach you but without success. Apparently, you told the doorman at the Ritz you were coming here, and that's how we found you."

The blood drained from al-Talib's face and he whispered, "In the name of Allah, please tell me they are okay."

Beer replied gently, "We're sorry. Kamal is dead. Fahda and Mutaib are in critical condition." Klein handed his phone to al-Talib. "Sir, here is an email from Director Howairini of State Security to the ambassador, describing present circumstances, which you can see was forwarded to me to show you." Al-Talib read the email, gasped, and his eyes became misty. He handed the watch back to the saleswoman, who disappeared with it.

"We have been sent to assist you," Beer continued. "King Abdullah has arranged for a private jet to fly you home immediately."

Al-Talib buried his face in his hands crying, then seconds later looked up and said, "May Allah bless the King."

"Yes, may Allah bless the King," Klein replied. Making eye contact with al-Talib, Klein continued in a sincere tone, "We can take you and your bodyguard to the airport in our consular limousine parked out front, behind your car. Our driver knows the fastest route to the airport. Or, if you prefer, you can go in your car and your driver can follow us. It is your choice, sir."

Al-Talib replied, "Achmed and I will go with you."

"Whatever you are most comfortable with, sir," Klein replied, knowing that regardless of al-Talib's choice, they had a plan. "Sir, we should go. Please follow me."

The group left Harrods, and Bareket was already there holding the back door open. As al-Talib climbed in, with Bareket behind him, and Klein said, "Is there anything in your car that you'd like to take with you?"

Al-Talib exclaimed, "Oh, thank you. I don't know where my head is right now. Achmed, would you please get my briefcase and laptop from the Mercedes?"

A minute or two later, al-Talib was sitting inside the limo, his briefcase and laptop on the floor, with his bodyguard Achmed sitting next to him. The moment the Israelis pulled away, a Saab pulled in front of and cut off al-Talib's Mercedes and the driver of the Saab jumped out of the car and ran inside Door 10. Al-Talib's driver cursed and began to back up so he could pull out and catch up to the limo. But just then, a taxi pulled up behind him, locking him in place. The driver leaped out of the Mercedes and frantically approached the cab. "You need to move! Now! I've got to go!"

Meroe returned a large smile. "Good day to you, sir. You could at least say *Please*?"

Exasperated, al-Talib's driver grunted and threw his arms up. "Please! I beg you!"

"My fare who called in for me should be out in a moment. Just hold on."

The driver pleaded futilely for the cabbie to back up even six feet. Panicked, he ran to the corner and onto Brompton Road, which fronted Harrods, desperately searching for the limo, but it was long gone. He returned to his car to see Meroe drive away with an empty car and a big smile.

The limo's occupants were in the car for less than a minute before Klein pulled out a gun with a silencer and shot Achmed in the middle of the forehead. Al-Talib exploded into a full-blown meltdown, which Beer, Klein and Bareket watched, amused. With the limo's reflective windows, nobody on the outside could see or hear what was going on inside. After a few minutes, al-Talib finally spoke. "You obviously do not work for Her Majesty's government. Who are you?"

"Your sworn enemy from Iran," replied Klein as he removed the battery from al-Talib's cell phone to assure it couldn't be tracked by cell towers.

Klein's preference was to kill al-Talib. In terms of the international Islamic terror regime, Klein considered him more dangerous than any misguided fanatical suicide bomber because al-Talib controlled and dispersed a fortune in dirty money. This time, however, he understood the importance of keeping al-Talib alive. Nobody had more secrets than al-Talib, and someone back home would extract them.

Al-Talib showed plenty of hatred but no fear. He brusquely asked, "So I assume you lied about my family's accident?"

"No. *We* caused the accident," responded Beer. "As the Koran teaches, *Qisas*…an eye for an eye. And we also used drones to blow up your oil fields at Abqaiq today."

"You Iranians are *Iblis*! You are Satan!" al-Talib yelled, pointing at Beer.

"Thank you! And I promise we are just getting started in creating chaos for you Saudis."

Al-Talib then asked, "How did you know I was at Harrods? And that I met with the ambassador?"

"Our Ministry of Intelligence is the best in the world. Sleep on that," Bareket said with a sneer. In fact, the Israelis knew everything about al-Talib's forty-eight hours in London, courtesy of Mossad's famous Unit 8200, which monitored all of his conversations: telephonic, electronic, and live, both within the Saudi embassy walls and in his hotel suite. The background information on his family had been accumulated over time in a file built by Mossad.

Beer pulled out a hypodermic syringe from a package on the seat and waved it at al-Talib. His eyes popped wide open, and he scooted back on the limo seat. Klein raised his index finger and said, "You should make this easy on yourself. If I wanted you dead, you already would be. This will only make you sleep."

As Beer moved toward him with the syringe, al-Talib began kicking. Klein leaped onto al-Talib and locked him down on the seat, allowing Beer to jab him in the arm. In seconds, al-Talib's eyes rolled back in his head and he was out cold.

Fifteen minutes later, the limo pulled into Biggin Hill Airport on the south edge of London, which catered to small planes and corporate jets. They found the hangar and its door opened and closed quickly, and the limo parked next to a jet. Four men carried al-Talib out of the car and stripped off his kaffiyah and gutra, redressing him into a black suit covered by a *tallis* with a tall black hat, converting al-Talib from Islamic fundamentalist terror financier to a Hasidic Jew. They lifted him into a simple white pine casket. Achmed's corpse was placed in a body bag and moved to another vehicle. He would be taken to a local funeral parlor and cremated as a homeless, unidentified pauper.

"Chaim, Dan, do you want to go onboard for a moment by yourselves?" Bareket asked.

"Why would we do that?" asked Beer.

"To say goodbye to Ori. We're taking him home."

Klein and Beer exchanged sad looks as they trudged up the steps of the Gulfstream G650. On the floor in the back of the cabin was a casket draped with the Israeli flag. Upon seeing it and having not yet had a moment to mourn their dear friend, Klein exhaled hard and tears flowed down his face. Beer rested his hand over his heart and closed his eyes tight. Klein inched toward the casket, removed the flag and draped it over a seat, and then opened the lid. Ori appeared peaceful, showing a half-smile.

After a few minutes, Klein wiped his eyes, kneeled down, and kissed Ori on the forehead. He muttered, "I love you, Uncle Ori. I'm sorry I dragged you into this thing."

"He was family to both of us," Beer added, fighting to keep his composure. "There was no way he wasn't coming here with us. You know that. This is not on you, Chaim."

Klein slung his arm around Beer's shoulder, pulling him in tight. They recited the *Kaddish*: "*Yizgadal v'yizkadash shemay reybah....*" Two minutes later, they stepped out of the Gulfstream to find Bareket, Meroe, and the other Israelis lined up to extend their condolences to Klein and Beer for the loss of their fallen friend. Bareket boarded the plane along with al-Talib and his briefcase and laptop. Next stop: Tel Aviv.

THE SAUDI EMBASSY WAS in a panic. Unsure what had happened to al-Talib, his driver contacted the embassy. Ambassador bin Nawaf had no clue what to do first. It took almost an hour before a decision was made at the highest levels in Riyadh to report the matter to British authorities as a potential kidnapping.

By then, the Gulfstream was at 37,000 feet over the southern tip of Germany.

Rafsani and Khaled had arrived at the embassy for their 3:00 p.m. meeting with al-Talib, only to learn about his disappearance from Harrods. Rafsani insisted that Saudi security interview Harrods employees and view the store's security tapes. Qatar Investment Authority, the current owner of Harrods, bypassed standard procedure and released the tapes to the Saudis.

When their group gathered in an embassy conference room and reviewed the tape of the Jewelry Room, Rafsani turned to Khaled the moment the kidnappers appeared on the screen and said coldly, "I know you recognize them. We will hunt them down and they will die for this."

12

Klein focused on the imposing, life-sized statue of King Richard I mounted on his horse, the king's muscles bulging from underneath his armor, his right arm brandishing a sword thrust high in the air, his fixed gaze reflecting arrogant invincibility. The weather-beaten bronze statue stood guard outside the main entrance to the Palace of Westminster, which housed Parliament. Big Ben dominated the blue sky at the far end of the government complex just one hundred yards away. Directly across the street sat Westminster Abbey, England's most historic church. The two buildings housed nearly 1,000 years of British and world history.

Klein repositioned himself to view the Lionheart's statue with the Abbey framing the background.

"What's with the statue?" Beer asked.

Klein showed him a picture on his cell phone. "Look here: a smaller version of this statue was in the chapel in Ethiopia and this *exact* view was painted on the chapel's ceiling. And the swords on this statue and that of King David are the same. So we need to go into the Abbey and find the sword. That's the purpose of the painting."

"That makes sense, but what are you getting at with the sword?"

"All right, hear me out. David's sword was called the Sword of the Righteous. It supposedly had magical and immense power. It had been kept at the Second Temple up to the time of its destruction, then it disappeared."

Beer nodded. "It supposedly bore a permanent stain from the blood of Goliath from when David cut off his head."

"Exactly. The statues from the chapel suggest that Richard the Lionheart and King David owned the same sword. Do you know what Richard called his sword?"

"I have no idea."

"Excalibur! He even carried it to the Third Crusade and gave it to his cousin Tancred of Sicily, but it disappeared again after that."

"Chaim, Excalibur belonged to King Arthur, who didn't exist!"

"But Dan, King David and his sword did. The Sword of the Righteous was real, not legend, and right here we can see it in Richard's hand. He simply called it Excalibur, so now everybody does." Klein crossed his arms over his chest.

"Explain to me how Richard ended up with David's sword."

"Maybe we'll find out in there," Klein said as he started walking toward Westminster Abbey.

A few minutes later, they visited the Abbey gift shop to buy a guidebook and were advised it would be better to come back the next day, since the Abbey was closing in fifteen minutes. Ignoring that advice, Klein and Beer entered the adjacent West door of the Abbey. They followed the map to the majestic Nave, its vaulted ceiling rising over one hundred feet. They walked past the grave of the Unknown Soldier and the tomb of explorer David Livingston. At the end of the Nave, they stood before the monument of Isaac Newton, with its famous globe of the heavens. Yards away sat the final resting place of Charles Darwin.

"It's amazing who's buried here," Klein said. "It's not just the royals and the scientists, but Dickens, Chaucer, Tennyson, Kipling, and others are buried in Poets' Corner."

"That's right," Beer said. "But tell me, how are we going to find what you're looking for? This church is massive. Every inch of it is filled with history and we don't have much time."

He motioned to Beer to follow him, and they speed-walked back to the quire, the worshipping heart of the Abbey.

For ten minutes, without success, they searched for a hiding place since they needed to stay in the building. Finally, they climbed into the wooden pews preceding the high altar to wait for the last tourists and worshipers to leave. They lay down flat in the second row, hidden from sight by the carved wooden walls surrounding the seats. An hour later, when there had been no noise for twenty minutes, they had the Abbey to themselves and continued their mission.

Klein slowly turned in a circle, searching for a clue. "There must be something here that ties our quest to King Richard or his sword. This is the most famous cemetery of the English monarchy, and Richard was one of the best known of all English kings."

"So let's find his grave." Beer studied the map of the Abbey's numerous chapels and monuments. After a minute, he shrugged. "His tomb isn't listed here. Richard the First, right?"

"That doesn't make sense." Klein typed in a Google search on his iPhone to find out where the Lionheart was buried. "He's not here. His brain, heart, and body are buried in separate locations across France. Where are the monarchs' tombs?"

Beer studied the map and pointed ahead. "We're close. They're up there on the left."

At the North Ambulatory, Klein exclaimed, "Look, there are lions everywhere!"

Seeing lions intricately carved into mantlepieces and columns, Beer asked, "So you think that's it? If Richard the Lionheart is our clue, we follow the lions?"

"Makes sense to me."

Beer agreed, then returned to the guidebook. "Edward the Third was also a great warrior king who created the Order of the Garter knighthood, modeled after King Arthur's Knights of the Round Table."

"Hmmm. So just like Richard, Edward the Third has a tie to Arthur," Klein said.

"Yes, and he also had a famous sword that he used in battle, which still exists today."

"Where is it?"

Beer peered into the guidebook. "Well, two floors below is the secret jewel chamber of Edward the Third, where he kept his treasure. Maybe it's there." Still reading, Beer quickly added, "Ah, the room is closed to the public. It will be difficult to get in."

Klein gave him a perplexed look. "Since when has that stopped us?"

"Aside from the fact that I think everything of value was moved to the Tower of London, the walls to the room are fifteen feet thick, there's no windows, and one huge metal door."

Klein cursed under his breath. "Not helpful. What's next?"

"There's another famous sword hanging on a wall somewhere behind us," Beer said with his nose buried in the guide. "It's where Edward the Third is buried, over in the chapel of Edward the Confessor."

They located the polished bronze effigy of Edward III, with his angular face and long beard modeled from his death mask. They scoured every inch around the king's memorial, looking for anything that might be relevant.

"It's not here," Klein said.

"Then let's try the Coronation Chair."

Seconds later, they were examining an ancient, intricately carved, high-backed wooden chair with matching spires on its corners. It looked anything but comfortable or regal.

"It's amazing that almost every sovereign since 1308 has been crowned in this crummy-looking chair," said Beer. "There are lions carved into each corner of the chair. And there," he added, pointing to a wall a few feet away, "is your sword. The book says it belonged to Edward the Third!"

Klein moved in closer to study the sword, looking dejected. "This is not the right sword."

"Sure it is," Beer retorted. "It's surrounded by lions. It was owned by Edward the Third. It's used in the monarch's coronation service. And the British think their monarchs serve by God's choice. Chaim, this *must* be the Sword of the Righteous!"

Klein studied it again and firmly replied, "No, it's too long and the pommel is different."

"What's a pummel?"

"Pommel...the thing at the end of the grip. Also, see the covering on the grip has three gold strips, and then the pommel has a green coat of arms engraved on it." He muttered, "That's not on David's sword. Besides, this is a ceremonial sword that goes with that shield up there. I guess I was wrong. Let's get out of here." Klein turned and started walking away, disappointment evident on his face. But after a few steps, he stopped and pointed. "What's that?" He stared inside a small dimly lit chapel, then moved toward an effigy of a knight in full armor against the back wall. "Who is this?" Klein asked.

Beer stepped back into better light, thumbing through his guide. "That's Sir Bernard Brocas."

"Who is he?" Klein asked impatiently. "I never heard of him. Why would he be buried with all of these kings and queens?"

"The guide says he was a favorite knight of Edward the Black Prince, the son of Edward the Third," Beer responded, reading straight from the book. He added, "This is really weird, Chaim. Brocas did nothing historically notable. But he's buried here and he's one of the only effigies in full armor, and look, he's got lions at his feet."

Klein had noticed them, but now his eyes were fixed on Brocas's sword.

Beer moved next to Klein. "Apparently nobody knows why the sword was added to the effigy long after Brocas died." Beer moved closer and said, "You know, this actually looks like the sword on the statue of Richard out there. Is that what you're thinking?"

Ignoring Beer, Klein bent over and rested his palm on the sword's concrete-like grip, slowly wrapping his fingers around it. Seconds later, Beer's eyes opened wide as the grey plaster-like top coating of the sword crumbled away.

A moment later, Klein held a glistening metal blade with a black grip and a solid gold pommel on the end. A red stain marked the blade about halfway up. Klein slowly pulled the sword from the side of the effigy and swung it around. To his amazement, it was the weight of a feather. He gripped it with both hands, and as he held it up vertically, the sword began to glow and emit a low hum. Klein slashed the air a few times, and each movement of the blade cutting the air sounded like the whoosh of the wind.

Klein looked over at Beer, who had inched back against the wall in awe. "Here, Dan, you want to hold it?"

Beer responded with an emphatic, "Absolutely not."

An instant later, a hissing sound and white gas filled the air from a vent right above Brocas's effigy. Before Klein and Beer could speak or comprehend what was happening, they fell to the floor, unconscious.

13

A dousing of cold water on their heads woke Klein and Beer. Through nuclear headaches, they sat up from lying flat on their backs on a thick royal blue rug with an inlaid gold pattern, the same as the carpeting in the House of Lords. Two royal guards in their formal reds stared them down from beneath their tall black furry hats. Seated nearby in a maroon velvet chair was a silver-haired woman in a flower-print dress with bright blue eyes, her pale skin accented by pink-painted cheeks. Her bright red lips formed a curious smile.

Dominating the oak and gold gilded walls was the thirty-foot long legendary painting of King Arthur with his sword raised, titled *The Admission of Sir Tristram to the Fellowship of the Round Table*. Other frescoes depicting the story of King Arthur adorned the walls. At the end of this ninety-foot-long room was a golden throne with a red velvet seat, placed on a pedestal under the Queen's coat of arms. The effigy of Sir Bernard Brocas with his sword propped up against it rested nearby—apparently transported here along with their unconscious bodies. Through a raised eyebrow, Klein asked, "You the Queen?"

The overweight, diminutive woman squealed with delight, pulled herself out of the chair, and waddled over to Klein and Beer. Through her proper English accent, she said, "No, no, no. I am only a baroness. My name is Baroness Jillian Collins. This is the Queen's Royal Robing Room, and you are in the Parliament building. So, may I ask, who are you?"

"Why should we tell you?" Klein replied.

"Because you trespassed in Westminster Abbey and broke priceless property belonging to Her Majesty's government. And you would have stolen it had we not stopped you."

Klein stared at the smiling lady, trying to size up their real measure of trouble.

The baroness again asked, "So, gentlemen, what are your names?"

When they didn't answer, the baroness stepped on Klein's hand and ground in her heel. He yelped and cursed. In a sarcastic tone, she exclaimed, "Oh my! I am so sorry! I pray you are all right." She pointed at Klein and said, "Let's see, you're Monkey See," and pointing at Beer, she added, "and you are Monkey Do." She laughed, pleased with herself. "Monkey See and Monkey Do. I like that!

"Fine," Klein said, "My name is Gabor Kanacz, and my friend is Jozsef Marko."

"And where are you from?"

"Budapest."

Turning to her guards, she said, "I told you they'd lie. That's their training."

"We have papers. We have proof," Klein replied indignantly.

"Of course you do, Mr. Klein and Mr. Beer."

Klein tried to keep his face blank, but a microscopic wince gave him away. Beer, however, ended any hope of continuing the charade. "How do you know who we are?"

"Chaim, right? And Daniel? But you like to be called Dan?"

Klein realized resistance was futile and sighed. "Yes," he said while Beer nodded.

The baroness announced, "I know *so* much about you! But first, Her Majesty's government thanks you for eliminating that dreadful terrorist Sawalha. You Israelis are so creative and effective in these matters." She softened her voice. "We're also sorry about the loss of Mr. Levin. I know you two were close. I understand he was such a good man."

Klein couldn't believe what he was hearing. "How do you know all this?"

"I am a member of the House of Lords and sit on the Intelligence and Security Committee that works closely with MI-5 and MI-6. Almost all of our work deals with terrorism. I had oversight on your mission. Again, I must say, you are spectacular at what you do."

"I guess I'm supposed to say thank you," Klein replied uncomfortably.

The baroness walked toward Brocas's effigy and demanded, "No games now! What were you doing with Sir Bernard?"

In an innocent voice, Klein replied, "We work at the Western Wall as archeologists, which makes us historians. Neither of us have been to London before. What better place to take in British history than Westminster Abbey? His tomb looked interesting."

The baroness sharply replied, "Don't give me that malarkey! I know you both work at the Wall, but Mr. Klein, I also know you are a highly skilled special forces soldier, proven from how you killed Sawalha and kidnapped Sheik al-Talib from Harrods. Yes, I know about that too." She clapped her hands in Klein's face. "Now I must insist that you stop playing games! I watched the entire security tape from the moment you entered the Abbey, including the removal of the sword from Sir Bernard's effigy. You were looking for something in particular. And you found it."

"This is all a misunderstanding," said Klein. "You've got it wrong."

The baroness turned to a guard and said, "Ian, please replace the sword."

Struggling with the heavy weapon, the guard placed the concrete sword on the effigy. Additional crust formed on the sword, and within seconds it morphed onto the effigy. Everyone stared at this remarkable transformation, and the baroness ordered, "Now, Ian, bring me the sword."

He took the grip and pulled, but the sword would not budge. He gave up after five seconds. "I'm sorry, ma'am, but it's stuck."

"Do it again, and use some elbow grease."

This time the guard grabbed the sword and pulled for around twenty seconds before begging forgiveness for his failure.

Looking at the other guard, she said, "Randall, you try."

The guard confidently walked up to the effigy, planted a leg on the base, grabbed the handle, and pulled with all his might until he fell backwards onto the floor. Baroness Collins glared at him, and he looked away guiltily. She then demanded, "Chaim, let's see you do it again."

"I don't know what you're—"

"Enough! I said I saw the tape of you in St. Edmunds Chapel with Sir Bernard's effigy!"

"I won't do it."

"Then I will put you both in jail in Finsbury Park and make sure every prisoner knows you're Israeli and being held for Sawalha's murder."

Klein reassessed his position. "Now that you put it that way, I'll do it." He approached the effigy and grabbed the sword's handle. Instantly, the plaster-like coating on the sword crumbled away, again revealing the shiny metal blade with its red stain. He picked up the sword and swung it around, awakening its bright glow and low hum, amazed at its unexplainable supernatural qualities.

Her face ashen, the baroness stood speechless. Randall dropped to a knee and crossed himself. Ian pointed at the painting of Arthur and stammered, "It's Excalibur! The sword lives!"

His eyes still fixated on the sword, Klein calmly replied, "You may call it Excalibur, but it is the Sword of the Righteous. The Sword of King David."

"*The* King David?" Ian asked.

"There is only one King David," Beer answered.

Randall asked the baroness, "Is he to be King of England? Like Arthur?"

She whispered, "No, Randall. Mr. Klein is the General of the Sons of Light."

Klein nearly dropped the sword. "Why would you say that?"

The baroness surprised her guards by ordering them to leave the room. Once they were gone, she nervously rambled, "I never thought this day would come. I thought it was a myth, but it's real."

Klein demanded again, "Why did you call me the General of the Sons of Light? Please answer my question!"

"It is my responsibility to know such things."

"*Your* responsibility?"

She looked to the skies, then said, "I am the Grand Master of the Poor Knights of Christ."

Not sure that he had heard her correctly, he asked, "You mean the Order of the Temple? The *Knights Templar*?"

Baroness Collins nodded.

"That's not possible," said Beer. "The order disappeared something like seven hundred years ago."

It was well accepted that King Philip of France was jealous of the Templar's immense wealth, power, and influence. Moreover, he owed them money and coveted theirs, so the French King accused them of heinous crimes they didn't commit. After that, on Friday the 13th of October 1307, he obtained an order from Pope Clement V, his cousin, that all Templars in France be arrested. Many were tortured, imprisoned, or murdered, including their Grand Master, Jacques de Molay, who was burned at the stake. And that was the end of the Knights Templar. Or so historians thought.

The baroness explained, "I know that's what the public believes, but King Philip did not extinguish the Templars. Actually, most French Templars escaped to other European countries and remained Templars. And, Edward the Second in England ignored the Pope's order to arrest the Templars. Certainly, no one ever claimed to find the Templar's famous treasure, and Philip only located a very small portion of it."

Shaking his head, Klein replied, "That happened a long time ago, Baroness. Treasure doesn't stay hidden for seven hundred years. It gets spent, embezzled, stolen, or maybe lost. If the Templars survived over all this time, their existence would have come out by now."

"Mr. Klein, how would you know if the Knights Templar stayed together all of these years, waiting for the right circumstance to resurface? Maybe once we were no longer an army, we carefully and quietly became bankers, statesmen, lawyers, and businessmen."

"Sorry, but I'm having a hard time accepting what you're saying," Klein replied.

The baroness pointed at Klein. "I think it is as preposterous that you're the General of the Sons of Light as it is that I am the Grand Master of the Knights Templar, isn't it? But they are both true. Tell me how we came to meet. Was it by coincidence or design?"

Klein stared at the floor in silence.

The baroness continued, "Chaim, the Knights Templar will now publicly resurface. For nearly seven hundred years, the story of the sword has been passed down from Grand Master to Grand Master. I was provided instructions, which I will follow. Because you are the General, you are the only outsider who may learn certain of the Templar's secrets. That will be the proof of who I am and that we exist."

Even though he had his doubts, Klein said, "I'm sorry for questioning you." He handed the sword to the baroness.

"Oh no, Chaim, this sword is now yours. We were merely its caretaker."

Klein was taken aback. "What do I do with it?"

"By legend, the sword wields immense power for those few who possess it. I suspect that one day soon you will know what to do with it."

"Did Richard the Lionheart own this sword?"

"For a time, he did—until he gave it to his cousin Tancred of Sicily."

Beer interjected, "I wonder if history would have been different if Richard had the sword in his final battle with Saladin at Jaffa."

"Possibly, but sadly the Crusades changed the world forever. Those wars still fuel the fire of the Islamic extremists' jihad against us, the infidels."

Klein asked, "Do you have any idea of what's next for me?"

"Obviously, I know that you already visited St. Mary's of Zion in Ethiopia. Otherwise, you wouldn't have known to come here. You had to have been in the Chapel cave and seen the Ark and the artwork. Chaim, the Templars built that room in the early 1500s. It is part of the *knowledge* passed down from Grand Master to Grand Master."

Klein rubbed his forehead, trying to take in all these new facts.

She continued, "Your responsibility is enormous, but if everyone does his or her part, perhaps this terrorist threat to peace that you have already been fighting will fade away. Then *all* men, regardless of race or religion, will believe it is far better to coexist."

"Baroness, respectfully, that's the most idealistic thing I've ever heard."

"The battle of the Sons of Light versus the Sons of Darkness *will* occur. It has already started. You're in the middle of it, and now we are as well."

"*You're* doing this with us?" Beer asked, dumbfounded.

"Yes, I am. And on one issue, Chaim, I need you to be truthful and tell me what you think of Muslims and the Arab world."

Klein spit out, "I hate terrorists. I have no problem killing whoever threatens my country, my family, or anyone else."

"I suspect that is one reason God picked you, but I asked your view on Muslims generally."

"I live in Israel and have many longtime Palestinian friends from school and growing up in Jerusalem. I've been close to my friend Malik since grade school. I genuinely believe the vast majority of

Muslims around the world want better lives for their families and are not guided by hate. I have no quarrel with Islam. I support the Muslims for Peace event that you probably heard about."

The baroness grasped Klein's hand. "I am so pleased to hear that. You should know that the MFP rally yesterday was approved by me, working with your government."

"Really?" Klein asked, surprised.

"Ask your Prime Minister," she said in a blunt tone. "You fixed a problem for us with Sawalha. We helped finance the MFP program here for you. It seems with what happened today, we are inextricably linked, Chaim. I hope we grow to like and trust each other."

"It would seem that should be a goal," Klein said, "but I have a lot to process. I didn't exactly expect to end up today with the Knights Templar as a partner. It sounds like quite a curious relationship."

"That's a fair statement. You'll see that we have immense financial capabilities and are a worldwide organization of extraordinary people. We exist because the legend of the Templar's treasure is true. Spies and informants warned us about Philip, and before he could act against us, we loaded most of our treasure, records, and secrets onto our own fleet of eighteen ships, which were brought here to England. Then, by our own design, we disappeared quietly into history."

After letting her point sink in, the baroness continued, "Consider that seven hundred years ago the Templars had the greatest wealth in the world. From then until now, the Grand Masters protected and wisely invested that treasure. Some people think our treasure was buried at Rosslyn Chapel or Oak Island in Nova Scotia, but that's not true. We converted our gold, silver, and gems into other assets that have since grown in value and produced great revenue. Especially our real estate holdings. We are wealthier than some nations."

"How will you use your money to help me?" Chaim asked.

"Yesterday, we helped Israel pay for the rally, but now the Knights Templar will permanently fund the MFP worldwide to assure its success. Defeating fundamentalism must come from within Islam. We must support mainstream Muslims so that they may stand united and tell the radicals they are wrong in their interpretations of the Koran. Just as important, we must educate those who do not know better. So, Chaim, take your sword and come with me."

The baroness led Klein and Beer through a maze of hallways, staircases, and an underground tunnel until they were back in Westminster Abbey. They exited a door adjacent to Poets' Corner into the octagonally shaped Chapter House, built 700 years ago for Benedictine monks. Once there, the baroness explained that the Chapter House had once been a meeting place for the King's Council and the Commons, the precursor to today's Parliament.

They passed through an alcove and stopped at an ancient heavy wooden door on which an engraved bronze plaque read "Librarian and Keeper of the Muniments." The door stood out due to its electronic security keypad and two unusual locks. While opening the door, she said, "Can you imagine? All these years, so many fascinating Templar documents maintained right here in this private Templar space."

Bookshelves covered three walls up to the eighteen-foot ceiling; the books' frayed bindings indicating their ancient state. The fourth wall held a wooden hutch stuffed with documents and artifacts. Next to the cabinet sat an intricately carved antique desk that Klein surmised once belonged to royalty.

When the baroness saw Klein looking above the desk at a framed picture of Winston Churchill, she said, "Sir Winston was also a Templar." Above Churchill's picture hung an 800-year-old, mint-condition white shield, emblazoned with a red cross in the middle, the symbol of the Knights Templars.

The baroness ordered Klein to sit at the desk. Then she took down the picture of Churchill, revealing a rectangular hole in the wall the size of a hardback novel. She instructed Chaim to explore the hole. Cautiously, he extended his arm in the hole until his elbow disappeared into the space. His fingers hit a flat area with a small opening. He concluded the shape of that space was a few inches round on top and maybe a half inch narrower at the bottom. Still feeling around, he considered the size and shape of the opening, then his eyes narrowed, and he asked Beer for his backpack.

Klein removed and unwrapped the cup of Jesus from the bag, noticing the baroness's astonishment. Klein said, "This cup was locked away inside the Temple Mount one thousand years before Westminster was even built. I'm pretty sure it fits into an open space in the back of this wall. Klein slid the chalice inside the cutout. He pulled his arm out empty-handed and said incredulously, "It's a perfect fit!"

The baroness smiled, opened her hands, and nodded.

A moment later, everyone could hear a grinding sound of the wall's bricks rubbing against each other. Six bricks began jutting in and out of the wall, until two fell with a thud onto the desk. Klein intuitively stuck his hand in the newly revealed hole and pulled out a wooden box with lions carved on the lid. His eyes opened wide, and he stared at the box before cautiously opening it. He found a document wrapped in navy blue silk, which he carefully unrolled at the baroness's insistence.

She said, "Imagine that...this scroll has been in that wall for hundreds of years, and tourists have walked by here every day thinking it's just the Church library. And all this time, Chaim, this room and that little space has been waiting for you. Only you, the person with Jesus's cup, could retrieve that scroll."

"How could anyone know to construct this?" Klein said excitedly. "And how did you know about the cup?"

"In my training to become Grand Master. Chaim, what the Templars found from digging around the Temple Mount all those years made them rich, powerful, and famous. It has always been said that they found the Ark of the Covenant, the Holy Grail, the Shroud of Turin, and the head of John the Baptist. But exactly what they found is unknown and lost to the ages because when King Phillip the Fourth arrested our Templar leaders, including Grand Master Jacques de Molay, he was unable to share many of our most important secrets with his successor. But I know about the cave in Ethiopia and that the cup you're holding is somehow part of a big plan that now involves you, and that cup validates you."

"But Baroness, how could you even know about the cup's existence?"

The baroness smiled. "Come now, Chaim. Everyone through history knew about the Holy Grail, although there have been many differences in opinion as to what really was the Holy Grail. We always assumed that it was simply the chalice you are holding, which could have been safely hidden elsewhere. It seems we were right because you found it in the Ark of the Covenant, which was probably only about one hundred meters from where the Knights Templar found their Ark."

"What does that document say?" asked Beer.

The baroness answered, "It is the deed to the property the Knights Templar took from their excavations at the Temple Mount. The document transfers all of that property back to you, upon your victory over the Sons of Darkness."

"Whatever property you have belongs to Israel," Klein said.

"I see no reason to discuss that right now. Do what you have to, and it will all be yours. You found an Ark and the cup. You found the sword. That led you to me, didn't it? So don't worry, we will help you along the way. We want you to succeed."

"That's fine! So I'll just get the cup back, and we'll be on our way."

The baroness wagged her finger. "Oh no Chaim, you get the sword and the scroll. I get the chalice."

Klein shrugged. "I guess that's a fair trade."

14

Kabul, Afghanistan

Since the mid-1990s, Kabul was a near-constant war zone, with car bombs and suicide bombers plaguing the city, leaving long stretches of skeletal, bombed-out buildings. Small red flags protruded from the dusty streets, marking landmines planted by the Soviets. The city reeked of sewage. Yet amid the rubble and filth, the people of Kabul lived their lives, walking the streets with their heads up, seemingly oblivious to the wars that plagued their city since 1979, when they were first invaded by the Russians.

With traffic at a standstill in the chaotic Kabul marketplace, Rafsani and Khaled exited their stalled taxi. Walking would be more time efficient. With both men clothed in the traditional Afghan garb, a *pakol* hat and a long, coat-like *chupan* over baggy pants, they blended into the sea of people.

After scanning the vicinity as part of his ongoing safety check, Rafsani said to Khaled, "You've exceeded my expectations in your training, but you are now facing the most difficult days of your life. We could die."

"If that is Allah's will, so be it."

Rafsani smiled, then walked into an intersection, ignoring multiple vehicles that nearly plowed into him. He turned in a semi-circle until he spotted the white dome and minarets of Kabul's tallest mosque. With Khaled in his wake, Rafsani headed toward the mosque, stopping now and again to be sure they weren't being followed. Minutes later, they entered a dimly lit internet café next to the mosque. The café was filled with an acrid combination of smoke, sweat, and the stench of human waste coming from the hole in the floor of a doorless bathroom. Four dirty folding tables lined the left wall, each holding three laptops. Half the seats were occupied by young men, oblivious to the environment.

Rafsani paid the attendant for an hour's time, and he sat with Khaled at the closest open computer. Once the internet screen appeared, Rafsani typed in www.TheRightHandofGod.com. Pictures of Islamic religious sites, including the Ka'aba and the Dome of the Rock appeared, followed by photos of Mujahedin, with scrolling letters proclaiming the glory of Allah and jihad. At a log-in window, Rafsani typed "RafsaniSonOfIraq." Another window opened, and he typed "WorldJihad."

An instant message popped up: "Why do you contact us?"

Rafsani typed: "I wish to see the Wise Man."

"For what purpose?"

"To bring him a Koran."

"Your location?"

"At father's home."

A moment later the screen turned black, as if the website had shut down.

"How long do you think we'll have to wait?" asked Khaled.

"Not long. They're expecting us."

Rafsani positioned his chair to view the passersby outside. As a rat scurried across the floor, Khaled pulled up a second chair and stretched his legs on it. Forty minutes later, a tiny, shoeless boy in a shredded tunic and pants torn off at the knees walked through the door. His eyes met Rafsani's, and with a high voice he asked, "Son of Iraq?"

Rafsani nodded, and the boy turned and left, motioning for the men to follow him. Rafsani and Khaled pushed past people as the nimble kid darted in and out of the thick crowd. The boy scooted into the marketplace where dilapidated merchant stalls lined up for blocks, selling everything from clothes, hardware, electronics, food, and jihadist materials to haircuts. The boy finally entered a shop filled with quilts and fabric bolts; the men followed him inside.

Without looking up, an old man in a black pakol working at a sewing machine instructed the visitors to sit in two plastic folding chairs. The boy disappeared.

Minutes later, an obese man waddled into the stall. He pulled open a black curtain next to the tailor and exited through a metal back door into an alley. Rafsani and Khaled followed, and as they passed through the door, they saw six men and three vans waiting for them. No words were spoken, but Rafsani understood what was next, and his slight nod indicated his submission. Black hoods were thrown over his and Khaled's head.

"Do not speak!" a voice commanded. "Words will be met with punishment."

Once Rafsani's van drove off, he coughed twice. About twenty seconds later, Khaled returned a light cough, confirming that they were being kept together.

So far, everything was happening the way Rafsani had predicted. However, he knew from experience that the process of face-to-face meetings with Ayman al-Zawahiri, the leader of al-Qaeda, was never the same. Security precautions were necessarily stringent. Silence was the rule, and their hoods would stay on until the ride was over, so nobody could identify anyone else. It was pointless to estimate where they were headed. This first ride could be a loop twenty times around Kabul or twenty miles straight out of town.

Even so, Rafsani could tell they were leaving the Afghan capital, as the city noise diminished and the van started climbing, indicating a trip into the mountains on the city outskirts. He expected another vehicle would take them for a second leg of the trip—possibly another after that—until al-Zawahiri's personal security team would make the final pick-up and delivery. The route and its participants were untraceable.

After what Rafsani estimated was about two hours, the van stopped. Still hooded, Rafsani and Khaled were shepherded into another van, but not before they were searched and again given the instruction of silence. The second ride took even longer, through broken, rising and falling winding roads, and the two hooded men took the opportunity to sleep. At the next stop, when their hoods were removed, they saw the dangerous Korengal Valley before them. The Valley of Death in Northeastern Afghanistan was a central focus of the U.S. war against the Taliban and al-Qaeda. Marked by their trademark black turbans, four of the five men greeting them in the travel party were Taliban. One carried a Russian-made, shoulder-launched, surface-to-air missile.

Rafsani looked out over the six-mile-long valley, bordered by craggy brown mountains on both sides, with scattered patches of massive cedar trees and the muddy, crooked Korengal River running through the middle of the rich green valley. Multiple villages of boxy stone houses with flat roofs meshed together into one complex were built into the steep-cliffed mountainsides.

Rafsani sized up the Korengali leader as being a crude man who feared nothing, having lived his whole life in this closed and untamed world. The Korengalis were born into violence and proudly relished their successes in battle over the Soviet Union, the Taliban, and now the United States. Out of financial necessity, they had finally made peace with the Taliban. Their valley was blessed with forests of income-producing, high-quality cedar. The government had tried to regulate and tax the Korengalis' sale of the wood, so ultimately an uneasy partnership was formed. The Taliban would smuggle cedar through Pakistan on treacherous paths using donkeys and in return, the Korengali would team up to fight the Americans.

Suddenly, an American F-16 roared out of nowhere from the south and disappeared to the north in seconds. Moments later, a few miles away, a deafening explosion was the prelude to a cone-shaped fireball that flashed halfway up a mountainside. The orange football field-sized fire turned into a grey mushroom cloud of smoke that expanded twentyfold as it rose hundreds of yards into the air.

Khaled stood transfixed by the visual of death and destruction. He had seen the effect of smaller bombs, both in his training with Rafsani and back home in Ramallah, but never the devastating effects of a one-ton bomb being dropped from a supersonic jet fighter. Rafsani watched Khaled's reaction and said, "You get it? One of those could land on us."

Khaled raised his eyebrows. "If it does, at least we won't feel it."

Their driver advised them that the bomb fell where their next switch was to occur. Rafsani then noticed the Korengali leader's visible angst while speaking on a handheld radio. He shut it off and angrily announced that everyone on the mountain was dead. He cursed Rafsani and Khaled as being bad luck and demanded the group immediately depart. As they started walking, Rafsani told the driver, "Tell them we need guns. We are soldiers. There could be an ambush."

His request was met with a sharp no.

Judging the group dynamics, Rafsani told Khaled the situation was unstable, and they had no ability to control it. Khaled stayed silent, but his adrenaline jumped at his mentor's ominous warning.

THE TRAIL INTO THE valley was filled with boulders and cedar trees, with each step downhill treacherous; the land was broken in steep, jutted angles, covered by rocks, overgrown tree roots, or slippery gravel. Nevertheless, the group moved quickly despite the fact that all the Taliban were wearing sandals. They soon broke into an open clearing that led them onto an uneven, two-foot-wide path hugging the side of the mountain on their left. On their right was a 500-foot drop to the bottom. As Rafsani admired the expansive panorama of the Korengal Valley, he said, "This is quite a view, isn't it?"

"Right. Amazing," muttered Khaled, who had yet to lift his eyes off the next step he was going to take, for fear it would be his last.

Thick bursts of machine gun and mortar fire started echoing through the valley. Speaking Pashto, the language of the Taliban, Rafsani asked the soldier ahead of him to get them weapons, since they were clearly headed into trouble. The young, rail-thin man with a spindly beard spun around and said, "I do not know who you are or where you are going. I was told to keep you safe. I cannot get you weapons. But you can trust me because *The Right Hand of God* is watching over us."

Hearing that, Rafsani asked, "So you're al-Qaeda? Are the others trustworthy?"

"I have never seen them before. I trust no one unless I know them."

Rafsani almost advised the man to not even trust those he knew, but instead he asked, "What's your name?"

"Tabur." The al-Qaeda soldier knew better than to ask the same question back.

"Tabur, please, we need weapons. Convince them."

"I am allowed my weapon because I am stationed here. These men are doing someone a favor by guiding you through the valley. They did not want to do this before, and they are even less happy now. I have to deliver you to the meeting point, but they don't."

"So, how do we defend ourselves if we encounter the Americans?"

"Pray," replied Tabur.

The group continued its trek and, to Khaled's relief, the path widened. Always observant of his surroundings, Rafsani spotted a white object flying above them that he knew was an American Predator drone, equipped with cameras that could read a license plate from two miles up. Given that they were in a wide-open section on a mostly unprotected mountainside, Rafsani knew they had been spotted, especially since they were carrying automatic weapons and an anti-aircraft missile. He also knew that mentioning it was pointless.

Ten minutes later, an Apache helicopter appeared on the horizon, bearing down on them at full speed. The Apache was a fast, highly maneuverable killing machine designed to destroy almost anything, including tanks and bunkers, with its sixteen Hellfire-guided missiles. Seconds later, an unending string of 50mm machine gun fire rained down on them. One Taliban's chest was ripped open, and two others who were shot tumbled down the mountain. Seeing the Korengalis running straight ahead, Rafsani yelled for Khalid and Tabur to run the opposite way.

One Taliban stood his ground, firing his machine gun at the Apache, a meaningless gesture since the helicopter was built to withstand automatic weapons. A stream of red-hot bullets cut his body in half. The Taliban with the shoulder-launched missile knelt down and aimed it straight ahead.

As bullets pierced the mountainside inches above his head, Khaled dove behind a massive boulder, and he was immediately flattened by Rafsani and Tabur. Rafsani was certain that one of the Apache's three-inch-long searing bullets would rip right through all three of them. At least death would be painless.

Seconds later, there were two nearly simultaneous explosions. The first was a deafening Hellfire missile that hit near the Taliban soldier, shaking the ground like an earthquake. A fireball flamed out in a fifty-foot radius, and a broiling heat wave fanned out five times that distance. Rock shrapnel shot through the air one hundred yards up like a volcanic eruption. A thick and choking layer of brown dust expanded so quickly it darkened the sky and carpeted the area like brown snow. The next explosion told them the Apache had been hit by the Taliban's missile, which was confirmed by the unmistakable sound of failing engines, high-winding rotors, and blades tailing off. The helicopter fell from the air and crashed into the mountainside. This was only momentary good news—Rafsani knew the U.S. would soon return with a vengeance.

Blanketed in brown grime, the three men struggled to stand up, their ears ringing. Rafsani glanced at the crater that now existed where the Taliban had stood his ground. He then saw the other side of the hole, where the one remaining Korengali was on one knee, staring at his dead friends. "Tabur, do you know the way down from here?"

"I know we're headed *that* way," he replied, pointing vaguely straight ahead.

Rafsani grunted and in one quick grab and twist on Tabur's shoulder, he snatched away Tabur's Kalashnikov. Quickly aiming, Rafsani shot the kneeling Korengali in the head, then handed the rifle back to Tabur. "You didn't trust him. I didn't trust him. I want our lives in my hands, not his. We need their weapons, and I'm making the decisions going forward. Let's go. Every second we stay here is a second closer to when the Americans come back, and when they do, they're not going to be happy."

"One thing is certain. That Taliban was either the bravest or craziest man I've ever seen," Khaled said. "Standing toe to toe in a fight with a helicopter is suicidal."

Tabur replied, "That, my friend, is jihad. I would have done the same thing if I had not promised to deliver you safely down the mountain. One day though, I will be a martyr."

Rafsani, Khaled, and Tabor carefully crawled into the crater and clawed their way back up on the other side. Twenty minutes later, they picked up weapons, a radio, and anything else off the corpses that might be useful.

"Quite an afternoon, Khaled?" Rafsani said with a biting smile.

"Well, this has not been fun, but it was a necessary event to turn me into a soldier. I still think I need to fire a weapon in battle and kill someone, to understand what that feels like."

Rafsani raised his eyebrows and replied, "I couldn't agree more."

RAFSANI, KHALED, AND TABUR hadn't yet covered 200 yards when they heard a helicopter approaching. Knowing it was the Americans, and since the men were in a wide-open path with no place to hide, Rafsani ordered them, "Drop your weapons, lie down flat and act like you're dead. No matter what, don't move an inch, don't twitch, don't cough."

Twenty seconds after they started playing possum, an Apache hovered above them, with a Blackhawk positioned off each wing. Rafsani knew their infrared sensors showed they were alive, so their only hope was that the Americans believed they were seriously wounded, near death and thus, would be left alone. When the helicopters finally dispersed, Rafsani announced, "We can't move until they recover their soldiers and head to their base. They'll come back here and if they see that we're gone, they'll find us and kill us."

As Rafsani predicted, thirty minutes later the Americans returned for a quick fly by. They waited five more minutes, retrieved their weapons, and started navigating down the mountain. Three hours later, when they reached the valley floor, Tabor radioed ahead to advise that they were safe and nearby.

It was a starless black night by the time they met up with a group of al-Qaeda and Taliban soldiers on a dirt road heading into Parquat, a village on the Korengal River controlled by the Taliban. "Praise to Allah," marked the response to the story of their bloody confrontation with the American helicopters and their "miraculous escape." Arrangements had already been made to feed and house Rafsani and Khaled for the night.

At sunrise, a new al-Qaeda guide, Nabil, arrived and drove them to another village. The Taliban already had lined up sixteen families on the road, and its leader was berating them, alleging that one of them had cooperated with the Americans, causing his friends' deaths. The young leader wore a long beard and a white robe, and he had a noticeable limp. He walked up and down the ranks of the impoverished, frightened villagers, threatening each one.

He stood before a timid man in his early twenties, demanding to know who had betrayed the Taliban, while the nervous man's three whimpering children clung to his leg. The rail-thin man repeatedly swore in the name of Allah that he knew nothing. Unmoved, the leader smacked him in the head with his pistol, knocking him to the ground, then ripped his tiny daughter away by her long black hair, causing shrieks from the child, her parents, and the villagers. The leader ordered silence, then slammed the girl to the ground. With his steel-toed boots, he repeatedly kicked her in the stomach and chest until one shot landed squarely in her face, crushing it, splattering blood and killing her. Anguished, the parents cried out and the leader warned the despondent father that he had five seconds to identify the spy. Despite the man's frantic plea that he knew nothing, the Taliban put the gun flush against the man's throat and pulled the trigger, stone-faced as he watched the father die a bloody, quick death. He next turned to an old man, demanding answers to his questions. When he failed to give a satisfactory response, the leader shot him in the head. His wife fell to her knees crying and collapsed onto her dead husband, embracing him as the Taliban emptied two bullets into her back.

Khaled's stomach turned and he grew faint, started hyperventilating, and looked away, fighting back tears. He glanced at a stone-faced Rafsani, who saw Khaled's reaction and whispered, "Khaled, stay calm. Check your emotions." Khaled took a deep breath to focus and regain his composure.

The leader then spun around and indiscriminately emptied his clip into the villagers, killing five more. He approached Rafsani and said, "That was for what they did to those who died yesterday, and for what they put you through."

"But these people didn't know anything," Khaled replied.

"Doesn't matter what they knew. The village now knows that cooperation with the Americans means you will die. Other villages will learn of this and understand the risk."

Khaled saw a little girl lying on the ground, gasping for air, bleeding profusely from her leg. He ran up to her, took off his belt and tightened it around her thigh to stop the bleeding, but it was too late and seconds later she died. He turned to find every Taliban soldier staring at him.

The leader sprinted toward Khaled, waving his pistol. "That was not your business!"

Khaled took a deep breath and stood his ground. "Those who violate the laws of Allah or interfere with jihad should be harshly punished. But certainly not innocent people or children who are fellow Muslims. We can never be respected if we act like animals."

"Respect? Who cares about respect! We rule by fear!" He pointed the gun at Khaled.

An instant later, Rafsani punched Khaled in the face, knocking him down. He stepped on Khaled's chest and said to the Taliban leader, "I apologize for my young friend. He is not thinking straight." Rafsani dropped to a knee, keeping Khaled pinned down, and hissed, "If you don't fix this now, you're dead."

Khaled stood back up and said to the Taliban leader, "I apologize to all of you. I am new to jihad and have not seen a child die before. I should not have done that. May Allah and you both please forgive me."

The leader returned the harshest of stares, but said, "Young one, I will let this pass, but only because I know that you are critical to this man you travel with, who I understand is an important leader of jihad. Out of respect for him, he can deal with you as he wishes."

Seeing that the situation was diffused, Rafsani turned to Nabil. "We must go now. My friend and I are already behind schedule. And you are right, I will deal with him later."

"I understand, but we have an attack planned against the Americans today. That is why there are so many soldiers here, with many more already in the mountains."

Rafsani responded, "We cannot be involved in that today."

"We fight the Americans every day. It is what we do."

"It is what *you* do. We are here for other business."

Visibly upset, the al-Qaeda guide answered harshly, "I was told you are a brave and important soldier for Allah. I am disappointed that you are afraid of combat."

While Rafsani couldn't argue with the Taliban, he could say anything to an al-Qaeda soldier.

"Nabil, I have been in more battles and life-threatening situations than everyone here combined. I fight the infidels every day. Just differently from the way you do. My friend and I are not engaging in battle today."

The soldier sneered, "Jihad means we all die in combat for Allah."

"Jihad does not mean you die for the sake of it at any time," Rafsani retorted. "You die for jihad at the right time."

"Today I decide that, not you. You will go into battle with us, and then I will take you to your rendezvous. You don't even know where to go, so if you wish to stay here, I will not return. You will still die in the Korengal."

Rafsani seethed. Normally, he would have killed Nabil right then, but he suspected he'd have his chance later.

Given the circumstances, Rafsani and Khaled boarded a truck headed to the Restrepo Outpost, which housed a small U.S. Army platoon on the side of a nearby Korengal mountain. They passed a one-legged man on the road slapping red paint on rocks to mark some of the 30 million still-live mines planted by the Soviets in the 1980s. In a nearby muddy field, fifteen green rusty tanks sat lined up in a row, abandoned by the Soviets. The Taliban platoon reached their destination halfway up the mountain and everyone climbed out of the truck.

THREE HUNDRED YARDS AWAY, an American Delta forces soldier set up a 66mm FLASH rocket launcher, a four-barrel bazooka that fired incendiary rockets armed with the new high-tech chemical TEA, which spontaneously combusts in air, burning at extremely high temperatures. TEA disintegrates skin and tissue on contact, and if its vapors are inhaled, it can melt internal organs. His spotter studied the video of enemy soldiers advancing from the west, measuring their distance at 936 feet. The Delta specialist lifted the four-foot-long FLASH onto his shoulder, centered the enemy through his scope, and pulled the trigger.

Seconds later, a fireball exploded in the middle of the Taliban and al-Qaeda soldiers about seventy-five yards from Rafsani, Khaled, and Nabil. Two thousand-degree flaming goo engulfed everything within a twenty-five-yard radius. Most of the men in that vicinity instantly melted to death. Those touched by no more than a nickel-sized amount of TEA had their limbs roasted off.

The intense heat was overwhelming, even where Rafsani and the Taliban patrol were standing. Nevertheless, the unit leader boldly moved forward with his shaken men tentatively following.

Rafsani stepped in front of Nabil while the others passed by. He claw-gripped the guide's Adam's apple and barked, "Nabil, I *will* die for jihad, but it will *not* be here. My friend and I have important business. You *will* lead us out of here right now to our rendezvous spot or I *will* kill you and find my own way, which I can do. Are we clear?"

Nabil nodded.

Rafsani fell to a knee and yelped in pain. The al-Qaeda and Taliban soldiers who just passed them spun around to see what happened. Grasping his foot, Rafsani moaned, "My ankle! I broke my ankle. Keep going! We will catch up."

The terrorists couldn't have cared less and continued forward. Khaled and Nabil assisted Rafsani, who was hopping on one foot as they moved away from the group. But the second they were out of view, they aggressively hiked back toward the valley. Even as the distance grew from the battlefield, the noise from helicopters and bombs made it clear the American offensive was in full force.

"Here we are," said Nabil. "This is always the rendezvous location."

Rafsani distrusted Nabil for jeopardizing his and Khaled's safety, but this spot actually made sense to him. After a two-day hike south out of the Korengal and through the mountains, they were shielded by trees next to the Kabul-Jalalabad Highway. The notorious, winding, heavily traveled four-lane highway, carved into craggy mountains, had been labeled the most dangerous road in the world due to its insane drivers, the Taliban shooting at cars, roadside bombings, and kidnappings. However, the six-car rest stop right below provided fast, easy access on and off the road.

Khaled got right into Nabil's face. "Unbelievable! Using the same rendezvous point every time? You've jeopardized our security and the people we're going to see!"

"What are you talking about?" the guide asked, obviously clueless.

"You're an al-Qaeda courier!" Khaled yelled. "Don't you realize that through drones, satellites, and spies, the Americans watch everything? You put us at risk! We could be under surveillance right now." Khaled glared at Nabil.

"That's ridiculous. You're wrong," Nabil defensively replied.

Rafsani was pleased that Khaled recognized the potential threat to their security and equally displeased that he had missed it. "Khaled, you're right. And Nabil, you've now twice put us in jeopardy!"

"I got you here safely."

"No, you're untrustworthy and reckless." Rafsani turned to Khaled. "You've handled yourself well since we arrived in Afghanistan, but trying to save that little girl was inexcusable. You both deserve punishment, so you will fight to the death. Whoever survives has the blessing of Allah."

"You have no right to force me to fight!" Nabil yelled, incensed.

Rafsani shrugged. "Then don't fight. Khaled, you heard my order."

Khaled simply nodded once.

Nabil grasped that he had no choice, and the two men squared off. Nabil was taller and heavier than the athletically built and focused Khaled, and the men circled each other.

Suddenly, Khaled turned toward Rafsani, standing perpendicular to Nabil, and said, "Wait, Omar, I have a question."

As Khaled expected and saw from his peripheral vision, Nabil let down his guard. In that instant, Khaled pounced with a quick half step toward Nabil, throwing a hard karate punch with his right hand into Nabil's nose, followed by a perfectly placed, equally hard left-handed punch into his Adam's apple. Nabil cried out in pain and stumbled backwards. Khaled continued his nonstop assault with blows to Nabil's stomach, followed by a series of fast, hard punches to his face and neck. Scowling at his barely conscious downed victim, Khaled put his left hand on Nabil's forehead, his right hand on the back of his neck, and in one quick jerk snapped his neck. Khaled spit on the dead man's face and rose to face Rafsani.

"Well, now we know you can kill someone up close and personal. That's a lot different from just pulling a trigger," Rafsani said. "Your diversion was perfect, and I loved that you showed no mercy in beating him and then ending it." Rafsani smacked Khaled on the arm and smiled. "How did it feel to take someone's life?"

"I felt nothing but contempt for Nabil. He had to die."

Rafsani didn't expect Khaled's coldness but was pleased that was Khaled's reaction. "So, Khaled, you handled yourself well at the airports. In Kabul, I let you run the motorcycle attack at the National Directorate of Intelligence, and you made all the right decisions, and fourteen traitors were killed. You've shown great bravery everywhere, including near the battle with the Americans and here today fighting Nabil."

"If that is what you think, I thank you and am humbled, Omar. But my error in judgment with the Taliban and the girl eliminated anything I did right. That could have been fatal for me and perhaps you, so from my view, this mission was a personal failure."

"Yes, what you did with the girl was stupid. You failed to keep your emotions in check. If you're going to be dumb, you better be tough, because otherwise, *you* will end up dead. You will always see children, old people, and others who could be innocent die. *They don't matter.* People die every day. We must stay alive until *we decide* it's time to die as shahid. We die under *our* terms. Do you understand?"

"I fully understand."

Rafsani retrieved Nabil's burner phone from his backpack, powered it up, and texted "Arrived" to the last number Nabil had called. A response came back: "Two hours."

RIGHT ON TIME, the sun now replaced by a sliver of the moon, a black Mercedes S550 pulled into the unlit rest area. A tall, thin man with grey hair and a long scraggly beard stepped out from the front passenger seat. He greeted Rafsani with hugs like a long-lost brother.

Abu Ahmed al-Cairo was Ayman al-Zawahiri's most trusted courier and was introduced to Khaled, as he was to everyone, as the Egyptian. The only person with direct contact and full confidence of Zawahiri was the Egyptian, who lived with the head of al-Qaeda for over twenty years. One of the most guarded secrets in the world was the Egyptian's existence and name.

"A Mercedes? Seriously? What about keeping us off the radar?" Rafsani said.

"It's a diplomatic car. Minister of Defense Asif insisted on loaning it to us, so we could get through border patrol."

A longstanding cooperative relationship existed between al-Qaeda and Pakistan, exemplified by Pakistan's sheltering bin Laden in Abbottabad for many years. Because Zawahiri could not electronically communicate with the outside world for security reasons, as was the case with bin Laden, he had to exchange messages with other al-Qaeda leaders through a series of untraceable couriers.

The Egyptian removed the SIM card from Nabil's cell phone, then tossed it down an adjacent ravine. Next, he obligatorily patted down Rafsani and Khaled, then dumped their backpacks as well. He opened the trunk, which contained a large cooler filled with water and towels, so the men could somewhat clean themselves. Clean thobes were waiting for them in the back seat, along with a bag filled with fruit and boiled chicken, which they ravenously attacked.

Forty minutes later, they approached a brightly lit border crossing separating Afghanistan from Pakistan. Twenty-foot-tall, barbed wire fences extended as far as the eye could see. Two tanks were stationed at each edge of the gate, their cannon barrels ominously staring down incoming traffic. Three jeeps armed with 120mm machine guns sat right inside the gate.

A platoon of armed soldiers stood sentry and as the Egyptian's vehicle pulled to a stop, four of them instantly surrounded the car. However, upon seeing the Egyptian's gold-stamped, red leather passport and diplomatic license plate, the car was waved through.

Upon clearing security, Rafsani said, "I know what happened to Sheik al-Talib."

"Who was it? The Israelis? Only they could kidnap a Saudi minister and make him disappear without a trace."

"Yes, but they made some mistakes. First, the murder of Mullah Sawalha and the kidnapping of Sheik al-Talib both happened in London within twenty-four hours of each other, and that is not a coincidence. Khaled, tell him about the restaurant."

Khaled said, "Three men came to the Mujahid Mosque for Friday afternoon prayers, and afterward they started an argument with Mullah Sawalha about the Muslims for Peace rally you probably heard about. Then we were having dinner with the Mullah in a restaurant when the same men came in passing out flyers for the MFP. This time, they started a fight with the Mullah that turned into a shootout, and the Mullah and one of their guys was killed. One of the murderers said something in Hebrew, so I knew they were Mossad. After that,

I read every obituary in their main newspapers, the *Jerusalem Post* and *Haaretz*, to figure out who was involved. Based on age and other factors, I concluded the dead Mossad agent was named Ori Levin. I sent a friend to the funeral to take pictures of everyone there. Omar and I studied the photos and identified the two other murderers, even though they were in disguise in London. So now we will find his friends and kill them."

"*You* figured that out?" asked the Egyptian.

"Yes."

"Now I understand why we put such great faith in you, my young friend," said the Egyptian. "But whatever you do, make sure you also kill their families."

The Mercedes soon pulled into a small airport on the outskirts of Peshawar. Surprised, Rafsani asked, "Isn't the General living here? Where are we going?"

"We know the Americans want to kill him, but they have no stomach for civilian casualties in a raid. So, we moved the General to Karachi, where he's hiding in the middle of sixteen million people. They'll never find him, and even if they did, they can't send in the Navy Seals like they did to kill Osama."

Three hours later, their Pakistan Airways jet landed at the modern Karachi Jinnah International Airport, and they were escorted through security as government VIPs. The Egyptian's driver pulled up in a Toyota Corolla, the most popular car in Pakistan, then jumped on the N10 Expressway, and fifteen minutes later he exited into the upscale Goth Shaikhan neighborhood. Passing high rises, office towers, cultural attractions, shops and restaurants, they parked in front of a tall apartment building on 26th Street only blocks from the Arabian Sea.

The Egyptian said, "It's late, but he wants to see you now so you can be on your way tomorrow morning." The Egyptian knocked on the door of Unit 801 four times as his signal, then used his keys to unlock two locks.

Zawahiri stood in the foyer, smiling broadly in his black turban-like kaffiyah, narrow wire-framed glasses, and floor-length white thobe.

Rafsani noticed that his once-long gray beard was trimmed to only three or four inches.

"*As-salaam alaikum*, Omar."

"*Wa-alaikum salaam*, General Ayman."

The two men exchanged the traditional Muslim double cheek kiss before Zawahiri acknowledged the Egyptian. Khaled was introduced next, and the al-Qaeda leader firmly grasped his hand, mentioning Khaled's rising star reputation.

Khaled had studied up to learn that Zawahiri was born in Egypt in 1951 to a wealthy family of doctors and politicians, and he had also become a surgeon. But by age fourteen, he had also joined the Muslim Brotherhood. When he was twenty-eight, he left for Afghanistan to fight the Soviets, where he met bin Laden, and they became close friends. At different times, Zawahiri was arrested by the Soviets for recruiting jihadists, placed on the United States terrorist watchlist with a $25 million bounty on his head, and sentenced to death in Egypt for killing sixty-two tourists. In 1998, as Emir, he merged Egyptian Islamic Jihad into al-Qaeda. By 2009, he had become al-Qaeda's military commander and in May 2011 became its leader after bin Laden's death. In 2015, he created a formal alliance with the Taliban and later, in a released audio message, he suggested that ISIS and al-Qaeda should merge.

Rafsani rested his right hand on Zawahiri's shoulder. "Ayman, are your new living arrangements working out? Are you safe here?"

Zawahiri smiled and spoke in an understated tone. "For more than twenty years I lived in caves and the most unseemly places in Afghanistan and Pakistan, in the worst of weather. I was always sick and nearly died twice. Now I live comfortably, eating and sleeping well, and nobody knows who I am, which you will understand shortly. I can even go outside and sit by the water to get fresh air."

"But that puts you and the organization at risk."

"Thank you for challenging me, Omar, because nobody does, but give me a moment and then you'll understand."

A few minutes later, Zawahiri walked out of his bedroom unrecognizable. While still wearing the same white thobe, he now donned a small white skull cap, dark horn-rimmed glasses, and his thin hair and shorter beard were black. Rafsani stared at him, stunned. "You dyed your hair?"

"It is not prohibited by Islam and this dye rinses out quickly. All of my pictures show me in a black kaffiyah with thin wire frame glasses and a long beard. So now, my friends, if I walked right by you on the street looking like this, would you know me?"

"No way," replied Khaled. Rafsani nodded in agreement.

"And nobody has, so I go outside every day. Actually, I would like some fresh air right now. Let's go for a walk." They exited the building into the warm and humid Karachi air.

Rafsani wasted no time. "So, Ayman, ISIS has surpassed al-Qaeda in the news, which is good for you, because it keeps al-Qaeda under the radar. But you're creating cells in Western Europe, Southeast Asia, India, and Eastern Africa. Given that ISIS has lost its money and territory in Iraq and Syria, al-Qaeda is already reemerging as the world leader of jihad and will grow stronger if it can strengthen its position in Syria and possibly attack Israel. In other words, you are well-positioned for the future."

"Yes, but it was a big loss that Osama's son Hamza was killed by the Americans. He would have succeeded his father," replied Zawahiri. "On the bright side, we are now in twenty-four countries and financially sound. The money has come from everywhere: the Taliban, significant donations, but also from ransom and extortion payments we've extracted from a few governments."

Rafsani was glad to hear it and said, "Our new ISIS leader, Amir al-Mawla, who succeeded Abu Bakr al-Baghdadi after the Americans killed him, has built an impressive inventory of cells through Europe and is growing ISIS' presence on the internet. ISIS may have lost Syria, but it is planting shahid throughout the West." He looked at Khaled.

"And I have handled some of that work in Europe," Khaled chimed in. "Over the last fifteen months I've been creating cells with Saudi money for the special mission Omar has been working on," said Khaled. "Right now, apart from our cells, al-Mawla tells me ISIS also has about seven thousand freedom fighters back in their European homes, who have completed their training in Syria and Iraq. That means we now have forty thousand soldiers from over one hundred countries trained throughout the world, and each one is waiting for his call to be a shahid."

"Allah's light shines down on you, Omar and Khaled. Your work is unprecedented. So, tell me your plans for Judgment Day."

"We have people carefully building cells in major cities in the United States, Europe, and the Far East," said Rafsani. "Every attack will be dramatic. Nothing simple like running over people on sidewalks. The goal is to damage infrastructure, kill many thousands, and ruin entire economies. But this is why I wanted to see you. After Judgment Day, we would like to merge al-Qaeda and ISIS, as you've previously suggested. Al-Mawla knows ISIS exists because of you and al-Qaeda Iraq. And soon he *will* need you. When everyone considers the options, symbolically and financially, it makes sense."

"Please tell al-Mawla that I completely agree." Zawahiri looked at Khaled. "I understand that in the past year you have become a bomb-making and weapons specialist and helped plan the assassinations of four infidels. Omar tells me that you are the best recruit that he has ever trained. That is high praise from someone with the highest standards. So, tell me what you think about all of this."

"I'm honored to work with Omar and to meet you. I am proud that on Judgment Day we will have spectacularly destroyed the infidels, and I will die a shahid."

Zawahiri frowned, shook his head, and wagged his finger. "You have much to learn, Khaled. Do you think Osama wanted to die?

No. Do you think Omar wants to die? No. Do you think I want to die? No. *We* must live. Our responsibility is to be leaders in the fight against the infidels. There are a million soldiers for Allah that can die honorably at any time as shahid. They are replaceable. *We* are not. Do you understand?"

Khaled bowed his head and humbly replied, "I do, General. Thank you for opening my eyes." He paused, then added, "I have promised Omar I would not let him down, and I will not let you down either."

Zawahiri replied, "I believe you and have faith in you."

15

Tel Aviv

"Since we've extracted every bit of information trapped in al-Talib's sick terrorist mind and on his laptop, I say we deliver his head in a gift-wrapped box to Al-Haqq." Dudi Bareket grinned at the five men sitting in the windowless Mossad conference room table. His proposal wasn't realistic, but Bareket had made his point.

Behind bookish round glasses, Mordechai Deckler, Chief of Staff to Prime Minister Zamir, tapped the table to secure his position to speak next. "Emotionally, extreme action would be appropriate retribution, given that Sheik al-Talib's plan threatens Israel's existence. But the fact is, we currently have the strongest relationship ever with Saudi Arabia, which remains in our long-term best interest. Killing al-Talib simply won't be helpful. Besides, we're not murderers."

Bareket rolled his eyes and shook his head. "I understand the importance of our economic relationship with the Saudis. And I appreciate that their sworn enemy is Iran, but they continue to fund terrorism directed against us and the West! Our relationship with them exists purely out of strategic convenience." Bareket pointed at Deckler. "We always have and always will kill our enemies, because their goal is to kill us first. We exact revenge when attacked because we must. Our enemies hate us, but they also fear us. And that includes Saudi Arabia."

"Dudi, do the Saudis know we have al-Talib?" Zamir asked.

"Not according to our agents on the ground. If they know they're not saying, because al-Talib directly links them to terrorism."

Boaz Mehrara, the youngest IDF General in the country, rose to address the room. His brilliance and imposing physical presence commanded everyone's attention. "Perhaps the missing laptop is more important to the Saudis than the missing minister. If they stay silent about his absence, they don't have to answer questions about his disappearance. Though, of course, their silence confirms they knew what he was planning."

Klein interjected, "We got lucky getting the laptop. We didn't know it was in his car."

"Can we tell the Saudis we learned of the kidnapping through informants and staged a search and rescue mission?" Deckler asked. "Then we could give him back as a goodwill gesture."

"*That* has potential," Zamir exclaimed. "They lie to us, we lie to them, and we both know the other is lying. We collected the information we needed from al-Talib. They get their minister back."

"That won't work," Mehrara said. "Talib knows we've been holding him, and that'll be the first thing he'll tell the Saudis."

Bareket looked away and replied, "Actually, Talib is at a safehouse in the Negev. He believes the Iranians are holding him prisoner."

Mehrara's eyes narrowed. "You just said you 'extracted every bit of information' from al-Talib, and now he thinks the Iranians are holding him. Just tell us Dudi, how did Mossad torture him?"

"We didn't."

"Then how did you get information from him?" asked Deckler, while rubbing his bald head. "I doubt he voluntarily answered your questions."

"We employed a harmless technique to make him speak freely during his interviews."

"Like what?" Zamir snapped, surprised by Bareket's revelation.

"An improved formula of Russia's SP-117 truth serum, so he won't remember anything."

"You drugged him? Is there more?" Zamir demanded.

"While he was under, we showed him a fake Al-Haqq website story about the car crash that we used to get him out of Harrods, and also we told him that we murdered his best friend. *We,* meaning Iran. Then we told him if he wasn't truthful with us, his daughters would be next and that we'd bring him body parts as proof."

"You don't call that torture?" Deckler said.

Bareket answered, "Absolutely not. We didn't physically hurt him, and he doesn't and won't remember what we did. In my book, that's not torture."

"Are you serious? That's psychological torture," Deckler replied.

"Not if he doesn't remember it," Bareket said, not backing down. "And even if he did, he'd still think we're Iranians. Otherwise, he has been treated extremely well. And please, you know that no country on earth has its existence threatened every day like Israel. We *do not* torture terrorists when they attack us and kill innocent civilians. Most countries do. But you know that Talib's computer revealed a globally coordinated terrorist attack. Should I really have stood down under the circumstances of this threat? Or should I have used every tactic necessary to protect us?"

Zamir smiled. "Frankly Dudi, given what al-Talib is responsible for, I think what you did is fine. If you beat the hell out of him a few times, I'd say he deserved that too. But don't do it now. Got it?"

"Yes, sir."

Having been uncharacteristically quiet, Norman Richards blurted out, "Deckler, you've lost touch with reality. Who *cares* if he was drugged? The Sheik is a fucking terrorist." Richards pulled a toothpick from his mouth and using it like a pointer continued, "What matters is that your Iranian story works, because Iran hates the Saudis, and the Saudis hate Iran."

Years earlier, when he was the CIA Station Chief in Jerusalem, with some help from Klein's cousin Debra, Richards stopped a plot by the infamous terrorist Carlos the Jackal to kill the American president. That had earned Richards the right to retire from fieldwork to a cushy job in Langley on the Middle East desk. Now he had been sent back to Israel to help prevent this new threat.

Richards looked at Klein. "He may be a little wacky, but I like Deckler's idea. You tell the world you sent Batman and his commando unit into Lebanon, which the Iranians control, to rescue al-Talib. That'll be one hell of a story. An Israeli commando unit saving a kidnapped Saudi minister from Iranian terrorists. The world will freak out." He laughed and added, *"The Jews did what?"*

Amused, Klein replied, "Batman? You think I'm *Batman*?"

"Yeah, I know all about you and your superhero record, and after you learn to fucking fly, I'll call you Superman. Till then, be happy with Batman."

Ignoring Richards's eccentric mouth, Zamir said, "Norman, we're *very* concerned about what we found on Talib's laptop. You saw it pertained to a coordinated global terrorist attack against Israel, America, and virtually every Western country. But there were no *details* about the plan. We saw only a few names like Khamenei, Nasrallah, al-Baghdadi, al-Mawla, and Zawahiri, and of course, wire transfers all over the globe. What have you and the CIA found?"

Without asking permission, Richards grabbed and lit one of Bareket's cigarettes. He leaned back in his chair and through a stream of smoke replied, "So far we've found shit. Nada."

"What about the money? Nobody traces money better than the United States," Mehrara said. "You have all the wire transfer information. Follow the money, right?"

Richards nodded. "We tried to trace the transfers out of a company called Altandy, Inc., in Dearborn, Michigan. We couldn't find an operating business with that name. The address was bad. The phone number on the bank account was bad. The person who signed the documents to open the bank account doesn't exist. We have a picture of him when he got a cashier's check to close the account, but there was no match in our facial recognition database. The man is a ghost. He and the money have disappeared."

"How about the bank?" asked Deckler. "Aren't banks required to investigate suspicious transactions, especially wire transfers?"

"The bank did not think the initial wires rose to the level of suspicious activity. Nothing was reviewed. So much for our Patriot Act."

Deckler frowned and sank into his chair. "Did you find anything about the New York or Washington transfers?"

Richards ran his fingers through his thick slicked-back gray hair. "Same deal, everywhere. We assume there are a number of fully operational cells in the United States, but so far, we've only met dead ends. We're working it really fucking hard."

"We know," said Bareket. "And we have two other leads you can help us track down."

"Happy to help. What do you have?"

A photo of an immensely built man with thick black curly hair and large dark brown eyes wearing an Iraqi Mukhabarat uniform popped onto the screen at the front of the room. "Omar Rafsani!" Richards declared. "What the fuck?"

"We believe he has a significant role in al-Talib's plans," replied Bareket.

"Well, now I get why you brought me here. Rafsani was Carlos the Jackal's protégé, along with the al-Sharif brothers, who nearly took out our government." Richards took a pensive drag off his cigarette.

"But Rafsani never went stateside. He stayed in Iraq to work for Saddam Hussein and became General of the Mukhabarat. Then he somehow escaped capture when Saddam was run out of Baghdad and helped al-Baghdadi grow ISIS out of the remnants of al-Qaeda Iraq. Now he's working with al-Mawla and we think, Zawahiri."

Bareket replied, "And Rafsani attended a meeting in Riyadh during the Haj with al-Talib and other state-sponsored terrorist leaders including Nasrallah. At that meeting, Rafsani even said he spoke for al-Qaeda. We believe that meeting is related to the terrorism attack plans on al-Talib's laptop."

"That's pretty damn interesting, but how did you learn about that meeting?" Richards asked.

"We have an agent inside the Saudi charity that al-Talib ran," Bareket answered proudly. "That's why we grabbed al-Talib when we could. Getting his laptop was a bonus."

Richards whistled. "No shit! *That* is fucking impressive. How'd you pull that off?"

"Sorry, Norman, you know I can't go there," Bareket said.

"Fine," Richards replied, not actually expecting the answer. "But I don't get the dynamics. I know Saddam hated al-Qaeda, so how could Rafsani work with al-Qaeda?"

"When bin Laden was in the Sudan, he paid Carlos to set up terrorist training camps there. Carlos mentored Rafsani and introduced him to bin Laden and they developed a relationship."

"I knew that Saddam and bin Laden both knew Carlos but not the rest," said Richards. "That ties everything together."

Bareket added, "Right, and Rafsani hated the U.S. so he had no problem with Zarqawi when he formed al-Qaeda Iraq, because he was so effective at disrupting the U.S. troops in Iraq. Then al-Qaeda Iraq morphed into ISIS. Rafsani was probably the only person in Iraq who could have pulled that off."

"Let me make sure I understand," Richards said. "The Iranians become uncomfortable partners with the Saudis on this grand terrorist scheme, then you kidnap al-Talib, a Saudi minister, and frame the Iranians for doing it?"

Bareket tilted his head, thinking, then said, "That's a fair statement."

"Holy shit, that's fucking awesome!" Richards said with a hearty laugh. "You Israelis have always been pretty damn smart. At some point that could make relations between them *very* rough."

"The thought never crossed my mind," Bareket said sarcastically.

Klein chimed in, "I just saw Rafsani and stood four feet away from him."

"What the fuck are you talking about?" exclaimed Richards.

"It was my team that was sent to London to kidnap al-Talib and kill Mullah Sawalha. Rafsani was with Sawalha when it all got crazy. I didn't realize who he was at the time."

"Sorry about Ori," Richards said. "I knew him a long time, and I know you and your dad knew him forever, but what the hell does all this have to do with me?"

"You know the British with their security cameras," Bareket said. "They had video of Rafsani on the street right after the incident. We identified someone with Rafsani."

"Who?"

Bareket softly answered, "You're not going to like this."

"Who?" Richards insisted.

"The grandson of your old friend Ghassan Kassem." A new picture appeared on the screen, showing Rafsani and Khaled Kassem walking in the Finsbury Park neighborhood.

Richards gasped. "Why in the fucking world would Khaled be with Rafsani in London?"

"That's what we'd like to know," answered Mehrara. "Actually, we *need* to know."

"His brother bombing the Wall doesn't make Khaled a terrorist. I've known him since the day he was born. Great kid. Super smart. Big heart. Wouldn't hurt a flea. There's no way he's a terrorist."

Deckler rubbed his gray goatee. "You've seen him, what, once in the past six years at a dinner party at his grandfather's house?" Deckler let that sink in with Richards. "You sure you know *everything* about him?"

Richards's eyes opened wide, and he fell back in his chair. "I know he's a good kid."

"Norman, sorry, but you need perspective about this," Bareket said. "You know we bulldozed the Kassem house a day after Mahmoud's bombing at the Wall. That could get even a good kid pretty upset, right?"

"Yes, but what is this, an inquisition?"

Bareket pointed at Richards. "And of course, Ramallah is ground zero for terrorist recruiting for Hamas and Rafsani has longstanding relationships with Hamas."

Richards's silence was his answer.

"So, Norman, from our thinking, Khaled is not just a perfect terrorist propaganda poster boy, but also…sorry, the perfect martyr."

Richards tapped his fingernails on the table. "And I'm here *because?*"

Bareket leaned forward. "Norman, we don't know what Rafsani and Khaled are up to. When we drugged al-Talib, all he told us is that he controlled the money, and that Rafsani is planning a multifaceted terrorist attack. His laptop only had the financial data we sent the CIA that you saw regarding tracing the money. Al-Talib was intentionally shielded from knowing the details of the attack, which as you know is pretty standard."

Zamir interrupted Bareket and said firmly, "We need you to visit Ghassan and see what he knows about Khaled."

"Seriously? He's not going to know jack shit," Richards answered.

Not backing down, Zamir replied, "Then you need to get him to find out."

Richards looked over the Israelis, then laughed. "I think you people have lost it, if your plan to stop an alleged major terrorist attack is *me*? And I thought *I* was the one with the alcohol problem."

Another photograph flashed onto the screen of a young man at a crowded funeral. Ignoring Richards's penchant for drama, Bareket explained, "This photo was taken at Ori's funeral. It's Khaled's best friend, Eyad, who was photographing everyone in attendance. You need to find out about him also. When will you go see Ghassan?"

"It's not happening," Richards replied, crossing his arms over his chest. "I'm not asking a dear friend to spy on his grandson. Even thinking I'd do it is fucking ridiculous." Walking to the door, he announced, "Goodbye, gentlemen, I'm out of here."

"Go get the Rabbi," Deckler told Bareket, who picked up a phone and gave an order. "Norman, please give us two more minutes. That's all—two minutes."

In a soft voice, Zamir said, "Norman, you know about the War Scroll and the battle between the Sons of Light versus the Sons of Darkness. Right?"

"Yeah, I learned about it sometime in my thirty years here. I know it's a bunch of mumbo jumbo apocalypto bullshit, written by a bunch of religious fanatics 2,000 years ago."

"I understand your skepticism," replied Zamir. "But listen, until something inexplicable happened with Chaim recently, I did not believe there was a God. If I said that publicly, I'd be removed as Prime Minister the next day. But I can't say that anymore."

"I don't believe in God either, or the fables written in anyone's Bible, including that there will be a final battle between good and evil," Richards said.

Chief Rabbi Schteinhardt entered the room, followed by a soldier carrying a heavy wooden box, which he placed on the conference table. Klein opened the lid, and everybody stood up to peer inside.

"You gonna part the Red Sea with that?" said Richards.

"Pick it up," Zamir said.

"Why?"

"Humor me," Zamir replied. "Pick it up!"

"Fine." Richards reached into the box and struggled to pull out a long grey plaster sword. He quickly placed it back on the table. "This is what was so important, a shitty old concrete sword?"

"Give it to me," said Mehrara, who picked up the sword. After holding it for about ten seconds, Mehrara passed it to Deckler, then Zamir, and each man struggled with its weight.

"Chaim, your turn," said the Prime Minister.

With one hand, Klein easily lifted the sword above his head. The plaster coating instantly started crumbling away, revealing a shiny metal blade with a black grip and gold pommel. He circled the sword in the air, and it began to hum and glow with an increasing brightness.

Klein stepped back from the others in the room and began slicing the air, a wind following each slash. Klein finally lowered the sword, looked at Richards, and shrugged. "Crazy, huh?"

Rabbi Schteinhardt softly chimed in, "Long ago, the ancient Israelites knew this as the Sword of King David, the Sword of the Righteous, forged by none other than God. It is hard to grasp concepts of something written by people about a great war 2000 years ago. But now you understand; there is something happening that is bigger than all of us. We need your help."

With his eyes glued onto the sword, Richards fumbled for a cigarette and muttered, "Holy shit." He looked at Klein and muttered, "Superman?"

General Mehrara answered, "No. Chaim is the General of the Sons of Light."

16

Paris

Hassen Tamimi looked across the table smiling at Chloe Dumas, Chaim Klein, Dan Beer, and Rafael Danzig, Klein's new bodyguard, all sitting in a windowless study room in the Sorbonne.

"Chloe, I appreciate what the Muslims for Peace is trying to accomplish," Tamimi said. "You are my dear friend and the best social anthropology professor in Paris, probably Europe, always writing, making speeches, and taking up good causes like the MFP. You're right. We Muslims must take back our religion from the fundamentalists before it's too late. Only *we* can save Islam. But I'm not the right person to lead the Muslims for Peace in France. "You *have* to do this. *You* can reach the masses. *You* have the contacts, reputation, and credibility."

Chloe Dumas leaned forward and pleaded, "There is no other Muslim leader in France with your name recognition and influence. You know I'm right," she said.

"I am not a prophet." He stroked his short salt-and-pepper beard and continued, "I am simply an imam at a mosque with thousands of worshipers—who numerous times have demanded my resignation and even called me the Imam of the Jews because I support cooperation with the Jewish people and seek solidarity with them. I've received many death threats because of this."

Dumas brushed her long blonde hair off her face and stared intently at Tamimi. "You *know* that you speak for the majority of your people. Your voice is important because you were previously a fundamentalist. How can you be so brave during your sermons but not expand your message to the moderate Muslims in France whom you've yet to reach?"

Tamimi stared hard at Chloe. "Are you suggesting that I'm a coward? I have said many things from the pulpit, but never that I wish to die as a martyr. If I antagonize the fundamentalists even more, they will most assuredly leave my five children as orphans."

"Hassen, I would never call you a coward. You are one of the bravest men in all of France," Dumas removed her large round glasses, revealing her big blue eyes. "You are a natural leader, and the moderate Muslims here believe in you, which is why you are the perfect choice to help lead this cause. You were the first to speak out against the extremists." Dumas paused, then softly said, "People follow brave leaders."

Born in Tunisia, Tamimi had studied Islamic fundamentalism at *madrasas* in Syria and Pakistan as a young man before moving to France in 2001. He became imam of the Grand Mosque of Paris, and once he came to better understand present-day Western life, he moved away from his radical views. In 2010 he joined the Conference of Imams, which published moderate *fatwas* for French Muslims. Over the years, Tamimi supported Muslim women's rights and French President Nicolas Sarkozy's effort to ban the burqa, and he established good relations with France's Jewish community. And he criticized the fundamentalists' reign of violence, murder, and terrorism as contrary to the true words of the Koran.

"I am not a leader, Chloe. I simply believe that Islam is being manipulated by foreign states, which have created an Islam of nationalists, and most Muslims don't want that. They want Islam adapted for their lives in France, and an imam who understands that."

"That's *exactly* what leadership is, Hassen!" said Dumas. "Islam is already the second largest religion in France. With high birth rates and continued immigration, in two or three generations, Muslims will compose a significant percentage of the population. The French are scared that the Islamists could dominate the National Assembly and imperil French culture. People here support Muslims who assimilate and make positive contributions to the country. That's why you need to speak out."

Tamimi raised his eyebrows and exhaled deeply. "A Frenchman who knows nothing about Islam and sees a woman covered from head to toe—what will he believe about us? The burqa is a sign of extremism, which is why I fight against it. It's either assimilate or segregate. Assimilation means better jobs, housing, education, maybe even freedom from prejudice."

"Frankly, we understand your concern about security," injected Beer. "The fundamentalists view you as a threat. That is an unfortunate reality. But we can give your family protection."

"Protection? Security? That is no way to live." Tamimi crossed his arms and stared at Beer. "This conversation is unsettling, Mr. Beer. I understand why Chloe is here. But I don't understand who you and these other two men are, except that you're Israeli. I have to assume the three of you are Mossad."

"How flattering," Danzig replied through Dumas, who served as the Israelis' French translator. "Usually, people presume I'm a librarian, a teacher, a store clerk, or something like that. Never once a spy." Danzig's average height supported a pudgy build that matched his pink face, framed by round wire-framed glasses and thinning, prematurely graying hair. "I promise you, Mr. Tamimi, we are not all Mossad."

"So what do you do?"

"I'm a strategist. I fix problems," Danzig said. "Big ones."

Beer chimed in, "And I *am* an archeologist, just like I said. The Israeli government sent us here because we are experts in Islamic culture. When we heard about the MFP growing in influence in France, we thought it could lead to a universal acceptance of Islam and a potential pathway to peace with Israel. So we decided to learn more about the organization, and now we're helping the Indonesians, who started the movement, and other nations make it grow."

Tamimi offered a noncommittal shoulder shrug. He glanced at Klein, signaling that he wanted to hear his story.

"From my perspective, the world is both anti-Semitic and anti-Islam," Klein said. I think the MFP can bridge relationships."

Tamimi shook his head and looked at Danzig. "Your words are vague. They suggest to me that Israel wants to use the MFP for propaganda."

Dumas snapped back, "You are wrong, Hassen! Israel is sincere and truly wants the MFP to be a success."

"That is why we are here now," said Beer. "Israel supports the MFP because we are *not* at war with Islam. We are fighting radicals, those whose actions make clear that they wish to eradicate us. We want life. We want peace. The entire civilized world wants peace!"

"Let's be clear, Mr. Tamimi," Danzig added, "should we all come to our senses, Israel will take substantial steps to prove its intentions are to create a true and lasting Middle East peace. First, we will support the immediate formation of a Palestinian state at the United Nations. Second, we will help rebuild Gaza and the West Bank, including its homes, schools, hospitals, and roads. So far, we have secured commitments from the United States, Great Britain, France, Germany, Canada, Japan, and even China to help us build that infrastructure. This means the citizens of the new Palestine will see a future filled with hope. In return, we insist that Hamas, Hezbollah, and the Arab states simply recognize our right to exist and give peace a chance."

Tamimi clasped his palms together. "Mr. Danzig, please know, your words sound so perfect, but you are a dreamer. Even if Israel and all these countries announce this plan to the world, Hamas, Hezbollah, al-Qaeda, ISIS, and the Iranians will do everything possible to stop it." Tamimi exhaled in frustration. "I sense you are honest and believe what you just promised, but respectfully, I find it *very* unlikely that the Israeli government actually will do all that."

Danzig responded, "Mr. Tamimi, Israel is surrounded by enemies who want nothing more than to incinerate the country. But for three thousand years, the Jewish people have survived constant, significant efforts to exterminate us…and yet we are still here." Danzig tapped the table with his index finger. "Unfortunately, we realize the distinct possibility, if not the probability, that at some point, and maybe soon, there will be a massive, orchestrated attack on Israel. If that happens, there will be all-out war. We don't want that. It could get very ugly."

Tamimi nodded.

"Given that reality, we must be practical," Danzig continued. "We will gamble and take the first substantial steps to prove to the world and to our enemies that we want peace. That means *we* must be the leaders in improving the lives of people in the West Bank and Gaza. If the Palestinians see meaningful change, we believe that will weaken Hamas. Maybe they'll even want to get onboard. This could defuse the rhetoric between the Arabs and the Jews, prevent a war, and create a future for everyone." Danzig paused and opened his palms toward Tamimi. "And if that plan doesn't work, at least we tried, and then we can blow each other to kingdom come. But we *will* take the first step."

Beer leaned in toward Tamimi. "Think about it: over the course of history, the Jews and the Arabs were not always enemies. Just imagine if our plan worked."

With an unsure smile, Tamimi said, "Your plan is a dream, but yes, if it worked, it would be incredible. But there are a *lot* of ifs."

Danzig placed his hand across his heart. "Of course. But what is better than to dream about peace and trying to make it work?"

"You can call it a dream, Mr. Tamimi, but let me tell you some realities," said Beer. "Would you believe Qatar has agreed to help Israel rebuild Gaza, and has already spent tens of millions of dollars there?"

"No."

"It's true. They've already funded a new power plant that will sit in Israel for Gaza's benefit."

"And you've heard about Saudi Arabia and Israel partnering in a number of ventures," added Klein. "Despite that terrible episode of the Crown Prince killing the journalist, he shows great promise in changing the face of peace with Israel."

Tamimi thought for a minute, then said in a firm voice, "You're probably right. It's worth the gamble."

Klein smacked his hands together and exclaimed, "Great, so you're in!"

"I didn't say that. I wish the MFP luck, but I will not get involved. I will not die for this cause."

Klein responded, "Then just go home, take a gun, put it in your mouth, and pull the trigger, because you're talking like a man who might as well be dead. You've given up hope and your sermons and public appearances are great big lies because even you don't believe them. I think you are a coward."

Tamimi's face reddened. "You can't talk to me like that!"

Klein pointed back at Tamimi. "I'm not done!"

Tamimi glared at Klein.

Klein collected his thoughts, then spoke in a disarmingly sincere voice. "You *chose* to put your life at risk the first time you bravely declared that moderate Muslims worldwide could save Islam from the fundamentalists. And I also know personally that sometimes, when you least expect it, you get pulled into something much bigger than whatever you have going in your own little world. And whether you like it or not, you do it because there's no choice. Literally, no choice, so you do it. Later you realize that it still is totally illogical, but you were meant to do that for which you were chosen. You are drawn to your destiny like a magnet. By a force you cannot explain." Klein looked away, then added softly, "I know you believe in what you're doing. You can't do what you do every day unless you believe it deep in your heart. I'm sorry about what I said. You are indeed a brave man. But Mr. Tamimi, you're already in this too deep to quit. You cannot get out because it's your responsibility to stay in—maybe it's your destiny."

Klein dropped his head. Beer was stunned that Klein opened up, given his generally unemotional interpersonal communications. Klein had always been a leader by his actions, seldom by his words.

Transfixed on Klein, Tamimi trembled as his eyes welled up. "Every time I prepare a sermon for my congregants about improving their lives and saving Islam, I tell myself 'Don't do this.' But a voice in my head tells me I *must* speak out." With tears streaming down his face, Tamimi said, "I will do this with you, because civilization is at a fragile precipice. Silence is not an option, but I am afraid of dying."

Klein moved to sit next to Tamimi, and he wrapped his arm around the imam's shoulder. "Hassen, you will find all the strength and courage necessary through Allah and those around you. But you should never fear dying. You should only fear not living and doing what you know must be done. That will give you the strength to see this through to its conclusion. We will prevail."

Tamimi looked lost in thought for a moment before saying, "You are not just some archeologist, Mr. Klein."

"I am! Daniel and I work together at the Temple Mount." He added, "But I've got something going on in my life right now, so I know exactly how you feel. I really want you to know that we will keep you safe." Klein knew the burden he had to carry in finding the Ten Commandments was one that could not be shared with just anyone.

Dumas cleared her throat. "Hassen, so you can understand the progress we've made, the MFP already has raised over three hundred million pounds just in England. It will also do that in France, which will help build the organization and get the word out here."

Tamimi's demeanor changed. His eyes opened wide. "That's a lot of money! How did they raise that? How is it being used? And why do you think you can match that success here in France?"

"Because we've already raised sixty million francs in just two weeks from French billionaires and companies, and we're just getting started. We're hiring social media experts and replicating the British website for France. We will show fundamentalist parents who want something better for their children that peace and prosperity beats hatred, killing, and poverty."

Tamimi folded his hands on the table and said, "Well, since I'm going to do this, I have my own requirements as well."

Dumas opened a black leather notepad holder, pulled a pen from her purse, and replied, "Okay. Tell me your list."

"A bulletproof vest, a full-time armed security guard and driver, and my family moved into an apartment building with quality security."

"Done," Danzig replied.

Tamimi continued: "A secretary, public relations specialist, a computer technician, printers, a copy machine, and a commitment that at least six other moderate imams will be hired to work in Paris."

"This is all easy stuff, including finding the imams," said Beer. "There are a lot more moderates out there than we even imagined. Your involvement with the MFP will help motivate them to help."

Tamimi scratched his forehead before adding, "I have one more request. I want a grade school and high school built in my hometown of Tunisia, staffed with moderate teachers."

"That's it?" asked Klein. Everyone had been expecting an even longer list of demands.

"For now. I'm sure there will be more."

"Fine. How much money do you want for yourself?" asked Danzig.

"Money?" Tamimi replied with a quizzical look. "My mosque already pays me. I don't want money. I want my family to be safe. I want the MFP to do what you promise. You find the money to build an organization and infrastructure, I'll use my mouth and contacts. Isn't that what we each bring to the table to make this work?"

Dumas closed her notepad, turned to the Israelis, and said with a broad smile, "I told you he's the real deal."

17

Chloe Dumas led the group out of the building onto the treelined Boulevard Saint Michel, a few blocks from the Seine. A broad mix of people casually strolled about, engaged in conversations while window shopping. Bumper-to-bumper traffic congested the road, and the constantly blaring horns gave life to the Latin Quarter neighborhood.

"Great meeting, Chloe," said Danzig, patting her gently on the back.

"I've known Tamimi for years and have spoken to him about the MFP a few times in the past two months to get him warmed up, but I think Chaim really closed the deal."

"So you think he'll do what he says?" asked Beer.

"Yes, if the MFP does what it promises. He's honorable."

"Good, then can we head over to the Tour de Temple now?" Klein asked.

"Before we go anywhere, I need to change clothes," said Dumas.

"Chloe, you don't need to do that. You look great," Beer said.

She gave Beer a dismissive glance, then said to Danzig, "I *always* bump into people I know, everywhere I go." She added a glare that warned: don't argue with me about this.

"How much time do you need, Chloe, and where do you want to meet?" Danzig said.

Klein brusquely said, "We need to head over to the Tour de Temple right now."

Dumas stepped in front of Klein. "Mr. Klein, the Temple Tower was demolished over two hundred years ago. There is nothing left of that entire Knights Templar complex. Nothing. A courthouse and Metro station sit where it used to be located. I can't imagine why you'd need to go there."

Adrenaline shot through Klein's body. "Ms. Dumas, it's none of your business. I need your cooperation. You're our tour guide today, and first, you say you need to change clothes. Then I tell you I need to go to the Tour de Temple, and you question me? This is really not helpful."

"You're absolutely right, Chaim. I apologize." She smiled and checked her watch. "I'll meet you in thirty minutes in front of the Metro station at Rue du Temple and Rue de Turbigo." She did an about-face and briskly walked away.

Once Dumas was out of earshot, Beer exclaimed, "What's with her? One moment she's totally awesome, and the next, she's fucking crazy!"

Klein added, "Danzig, this isn't going to work. Just call and tell her thank you, and we're going on our own. It's not hard to find the Tour de Temple."

Danzig returned a blank stare. "Chaim, I'm in charge of your security. Explain to me why we have to go there."

Klein shook his head, then replied, "When I was in Ethiopia, there was a fresco on the ceiling of the chapel that I came to understand depicted the Knights Templar complex. I want to see it. Here, take a look." Klein pulled out his phone and showed Danzig a picture.

"Makes sense. But Chloe knows her way around Paris better than us. We're sticking with her. Let's go."

THIRTY MINUTES LATER AT the Temple Metro stop, Klein, Danzig, and Beer were engrossed in conversation about how the water aquifer in Gaza was about to run dry, which would leave the Palestinians living there without a fresh water supply, when they were startled by the interruption of a woman speaking impeccable Hebrew.

"As you can see, there is nothing left of the Tour de Temple." The thin woman with shoulder-length brown hair and dark eyes opened her arms broadly and said loudly, "Almost nine hundred years ago, after the Knights Templar were formed, King Louis the Seventh gave them this property. They built a tower and called it the Tour de Cesar. In this large Gothic church many important Templars were buried. There was also a palace and a second four-story tower, which was known as the Tour de Temple. That tower, which is what you wanted to see, housed chapter meeting rooms, a justice room, a preceptory, a dungeon, and both the Temple treasures, and the Royal Treasures."

She took a breath. "Unfortunately, as I assume you know, but maybe not, on Friday the thirteenth of October 1307, King Phillip the Fourth orchestrated a raid and arrested every Templar he could find in France and held its leaders Jacques de Molay, Geoffrey de Charnay, and Hugues de Payraud in the temple dungeon, until they were burned at the stake. Brutal! That's how the Friday the 13th superstition came to pass. But, as justice would have it, 486 years later in 1792 during the French Revolution, King Louis the Sixteenth and Marie Antoinette were also imprisoned in the Temple dungeon before they were guillotined. Then, after the revolution, Napoleon ordered the Templar complex demolished. What a pity! It would have been fascinating to explore a Medieval fortress—you know, like the Tower of London? But there, now you have it. We can leave."

Stunned, the men stared at her. Klein finally said, "Do you know Chloe Dumas? Who are you?"

She stuck out her hand. "I am Galit Kevetch. Nice to see you again." She pulled a pair of large round glasses from her shoulder bag, put them on, and in the same perfect French accent they'd heard only half an hour earlier, she said cheerfully, "Yes, of course, I know Chloe well. She is one of my favorite people."

Klein dropped his hand from hers and with his eyes wide open, even though he knew the answer, he asked, "You are *the* Galit Kevetch? From Jerusalem with three sisters?"

Before she could answer, Beer added, "The Olympic judo champion?"

"Chaim, you *do* remember me?"

Klein paused, then said, "All too well," wanting to leave it at that.

"Galit, you never told me that you knew Chaim," Danzig said with a frown.

"You didn't ask."

"I assume it's been a long time since you've seen each other?"

"Not long enough," Klein replied. "And I assume it's been a long time since you told the truth, given that this morning, you said you never met Chloe Dumas."

"I didn't lie," Danzig said. "I had only met Galit—not her alter ego, Chloe."

Beer and Klein both gave Danzig the same *Are you serious?* look.

Unable to hold back, Galit said in a snotty tone, "I can't believe the big, bad Chaim Klein still has an attitude problem after all these years."

Klein thought to himself, *Oh well, here we go,* and he snapped back, "I think I liked you more as a smart, tall, blue-eyed blonde with big boobs."

"Nice to see you too, Chaim. You know, I never got the chance to ask you, is it true that my friend Schprintze shot you? As I heard the story, she aimed her gun at you, and you yelled at her, 'Never point a gun at someone unless you plan to shoot them,' and then she shot you. Did I get that right?" Her grin confirmed to everyone she had nailed it.

Klein winced. "Yes, but I admit to gaining a healthy respect for her after that."

"I have more stories about Chaim, if you gentlemen would like to hear them."

"And I have some stories about Galit ..." Klein stopped, realizing if he finished his thought, she would win the war of words. He knew she'd remember beating him in an IDF self-defense tournament.

Klein glared at Galit, who smiled smugly.

Beer injected, "This should be a fun day."

"Everyone, shut up!" Danzig ordered. "Chaim, you signed off on me handling your security. We cannot have you at risk. Believe it or not, Galit is our best European agent, and is joining the team, starting now."

"She's the best?" Klein frowned. "I find that hard to believe."

"Undoubtedly. She has skills that *none* of our other agents have. And Galit, other than discussing the MFP because of your connection to Tamimi, we couldn't yet tell you what's going on. When you learn about Chaim, your head will spin."

"My stomach is already turning. But I know, Chaim is our greatest Sayaret commando leader. He is a *fabulous* terrorist assassin."

Danzig yelled, "Listen, whatever the history is between the two of you—"

"Stop. I don't need a lecture," interrupted Klein. He looked at Galit. "Okay, to be honest, I always thought you were super smart, and I was in awe of your talent, especially *that* day. And today you were great with Tamimi. Plus, your disguise had me completely fooled. But you don't know me today, any more than I know you. Right now we have to get along." He stuck out his hand. "Deal?"

Surprised, she shook his hand. "Thank you, Chaim. I've been living in Paris as Chloe Dumas, along with some other aliases, for a long time now. I'll say this, if you think I like wearing that whole disguise, and especially the big, padded bra and high heels, living as a fictional character every day, you're wrong." She smiled. "But no one in Paris knows *Galit*. So, since we're past that, and given that the Templar complex is long gone, why come here?"

"Because underneath where the tower used to stand is a catacomb that I need to see." Klein considered telling Galit the whole story but concluded that was too much information for now. "Honestly, I don't know what I'm looking for, though I'll know it when I see it. I think art owned by the Louvre is stored in a catacomb in that location, except it's closed to the public."

"I've never heard about that catacomb, so I'm not sure if we get there through the subway or the courthouse. But I can call someone who would know."

A moment later, Galit was speaking to someone in her Chloe Dumas voice. She hung up and said, "A friend of *Chloe's* is the Curator of Greek and Roman Antiquities at the Louvre. She knew about the catacomb, and acknowledged it belongs to the Louvre. It's underneath the Palais du Justice but has no public access. She says there's nothing but bones down there."

"If it has nothing but bones, then why does the Louvre control it?" Klein said.

"Let's just get into the courthouse, find the catacomb, and see what's in it," ordered Danzig, already walking away.

"Raphael, I have a question," said Beer.

Danzig turned, ran up to Beer, and poked him in the chest. "I told you before, do not call me Raphael—ever. It's Danzig. Only Danzig. Got it?" Danzig turned and stormed toward the courthouse.

Beer saw Klein laughing. "Chaim, he goes crazy on me because I call him by his first name?"

"Dan, he warned you. Take him seriously. Next time, he *will* hurt you."

Beer looked clueless, and Galit chimed in, "You know about Raphael the Angel, don't you?"

"He is the Angel of Healing in Judaism, Christianity, and Islam."

"And you know Danzig's background?" she asked.

"For a while, he was Netanyahu's personal bodyguard," Beer said.

168

"Danzig was an assassin, who still has more kills than anyone. Because of all the people he killed, he hates that his name represents the Angel of Healing. So just call him Danzig."

"That's ridiculous. Is he nuts?"

Galit and Klein looked at each other, and Klein answered, "A little. But he's also brilliant and really good at what he does."

"That is true. I've worked with him extensively." Galit's comment confirmed she was added to the team by Danzig, not Bareket.

A MINUTE LATER, THE group entered the courthouse and walked down a grand marble staircase to the bottom floor, peeking into a noisy cafeteria filled with attorneys, clerks, and civilians. Seconds later, they moved into a dimly lit hallway off the cafeteria.

"We need to find the entrance to the catacomb quickly, or we could have a problem with security, just wandering around the courthouse," said Danzig. Klein and Galit both discreetly looked to the ceiling corners to locate cameras.

Danzig grabbed the brass doorknob of the nearest room and found it locked. He told the group, "Too many people coming in and out of the cafeteria. Act like you're in a discussion and move closer together to give me cover."

Danzig pulled a cell phone-sized tool kit from his jacket and dropped to one knee. The others formed a protective circle around him while he fiddled with the lock.

"I can't believe you actually carry a lock pick," Klein said.

"I'm full of surprises. I always have a pick, a gun, and a knife on me."

"Always?" Klein asked.

"Are you fucking deaf, Chaim?"

"Let me guess," said Kevetch. "Also, a passport, a fake ID, and a lot of money."

"Good memory."

"I still do the same."

"Good training."

Looking at Galit, Klein asked, "Seriously, you too?"

She tilted her head and smiled. "Are you deaf?"

A moment later, Danzig had the door open and told the others not to move while he slipped inside. He quickly returned, advising that the room was stuffed with boxes containing old case files. As the group moved toward the next room, Klein pulled out his cell phone and started scrolling through data. "Dan, remember in Ethiopia when I was in the Chapel where the Ark was located?"

"Of course."

Galit gave Klein a perplexed look. "What are you talking about? What ark?"

Klein handed his phone to Beer, and Galit looked over his shoulder. "So here's the photo I took of the fresco that I later figured out was the Templar complex. Then, after we met the baroness, I read everything I could find about the Knights Templar, and what happened to their complex here. Just this morning, I was going through my notes, and there's a history of Paris that said the remnants of the fortifications of the Templar complex were located at 69 and 71 Rue du Temple."

"Are you saying we should go look there?"

"No. Look at the number on the door here, 115. This building is massive. It's impossible for us to check every room, even on this floor. Why don't we at least take a shot and find rooms 169 and 171 and see what's there?"

"Chaim's right about our inability to cover this building. We have nothing to lose," Danzig replied.

Exasperated, Galit said, "Will someone tell me what is going on? I don't have a clue."

"You know I'm an archeologist, right?" Klein said rhetorically, adding, "I ended up in a cave in Ethiopia looking for an extremely rare and valuable artifact, and some things I saw in the cave lead me to here. I'll tell you more when we have time."

Klein turned away, observing that the room numbers were increasing to his left, so he started walking in that direction, with the others following. He turned at the end of a short corridor, well away from the cafeteria. He stopped before Room 169 and confirmed 171 was next door. "This is it. Open it up."

Danzig dropped to one knee and remarked that the door had two unique locks, not like what he had opened in Room 115. Galit got to work on the door at Room 171.

Both sets of locks were opened, and the group entered to find that the two rooms were combined into one large conference room with a huge ornate table, matching and immaculate antique furniture, and ten locked file cabinets. Across the room, next to a massive hutch, was an intricately carved double door. Everyone's attention was drawn to its golden doorknobs in the shape of skulls. Galit quickly agreed she'd never seen anything like the double locks on those doors.

Although it took almost ten minutes, they got the doors open. Klein walked through first but stopped to turn on his cell phone flashlight. He found a light switch and advised the others that only a few feet ahead lay a long stretch of stairs going down.

Klein took only two steps down before he yelled back to Beer, "Ron, there is a fresco on the wall here identical to one that I saw with the Ark in the chapel in Ethiopia."

"Obviously we're in the right place."

Galit exclaimed, "What do you mean by the Ark?"

Looking away, Klein said, "I found the Ark of the Covenant. I also saw another one in Ethiopia."

"That can't be."

"Believe it," Klein blandly replied.

"I don't know if that is utterly remarkable, or if I should wonder exactly what I just got myself into," Galit said.

Klein thought about it. "Both."

He then led the group down the equivalent of three flights of stairs. At the bottom, they gazed in awe at the most unique catacomb in the world. The twenty-five-foot-high plastered ceiling was filled with religious frescoes. An ornate multitiered crystal chandelier trimmed with carved gold moldings, holding electric candles, hung in the center of the ceiling. Rows of a morbid pattern of skulls and bones sitting on shelves alternated with foot wide red Rance marble columns and arches, all accented by rounded mirrors. Across the room stood sixteen-foot-tall polished mahogany double doors with golden handles.

"This is incredible," Galit declared. "Except for the skulls and bones, this room is modeled after the Hall of Mirrors at Versailles, even the wooden floor. Why would anyone build this?"

Klein turned on another light switch, transforming the room to near daylight as the huge chandelier's light bounced off the room's hundreds of mirrors. Given that the back of every cherrywood shelf had a slit cut into it, a reddish hue eerily illuminated the skulls and bones. A gleaming bronze tag on a shelf across the room caught Klein's eye.

He walked over, read it, and announced, "This is not just any catacomb. This is a Knights Templar mausoleum." He pointed to the skull above the bronze tag and announced, "Jacques de Molay, the last known Grand Master of the Templars. Look closely at the names carved into the shelves. They're all Templars."

Galit turned in a full circle to visually explore the room before declaring, "How can the public not know this catacomb exists? And it's spotlessly clean! Who takes care of this place?"

"The Knights Templar," Klein replied with certainty.

Galit shot back, "Chaim, they're extinct. Everyone knows that."

"Everyone's wrong. I'm also certain that what I came to see is behind those doors, and I have to go in by myself."

He walked over, opened the double doors, and was met by a royal blue curtain, identical to the one in Ethiopia. He pulled it open and entered a room where an Ark of the Covenant sat on a simple pink Jerusalem stone platform. There was no light coming from the Ark, but slowly, as Klein approached it, electric sparks began to shoot between the two cherubim on the Ark's lid. Stunned that the Ark had come to life, Klein dropped to one knee and prayed for personal strength.

He scanned the sanctuary, marveling at the brightly colored frescoes tattooing the chapel wall and ceiling. Sculptures of Moses and David, similar to those located in St. Mary of Zion, lined a wall. He focused on the face of a third statue, a man holding a sword. The inscription carved into its white marble base were the words of Isaiah: "Nation shall not lift up sword against nation. Neither shall they know war anymore." He snapped a picture of the statue with his cell phone. He next saw a painting across the room of a large Gothic church, realizing it was positioned over a small rug with a white-and-blue cup stitched in its center. He took a photo of the painting, sure that he had seen the same depiction in Ethiopia.

Moments later, he reentered the great hall and announced, "There was another Ark in there. Identical to the other two. Also, a rug with the cup."

"*Your* cup?" Beer asked, knowing the answer.

"Technically, I believe it belonged to Jesus."

With her mouth gaping open, Galit took a stunned step backwards. Klein showed her the photo of the painting. "This is Chartres Cathedral, right?"

"Yes, it's about fifty miles from here."

"That's our next stop."

Klein then showed the group the picture of the statue of the man.

"That's Chaim's sword!" Beer exclaimed. He looked at Danzig and Galit. "He has the Sword of David. The Sword of the Righteous."

Danzig frowned. "You guys are real jokers."

"You think so?" Klein displayed the picture of the statue a second time. "Who is that?"

Galit and Danzig focused on the picture, shaking their heads in disbelief at its striking resemblance to Klein. Galit stepped in front of Klein. "Who *are* you?"

Without hesitation, Chaim replied, "The General of the Sons of Light."

18

Chartres, France

Klein stood near the north entrance to the 1,200-year-old Chartres Cathedral, marveling at the church's magnificent architecture. Perched on a hill in the beautiful town of Chartres by the Eure River, its soaring 349 and 377-foot-tall contrasting spires were visible from miles away in the surrounding golden meadowed countryside. Its 167 stained glass windows were world renowned for their intensely bright color and design. The front Royal Door was framed by a 60-foot border with dozens of intricately carved white marble sculptures and two equally ornate 18-foot-tall wooden doors. "If you think this is incredible, wait until you see the inside," Klein said. "After Ethiopia, I researched the art and history of this place at length."

"It's definitely one of the world's most beautiful churches," Galit replied. "But I still don't understand why we're here."

Instead of answering, Klein walked toward the entrance. He stopped at a stone pillar near the Royal Door and pointed at it. "*This* is why we are here."

Beer moved in for a closer look. "It's the Ark of the Covenant."

"That's good, but now what?" Galit asked.

"I don't know until I know," Klein replied.

"What does *that* mean?" snapped Danzig. "*I don't know until I know?* You dragged us out here. I want a plan."

"It means exactly what he said," Beer answered. "He doesn't know until he knows."

"Do you guys rehearse this shit just to mess with me?" Danzig yelled.

Klein snapped back, "Danzig, I'm supposed to find something here—I don't know what it is. God doesn't talk to me. I don't see burning bushes. I'm not trying to be evasive."

"You don't sound evasive. You sound like an idiot."

"Whatever. But you're not helpful, and this is *my* operation. So if you don't like how this is going, when we get back to Jerusalem, I'll get someone else."

"Chaim, I've known Danzig forever," Galit injected. "He sees the world only in black and white. This whole biblical thing is just way too gray for him." Galit turned to Danzig and ordered, "Be-have!"

During the drive from Paris, Klein explained to everyone the church's art, relics, and history, impressing Galit with his knowledge. Most notable was the Virgin Mary's tunic, the Sancta Camisia, given to the cathedral by Charlemagne in 876. But more relevant, the Knights Templar reportedly stored relics here that they had found in the Temple Mount. Klein led them to Chartres's crypt, built by the Templars as a secret underground chamber. It was the third largest crypt in the world, behind St. Peter's and Canterbury, but perhaps it was more mystifying than all others. Shrouded in secrecy, the crypt contained no tombs.

As they reached the crypt, they were interrupted by a woman with a proper English accent. "Mr. Klein, Mr. Beer, what an incredible coincidence, bumping into you here."

Klein spun around, confirming that which he instantly knew. Smiling at an elderly woman in a bright print silk dress, he said, "Baroness Collins, why is it I'm not at all surprised to see you?"

She returned a smile and gestured at the two casually dressed men flanking her. "You remember my Royal Guardsmen, Ian and Randall?"

"Of course," replied Beer, sticking his hand out to shake Ian's. As the guard stiffly grabbed it, Beer added, "I didn't recognize you ladies without your tall black furry hats." Beer remembered how Ian and Randall mistreated him and Klein in London, and he relished teasing them now.

"Was that supposed to be humorous?" Ian said, frowning.

"I didn't think that was humorous one bit," Randall added.

In a bad fake English accent, Beer replied, "I was serious. I would never be humorous at your expense."

Ian took a threatening step toward Beer, and Danzig moved between them and grumbled, "Lady, I don't know who you and your boys are, but we're kind of busy. Now that you've said hello, move on!"

"No! These people are friends," Klein said. "If they're here right now, I'm certain it's to be helpful."

"Mr. Danzig, with your superb skill set and record of success as a coldblooded killer, I'm amazed to discover that you are quite simply a dumb, blunt instrument completely lacking in social skills." A fake smile was plastered on the baroness's face.

"How do you know who I am?" Danzig asked with a shocked expression.

"Does that really matter, *Raphael*?"

"Lady, this is not going to work out well for you," Danzig said, his voice rising.

The baroness studied Danzig. "I told Prime Minister Zamir this mission was too sensitive to be put at risk by your unprofessional, temperamental conduct, Mr. Danzig. I simply won't have it."

Amused, Klein and Beer watched the exchange. Unamused, Galit was trying to size up the situation.

"Why were *you* discussing *me* with Zamir?" Danzig demanded.

"If Mr. Klein did not tell you, then I shall not either," the baroness replied.

Having heard enough, Klein stepped forward. "Baroness Collins is a member of the House of Lords. She sits on its Intelligence and Security Committee and has provided funding for the MFP. Let's be clear, Danzig, I trust her more than I trust you."

Pleased, the baroness turned to Galit. "We've not met. Your name is…?"

"Nina Small."

"Nina Small? How interesting! This morning, a blonde French woman named Chloe Dumas and your friends met with Hassen Tamimi. Then Miss Dumas left them, and thirty minutes later, a brunette woman met them at the Palais de Justice. I assume that was you. But then, Chloe Dumas called a woman at the Louvre asking about an obscure catacomb located under the courthouse. That woman called Ms. Dumas back, even though she wasn't at the courthouse. You were. And of course, Chaim found what he needed in the catacomb, which led him here, where we have been patiently waiting."

After an intentionally long pause, the baroness asked in an innocent tone, "So Miss Small, by chance do you know Chloe Dumas or…Galit Kevetch?"

"Who else knows my cover?" Galit replied calmly, though her eyes showed concern.

The baroness gently took Galit's hands. "No one. And I promise it will stay that way. We are partners with Israel on Chaim's mission. Prime Minister Zamir and Mossad Director Bareket told me *all* about you. Once I read your dossier, I strongly supported your involvement. But I remain skeptical about Mr. Danzig. He is quite the bore."

It took a few seconds for Galit to absorb the baroness's remark. "So Chaim's treasure hunt is a joint mission of Great Britain and Israel?"

"Not quite. Technically, it's the Knights Templar and Israel."

Danzig burst out laughing, but Galit, startled, asked, "You really mean the crusading Knights Templar, that have been extinct for about eight hundred years?"

"Yes, except that we've never been extinct. Not for a day. We perpetuated that myth, first as a matter of self-preservation, then, later, as a matter of prudence."

"And how would you know that, since nobody else seems to?" Galit asked.

"Because, Miss Kevetch, I am the Grand Master of the Knights Templar." The reply was stated so quickly and with such conviction that it left no doubt as to the truth. "Chaim and Daniel accept it. Your Prime Minister and Dudi Bareket accept it. Shouldn't you?"

Galit glanced at Klein, who nodded. "I guess. But it just seems so…impossible."

"Yes, it does." The baroness turned to Danzig and asked, "And you, sir?"

Danzig stared at the ground, then looked up. "I'm not going to speculate on the Knights Templar, but it does seem there is something unusual happening with Chaim. Baroness Collins, I apologize for my behavior a few minutes ago. I was sent to protect Chaim, and that I will do."

"Well, that's progress! Maybe there is hope for you." Turning to Galit, the baroness said, "And you might be interested to know that the President-Director of the Louvre is also a Templar."

"Really?" she replied with wide eyes. "So my friend at the Louvre called him, and then he called you?"

"I'll put it like this. The Knights Templar is like a large international corporation. As a senior representative of our French chapter, he reports to me."

Klein interrupted, "So how did you know to find me in Paris?"

"Your government has been marvelously cooperative and gave us a head's up. We've been following you since you landed, because now,

Chaim, you need my help. You could walk around this church for a year and never find that which you *must see.*"

"You mean another relic? The Sancta Camisia?"

"No, Chaim. You are here to gain knowledge. To learn something that only a few people in the history of civilization have known. Come."

As the group walked back upstairs, the baroness lectured, "Chartres has the strongest historical tie of any church to the Knights Templar. The carving of the Ark by the outside door exists because in the Middle Ages, the crypt held both the Templar treasure and the Ark that Chaim saw today in Paris. That Ark, by the way, was found by the Templars when they were digging around the Temple Mount. That means the Jews of ancient Israel had two Arks. The Templar's treasure, however, helped pay for the building of Chartres and many other cathedrals in Europe, including Notre Dame. Most of them, including those here, have statues of Solomon in their west portal. Also, the twin towers outside face west and resemble the Second Temple's two pillars, Joichin and Boaz."

"Baroness Collins, what happened to the rest of the treasure the Templars found at the Temple Mount?" Galit asked.

"Frankly, that treasure was enormous, and then it grew significantly from personal contributions and prudent investments. Fortunately, around 1153, our Fourth Grand Master, Bertrand de Blandefort, began transforming the Templars into something akin to a modern-day corporation. We started purchasing real estate throughout Europe, especially in London and Paris, some of which we still own, along with other properties acquired over time. We also bought works of art by the Grand Masters. Ask Chaim how many pieces of Michelangelo and da Vinci he has seen that the rest of the world has not. When King Phillip tried to exterminate us in 1307, he found some of our treasure, but not very much. After that, to reduce risk, we spread out the treasure and even started using banks. As long rumored, some of this was moved to Rosslyn Chapel near Edinburgh and some to Rennes-le-Château, where it remains. Everything we own has been hidden in layers of trusts and companies. No one except us could ever figure out what is or is not a Templar asset. In the 1700s we even funded the Masons in America, many of whom were its founding fathers. Now we are using our treasure to fund the MFP."

"Baroness, are you aware of the Copper Scroll?" Beer asked. "It's one of the Dead Sea Scrolls found at Qumran."

"Of course. It accurately described the Temple's treasure that we found as including great quantities of gold, sacred vessels, and at least twenty-four types of other treasure."

"I'm sorry ma'am, but you mean *stole*," Klein said bluntly, but in a polite tone. "You just admitted that for one thousand years the Knights Templars have grown and profited with property that belongs to the Jewish people and Israel."

The baroness sighed and looked a bit sad. "You're completely right, Chaim. And forever, your people have been mistreated throughout the world, including by English kings who persecuted the Jews in the Middle Ages. Even by the Lionheart. We can't change the past, but we *will* change the future with financial reparations to Israel, as I promised you in London. And if the MFP succeeds, it could help achieve peace in the Middle East, which would vastly improve the quality of life in Israel. This is very important to us, given that we and the Church started the whole mess in the Middle East with the Crusades."

By then, the group had walked outside of the cathedral and was standing in front of Chartres's West Royal Portal. The baroness pointed at a mosaic above the door. "Who knows what that is?"

Galit replied, "That's the *Last Judgment*. Jesus is surrounded by the Four Apostles."

"Good. What else do you see?"

"His right hand is raised, making a blessing."

"And his left hand?"

"Obviously, he's holding a book."

"Yes, but it's not just any book. That is the *Book of Life*, and this mosaic is foundational to everything else you will see inside."

Baroness Collins scurried into the cathedral with the others following behind and pointed up at a window with mostly red stained glass. "See that? It's King David. How many cathedrals do you think have a stained-glass window of King David?"

Not waiting for an answer, she spun and pointed at the large mural directly in front of them. "Again, *The Last Judgment*, with Jesus surrounded by the four beasts of the Apocalypse from John's Revelations. Galit, do you know who they are?"

"Matthew, Mark, Luke, and John."

"Correct. The beast with the human face is Matthew, representing Aquarius. The Lion is Mark, representing Leo. The ox is Luke—Taurus. The eagle is John, being Scorpio. Chaim, what do you think the halo above Jesus's head represents?"

"It's a halo. I don't know."

"It is the rebirth of the sun. That halo sun actually symbolizes the Galactic Cross and the End Times of the Revelation."

The baroness grabbed Klein's arm and they walked eighty feet up the aisle and stopped. She bent over and pointed at a nail sticking out of the square brown stone floor. "See that nail? Chartres's windows are aligned to the light of the summer solstice." Pointing up, she said, "That is the window of St. Apollinaire, which depicts the Roman sun God, Apollo. Every June 21st, the day of the summer solstice and on no other day of the year, a precise beam of light shoots through that window directly onto this nail. How somebody figured that out nearly a millennium ago is beyond comprehension. And as you'll see, the message of the nail and June 21st is even more important than the engineering."

The group followed the baroness into the ambulatory, and she pointed above a nearby door. "All right, now see that large zodiac dial there? This is very unusual. Why would that mural of *The Last Judgment* at the front door or this zodiac dial even be here? Christianity rejects astrology as paganism! It's true that some cathedrals contain an occasional window or mural with astrology. But Chartres is *filled* with astrological and apocalyptical symbolism. Look at the large Rose Window over there depicting the Apocalypse and then, that long stained-glass window called the Zodiac Window. You can see that Taurus was replaced by Gemini, which ends on *June 21st*"

"Baroness, is this all tied to the Great Celestial Event that the doomsdayers predicted would happen on June 21, 2012?" asked Galit. "Wasn't the world supposed to come to an end?

"Galit, no one could accurately predict two thousand years ago that exactly on June 21, 2012, the world would come to an end. But somehow Judaism, Christianity, and Islam each foresaw a final great war. End of Days, the Apocalypse, the War Scroll—they all basically say the same thing."

Beer added, "I don't understand. Are you suggesting that all this art in Chartres symbolizes the Apocalypse, astrology, and I guess, Israel—or Chaim?"

A smile stretched across the baroness's plump face. "Yes, you and Galit are both right! Daniel, only Chartres has these special features. This cathedral has an extraordinary tie to Israel. The Ark at the door, the Statue of Solomon, the window of David, the twin towers, and even the crypt. So first, consider astrology. The predicted timing of the Apocalypse was off by some years but look at the world now." The baroness stopped, looked down, then looked back up, misty eyed. "It *feels* like the world is collapsing upon us, that the Apocalypse is near, heightened terrorism, the nearly worldwide rise of the militant right, a global recession, and the planet is literally burning up. Then, consider how the symbolic references from here to the Temple in Jerusalem and the Ark of the Covenant all merge together to help symbolize you, Chaim, the General of the Sons of Light, who must stand strong in the battle against the Sons of Darkness. Now the Knights Templar can redeem its past sins and help you, and we must do it together.

And with the help of others, we can bring balance and order back to this earth."

"Frankly, it's hard to dispute that the world *could be* headed toward a massive world war, like an apocalypse," Klein said. "I've seen up close that the Islamic fundamentalist terrorists *want to die* for Allah and do not care if their families die. That is a hard enemy to defeat."

The baroness paused, then somberly added, "Only one day of bad events *anywhere* could spin the entire world out of control. Chaim, once you pulled the sword from Bernard Brocas's effigy, and we learned you found the Ark and had the Chalice, we, the Knights Templar, realized that everything was in motion, as foreseen ages ago."

The others understood acutely that the baroness's conclusions could be a grim reality; after all, they were Israeli and knew all too well about living with the constant threat of violence. Baroness Collins focused on Klein. "Chaim, nothing that's happened to you—nor the artifacts and art in this cathedral—is coincidence. This is *your* battle. I know you've been fighting against terrorism since you joined the IDF at eighteen. Now, your battle is to change the dangerous path the world is on. Who knows what's possible when you find the Ten Commandments and reunite them with the Ark? Maybe then, everyone can learn to coexist."

Chaim stayed silent, frowning for a few seconds. "That's wishful thinking. But I don't think we can change the ingrained thinking of millions of Islamic fundamentalists."

"Yes, right now it sounds absolutely ridiculous. But so is the fact that you've found three Arks and that sword. You cannot deny what has already been set in motion! I know you accept your role as the General."

Chaim nodded, then looked away.

To get his attention, she snapped her fingers in his face. "If you succeed, Chaim, our hope is that your work will usher humanity into an Age of Enlightenment."

"The Age of *what?*" Klein said.

"The Age of Enlightenment marks mankind's intellectual and social acceptance of all people—simply meaning: world peace. The War Scroll even says, 'In the end, all of Darkness is to be destroyed and Light will live in peace for all eternity.' It will be the rebirth of man. It can happen. The MFP is already gaining worldwide support. It's why Israel has committed to new levels of cooperation to help the Palestinians. It won't be easy, but peace could be within our grasp."

After another long silence, Klein rubbed his forehead and exhaled deeply. "But I still don't have a clue where the Ten Commandments are located."

"No, you don't. But I do."

Klein's eyes popped open. "Are you serious? Why didn't you tell me this before?"

"Because you had to prove yourself and get to this point on your own. You had to believe in your mission. I could offer you only limited help you until now."

"Okay, fine. So let's just go get the tablets right now!"

"That's not so simple."

"Why?"

In a matter-of-fact tone, the baroness said, "The Ten Commandments are *somewhere* in the Vatican. We will have to go steal them."

The entire group was stunned. Danzig exclaimed, "You're shitting me!"

Baroness Collins looked to the skies and replied, "No, Mr. Danzig, I am not 'shitting you.'"

"The Vatican is impregnable," replied Danzig, everyone concurring. "And it sounds like you don't even know where in the Vatican they're hidden?"

"Yes, Mr. Danzig, that is true, but I'm optimistic that we'll figure it out."

As the group walked out the front door of Chartres Cathedral, a young man with a scruffy beard wearing a New York Yankees baseball cap, a polo shirt, and sunglasses, pulled out his cell phone. A moment later, he said, "Omar, this is Eyad. They just left the cathedral. I'll stay on them. Say hello to Khaled for me."

19

Jerusalem

Norman Richards strode briskly through the Damascus Gate into Jerusalem's Old City. When he served as the CIA's Jerusalem Station Chief, he entered the Arab Quarter through this gate countless times. Now, seldom back in Jerusalem after he stopped a terrorist attack at the President's Inaugural National Ball over a decade ago, he was revisiting a place he did not miss one bit.

Completed by Suleiman the Magnificent in 1537, the eighteen-foot-tall gate was flanked by twin towers that jutted out, featuring turrets and arrow-shaped slits, providing evidence of the violence and death that had all too often plagued Jerusalem over its 3,000-year history.

Richards was immediately thrust into the bustle of the noisy and colorful *souk*. Israeli Arabs operating out of closet-sized shops, make-shift stalls, and pushcarts lined the walls along the narrow stone street, otherwise filled by a moving swarm of people. Only the locals received a bargain from these expert hagglers who sold everything from food, clothing, toys, electronics, and souvenir knick-knacks, including ornate daggers made in China.

Richards remembered every turn on the winding, sporadically marked Arab Quarter streets to The Flying Horse coffee shop. Minutes later, he walked into the restaurant, unsurprised that absolutely nothing had changed. Dozens of hookahs in various shapes, sizes, and colors sat on three shelves to his left. A group of men sat at two small rickety linoleum tables talking politics. The owner, an obese man with a full head of white fluffy hair and wearing a plaid shirt, rested in a worn maroon leather chair behind a glass counter. He offered Richards an almost imperceptible smile, followed by a discreet eye movement signaling him to the back room.

Richards strolled into a larger room decorated with red brick wallpaper and filled with about twenty tables. Only one was taken by an old man who sat focused on his newspaper, flanked by two imposing bodyguards. They rose and approached Richards. In anticipation, Richards moved into a wide stance and raised his arms above his head. They quickly completed their weapons search, inspected the contents of a shopping bag he carried, and cleared him. Richards approached the old man and said, "As-salaam alaykum. I have missed you."

Ghassan Kassem, short and stooped, was already standing, waiting for his guest. "And upon you be peace." He moved in closer, and the men shook hands and lightly touched foreheads, a traditional Arab greeting. "My good friend, I have missed you as well."

Richards looked over Kassem's perfectly pressed white shirt, black pants, and polished black shoes. "You wore that outfit the last time I saw you."

"And how would you remember that?"

"Easy. You've worn that outfit *every* time I've seen you."

Kassem returned a big smile. "I seem to recall we've had this conversation."

"Many times."

Both men laughed. Handing the bag to Kassem, Richards said, "I brought you a gift."

Kassem looked in the bag, then burst out laughing as he pulled out a new blue jean jacket. He held it up for inspection. For decades, Richards was known for always wearing a beat-up blue jean jacket, and Kassem had teased him about it incessantly.

"You know I will never wear this."

"Of course."

Kassem's smile faded and he asked, "I'm curious, Norman, are you still not drinking?"

"Clean and sober and I don't miss the booze one bit...until I do."

"Tobacco?"

"A man has to have one vice, doesn't he?"

"No."

"Look in the bag. I also brought you some Montecristo No. 2's. Still your favorite?"

Kassem pulled out the cigars. "I stand corrected. Perhaps one vice is acceptable." He added, "Are you still fighting?"

While lighting a cigarette, Richards said, "Yep. I still like to pick a fight every so often. It helps me keep my sunny disposition."

Kassem shook his head. "You'll never grow up, will you?"

"You don't understand."

"No, I don't. You're in your sixties. It's crazy."

"Okay, when you're young, you can drink and fight. When you're old, you can't drink and fight, unless you want to get hurt. So, I don't drink anymore—but I still fight."

Kassem wagged his finger at Richards. "And you are still quite the character."

"I sure hope so." Richards leaned closer to Kassem and said, "Ghassan, I hate saying this, but you don't look so good."

Kassem nodded. "I'm old and tired. Life is not good."

"You've *always* been the eternal optimist! Talk to me. Is it your health or are you just beaten down from everything that's happened since Mahmoud blew himself up? That would certainly be understandable."

With sad eyes and in a whisper, he replied, "You know me well, Norman. Yes, everything in my life changed for the worse after the attack. So many people, including the media, call me the ultimate hypocrite, even slanderously suggesting that I put Mahmoud up to it. I worked fifty years so my people could have a Palestinian state and peace with Israel. Now that hope is gone."

Richards placed his hand on top of Kassem's. "It's not your fault that Mahmoud turned. And you've *never* been able to control the peace process. But you were nominated for the Nobel Peace Prize! You put yourself at risk for your people every day for those fifty years and you made tremendous progress working with the Israelis."

"Norman, stop! This is not helpful."

"No!" Richards exclaimed. "Your work led to a hundred programs and positive changes in relations between the two sides."

"But we are no closer to peace, especially since neither Hamas nor the Palestinian Authority give any indication that they want it. So it's not happening."

Richards lowered his voice. "What about the MFP? You have to like what it's doing. They quote you in all of their printed materials, which are circulated across the globe. They call you the 'guiding light leader' of the movement for moderate Islam and peace. The MFP is gaining traction everywhere, even in Israel."

Kassem said with a combination of anger and sadness, "You don't understand! I agree the MFP is doing great work, but people in Gaza and the West Bank call me a fraud!" He fell back in his chair and crossed his arms. "Norman, I know you mean well, but I also know you didn't come all this way to give me a civics lesson. So, what do you want from me?"

"Okay, sorry, we'll do it your way. Unfortunately, what I need to discuss with you won't make you feel better. It's going to make you feel worse."

"There is nothing you can say that will make me feel worse."

"It's about your grandson Khaled."

Kassem put his hand up. "I already know that he has taken up with the jihadists. The day after Mahmoud's attack, the Israelis killed a Hamas recruiter in front of my family, then they bulldozed the house. You should have seen the hatred in Khaled's eyes. Then one day shortly afterward, Khaled and his friend Eyad said they were going to play soccer and we haven't seen them since. I am aware that Khaled's involved in something bad, so you've wasted your time coming all this way to tell me that."

Richards pulled a photograph from his shirt pocket and placed it on the table. "Do you know who that is?"

"No."

"Omar Rafsani."

Kassem sat up straight. "Saddam Hussein's Rafsani? From the Mukhabarat?"

Richards nodded.

"Wasn't he captured and executed by the Americans along with the rest of Hussein's criminals?"

"He escaped. Even though bin Laden and Hussein hated each other, somehow Rafsani became one of bin Laden's senior operatives. And everyone knows, much of Hussein's military helped lead the Islamic State. So what does this tell you?"

"Rafsani is connected to ISIS and al-Qaeda."

"Connected would be an understatement. Some time ago, during the Haj, Rafsani attended a meeting in Mecca with representatives of Iran, Hezbollah, Hamas, and other groups to plan a massive world-wide terrorist attack funded by a Saudi charity."

"What does this have to do with Khaled?"

Richards placed on the table a second photo, showing Khaled having a meal with Rafsani. Kassem's eyes opened wide at the sight. "Where was this taken? Why was Khaled with Rafsani?"

"This picture came off London's street security system. Rafsani and Khaled were having dinner with a radical imam when someone came in and assassinated the cleric. They were lucky not to be killed. We know that for over the past year Khaled has traveled with Rafsani to numerous European cities and also to Afghanistan or Pakistan, possibly meeting with Zawahiri."

Kassem planted his forehead in his hand and mumbled, "Zawahiri?"

Richards nodded, placing another photo in front of Kassem. "And here's Eyad. You're right, Ghassan, he's also working with Khaled and Rafsani."

"Eyad was always trouble." Kassem frowned. "So obviously, Khaled is working with Rafsani and either al-Qaeda or ISIS."

Richards leaned in to look Kassem square in the eyes. "Ghassan, it goes well beyond that. We are fairly certain Khaled is helping Rafsani orchestrate a massive terrorist attack. Something totally unprecedented."

Kassem said loudly, "Now I see! You're here to get information on my grandson so you can find him and kill him, aren't you?"

"I don't want anything bad to happen to Khaled. But you need to understand, this threat is real. Otherwise, I wouldn't be here. I've seen classified material that indicates tens of thousands, maybe even hundreds of thousands of people will die unless this attack is stopped." Richards paused a moment to allow his message to sink in. "Ghassan, you can be old and tired and depressed and do nothing to prevent this from happening, or you can use whatever knowledge and energy you have left to help us stop it."

Kassem shook his head. "I am in an impossible situation. I need to think about this."

"No, you don't. I remember that Muhammad Ali was your hero because he stood up for what he believed in at great personal sacrifice."

"That's true. I was more excited to meet him than the pope and other world leaders."

"You say you're old and tired. Well, Ali said, 'Don't count the days. Make the days count.' Take his advice."

"You're quoting Ali to convince me to hand over information on my grandson?"

"You're damn right. Especially since you believe everything you worked for, including your reputation, was destroyed by Mahmoud." Richards quickly glanced at a note in his pocket. "Your hero also said, 'Don't ever back down from a fight that you know is something worth fighting for, even if you may not win.'" Richards grabbed Kassem's hand. "This is your opportunity to fight for your name and to fight once again for *all* your people. You can help save thousands of lives— if you don't try and that attack occurs, how would you feel?"

Kassem leaned back and sighed. "When did you become an expert on Muhammed Ali?"

"Yesterday."

"Okay. No one's fought for me for quite some time. So at least you have. You've always been a true friend."

"It's reciprocal, but you have many friends waiting for you to reemerge. The only thing lost is time. You can still help lead the creation of a Palestinian state and make a true peace with Israel."

"And to do that, I must spy on my grandson and possibly become a martyr."

Through a thick stream of smoke, Richards replied, "That's right, but maybe you might make a difference and save his life. Do you want to lose another grandson?"

20

Tel Aviv

Prime Minister Zamir took a gulp from yet another cup of black coffee. At 8:35 a.m., it was already his fifth that day. Since the attacks began last night, no one on his staff had slept. Coffee alone was keeping him and much of Israel's leadership functional.

Hezbollah's strikes had been an unequivocal declaration of war. From Syrian territory just beyond the Golan Heights, the terrorist group had showered northern Israeli towns with over 300 short-range missiles—most of which had fortunately been stopped by Israel's defensive Iron Dome. About 45 miles to the west in Lebanon, another 400 missiles had hit populated areas close to the border. So far, over 150 Israelis had died.

On the top floor of the Ministry of Defense building, the Situation Room was uncharacteristically quiet. Zamir's steely blue eyes darted around the table seated with generals and government ministers before he broke the silence. "I want the most severe retaliation possible," Zamir said. "Whatever we do, we'll be criticized by international public opinion. Hezbollah fires its missiles at us, then hides among civilians in Lebanese towns. We must go after them. Hezbollah started this war and we're going to finish it. Our obligation is to keep our people safe." He pointed at the man sitting opposite him. "General, do what you must to shut down Hezbollah and kill Nasrallah."

IDF Chief of Staff General Barak Mehrara responded with a stern nod. "Sir, we know that along the northern border, roughly half the Lebanese houses are used by Hezbollah to store weapons and hide their soldiers. That's why the Golani Brigade has been specifically trained to deal with Hezbollah's tunnels and hit and run tactics." Mehrara turned to Northern Command Major General Akiva Weisman. "We'll drop leaflets from helicopters, advising Palestinian civilians to vacate any of the towns occupied by Hezbollah. Tell them our Golani Brigade will destroy every home that hides a tunnel or is found storing weapons. But before you fire on Hezbollah's missile batteries in residential areas, confirm their satellite coordinates. We want to minimize civilian deaths unless they're aiding Hezbollah."

Weisman replied, "Their rocket launchers are small and mobile. Hezbollah fires rockets from one place, then moves quickly to the next. Spotting and destroying their launchers is extremely difficult."

"Maybe in this war, our drones will do better," Zamir said.

"Do I have permission for another incursion into the Bekaa Valley, including destroying their poppy fields?" Weisman asked.

Zamir smiled. "General, that would be perfect."

Since the mid-1980s, Hezbollah had controlled the Bekaa Valley, known for its cannabis and poppy fields and its production facilities for hashish and heroin. A significant amount of Europe's drug supply originated out of the valley, earning Hezbollah many millions of dollars, which funded its political operations. Hezbollah's other revenue sources included cash from Iran as well as profits from European drug dealing, car theft, and counterfeit goods. Hezbollah was not the

Islamic Party of God, but rather the Party of Thugs, Zamir had said on more than one occasion.

Bareket chimed in, "Destroying their poppy fields might hurt them more than taking out their missile batteries."

Zamir leaned back in his chair. "That's good, but no matter how successful this campaign may be, we must kill Sheik Nasrallah. General Mehrara has designated Sayaret Duvdevan with responsibility for taking him out."

The conversation was interrupted by a knock on the door. A soldier entered and announced, "Mr. Prime Minister, Lieutenant Chaim Klein and Chief Rabbi Schteinhardt are here to see you."

Zamir stood and looked at his staff. "Gentlemen, excuse me, but I need to clear the room for fifteen minutes."

Everyone but Dudi Bareket and Mehrara filed out. Klein entered, dressed in full battle gear, pistol at his side, a Micro-Tavor assault rifle draped around his shoulder, helmet in hand. Chief Rabbi Schteinhardt walked in behind him.

Before Zamir could say a word, Klein said, "Sir, since my unit has been called for duty, you need to send me into Lebanon with them. They're leaving in two hours. I need to be there."

"Chaim, this is complicated," said Zamir. "Your reports from Ethiopia, London, and Paris are astounding. If I didn't know you had written them, I would have thought it was fiction. Now your Duvdevan unit is about to go on a highly dangerous mission. There's a strong chance no one will return. But your work finding the tablets must continue. I cannot risk having you killed in action. This is not to protect you but rather to protect the future of the country."

"I don't need you to protect me. We're at war. I should be in it." Klein looked at the Chief Rabbi. "Will you please tell him?"

"Mr. Prime Minister, the Old Testament contains many fables— for instance, God speaking to Moses through the Burning Bush. Logically, it seems hard to accept that God truly ever spoke to any single man, whether it was Moses, Jesus, Muhammad, or any other prophet. Yet after two thousand years, *only* Chaim was able to unearth the Ark of the Covenant. Even if he is not having a direct conversation with God, somehow they seem to be having communication." The Rabbi looked up. "None of this is a coincidence. Chaim is neither a prophet nor the Messiah. But he is the General of the Sons of Light. Our enemy has attacked us, and Chaim must lead his unit into battle. I don't know if he will live or die. But I do know you should not interfere with his destiny."

Zamir looked torn. While the others took their seats around the table, he paced back and forth, contemplating the situation.

"Eli, Duvdevan will have all the air support needed," Bareket said. "Chaim is the best special forces leader we have, and his unit will work better if he's there to lead them."

Zamir glanced back and forth at Schteinhardt and Klein. Finally, with a casual hand gesture, he softly said, "Go."

Bekaa Valley, Lebanon

The twenty-four Sayeret Duvdevan soldiers separated into two Sikorsky UH-60 Black Hawk helicopters. As they lifted off, Klein addressed them through integrated speakers, "Duvdevan, we are headed to Baalbek in the Bekaa Valley. Our target is a hospital; Sheik Nasrallah is reportedly there for a meeting. He thinks we won't attack a hospital, but he's wrong. Three things to remember. First, if you see Nasrallah, *kill him* on sight. Take pictures for proof. If possible, take his body. Second, do not kill civilians or any wounded Hezbollah soldiers in hospital beds. Third, upon landing, we expect about seventy enemy troops and a firefight. Be careful and be smart.

"Team Aleph, set the perimeter and provide cover for Beit and Gimel. Team Beit, we believe Hezbollah leadership is meeting in a conference room on the first floor. You know what to do if Nasrallah is there. All other Hezbollah leaders are to be taken prisoner.

Team Gimel, the warehouse next to the hospital is a weapons depot. Destroy it."

This mission had been put together with little notice, so Klein knew the intelligence reports were suspect. But he also knew Duvdevan was among the world's best-trained, most experienced, and best-equipped special forces units. Each member was a walking arsenal, carrying a Para Micro Uzi and a Glock 19c with multiple magazines for both weapons, a hunting knife and a throwing blade, hand grenades, flash grenades and smoke grenades, and two pre-wired plastic explosive bombs with timers. They had night vision goggles and their helmets were outfitted with earpieces and microphones set to the same frequency so that everyone was linked together.

Klein grabbed the microphone again. "Landing in two minutes. We've got thirty minutes to get in, do what we have to, and get out. Don't forget, we're cutting the power. We can operate in darkness; they can't."

Liav Samuels was the least imposing of the Duvdevan both because of his diminutive size and baby face. But he was a fearless, industrious soldier and a brilliant electrical engineer. If anyone could cut power to a building or a city without getting electrocuted in the process, it was Samuels. He was also Klein's close longtime friend.

Klein stood at the exit hatch and moments later the Black Hawks touched down in a parking lot. "Hospital, forty yards straight ahead. Let's go!" Klein leaped out first, landing crouched low like a cat, his Uzi in firing position. He sized up the area and saw two Israeli Apache attack helicopters hovering a hundred feet above, providing backup support.

Two teenage boys sprinted from behind a car toward Klein's helicopter with lit Molotov cocktails. As they were poised to throw their gasoline bombs, Klein raised his Uzi and cut them down. When they fell, the bottles broke next to their bodies, igniting their corpses.

Klein's soldiers emptied out of the helicopters and Samuels joined his leader and friend.

"Keep low, move fast!" Klein ordered.

To set a perimeter, the Team Aleph soldiers split in half. As the Beit commandos darted toward the hospital, a middle-aged civilian ran toward them, firing a pistol. Almost instantly, he was shot dead.

At the same time, eight Hezbollah dashed out the hospital's front door, brandishing pistols. Underequipped and outmanned, they were killed within seconds. Moments later, another dozen Hezbollah rushed from the same door, engaging the entire Beit unit in close contact combat.

Klein spotted another group of Hezbollah running toward them from the warehouse on the right, weapons drawn.

"Right flank! Right flank!" Klein yelled above the chaos.

Klein and Samuels dove to the ground. Klein lobbed a smoke grenade at the oncoming terrorists. The thick white smoke allowed Klein and Samuels to each spray a clip of thirty-one bullets into the enemy with their Uzis. Up above, an Apache flew behind the Hezbollah and helped mow them down. As the smoke dissipated, they could see that the ground in front of the two men was strewn with corpses.

Klein jumped back to his feet as three Hezbollah charged. The closest attacker was immediately upon him, his pistol drawn. Klein jumped to the side, spun, and kicked the man in the back, shooting him twice. Two other Hezbollah brandishing knives and pistols were about fifteen feet away. Klein made a leaping somersault, and both fired and missed him.

One attacker was now two feet from Klein's face with a gun and the other was moving to stab him. Just before the attacker with the gun fired, Klein dropped to his knees and shot him in the stomach from a foot away. As the soldier with the knife lunged toward the Israeli, Klein jump-kicked his enemy in the face, grabbed his forehead with one hand and the back of his neck with the other, and then snapped away his life with one brutal twist.

Twenty feet away, another Hezbollah soldier had Samuels pinned down, his knife inching toward Samuels's eye. Klein fired two shots at the attacker, who jerked up erect, then tumbled over.

Klein surveyed the carnage; there were dead bodies everywhere. Duvdevan had secured the area but at a high cost: three dead Israelis. Klein knew it could have been worse. He announced into his com link, "Beit, get me as many Hezbollah hostages as possible. Gimel, set the explosives for twenty-five minutes."

Once inside the hospital, the Beit soldiers spread out, cautious of a confrontation lurking behind every door and corner. Klein and Samuels ran down a stairwell to the basement. Using hand signals, they moved silently, stepping into a room with their Uzis in firing position, then reversing the choreographed move to exit. When Samuels opened a door and did not walk out immediately, Klein burst in to provide backup.

He found Samuels pointing his weapon at about twenty petrified doctors and nurses, huddled together in a storage room.

Klein asked them in Arabic the location of the generators. No one answered. Klein didn't have time for this. He approached the oldest doctor, placed his knife on the man's throat, and asked the question again, giving a five second warning.

The doctor looked away. Klein stepped behind him and made a long but negligible cut on his throat. The doctor screamed that he would take Klein to the generator.

Klein warned the group that if they left the room before he returned, they would all be killed when found. Samuels knew that Klein was serious.

The doctor led them through a maze of hallways that came to a dead end at a locked metal door. Samuels set up a plastic explosive and they moved away.

Seconds later, a loud blast blew the door inside the room. A filthy equipment room was stuffed with electrical panels, equipment, and tools.

Samuels approached a tall electrical panel with switches and hundreds of tiny white lights. Grabbing three large red handles, he pulled them down. The panel lights went dark, but ten seconds later, they kicked back on. Samuels moved to another panel that glowed with red and green diodes as a car-sized generator behind it started churning away.

Pointing at the panel, Samuels said to Klein, "You take this one and I'll get the generator. Set your explosive for a minute, but don't push the button yet, okay? Can you handle that?"

Klein laughed at his friend's humor. They quickly affixed their plastic explosives, then hustled from the room and back down the hall, the doctor in tow.

Klein said, "That's it, Liav? I dragged you all the way here just to blow up a generator?"

"Yep. It's easier to knock something down than it is to put it back together," Samuels said, grinning.

A few seconds later, two nearly simultaneous explosions echoed off the walls. This time the lights went out and didn't come back on. Klein and Samuels put on night vision goggles. The doctor now couldn't see an inch from his nose, and Klein took advantage of the situation. He slammed the old doctor against a wall, then punched him in the stomach and smacked him repeatedly in the face. "Where is Nasrallah? Tell me! Where?"

The trembling doctor's knees buckled. Klein yanked him straight up, then pulled out his knife, and again placed the cold blade on the doctor's neck.

Tears streaming down his face, the doctor stammered, "He left hours ago. Long before the bombing. I swear on the lives of my children. He visited the wounded, met with some people, and left."

"What about the other Hezbollah leaders? Where are they?"

"Down here, in another room."

"How many are there?"

"About ten."

Klein believed him. He said in a calm voice, "If you take me to them, I promise that neither you nor anyone else on your medical staff will be harmed. But if you don't help me, I will line your staff up against a wall and execute them. You will live, so their deaths will be in your head forever. Do you understand?"

The doctor repeatedly nodded. "I will do whatever you ask."

Klein flicked on his com link. "Beit, have you found anyone significant?"

A chorus of no's resounded through his earpiece.

"Okay, come find me and Samuels in the basement. Hurry! Air One, we need ten more minutes. Aleph and Gimel, get to the lobby with every Hezbollah soldier capable of walking."

The doctor led Klein and Samuels to the entrance of the room sheltering the Hezbollah leaders. The two Israelis waited until four more Duvdevan joined them.

Klein whispered to Samuels, "To get out of here alive, we need these criminals as hostages." He removed a flash grenade pinned to his shirt and signaled directions to position the men.

Motioning for everyone to close their eyes, Klein opened the door and tossed in the flash grenade. The concussive sound and blinding white light caused a chorus of shrieks. Duvdevan stormed the room, and in seconds overpowered the shocked and still-blinded terrorists.

Two minutes later, fourteen high-level Hezbollah captives were lined up, lying on their stomachs, and hands locked behind their backs with unbreakable zip ties.

Samuels brought the doctor back to the medical staff, cautioning them that for their own safety, they should stay put for another fifteen minutes.

Klein carefully examined the faces of the high-profile prisoners who had been hiding. Finally, Klein focused on a thin man with a scraggly beard and small eyes, instantly knowing who he was. Klein pulled him to his feet by his thick grey curly hair. "Where is Nasrallah?"

The Hezbollah spit on Klein.

Klein punched him in the nose, intentionally breaking it, spraying blood everywhere. Klein yelled, "Where is he?" The man grunted and refused Klein's repeated demands for information.

The Hezbollah soldier laughed, drawing cheers of support from his comrades. Klein pulled out his Glock and fired a shot point-blank into the man's kneecap. The terrorist crumbled to the ground, screaming. Klein kicked him hard in the groin, then stepped on his throat. "Where is he?"

The man was gasping but continued to show his defiance, muttering Allah's name. Klein knew this man wanted to die a martyr, so he changed course. "Ahmed Kuntar, I will not kill you. Instead, you'll rot in prison with your brother Samir."

"Jew pig. You know one day we will either be released or traded for one of you, so we will win, and you will lose, again."

"Kuntar, thank you for confirming your identity."

Two Duvdevan pulled Kuntar to his feet and held him up. "Your knee was payback for the little girl your brother killed."

"Allah blessed me for helping massacre that family."

Klein then shot him in the hip and said, "And that's for the father." After Klein put his gun away, he snapped Kuntar's collarbone, adding, "That's for the other little girl." Finally, with Kuntar back on the ground nearly unconscious, he stomped on both hands repeatedly. "That's for what the mother had to go through, and to assure you'll never make another bomb." Klein felt satisfied doling out his own justice to Kuntar, a notorious, long sought-after terrorist.

Klein and the other Sayaret members dragged the Hezbollah prisoners upstairs into the hospital lobby. Teams Beit and Gimel held sixteen additional hostages.

As the roar of incoming Israeli helicopters grew louder, the Duvdevan unit circled around Klein. "Just like always, getting in is easier than getting out," Klein said. "We have no idea how many enemies are now out there, but let's assume it's going to be crazier than when we landed. But at least we have valuable prisoners, so maybe not. Follow my lead."

When the first Black Hawk touched down, with cover, Klein and two other Duvdevan carried the dead Israelis to the closest helicopter.

Next, Klein grabbed a Hezbollah, put a gun to his head, and walked with his body flush against the enemy, using him as a human shield.

Samuels followed a few steps behind, positioned identically with another Hezbollah hostage, and they boarded the first Black Hawk. One by one, the rest followed until all of the soldiers with their captives were on board.

Klein was last to board the second Black Hawk. As he sat in the jump seat, the helicopter rose off the ground. He glanced through the open door, spotting Samuels in the jump seat of the other Black Hawk, now a hundred feet off the ground.

Klein waved and Samuels returned a two-finger salute.

A second later, a loud explosion and a flash of fire shook Samuels's Black Hawk. It banked hard to the left and dropped like a brick falling from the sky.

Klein helplessly watched the helicopter spin wildly out of control. It exploded into a fireball when it hit the ground.

Klein fell to his knees, buried his head in his hands, and screamed, "Oh God! No! Not again!"

A moment later a series of explosions ripped a weapons depot apart below them. As the Israeli squadron flew higher and sped away, more blasts could be heard—until there was one massive explosion, indicating the ignition of a cache of Iranian missiles.

Klein was dazed. Liav: another lost friend. Images of his previously murdered Duvdevan brothers Schlomo and Micah and his cousin Debra filled his head. Plus, now fifteen more dead Duvdevan. No captured sheik. A failed mission.

A rage came over him. He jumped up, grabbed a Hezbollah captive, dragged him to the hatch door and threw him out, 600 feet off the ground.

All eyes were on Klein, but nobody said a word. The Israelis understood Klein's hurt and anger. Klein felt a cold, burning emptiness in his heart. He turned and looked away so nobody could see the tears pour from his eyes.

21

Istanbul

Istanbul was Professor Yussef Hosnu's favorite place to visit. There he could speak Arabic, pray at some of Islam's most beautiful mosques, eat gourmet food, enjoy artistic and intellectual culture, and sleep in luxury at the Kempinski Hotel, formerly a Sultan's palace.

Once called Constantinople, the magnificent city was as significant as any in world history. Situated on the Silk Road, it had served as an imperial capital during the Roman, Byzantine, and Ottoman empires for 2,000 years. Until recently, it was a religious center where Christians, Muslims, and Jews peacefully coexisted. Now, it was a culturally advanced and cosmopolitan metropolis. Ancient yet modern, teeming with 16 million people, Istanbul boasted a long list of splendid architectural and historical structures, making the city one of the world's favorite tourist destinations.

Hosnu wove his way through the Kempinski Hotel's chic and crowded outdoor restaurant, situated on the edge of the Bosphorus strait. Two magnificent yachts cruised only fifty yards away, and dozens of ships floated further down the wide waterway.

A cloudless azure sky framed the Bosphorus, the wide body of water separating Istanbul into thirds while dividing it onto two continents. Asia sat to the east, and Europe, with its magnificent mosques and palaces just off the Golden Horn, was in the west. The Black Sea buffered Turkey from Russia to the north, which partly explained why Turkey was a member of NATO. More problematic was that Turkey shared its southern border with Lebanon, Syria, Iraq, and Iran; it was sitting atop perhaps the most complex and dangerous hotbed of right-wing fundamentalist Islam in the world. Turkey had few friends in this part of the world.

Hosnu approached two well-dressed men sitting at a table, engrossed in conversation. They rose from their white wrought iron chairs and exchanged traditional Muslim greetings.

"My, what do we have here!" Hosnu said, smiling. A lunch buffet lay before him with sliced fruit; a basket of croissants and pastries; a tray with tomato and cucumbers garnished with cheeses, nuts, and olives; and another plate of sliced lamb and chicken. He picked up a few olives and popped them into his mouth.

"Who likes to talk on an empty stomach?" replied Rafsani.

"Nothing but the best for you, Professor," added Khaled as they all sat down.

Dr. Yussef Hosnu was an esteemed Professor of Middle East Studies at The Ohio State University. Hiding under the guise of educational respectability, Hosnu spent the last twenty years travelling America lecturing at conferences and rallies on his Wahhabi fundamentalist version of Middle East history and the Koran, spewing anti-American, anti-Zionist rhetoric. In the process, he indoctrinated tens of thousands of American Muslims, raised millions of dollars, and established a U.S. based Islamic fundamentalist network, sheltered behind the doors of mosques and so-called charities. All along, his principal mission was to work with Rafsani and the now-missing

Abdullah al-Talib to create a network of terrorist cells throughout the United States that would engage simultaneously with those created by Rafsani.

Moments later, two waiters in white shirts and black bow ties appeared. One filled Hosnu's crystal water goblet, while the other poured Dom Perignon into a champagne flute. Once the waiters left, Hosnu said, "Omar, Khaled, I am so pleased to see you, but before we get to business, *why* are you wearing suits?"

"It's a good look, isn't it?" Rafsani said. He opened his navy-blue jacket to show Hosnu the label. "Canali." Glancing at Khaled, he added, "Armani, right?"

"No, Zegna. The gray pinstripe is the Armani," Khaled replied. Focusing on Hosnu, he added, "We went shopping in Rome and stocked up."

Hosnu shook his head. "Why would you *need* suits? I don't understand."

"For days like this," replied Khaled.

"You put on a suit for me?"

"Of course. We're at the Kempinski. Security is everywhere, but we don't even get a glance," Rafsani said confidently. "I learned from Carlos long ago: Don't stand out. Blend in. "

"You're a respected professor from the United States," Khaled said. "And when you're stopped by airport security, it's because you look Muslim. But then, since you dress well and you're a college professor, passport control lets you right through, right?"

"Yes, that even happened today. When I told them I'm here to lecture tomorrow at Istanbul University, security couldn't have been nicer."

"Clothes and title legitimize anyone," said Rafsani. "Imagine this. We've flown all over the world on 'business' the past two years, and we wear suits to establish our cover as partners in a London-based law firm. We carry fake brochures and business cards, and we have a fake website with our pictures and CVs. There are even fake press releases that tout our success as lawyers that show up if you Google our aliases. We paid a lot for all of that, as well as perfect false passports. Basically, we go wherever we want without trouble and always in suits."

"I love it. Terrorists posing as lawyers. Great irony." Hosnu laughed. "But are you actually spending a lot of time in London?"

"Not anymore," Rafsani replied. "These days we're here more, helping ISIS recruits from other countries get where we need them to go. Thanks to Khaled's work when he was in the U.S. with you, we've had about thirty American ISIS recruits come through Istanbul."

"Excellent," Hosnu said through a mouthful of chicken. "So, Omar, tell me how you think ISIS survives after what's happened in Syria and Iraq."

Omar nodded and smiled. "Obviously, ISIS started out strong, then failed badly there. But more recently, we've done very well spreading our message through the internet and in fundamentalist mosques. Technically, the ISIS army is in trouble, but the individuals and especially the sleeper cells who make up ISIS are thriving. Ultimately, we will win the war against the West because as individuals our cells are invisible, and we have infiltrated *everywhere*. The infidels will never find us."

"And we will kill the nonbelievers and change the world," Khaled confidently added.

"Khaled, you've changed since we were together in America."

After Khaled had gone through a few months of training with Rafsani in locales around the Middle East and Northern Africa, he was sent to America to learn from the Professor and his protégé, Ismael Nadal, who was always referred to as the Engineer, about setting up a terrorist network, money laundering, the dark web, and managing websites. Just being Mahmoud's brother made Khaled someone people wanted to meet. Khaled especially stood out during a six-city fundraising tour with Hosnu for the Council of Islamic American Refugees, during which he became a star for his passionate and vitriolic anti-West speeches.

"Thanks to Omar, I've seen, done, and learned a lot since then. I'm *not* the same person that you met last year. I truly understand now why we must succeed in our mission. It's not about me seeking revenge. This war is for all of our people." Khaled glanced at Rafsani and added, "Omar, you built me. You are my teacher. You are my mentor. You are my brother."

Rafsani smiled and squeezed Khaled's shoulder. "Yes, and we will finally avenge all injustices committed against Islam. So, Yussef, I need to know if our cells are all set."

"Of course. We have numerous cells in our target cities in America, plus those you set up in Europe and Asia. No cell anywhere in the world can communicate with any other cell, nor do they know where any other cell in our network even exists. This vastly decreases risk. So if something goes wrong in Washington, the other cells in the U.S. and everywhere else remain secure."

"How do the cells know what to do, and when we are going to launch?"

"We communicate through a private chatroom on a website on the dark web."

"I've heard about the dark web, but I don't know how it works," Rafsani said. "Walk me through it."

"Of course. The internet most of the world uses every day includes commercial websites, social media, news, and email. But that's actually maybe just five percent of the entire internet. The rest is on the dark web. To get onto it, I downloaded software from Torproject.org. It's a free open network router program known as Tor, which anyone can find through Google. Inside the dark web, our website posts anti-West articles and violent videos that show how we punish the infidels. But more important, we use this website to recruit and communicate."

"But why use the dark web?" Rafsani interrupted. "Wouldn't it be easier for more like-minded Islamic brothers to find us on a website on the regular internet?"

"No. Governments not only monitor and shut down those web-sites, but more important, on the regular internet, they can trace the websites' IP addresses and emails," Khaled said.

"How do you know that?" Rafsani asked, pleasantly surprised at his protégé.

"You're old! How do you *not* know that?"

Hosnu laughed. "Kudos to Khaled. Anyway, Tor bounces every one of its communications through a distribution network of about twenty-seven relays around the world. This prevents governments from tracing our IP address or communications, so the identity and location of anyone online in the dark web remains unknown. Ironically, Tor was created to protect sensitive data for the U.S. intelligence agencies, military, and American businesses, so *they* could operate in secrecy. Now groups like ours use it to stay hidden. But we also have encrypted emails using Tutanota, which is a secure email server." Hosnu took a quick sip of champagne and raised his glass. "The proof that the technology works is that no one has found me."

"Omar, the dark web is also an online black market," Khaled injected. "Everything is for sale. Weapons, drugs, murder, children, women, men…anything!"

"So Yussef, what's our website called?"

"*Kill the Infidels.* A perfect name for recruiting the martyrs we seek."

"I like it," Rafsani replied with a grin. "But how do you recruit those who contact you, if the website and emails are anonymous?"

"While the intelligence services can't trace our communications, we know they monitor our website with agents whose sole job is to try to infiltrate us. And also, most Western governments share intelligence. Therefore, we communicate very slowly with every potential new recruit. When we're totally comfortable that we've collected and verified enough information about that recruit, a local cell leader makes direct contact."

"But how can you be truly confident the recruit is *not* an undercover agent?"

"We have a test. After we've vetted a candidate, we pick a random woman in their city and we order the recruit to immediately kill her up close, with our cell leader as a witness. Undercover agents would not go that far. If the recruit passes that test, they become part of the cell. If they refuse orders, we kill them. And if we're wrong and have been infiltrated, only that one cell is at risk."

"Yussef, it is brilliant!" Rafsani exclaimed.

"So how many cells are fully operational and ready to launch?" Khaled asked.

Hosnu frowned, "Only forty-two, which includes the European cells you handed off to me. I wanted sixty, as we discussed in Mecca. It just takes so much time to recruit and stay on top of everything." Hosnu looked down and whispered, "I'm sorry."

Rafsani's chin jutted forward. "Sorry! Are you kidding? Forty-two cells? That's incredible!"

"Yussef, including the six in the Middle East that we put together, that gives us forty-eight," Khaled said. "Seriously, think about how the world reacts when there is just one attack, anywhere. With forty-eight, there will be unimaginable chaos everywhere."

"Khaled is correct," said Rafsani. "You have done Allah's work. So, tell me, what do you have planned for the cities?"

Hosnu rubbed his chin. "Well, in Paris, I have one cell of ten men *and* women who will open fire on the crowd at the Louvre's outdoor plaza with automatic weapons. Then they'll spread out and attack the galleries. In Rome, we'll storm St. Peter's Basilica, make it a blood-bath, and destroy everything with hand grenades. Florence is an easy target. The Uffizi Gallery has long lines with little security, and we will just mow the people down. Then we'll set fire in the Vasari Corridor and burn the art. Did you know that in 1993 the Mafia bombed the Uffizi, and the Italians still haven't provided real security?"

"What about London?" Rafsani asked.

Hosnu held up three fingers. "Our three separate cells will attack both symbolic and high-impact locations to maximize damage. We'll use an RPG on Ten Downing Street, shoot our way into Westminster Abbey, and blow up the base of the Eye so that the Ferris wheel crashes down into the Thames with everyone in it. *That* video will go viral."

"Great targets," said Khaled. "All extremely high-profile locations. That'll shake up the British."

"That's the goal. In many other cities, we have easier attacks planned—in subways, shopping malls, and public places, like the square in Prague, where automatic weapons and hand grenades can do significant damage quickly. The world will soon understand that no place or person is safe from us."

Rafsani raised his index finger. "That's what they should believe, because it is true."

"My job was to plan a war on the streets of the Western cities," Hosnu said.

"And clearly, you did. So tell me your plans for America."

Hosnu opened his arms wide and said, "As the expression goes in the United States, *they are fucked!* We have cells in twenty-three cities, many with multiple cells. In Washington, our main target is the West Wing of the White House. Using the surface-to-air missile that you found for me, we'll fire it from a van on Seventeenth Street by the Old Executive Office Building. We don't even have to kill the president. Just blowing up the White House will be good enough. By the way, Omar, how did you get that weapon?"

Rafsani shrugged. "We have friends everywhere."

"What about the second cell in Washington?" Khaled asked.

"It will storm the Holocaust Museum with automatic weapons. The cell has built a dozen sarin gas canisters that they'll drop throughout the building, killing everyone. I love the symbolism of that attack."

"As will the rest of the Islamic world," said Rafsani. "Okay, the big one: what about New York? You told me before that you have put more time and effort there than anywhere else."

Hosnu looked to the heavens and mouthed "Praise Allah." He then said, "A moving van packed with C-4 will explode in the middle of the Holland Tunnel. The resulting fireball should incinerate everyone in the tunnel. But even if it doesn't, the fans that suck out the carbon dioxide in the tunnel will be destroyed, so any survivors will suffocate. Two minutes later, we have a dive team that will blow four large holes in the tunnel and flood it. We also have men planted inside the New York City sewer department who will shut down the pumps at Canal Street, SoHo, and Tribeca. Those areas will flood, as will the West Side subway lines. Many more will die in New York on Kill the Infidels Day than on 9/11."

"I don't know how you came up with that plan for New York, Yussef, but it is extremely impressive."

"Thank you. But you know I had help from Ismael Nadal, the engineer I told you about. He is brilliant! Khaled, you remember him from Chicago, don't you?"

"He's hard to forget. Very intense guy." Khaled looked at Rafsani and said, "Even more than you."

"I like him already," Rafsani replied. "Anything else, Yussef?"

"Of course! We'll target airport terminal entrances with carry-on suitcase bombs and automatic weapons, just like the attack here in Istanbul a few years ago. We'll also use carry-ons at the busy shopping centers, office buildings, hotels, and landmarks, most of which are totally defenseless. Each carry-on can hold fifty pounds of explosives, and we only need one person per attack. That way, each cell can spread out their attacks to many locations within one city. Think about it: every day you see people walking through the streets pulling carry-on suitcases. It's foolproof."

"How many single-person attacks do you have planned?" Khaled asked.

Hosnu scratched his head. "At least three hundred. Probably more. Also, for maximum impact we will hit every target in the U.S. and Canada at exactly 1:00 p.m. Eastern. Every city will be well into its business day because it will already be 10:00 a.m. on the West

Coast. By then, all the attacks on the European and Asian cities will have been executed. The globe will be in chaos."

Both Khaled and Rafsani were briefly stunned silent. After a few moments, Rafsani added, "There won't be enough newsprint or television airtime to cover all the attacks that day."

Khaled asked, "Given all of your plans for the U.S., how did you buy so many guns for your shahid?"

"Seriously? The easiest thing to get were guns. Anyone can get a gun in America, including automatic weapons. Even mentally ill people can legally buy them."

Rafsani burst out laughing but Hosnu quickly said, "No, I'm serious."

"Really?"

Hosnu nodded vigorously.

"Even I don't want crazy people having guns," Rafsani declared. "Too unpredictable."

"Omar, who cares? If the Americans want to kill each other, that's good for us," said Khaled. "Second and much more important, Yussef, what can we do to thank you? Do you want more money? A new car, maybe a Ferrari? A villa somewhere?"

"No, nothing," Hosnu politely replied. "Just knowing that you're pleased with my work is enough. I don't need any more money or possessions."

"Okay, but if you change your mind, let us know. You've certainly earned it," said Khaled.

"Thank you. So, if you don't mind, I'd love to know where you set up cells in the Middle East."

"Riyadh, Cairo, Amman, Abu Dhabi, Kuwait City, and Jerusalem," Rafsani replied, "which is where Khaled and I will be on Kill the Infidels Day. Those attacks will redraw the map of the Middle East."

"Riyadh? I don't understand. Hasn't the Kingdom provided almost all of our funding?"

Rafsani shrugged. "Maybe so, but the Kingdom has to go. They're trying to modernize. They do business with the Israelis. It has served its purpose."

"You know it won't be easy to hide in or escape from Jerusalem on Judgment Day," said Hosnu. "So why put yourself at risk there?"

"We will be in the middle of the battle that day, not on the sidelines," Rafsani replied emphatically. Once all these attacks hit our enemies and they're preoccupied dealing with them, my people in ISIS, the Iranians, Syria, and Hezbollah will attack Israel from all directions. And we'll also use chemical weapons I salvaged from Iraq."

"*You* have them?" Hosnu said, visibly surprised.

"Of course. That's why the U.S. couldn't find the 'weapons of mass destruction' that Bush swore existed when he invaded Iraq. Bush and the CIA were right, and I'll prove it to them when we use those weapons against Israel. Anyway, Khaled and I will be in Jerusalem when we seize it back from the Jews. I promise to burn the city, just like the Romans did two thousand years ago."

"I can't wait!" Hosnu exclaimed. "How long before Judgment Day?"

"Very soon."

"Excellent. So, Omar, one last thing. I know you need to give the final order on when the attacks will commence. I need to make sure that Khaled has Tor *today* and the Kill the Infidels website loaded onto his laptop, and that he's well trained using it. That means we'll be able to communicate freely between us, in addition to launching the attack message yourself."

Hosnu handed a thumb drive to Khaled. "Do not lose that! It's the entire database on the cells plans and all Kill the Infidels cell numbers and email addresses. The only other copy is on my laptop. That's why my Mac never leaves my side."

"Yussef, we are so grateful," said Rafsani. "You've left nothing to chance. Allah himself will greet you in heaven, hopefully many years from now." He clasped his hands together and pointed them at Hosnu with a smile.

Hosnu glanced at his watch. "We have done Allah's work together, my brothers. Please forgive me, but I need to meet with the president of Istanbul University, where I am speaking. You know I must keep up appearances to protect my cover."

"Yes, of course, but we must toast before you go," Rafsani said.

All three raised their champagne flutes and followed Rafsani's lead in clinking their glasses, repeating, "To killing the infidels."

"Yussef, what time would be good for us to meet tonight?" asked Khaled.

"I have a 7:30 dinner appointment, so how about ten o'clock? Room 430. Knock five times and bring your laptop."

The moment Hosnu left, Rafsani said, "He must die. He knows everything. He's done superb work, but his existence is now a risk to us."

"I assumed as much and have a plan. Once I have Tor and the website working, I will kill him. It will look like a suicide."

"You have learned well, Khaled. I'm proud of the man you've become."

Khaled lowered his eyes. "I humbly owe you everything. I am the man you made."

22

Jerusalem

Klein and Beer had just finished giving Baroness Collins, Galit, and Danzig the VIP tour of the tunnels under the Temple Mount, and Klein was looking forward to showing them the Ark. They passed the illuminated sign that advised they were at the spot closest to the Foundation Stone and the Holy of the Holies, and they approached a short set of stairs up to a metal door underneath another sign that read: Danger-Electrical.

Klein unlocked the door with a key, and everyone slipped inside to find another door a few feet up. He punched in a twelve-digit keypad code, the door swung open, and the group followed Klein, who was carrying a lantern, through a series of hallways. Finally, Klein stopped at a stone wall, lifted the lantern, and peered through the light at the ridges between every stone, using his free hand to feel around. He kept moving until he found what he wanted. He put down the lantern, outstretched his arms evenly, and pushed against two blocks.

217

A moment later, the blocks shifted backward into the wall. Thirty seconds later, a hidden doorway and the tiny room beyond were revealed. As they entered, the lantern's light reflected off the gold-adorned Ark and the two golden cherubim perched on its lid.

He walked to the back wall and effortlessly picked up his sword in its dormant, crusted state. The sword transformed into a gleaming blade, humming as he spun it around. Seconds later, orange and white sparks crackled between the two cherubim. The more Klein swung the sword, the more the Ark's lid sung back with greater flashes of crackling light, as if it was in direct communication with Klein and the sword.

Her hands on her cheeks, the baroness gasped. "The Ark of the Covenant is alive! God is with us in this room!"

Galit's eyes were transfixed on the Ark. Tears ran down her face.

Pale and visibly shaken, Danzig whispered, "It's proof that the Burning Bush and Moses coming down Mount Sinai with the tablets were real."

Klein smiled faintly, pleased that this was the first time *this* Ark responded to him. "Yes Danzig, this is all real, which drives home why we must find the Ten Commandments. Whether they're in the Vatican or somewhere else." He looked at Galit and said in a matter-of-fact tone, "You're the smartest one here. What do you think?"

Galit dried her eyes with the sleeve of her sweater, then said, "From a historical standpoint, I'm skeptical the tablets are in the Vatican. I've researched and found nothing about anyone seeing, selling, or owning them since the destruction of the Second Temple. But also, going back two thousand years, both Josephus and the Arch of Titus recorded that Titus took mostly gold, silver, and the large menorah from the Second Temple. Also, the Romans wouldn't have had an interest in the Ten Commandments. They were pagans who worshipped idols, so they'd see the tablets as worthless pieces of stone. Even if they were brought back to Rome for some reason, they wouldn't have given them to the

Christians. At the time, the Romans were killing Christians, sending them into the Colosseum to fight lions."

Beer added, "Further, there was no Vatican back then. The Catholic Church's first cathedral in Rome was constructed by Constantine in the 300s and St. Peter's wasn't built until around 1600. So there's no way that the Ten Commandments made it to Rome in 70 A.D., when there was no place to keep them safe."

Klein turned to Baroness Collins. "I'm sorry, Baroness, but there are no facts to suggest that the Ten Commandments are in the Vatican. And if miraculously they are there, it's impossible to think that we can break in, hunt around, find and steal them from a super high-security building, then get out safely."

The baroness retorted, "So you've no idea where to find them, Chaim?"

"That's right."

"But somehow all along you've *known* that you were destined to find the Ten Commandments—that's what propelled you on this long, unusual journey…Ethiopia, London, Paris, Chartres."

In a strong voice, Klein replied, "Yes, I believe the Ten Commandments are out there. I'm just not convinced they're in Rome, and I don't think we should go there."

The baroness folded her arms across her chest, then said loudly, "But they *are* there! Do you think I'd waste my time going to Rome putting both the Knights Templar and you at risk? Haven't we been completely supportive of your mission, including funding that put over 100 million pounds into the MFP coffers? Like it or not and believe it or not, Chaim, I *know* they are there."

"Respectfully, simply saying that we need to go the Vatican doesn't make it happen," Klein said.

The baroness snorted, then focused on Galit. "Miss Kevetch, as our history expert, let's talk about how the Knights Templar came to power."

Galit looked at Klein for guidance, who shrugged. "I already know the story, Galit," he said, "but give me the lecture anyway. Maybe one of us will have a revelation."

Galit sighed. "Well, the Knights Templar were founded in 1119 when the original nine Catholic knights travelled from Europe to Jerusalem and presented themselves to King Baldwin the Second, offering to serve him however he needed. About a year later, the King granted the Templars permission to set up residence on the Temple Mount. After that, they dug everywhere around this area for about nine years, no doubt looking for the treasure that legend said was hidden away. The Romans didn't find it. But then, suddenly, the Templars returned to Europe and became phenomenally wealthy, which also made them famous and powerful. That enabled them to build a diverse commercial empire. It's always been said that the Templars found the Temple's treasure, including something of great religious significance."

The baroness added with a raised finger, "In fact, Galit, hasn't the story for a thousand years been that the Knights Templar found the Ark of the Covenant?"

"Yes, and I presume that was the Ark that Chaim saw in Paris."

"Wait a second!" Klein interrupted. "How can the High Priest's parchment I found in here say that Roman soldiers ended up with the Ten Commandments, but no one actually thinks the Romans took them to Rome?"

The baroness walked up to him. "Chaim, hasn't this adventure taught you that anything is possible?"

Klein shrugged noncommittally.

"The High Priest you found entombed couldn't possibly know what happened to the tablets *after* the door closed since he was locked away in this room, correct?"

"True," Klein said.

"Which means that anything could have happened to the tablets after that battle," said the baroness.

"I guess so."

"Did you, or anyone for that matter, ever consider that *maybe* when the Knights Templar were digging around the Temple Mount, they found the corpse of *another* Jewish priest hidden away, clutching the tablets to his chest?"

Everyone's head jerked toward the baroness. "And maybe when they found the priest," she added, "he too had a parchment note, one which said that he bartered gold in a trade with two Roman soldiers in exchange for the tablets and his life." After a purposeful pause, she asked, "What do you think the Roman soldiers would want more, gold—or two pieces of worthless stone with Hebrew printing on them?" Without waiting for an answer, the baroness said, "And by the way, Chaim, we still have that parchment in the Templar library in Westminster Abbey."

After a few seconds, Klein replied, "If the Templars had the Ten Commandments, why would we have to go to the Vatican to get them?"

"Don't get ahead of yourself, Chaim! We need to jump forward one thousand years to when Christianity was the dominant religion in Europe. Consider that while the Templars didn't find the Ark you found, they *did* find the treasure and the Ark that's now in Paris. And just as importantly, they found the priest with the Ten Commandments. They knew those tablets were even more valuable than the gold and jewels because they were written by the finger of God. So, with these two most profound religious artifacts and the Temple treasure, they went to Rome to visit Pope Innocent the Second, and they showed him the tablets, the remains of the Jewish priest, and his parchment." Baroness Collins let her story sink in before confidently concluding, "Imagine that…one thousand years after the fall of the Second Temple, the Ark of the Covenant and the Ten Commandments were found by the Knights Templar."

Everyone processed the baroness's astonishing pronouncement until Galit said, "And that's just around the time the Council of Troyes recognized the Templars as a military *and religious* order!"

"Yes, and after that, Pope Innocent issued a papal bull that the Knights Templar would pay no taxes, could pass through any country's border without interference, and would be answerable only to the Church," the baroness said. "In part, that's how Templars grew so powerful throughout Europe."

"This is all very interesting," Beer said, "but it still doesn't explain how the Church ended up with the Ten Commandments. Are you suggesting that the Templars traded the tablets to the Pope in exchange for power and influence?"

"That makes sense," Danzig chimed in. "The Pope got the tablets to show the people that he is the voice of God on Earth, and for two pieces of stone, the Templars became such a dominant force in Europe that they remain legendary to this day."

"Mr. Danzig, I admit that actually sounds quite feasible, but unfortunately, it's not what happened," Baroness Collins said, shaking her head. "The first time the Templars met the Pope, they showed him the tablets, and after quite a negotiation, they pledged their full loyalty to the Church. Then, with his agreement, the Templars kept the tablets so they would remain safe. The Pope understood the symbolic power of the tablets, but he had little security and many enemies—most of whom were powerful kings. From this, the Pope and the Templars forged a strong relationship, built on the Templars' army and money and their promise to protect the Ten Commandments."

"So how did the tablets wind up in the Vatican?" Klein asked.

The baroness frowned. "Because two hundred years later, another Pope betrayed the Templars."

"You mean the story with King Philip?" Klein asked.

The baroness stared at the Ark before responding. "In the early 1300s, King Philip the Fourth of France found himself in a difficult spot with the Templars. He had inherited land in Champagne where the Templars were headquartered, and as we know, by that time, they were an unstoppable financial force, doing whatever they wished, plus they also had that powerful army. So, to poke Philip in the eye, they announced their intention to form their own state; not long after they supported a successful coup of the King of Cyprus. Now, if that wasn't enough to make a king insecure, Philip was broke and in debt to the Templars."

"Hmmm, so Philip had no cards, and the Templars threatened his monarchy," Beer said.

"Wrong. Philip held a trump card that the Templars didn't contemplate. The House of France had an even stronger alliance to the Church than did the Templars, because five French kings already had led their armies into the Crusades for the Popes, and Philip and the Pope were related to boot. Philip, who was morally bankrupt and hated the Templars, saw getting his hands on their fortune as the only way to solve his financial problems. That was why, on the very day in 1307 that Pope Clement the Fifth was inaugurated, the King concocted the accusations that the Templars committed usury, fraud, heresy, and sodomy, causing a great public outcry against them. He extracted false confessions from their leaders through torture of the most medieval kind."

"Listen, Baroness, we all know the Friday the thirteenth story," said Danzig. "Tell us something we don't know."

She glared at him. "You sir, are utterly impossible."

Danzig nodded. "Probably, but seriously, come on already!"

The baroness ignored Danzig and continued, "Everyone knows Philip arrested dozens of Templars, including Grand Master Jacques de Molay. Then, two years into a trial with the thinnest of evidence against the Templars, Pope Clement struck a three-way deal that included de Molay and some other Templars being burned at the stake. In exchange for sparing the remaining Templars, they had to disband in France and leave Philip some money and their buildings in Champagne. Fortunately, most of our treasure was secure; it had already been moved on our ships to England or spread out across Europe. Those extraordinary assets have kept us a silent but powerful institution that exists and thrives today." Baroness Collins shook her head and continued. "And the Pope's extortionate 'fee' for this betrayal was his taking possession of the Ten Commandments, in return for the lives he spared and the money he claimed to have saved them. In the Pope's absurd and greedy view, everyone got what they needed."

Beer had been Googling on his iPhone. He read from his screen, "But Baroness, the Chinon Parchment found in the Vatican archives in 2001 says that in August 1308, Pope Clement absolved de Molay and the Templars, then reinstated them to the Church. That was equivalent to a full pardon. Couldn't they have reasserted themselves, including in France?"

"Too little too late. The damage was done. De Molay was dead, the Ten Commandments were gone, and we lost Champagne. The Templars concluded that the best plan to survive was to keep themselves secret, to protect their holdings and people. We also had trust issues with the Pope. But I think in a different way, you'll see the Chinon Parchment may still prove helpful."

"So that's a really incredible story, Baroness," said Danzig. "But I'm wondering how we can get in and out of the Vatican in one piece, much less with the Ten Commandments in our possession. Explain that to me."

Even though his point was legitimate, knowing that Danzig was just trying to needle her, the baroness smiled. "You certainly like to mix it up, don't you Mr. Danzig?"

"Absolutely. And being an eternal pessimist, I can't imagine a crazier, more farfetched operation than what you're proposing. I have one job: to keep Chaim safe. There's no chance to do that with this ridiculous scheme of yours."

The baroness sighed heavily. "I don't know how you all tolerate him."

"It's difficult," Klein replied, "but he's really good at his job."

Baroness Collins turned away from Danzig and focused on Klein. "Chaim, when I was a teenager, about thirty others and I, all of whom were born of the right Templar-related bloodline, started our education to be future leaders of the Knights Templar. Then one day, the timing was such that I was elected by our ruling body, the Knights High Council, to assume the magnificent responsibility of becoming the Grand Master. It's difficult to understand these things, but there is factual knowledge of historical events unknown to the public that has been passed down through many generations of Grand Masters, including me. Without a doubt, the facts I related to you about how Pope Clement obtained the Ten Commandments happened. I wish it weren't true, but it is."

"Why didn't you just tell us this before?" Klein asked.

"I couldn't. My vows as Grand Master require that I live with many secrets. But now it's time for some of these secrets to come to light. You now know more about the Ten Commandments and the Vatican than almost all of my colleagues on the High Council."

"So you're breaking your vows?"

"I couldn't tell you sooner. I had to see what you were made of. Can't you see that I believe in you, and that it's now or never for this mission, which we can *only* do together? We must succeed. Too much is at stake." Putting her hands on her hips, she demanded, "Chaim, I need your answer! Are we going to Rome?"

"Baroness, I know you are truthful and honorable. But please tell me how you know the tablets are still in the Vatican."

"I've said more than I should have. For hundreds of years, they were hidden in Castel Sant'Angelo. Then at some point, they were moved inside the Vatican. They are there."

Klein stared at her quizzically.

"You don't tell me everything either, Chaim."

"That's fair."

The baroness sighed and tried once more. "Chaim, it is the Knights Templar's responsibility to recover the Ten Commandments and return them to Jerusalem." Pointing at the Ark she added, "None of this is coincidence. It is all of God's design. You know this is true. Help us fulfill our destiny to bring about a new age of enlightenment.

An age of peace." She then grabbed Klein's hand. "I've never said this to anyone before, but I beg you, please, trust me."

Galit leaned into Klein. "Chaim, many inexplicable things have happened to you since you found the Ark of the Covenant. Why is the baroness's story any different from yours? It may seem illogical, but clearly the Knights Templar are very real. It seems to me that the two of you are...*partners?*"

Klein remained stone-faced and looked at Beer. "What do you think?"

"Chaim, this is not something we vote on. It's up to you, but I trust the baroness."

"Danzig?"

"Even if she's right, breaking into the Vatican is just too risky. But regardless, I'm here to protect you, and will support whatever decision you make, especially after seeing this room today."

Klein stared at the Ark, then his gaze moved to the baroness. "Baroness Collins—and all of you—have had to put your trust and faith in me. I need to return that trust to her and the Knights Templars."

A broad smile overtook the baroness's face, but then she turned serious. "Thank you, Chaim, but we have work to do. Anyone can get in and out of the Vatican. The hard part is getting out with the tablets."

PART THREE

23

Rome

A black Mercedes darted through traffic on the Lungotevere Castello, centered between the Tiber River and the infamous Castel Sant'Angelo, the former papal prison. Seconds later, the road turned into Via della Conciliazione, and vehicle traffic came to a dead stop, revealing St. Peter's Square and its basilica in its full glory. The passengers in the Mercedes were uncharacteristically quiet, captivated by the sight of the Vatican, the symbolic home to the Roman Catholic Church and its 1.3 billion followers.

The iconic Renaissance dome of St. Peter's Basilica dominated the landscape, designed by Michelangelo and completed after his death by Giacometti della Porta in 1546. The present basilica replaced Constantine's first basilica, which had been constructed on top of ancient grottos, catacombs, and the graveyard where the apostle Paul was martyred and buried 2,000 years ago, and where his remains were found and validated in 1968 by Pope Paul VI. Tucked away in this small city-state was one of the greatest museums and art collections in the world, as well as the renowned Vatican Apostolic Archive—formerly known as the Vatican Secret Archives.

Already at 8:45 a.m., a swarm of the faithful flooded the sidewalks to celebrate the Pope's 10:00 a.m. Jubilee for Peace at St. Peter's. The Mercedes's driver, Ezana Meroe, bellowed through his thick Ethiopian accent, "Too many people. Too many cars. Time for you to walk," and he immediately pulled over.

Klein leaned forward from his seat behind Meroe. "Ezana, one more time…what is your route?"

"I make the next right, then turn left two blocks up at Catalone and follow that five blocks to Porta Angelica, then right again. A white produce truck with 'Carbone' printed on the back will exit a parking space, and that will be mine."

"Our Mossad agent has confirmed he's there, holding the space for you," said Beer. "When you see him, beep your horn three times as the signal."

Meroe nodded.

"Good. And Ezana, no matter what, do not leave this car unless I call and instruct you to bring the package to St. Anne's Gate," Klein said.

"I know," Meroe replied. "May God be with you."

"He'd better be," Klein said under his breath.

The passengers stepped out of the car. Galit and Baroness Collins had disguised themselves as elderly nuns. Galit donned a short gray wig, small round glasses, and a fake mole; the 72 year-old baroness already looked the part. Klein and Beer were dressed as Catholic priests, and Danzig's costume as a Russian Orthodox priest with a long grey beard was the most dramatic.

"This is exciting!" exclaimed the baroness.

"Are you kidding?" Galit answered angrily. "This is dangerous! Arguably, crazy!"

"You don't understand. I've had a rich, full, fascinating life, but I never dreamed I'd go searching for the Ten Commandments in the Vatican! Even if we get caught today, I'm an old lady. What are they going to do to me?"

"Put you in a cold, dark cell," replied Danzig, in a tone suggesting he spoke with knowledge.

"And maybe you will just disappear," added Klein."

"Oh, that's silly. The Pope would never do those things. He is such a good man."

"The Pope might not, but those who work for him might," said Galit.

"Well, I don't think you're right."

"Think again," replied Klein in a frank tone that startled the baroness. He then commanded, "We know the plan. Time to execute. First, communication check."

Simultaneously, everyone walked in different directions, pulled out their iPhones, and clicked a sequence of buttons in the systems screen. Klein waited ten seconds and said, "Sister Jillian?"

"I hear you perfectly. Can you hear me?" replied the baroness. Earlier, each member of the team had placed into his or her right ear a Mossad-designed, state-of-the-art, nearly invisible audio and GPS transmitter hooked up to a satellite.

"Sister Chloe?"

"We're good," replied Galit.

"Father Daniel?"

"Clear."

"Father Rafael, remember, do not hurt anyone, no matter what. Understood?"

"I'll try."

"That's not a request. It's an order," Klein said. He continued, "God? Can you hear me?"

"Chaim, stop calling me that," Mossad Director Bareket tersely replied.

"Sorry, but if we get caught today, it will take God to get us out of here. All right, disperse and camera check."

Each team member tapped buttons on their phone screens, activating their GPS and undetectable body cameras hidden in their clothing. All had their own color-coded markers on the screen showing their precise locations, which could be viewed by everyone else.

Seconds later, Bareket said, "Video and GPS up. Good luck."

They walked separately toward the Vatican amidst the thick crowd. Bareket watched them from a van with a satellite feed, parked in front of a store specializing in robes and headpieces for bishops and cardinals.

Today's Jubilee of Peace had been initiated by Pope John XXIV only a year into his papacy. As Cardinal Guido Pellegrini of Florence, he had witnessed mass death, destruction, and despair during his frequent travels as a Church emissary to the site of war zones and terrorist attacks in Europe and the Middle East. As Pope, he had stated his intention to use his influential pulpit to send a global message of peace.

The Pope understood that in the Middle East, each unnecessary death by the enemy ensured another generation's hate, guaranteeing violence and perpetuating the vicious cycle of mutual destruction. It mattered not whether the victim was Israeli or Palestinian, Sunni or Shiite, Westerner or Islamic Fundamentalist. His psyche had been greatly affected by witnessing the suffering of countless defenseless people, so he took the name "John" to honor the last Pope of that name who reigned from 1958 to 1963 and whose reformist ideals influenced subsequent popes. Perhaps the world's countries were incapable of bringing about peace, but that wouldn't stop Pope John from trying. The Jubilee of Peace was the first step.

Jubilees were reserved for religious celebrations, such as the Great Jubilee of 2000. But after John Paul II held separate special Jubilees for sick people and health care workers, migrants, prisoners, statesmen, and politicians—all kinds of social justice issues—precedent had been established for John to call the Jubilee for Peace. A long list of world government, religious, and social leaders had agreed to participate, with over 700,000 people from over fifty countries attending. In the front row of world leaders, by the dual-purpose stage and pulpit, sat Israeli Prime Minister Eli Zamir. Not far away was the Crown Prince of Saudi Arabia.

When they reached the obelisk in the middle of the square, the baroness and Galit moved to the left in order to enter the Vatican from the south. The men moved to the north entrance.

Over their earpieces, Bareket announced, "Listen up! We've tapped into the Swiss Guard radio feed and computers. Most of the dignitaries are already seated. The Swiss Guard and Vatican police are protecting the VIPs with help from Italian, British, and American security. There are twenty-two rooftop sharpshooters and plainclothes officers everywhere. Also, the live feed from the museum, archives, and the sacristy show that they are empty, as expected. Chaim, it's now or never."

"It's now. Let's pick up the pace!" Klein replied.

"Yes, move fast," Bareket added. "The Swiss Guard just ordered security to cut off all VIP seating in fifteen minutes, to avoid distractions when the Pope walks out. If you're not in line by then, you're not getting in."

Galit took the baroness's black shoulder bag and slung it around her shoulder and was now carrying two bags. She grabbed the baroness's hand and with an apologetic smile, Galit politely but aggressively pushed through the crowd, towing the baroness along. They passed through the semi-circled columns framing St. Peter's Square, leading up to the front of the plaza and the basilica. Minutes later, they reached the iron security gate adjacent to the Dono di Maria Hostel.

Only three people stood in the VIP line ahead of them. When it was their turn, Galit smiled at the Vatican Central Security Corps policeman and handed the navy blue-suited officer her counterfeit, barcoded ticket. He scanned it and sent her through the metal detector, passing their bags quickly through the x-ray machine. She stepped to a table and was greeted by a young woman in an elegant black suit. Galit handed her the picture ID she'd received from Klein that morning, identifying her as Sister Chloe Dumas from the Church of the Holy Sepulcher in Jerusalem. The woman checked the ID against her laptop database, then handed the ID back to Galit and welcomed her to the Vatican.

Baroness Collins reached the table. Her false ID was in the name of Mia Arya, also from the Church of the Holy Sepulcher. She said, "I need to use the restroom before sitting for two hours. Do I have time?"

The woman smiled and replied, "Of course you do, Sister Mia, though you should hurry, because Pope John will appear in ten minutes, and you'll need to be in your seat by that time. The closest restroom is straight back at the entrance to Audience Hall."

As they walked away, the baroness said, "Honestly, I was concerned that the tickets and ID cards wouldn't work, but they did! How did you get them?"

Galit didn't want to answer the question but decided it was easier to simply do so. "Mossad used Prime Minister Zamir's ticket to create a barcode and hologram seal that would match the Vatican's data points. They then located the attendance list on the Vatican computers and inserted our aliases. They did their job, and now it's our turn."

About 300 yards away, Klein, Beer, and Danzig meandered about the colonnade on the north side of St. Peter's Square, waiting to see if the women's forged tickets worked. Once Baroness Collins and Galit were clear, the men approached the security entrance at St. Anne's Gate, where two Swiss Guards stood sentry. By then there was no line, and with their own fake IDs, they quickly passed security just as orchestral music began to ring out in the distance.

They headed up the gray brick road to the Barracks of the Pontifical Swiss Guard, forty yards away. While walking, Danzig picked at the stitching on the inside of his cassock sleeve, removing ceramic lock picks. When they reached the black metal gate, Klein checked to make sure no one was in sight. Danzig stared at the lock. "Chaim, this is a unique key lock from the 1800s. I do doors, not gates." He dropped to a knee and added, "Sorry, slim chance. But I'll try."

Klein said forcefully, "Dan and I have been on this hunt for nearly two years. We are *done* if you can't get us in."

"This is hopeless," Danzig replied. Then in one quick movement with his right hand holding two picks, he twisted the gate handle with his left, and the gate flung open. Danzig smirked, to show he had just been messing with them.

Klein bit his bottom lip. "Not funny. You benzonah."

"That's me." Danzig jimmied open the lock on the wooden door to the barracks. They scooted inside, finding a large, well-furnished sitting room with cherrywood walls, garnished with antiques, couches, chairs, tables, and Swiss Guard historical artifacts. The group followed Klein down a hallway and into the basketball court-sized wardrobe room.

One wall was filled with racks holding the traditional Swiss Guard blue, mustard, and red striped Renaissance uniforms and the less familiar simple royal blue knickered uniforms with white page boy collars. Alphabetized name tags were clipped to the sleeve of each uniform. Shelves on another wall held silver helmets, breastplates, and navy helmets graced with thick red plumed feathers. Wooden cubicles were filled with belts, gloves, and berets. Slotted round boxes housed the six-foot tall halberd spears that Swiss Guards carried on formal occasions.

Unexpectedly, a loud Italian voice startled them. "Priests? I don't understand? What are you doing here? How did you get in?"

The Israelis spun around finding a young, helmetless Swiss Guardsman in his colorful uniform. Danzig opened his arms wide and approached him slowly with a big smile. Politely, Danzig replied in Italian, "My son, the front door was open, and we were concerned that something was wrong." The soldier's uncomfortable smile showed that he knew it was a lie. Sensing his uncertainty, Danzig jerked his head and pointed to the right, causing the guard to look that way. He then threw his left fist into the side of the guard's head, and the man crumbled to the ground, unconscious.

Klein seldom swore, but he shouted, "Fuck! Danzig, I told you ten times, no violence!"

Unfazed, Danzig retorted, "Would you prefer that he radioed for help? How would that have worked out? There was no choice."

Beer rubbed his chin and said, "Chaim, he has a point."

"I hate to say it," Bareket added through their earpieces, "but Danzig did what he had to."

In the background, Galit chimed in, "So you know, we're hiding in the bathroom and have been watching you. Chaim, I've seen Danzig use that trick before. It never fails."

Klein growled, disturbed by the turn of events. He knew Danzig had done the right thing, but he also knew a missing Swiss Guardsman was a problem.

Danzig ordered, "Dan, find a place to hide the body."

Beer hustled out of the room.

Exasperated, Klein said, "Please tell me he's not dead."

"No, only a concussion," said Danzig. "He'll be out for a while. Forget about him. Right now, we need to get you and Dan into uniforms."

After trying on four different Renaissance uniform jackets, Klein said, "I can't figure out how these things fit. What do I do?"

"There is a uniform that will fit you," said a new voice from the doorway. "You just don't know what to look for."

Klein and Danzig spun around, speechless at being discovered a second time in two minutes by another member of the Swiss Guard.

The guard peered down at his comrade. "I assume Zinncino discovered you, so you hurt him? Please tell me he's not dead. Hurt I can deal with. Dead is a problem."

"He's only unconscious," Danzig replied, starting to walk toward the soldier.

The guard pulled out a Heckler & Koch MP7 and pointed it at the men. "Stay still, my friends. You may have taken him down, but you won't get near me."

Beer reappeared, sneaking up on the Swiss Guard from behind. When he was a foot away, the soldier spun around with the gun pointed inches from Beer's head. "Move, twitch, or breathe and I'll give you a third nostril."

The guard studied each of the Israelis, then pointed at them. "Okay, you're Chaim Klein, you're Rafael Danzig, and that makes you Daniel Beer." Looking down at Zinncino, he added, "And from what Baroness Collins has told me about you, I assume it was Mr. Danzig who hurt my soldier. I am Lorenzo Bruno Pagano, Commandant of the Pontifical Swiss Guard."

The Israelis froze, deflated. Bareket exclaimed, "We've been played by the baroness! I can't believe we didn't see this coming."

Klein yelled, "Baroness, I promise that one day, when we get out of this, I will hunt you down like the terrorists I have assassinated, and I will kill you."

"Chaim, that sounds rather harsh," Baroness Collins calmly replied in the earpiece. "Why don't you just ask him why he's here and see what happens after that?"

Klein reflected for a few seconds. "The baroness told me to ask why you're here."

"I'm here because a few weeks ago, she asked me to help you borrow Swiss Guard uniforms for a few hours, so you could search the Vatican for an important artifact, and if you found it, you would take it with you."

Klein shot right back, "You expect us to believe the Commandant of the Swiss Guard is going to voluntarily become an accomplice to a grand theft in the Vatican?"

"There's no way," Beer added.

"You must think we're stupid," Danzig tossed in.

"I understand," Pagano said. "If you just took me on face value, I'd take you for fools." With a raised index finger, he said, "But what if I'm a Knights Templar? Would that change your thinking?"

"That's bullshit!" exclaimed Danzig. "You're not a Templar."

"You say that not knowing the history. The fact is, the Swiss Guard and Switzerland both exist because of the Knights Templar. The Templars convinced the Swiss Guard to defend the Pope in the early 1500s during the Sack of Rome. And we've done that ever since. It is no coincidence that the Swiss flag is an inversion of the Templar cross." Pagano paused and held his head high. "And as the seneschal of the Swiss chapter, I am an advisor to the Grand Master, Baroness Collins. So, when she called and asked me to do this, I knew I must do my duty."

The baroness added, "It's all true. I didn't tell you about this, because my request for assistance was unprecedented, and I really didn't know if he'd show up. But he did."

Beer wasn't convinced. "Baroness, it makes no sense that two hundred years after the Pope sided with Philip and ruined the Templars, they would still protect him during the Sack of Rome."

"But they did, for one good reason. They knew from sixteen years earlier that the Pope had the Ten Commandments. The tablets *had* to remain safe, and the Templars were hoping that one day exactly what is about to happen, would happen. And that's why I always said that the Ten Commandments were in the Vatican."

Klein replied, "Well, we're here, so we might as well go with it."

"Commandant Pagano will fit you with a uniform, then we're on our own," the Baroness said.

Beer looked at Pagano. "What do we do about Zinncino?"

"Lock him in the armory room closet up the hall. No one will hear him there for a while." Pagano grunted, shaking his head in self-disgust for allowing his comrade to be treated in such a manner.

Klein, Beer, and Danzig quickly deposited Zinncino in the closet, then returned to the wardrobe room.

"Klein, go pick up the uniform for Margolis. Beer, find the Altmann uniform," said Pagano. "You're each about the same size. Then I'll help you dress. We need to hurry. I've already been here too long, and so have you."

Ten minutes later, Klein and Beer were transformed from priests into colorful Swiss Guards carrying halberd spears. Standing at the barracks' front door, Pagano said, "I don't know what you're looking for, but there is nothing significant hidden in the museum. If it's a document, it's in the Apostolic Archive, which is massive, and you'll never find what you want. The archive's underground bunker is even larger and impossible to sneak into. So use your time wisely." He checked his watch and added, "I must be on my way."

"Thank you for trusting and helping us, sir," Klein said, with an extended hand that Pagano ignored.

"Let's be clear. I don't trust you and I didn't help *you*. I did this for Baroness Collins and the Templars." As he walked away, he called over his shoulder, "This never happened. If you get caught, you'll be immediately arrested as a threat to the Pope. And if you hurt anyone else, I'll shoot you, because I can. No trial. No prison. Shot!"

Klein looked at Danzig. "I think he means it."

"So do I," Danzig replied.

Bareket announced, "It's 10:30. You have less than two hours before the Jubilee service ends. The Sisters have passed through St. Peter's Cathedral and are in the hallway leading into the Sistine Chapel, headed to the archive."

"We're already behind schedule," Klein announced. "We should listen to Pagano. Since the odds of finding anything in the archive or even getting into the underground bunker are low, we'll target the sacristy."

Klein always thought the sacristy, or the treasury, was the logical place where the Ten Commandments could be safely hidden. The sacristy stored over 5,000 priceless liturgical items: gold and jewel-encrusted chalices and candlesticks, precious gems, papal jewelry, and hand-embroidered robes, vestments, and tiaras, along with other priceless pieces used in religious services. The sacristy was where the Church's most valuable artifacts were locked away, and what could be more valuable than the Ten Commandments?

Baroness Collins and Galit exited from a small door in the Sistine Chapel and stood at the bottom of Bernini's long Scala Regia marble staircase, framed by its vaulted ceiling and marble columns. The others joined them, and they walked up the steps, opening a twenty-foot wooden door into St. Peter's Cathedral. They entered by the Chapel of the Blessed and Bernini's Tabernacle, crossing the nave and its breathtaking view of the cathedral. Maintenance workers were spread out across St. Peter's vast expanse, moving chairs, polishing the floor, and off in the distance, cleaning the great altar canopy, Bernini's ninety-ton Baldacchino, which stood directly over St. Peter's tomb. Klein's group passed the white marble monument to Leo IX and opened a door into the Necropolis that took them out of the basilica and into the sacristy.

Danzig already held his lock picks when he found the locked door. Within seconds he had it open, and they entered the sacristy vestment room. It was round, with a two-story ceiling, an asymmetrical multi-colored granite floor, and intricately carved gray stone walls accented by sections of gray, alabaster, and gold granite wall insets. They moved through an arched entrance to the other sacristy rooms, stopping to glance down the numerous hallways.

Klein sighed. "This won't be any easier than if we tried to search the archives. There are seven floors with at least sixty rooms, with everything locked in cabinets. Danzig and Galit can each only be in one room at a time."

Bareket added, "You're down to eighty minutes. When the service ends, this is where every priest will go to deposit their ceremonial wardrobe."

"Got it," Klein said. "Okay, this floor contains the basic items used in religious services. I'd think something as secret as the Ten Commandments would not be kept in a high-traffic area. Let's start on the second floor."

"Dudi, there's video everywhere," Galit said, after spotting a hidden camera. "You did a bypass and inserted blank loops, right?"

"Of course. Vatican Security has been watching screens with empty rooms every place you've been."

Clueless as to where they could find the tablets, the group moved room by room on the second floor without success. No two rooms were the same. They realized that each room stored the same type of item, such as jeweled goblets, ancient papal tiaras, or golden candlesticks. The artifacts were displayed in a variety of windowed cabinets and closed dark wooden hutches or lined up on shelves. After half an hour, the group realized they were wasting time and everyone spread out.

Twenty minutes later, still only on the third floor and frustrated, Klein called the team back together. "Baroness, this isn't working and we're running out of time. Is there anything you can think of symbolic to the Ark or Ten Commandments that's located inside the Vatican? Maybe we'll get lucky there."

Baroness Collins rubbed her temples, then covered her eyes in thought. She said in a soft, cracked voice, "No, I think I might have let you down. I am so sorry."

"Wait a second," Galit said. "I have a thought."

"What is it?" Klein replied, not expecting a breakthrough.

"You know the huge obelisk in the middle of St. Peter's Square? It's actually a zodiac sundial. There are twelve white marble stones for each zodiac sign surrounding the obelisk. You remember we learned from Baroness Collins that the zodiac is partly symbolic of the Age of Enlightenment, which, as I understand it, requires the tablets be found and reunited with the Ark."

Everyone was laser focused on Galit. "Go on," Klein said.

"Well, maybe something else in the Vatican is a clue. Maybe another zodiac window? Or something like the Apollo window with the nail in the floor?"

"The St. Apolli*naire* window," the baroness corrected. "Good thinking, Galit. But I don't know the art in the Vatican well enough."

"Well, here's a reach," Danzig injected. "June 21st seems to be an important day for all of this zodiac mumbo jumbo, doesn't it, Baroness? And it's tied to that window. Maybe something in here relates to that date?"

"Right, like meaning the number 621 for June 21," Beer said. "All of these rooms are numbered. Why don't we look at that room?"

Klein glanced at his watch. "We have just thirty minutes. Let's spread out and look for some art-based clue. Danzig, see if there's a room 621, and if so, what's in it."

They dispersed, and Danzig hustled upstairs, quickly finding room 621 with the Italian word *volta* stenciled in gold paint on the door. Danzig was fluent in Italian; he smiled and rubbed his hands together. "Who knows what volta means?" he announced through his transmitter.

Simultaneously, the baroness and Galit answered, "Vault."

"Quick, everyone, get up to the sixth floor," Klein ordered.

A minute later, Danzig already had the double-locked door open. The room looked much like a bank vault filled with numbered safety deposit boxes. A pink marble table stood in the center of the room flanked by two chairs.

Klein stared at the metal boxes, then put his hand on the largest box, located at eye level and said confidently, "They're in here."

"How do you know?" asked Galit.

Klein was speechless for a moment, then said, "Bad answer. But it's because I just do."

Looking deflated, Danzig said, "The only way to get into safety deposit boxes is to drill them. They have unique tumbler systems."

Klein returned a blank stare and muttered, "That can't be."

Galit dropped her bag on the table. "I can do it. I have acid with me that will burn through the lock."

"You brought acid with you?"

She nodded and pulled a pen-shaped item out of her bag. "You have no idea how many burglaries I've committed for Mossad. I've learned you never know what you need when you're trying to steal something." Galit removed the cap from the device and inserted its needle point into the top of the lock, then pushed a button, resulting in a hissing sound and a foul-smelling vapor. She pushed hard into the lock and the door swung open. She opened the cabinet door and, wide-eyed, exclaimed, "Oh my God, I can't believe it!"

Everyone crowded around her to see a polished mahogany box, which was marked by an engraved bronze plaque that read, "*I Dieci Comandamenti.*"

"We found them!" yelled Beer, turning to give Danzig a hug.

Baroness Collins rested her hand on her heart. "This is amazing."

Danzig added, "Never in a million years would I have thought this possible."

Klein stood silently; his head bowed. He looked up and said softly, "We need to take these and go."

Galit pulled the wooden box from its compartment, placed it on the table, and said, "Chaim, this honor belongs to you."

As Klein put his hand on the lid, the group was startled by a loud voice coming from the door.

"You are not taking that out of here!"

The group turned to see Commandant Pagano and five Swiss Guards standing there, with pistols aimed at them.

24

"You lying, good-for-nothing, bloody, buggering traitor bastard!" screamed the infuriated baroness, shaking a fist. "One way or the other, you will pay for this!" She bolted toward Pagano, but just as her leg swung backwards to kick him, two Swiss Guards restrained her, one on each arm, locking her in place.

Pagano stood stone-faced, observing Baroness Collins's tirade.

Galit whispered to Klein, "I don't know if I'm more surprised that we just got caught or by her reaction."

"Damn it, Galit! Don't talk about me in the third person!" the baroness snapped. "I'm not deaf. I'm standing right here. And yes, I'm mad as hell and can be quite nasty when I need to be!" Glaring at Pagano, she yelled, "You have no idea the damage you just did. So many positive things to help the world depend on us taking those tablets."

Pagano shrugged dismissively.

The baroness moved her glare from one Swiss Guard to another. "You disgusting weasels, take your filthy hands off of me." The guards looked at Pagano, who nodded, and they released their grip. She shook out her arms, looked at Klein, and said, "Chaim, now I understand why you said in the barracks that you wanted to kill me when you thought I betrayed you."

"That's really not helpful right now, Baroness," said Klein. "I knew there was risk in trying this, but I didn't think we'd actually find the tablets and *then* get caught."

"That's life," Pagano said, grabbing the halberds from Klein and Beer. "I don't doubt that whatever you had planned for the Ten Commandments is important to you. I actually would have let you steal many other things from the Vatican, but not these."

"They don't belong to the Church," said Klein. "They belong to my people."

Pagano shook his head. "Your people haven't owned them for two thousand years. You know what they say about possession of property?"

"I don't suppose it has occurred to you that just maybe *your* Knights Templars and *your* baroness worked with me for a good reason."

"Perhaps. But what might be a good reason for you might not be a good reason for others."

Klein sneered at Pagano.

"By the way, Commandant, how did you know where we were?" Danzig asked.

"Mr. Klein, I'm proud to be a Swiss Guard and a Knights Templar. But when Grand Master Collins asked me to outfit two strangers in Swiss Guard uniforms so that they could stroll around Vatican property on the day of the Jubilee for Peace to steal something, of course I had to implement *some* security measures. The Swiss Guard is technologically adept. I cloned your communications devices in the barracks, so we not only listened to you but watched you on live video every step of the way. We also quickly detected the false loop your specialists inserted into our video surveillance system, so we never lost sight of you. The Ten Commandments may be the only item in the Vatican that is utterly irreplaceable. I cannot let you take them."

Klein was expressionless but seethed underneath. A few blocks away, Bareket cringed, concluding this was probably the end of his Mossad career.

Pagano checked his watch. "The Jubilee service is ending. I need to escort the Pope." Looking at the other Swiss Guards, he said, "You know where to take them. Make sure no one sees you. Go through back halls." Pointing at the Israelis, he added, "They are highly trained. If they try to escape, shoot to kill." As he walked past Baroness Collins, she gave him the hard kick in the shin that she had missed before.

Pagano grimaced, but said nothing and walked away.

Galit put her arm around the baroness's shoulder and squeezed. "I bet that felt good."

"It sounds like we're headed to a jail cell," Danzig said.

"Probably in the underground bunker," replied Galit.

The group was led through a long, circuitous route of hallways and stairwells. They finally passed through a doorway framed by thick gold draperies into a large formal room with frescoes bordering its gold inlay ceiling. Tall book cabinets lined the walls, with a sitting area near the entrance. Thirty feet away sat a large desk with side chairs.

"I don't know where we are, but this sure isn't prison," Beer said. A few minutes later, Pagano entered the room and sent away the two Swiss Guards.

Baroness Collins rushed toward Pagano, but he held up his hand. "You got your one free kick. If you do that again, I will defend myself, and you won't like the result. Am I clear?"

Her nostrils flared and she said with a snarl, "The Knights Templar were built on loyalty and honor. I'm not done with you. You are a traitor and for that you will pay."

Pagano calmly replied, "I pledged a duty to the Knights Templar, but I also pledged my life to the Pope. That's what Papal Swiss Guards do, and I am their Commandant. I had to make a choice: the Church or the Templars. I fulfilled my duty to the Templars. I helped get you into the Vatican, got your men dressed as Swiss Guards, and told you where not to go." Pagano was interrupted by three loud knocks on the door.

As it opened, he added, "And I also arranged an audience for you with the Holy Father, Pope John."

Resplendent in a white floor-length robe stitched with gold and red threads, the Pope strutted into his library like a forty-year-old man, in contrast to his seventy-one years. His thinning gray hair was combed straight back; his strong jaw and steely blue eyes peered through narrow wire-frame glasses. He studied Klein, then glanced at the other intruders, who were again shocked into momentary silence.

Speaking in English with dramatic inflection, Pope John said, "What an interesting day. I invite your prime minister to my Jubilee for World Peace, where I seat him up front, only to learn that his agents have broken into my home—our Church—to steal a very special object. I normally use this room to meet dignitaries and heads of state, and instead I end up with thieves. This is *extremely* disappointing. I can't wait to hear the story that you will now try to dream up to explain this outrageous conduct." The Pope crossed his arms over his chest and stared at Klein.

"Your Excellency—"

"Holiness, not Excellency," he replied sharply. "I am not a king. I am the Pope."

"I am sorry for not knowing how to address you. I certainly did not expect to meet you today."

Pope John made the slightest of smiles. "No, I suppose not. But you did try to steal from us. So it seems that we are off to quite a bad start."

"Yes, we are. I admit that today is not working out quite how I imagined." Klein took a deep breath and continued in a stronger voice. "But you have what I need, and I need it badly."

The Pope considered Klein's comment. "So you don't apologize… and you're more upset about not getting what you came for than getting caught trying to steal it?"

Klein considered the Pope's question. "Since you put it that way, I'd have to agree."

"That is greater honesty than I expected. Now I am curious about your motivations. I will ask you two questions, and you better have good answers to them. I understand your name is Chaim Klein. Now tell me Mr. Klein, first, why do you believe you need the Ten Commandments and second, how did you know they were in the Vatican?"

Klein looked the Pope in the eyes and nervously blurted out, "I accidentally found the Ark of the Covenant hidden in a chamber underneath the Temple Mount, which was placed there on the day the Romans destroyed the Second Temple in 70 A.D. I then learned from Israel's Chief Rabbi that according to the War Scroll, which is one of the Dead Sea Scrolls, that I am the General of the Sons of Light and responsible for finding and reuniting the Ten Commandments with the Ark of the Covenant. My story is true, and I can prove it. I *was* trying to be a thief today, but I am *not* a liar. I have a friend near St. Anne's Gate. His name is Ezana Meroe and he needs to bring me a package. When you see it, you will understand why I need the tablets."

"That is quite a mouthful. It suggests you are supposed to lead an army to defeat the Sons of Darkness in the Armageddon. The end of days." The Pope glanced first at Pagano, then at his most trusted advisor, the Vatican's Secretary of State Cardinal Bernardo Marino, to measure their expressions. "Mr. Klein, you're either a very creative storyteller and think that outrageous lies will get you out of this, or somehow your story, as improbable as it seems, could be true. Certainly, our respective religions have prophesied a variation of your story. Perhaps I should see your package and pass my own judgment?"

"Yes, I told him he might have to come here with the package. May I call him, please? He knows to go to St. Anne's Gate. His name is Ezana Meroe."

The Pope instructed Pagano to find Meroe. Pagano whispered instructions to two Swiss Guards, who quickly departed.

Looking at the baroness, Klein said, "This is Baroness Jillian Collins of the House of Lords in Great Britain. She can explain how we knew the tablets were here."

The Pope nodded, giving her permission to speak.

The baroness stood erect and declared in a strong voice, "I am the Grand Master of the Knights Templar."

"So I've been told. Another interesting story."

"My proof is simple and irrefutable, Your Holiness. I know that in 1308, after King Philip forced Pope Clement to convict the Templars for heresy, Jacques de Molay, the Grand Master, struck a deal with the Pope. They traded about a dozen Templar lives, some money, freedom, and the Ten Commandments. In return, they received a papal pardon and absolution through the Chinon Parchment. Notably, during the Sack of Rome only a few years later, it was the Templars in England who convinced the Swiss Guards, who were mostly Templars, to protect Pope Clement and the Tablets when he escaped to Castel Sant'Angelo."

The Pope frowned. "Baroness, the whole world knows about the Chinon Parchment. Why should I believe your version of history?"

"For two reasons. Commandant Pagano, whom I know you trust, will confirm that a member of this Swiss Guard has been the Knights Templar Swiss seneschal since the Swiss Guard's inception. Ask him."

Standing behind the baroness and Klein, Pagano nodded his affirmation.

"Second, there is no other truthful explanation as to how the Church came into possession of the Ten Commandments." The baroness reached into her shoulder bag, pulled out a leather valise, and removed a yellowed document. "See, there are two *original* copies of the Chinon Parchment. Actually, the second copy was found in the Apostolic Archive in 2001, and that's what the Vatican released to the public. But you also have the left half of the *first* copy in your secret papers that only you, I, and a few other people in the Vatican even know about. This is the right half." She handed it to the Pope. "When you put the torn halves side by side, they will fit together perfectly. And you well know that the Knights Templar convinced the Swiss Guard to protect the Pope and the Ten Commandments during the Sack of Rome."

Surprised by the baroness's tone and accurate declaration of facts she shouldn't have known, he replied, "What you say is true, and we will retrieve our half of that document right now to see how they line up." He nodded at Cardinal Marino, which was understood to be an order.

"I suspect we will be here for a while," Pope John said. "Baroness Collins and Mr. Klein, please join me at my desk." Pagano directed Galit, Beer, and Danzig to nearby chairs.

An aide pulled out the Pope's high-backed, white-padded chair for him, and Klein and Baroness Collins sat down across from him. A few minutes later, accompanied by two Swiss Guards, Meroe entered the room, hugging a long, narrow, brown wooden box. Cardinal Marino reappeared, holding a folder. Pope John opened it, revealing a torn yellowed parchment with tiny Latin words that filled most of the page, followed by two sentences and three different colored wax seals at the bottom. The Pope lined up the two halves of the document, and when he rubbed his chin and stared at the ceiling, it confirmed what the baroness already knew.

"I assume you're satisfied with the match, Your Holiness, so may I have my half back, please?"

The Pope slid it across the table. The baroness pulled a tiny amber bottle with a rubber dropper top from her bag and squeezed a few drops of a clear liquid on the top of the document. She then dabbed her handkerchief in the liquid and spread it across the top.

"What are you doing?" the Pope exclaimed. "You'll ruin the document!"

"Did Your Holiness know that invisible ink has been used for over two thousand years, even by the ancient Greeks and Romans? This is just sodium hydroxide. Let's give it a few seconds." Almost immediately, previously unseen words rose to the paper's surface.

The Pope fell back in his chair. "There is nothing like that in our document or I would know about it!"

"So you think," Baroness Collins replied. Before anyone could stop her, she leaned forward and squeezed a few drops on the top of the Vatican's half of the parchment.

"How dare you!" the Pope yelled.

The baroness raised her hand to stop the approaching Swiss Guard and calmly answered, "Please just give it a moment and take a look. Your document is fine."

Seconds later, words appeared. The baroness again moved her half of the document next to the Pope's, and the document's long-hidden message lined up perfectly.

The Pope read the Latin words silently. When he finished, he stared at the baroness. She handed him a note and said, "This is the message. Am I right?"

He read it and alternated between staring at her and the document.

"Would Your Holiness prefer to read the message aloud, or should I?"

The Pope focused on the message a second time, then read off the combined document, "When this document is made whole, the Knights Templars again shall be the rightful owners of the tablets that state the law of God as presented to the prophet Moses."

"And underneath the message on your half, the document is signed by Pope Clement, and that signature matches the one at the bottom?"

"It appears to be."

"Your Holiness, can you read the signature on my half?"

After studying it, he shook his head no.

"It is that of Jacques de Molay. This secret message reflects the arrangement that he made with Pope Clement. You know that de Molay sacrificed his and other Templar lives to save the rest of the Order and most of their treasure, and in return, Pope Clement received the Ten Commandments for safekeeping. They validated their transaction in invisible ink because, at that time, the world couldn't know this astonishing secret. Imagine if back then, or for that matter even now, this full copy of the Chinon Parchment fell into the wrong hands. De Molay and Pope Clement clearly contemplated that this day would come." She paused, and in an understated tone, added, "Your Holiness, that day is today. The Ten Commandments now belong to me."

The Pope folded his hands on the desk. "It's an old contract but apparently a valid one." He paused, then asked, "So if I may, Baroness, what plans do you have for the tablets?"

"I'm giving them to Mr. Klein."

Klein exhaled heavily and rested his hand on top of hers.

"Why would you do that? You call in a 700 year-old contract for the most valuable religious artifact in existence, and you hand it over to him?"

"He *is* the General of the Sons of Light."

"Which is nothing more than an ancient tale."

"Oh, but you accept that the Ten Commandments are real and that Jesus turned water into wine? And you acknowledge that Christianity, Judaism, and Islam all accept some version of the Apocalypse as part of their religious doctrine?"

The Pope frowned and looked away.

Klein motioned to Meroe to bring him the wooden box that remained clutched to his chest. Meroe placed it gently on the Pope's desk and opened the lid. The Pope looked inside, and his eyebrows furrowed. "It's an old plaster sword, obviously made for some artistic endeavor."

"Would Your Holiness please pick it up and show it to everyone?" Klein said.

Pagano stepped forward. "I will pick up the sword first, but not until you and the baroness move away from the Holy Father and stand back by your friends."

Klein helped Baroness Collins out of her chair, and they rejoined the other Israelis.

Pagano reached inside the box and ultimately, with a two-handed effort, he succeeded in pulling out the sword. Once it was balanced against his shoulder, he said, "There is nothing special about this sword except that since it's like concrete, it's heavy."

"Your Holiness, would you please try?" Klein replied.

"Fine, let me see it."

Pagano carefully handed the sword to the Pope, who struggled with its weight and in only a few seconds, Pagano took it back. Perturbed, the Pope stared coldly at Klein and said, "This appears to be a waste of my time."

"No, now it's my turn," said Klein.

Pagano leaned the sword against the desk, then removed his sidearm and pointed it at Klein. "If you take one threatening step toward the Pope, I will shoot you."

"That seems to be a theme with you," Klein said. "I'm not here to hurt his Holiness." Then, with one hand, Klein grabbed the sword in the middle of the blade, effortlessly lifted it above his head and declared, "This is the Sword of David! The Sword of the Righteous! The sword the British have called Excalibur! *This is my sword!*"

As he was speaking, the grey plaster crumbled away, transforming into a shiny, glowing metallic blade. The sword began to hum, and Klein moved his hand down to the black grip and gold pommel and began slicing it through the air. Each movement caused a wind gust and loud swishing sound. The more he swung the sword, the more ferocious the wind.

Everyone in the room was transfixed by the sword, even those who had seen this demonstration before. After a minute, Klein put down the sword and said, "I found this in Westminster Abbey while searching for the Ten Commandments. It transformed when I touched it, and this only happens for me." He handed it to Danzig. In seconds, the sword morphed back into its plaster form.

Klein took it back a second time and again it came alive.

The Pope approached Klein and said solemnly, "It appears you *are* the General of the Sons of Light. I have been chosen by the Cardinals to lead my people, but you have been chosen by God to lead all people."

"That's not really true, Your Holiness. I am neither a prophet nor the Messiah," Klein replied emphatically. "I am simply a man who was inexplicably sent on a mission, and I still don't know why. I've not spoken to God as Moses did with the Burning Bush. But I do hope my connection to this sword helps you believe why I need to reunite the Ten Commandments with the Ark of the Covenant."

"You may not have spoken to God, but he's spoken to you. And with what I've seen today between the Chinon Parchment and your sword, how can I, of all people, not believe? I do believe. I also have no right to ask, but I must. What is next in your journey?"

"I don't know. I don't yet understand my role as General of the Sons of Light in this battle against evil. Until a few years ago, I was a Special Forces officer and killed many in battle and some by assassination, but these were always terrorists out to kill my people. Right now, it seems to me we are in a world war involving the Islamic fundamentalist terrorists, and it's only getting worse. But I don't believe that more war is the answer. War only brings death. I no longer want to fight and kill. I want to fight for life."

For many seconds, the room was silent. The other Israelis were both surprised and moved by Klein's announcement, especially Galit, who stepped forward and placed her hand on his shoulder.

Pope John asked, "So you see this as a fight against the Islamic fundamentalists?"

"Yes, and so should you. ISIS, al-Qaeda, Hezbollah, and countless other terrorist groups have declared jihad against the free world. I know your life is constantly threatened by them. In their eyes, the West is the enemy. And the Catholic Church had its role in the Crusades and helped create the animosity that exists to this day with the fundamentalists. The Islamists want an eye for an eye and to finish us off."

"Well, that's blunt and not terribly diplomatic, but unfortunately accurate."

"I never claimed to be a diplomat."

"That's refreshing. I appreciate your candor, and I like your thinking. You're right. We need to fight for life."

"Your Holiness, may I please have a moment with my friends?"

"By all means."

Klein huddled with the baroness and the Israelis, and after a few minutes, he again stood before the Pope. "I'm honored that you have shown faith in me today, so now, we wish to show our faith in you. We believe that while terrorists have to be stopped as a matter of preservation of life, *Islam must be supported*. Islam is a peaceful religion. We wish to support Muslim countries and their people, wherever they live."

"That is quite a statement. I don't believe I've heard or read anything that strong coming from the Israeli government."

"Not in those words, Your Holiness, but Israel has continually tried to help the Palestinian people and every time they do, either Hamas or the Palestinian Authority negatively propagandize it. I know from personal conversations with Prime Minister Zamir that he is not anti-Islam."

"I am aware. It is why he was seated in the front row today."

"Good, so, please Your Holiness, I humbly ask for your commitment that the next thing I tell you remains strictly confidential, at least for now."

"You have my word."

"I assume you are familiar with the Muslims for Peace?"

"Of course," the Pope replied.

"What the world doesn't need to know yet is that the MFP has been partially supported by both Israel and the Knights Templar, because we know we can't change Islam. Change has to come from within Islam's own people."

The baroness chimed in, "First we contributed one hundred million pounds and then just this week we gave another one hundred and fifty million. And we're ready to give more."

The Pope clasped his hands together and sat back down at his desk. "My friends, this is wonderful. Israel, the country that would be least expected to support the MFP, turns out to be a significant player in reaching out to the Muslim world. And the Knights Templar, which supposedly disappeared seven hundred years ago and fought for the Church in the Crusades against Islam, is a financial participant."

Klein raised his index finger. "There is more. We, meaning Israel and the Knights Templar, respectfully ask Your Holiness to consider joining our effort. The Ten Commandments are foundational to Judaism, Christianity, and Islam. We humbly ask you to participate in a service in Jerusalem when the Tablets are returned to the Ark of the Covenant and to help us reach out to the Islamic community, whether through the MFP or on your own."

Pope John leaned in toward Klein and said, "Well, that is an interesting proposition."

"What makes you think the Palestinian Authority will even allow you access to the Temple Mount for your ceremony?" injected Cardinal Marino. "It is *their* Temple Mount, not Israel's."

"He has a point, Mr. Klein," said the Pope. "The Dome of the Rock is located on top of where the Second Temple stood. Are you intending to put the Ark of the Covenant and the Ten Commandments on the Foundation Stone inside the shrine?"

"To me, that would be the goal. The Palestinian Authority is already a big beneficiary of the MFP. I'm hoping that everyone will see the advantages of cooperating," Klein said.

"You are quite an optimist," replied the Cardinal.

Klein grinned. "After traveling around the world searching for the Ten Commandments and somehow finding them, how can I not be an optimist? That which I thought was impossible actually happened."

The Pope pointed at Klein. "*You* are an optimist." He pointed at the Cardinal. "He is my pragmatist. I think with my heart. He thinks with his head."

Sensing an opportunity, Galit stepped forward. "Holy Father, Cardinal Marino, my name is Galit Kevetch. I've been involved with the MFP almost from its inception. I think it would be helpful if I walk you through what we believe the MFP can accomplish—for instance, in Saudi Arabia."

"Please do, Miss Kevetch," the Pope replied.

"Thank you. As you know, for about seventy years, the Saudis have sold oil across the globe and made a fortune, especially when it was at one hundred dollars a barrel. This allowed up to ninety percent of Saudi citizens to work for the government and get free health care and subsidized utilities. But those days are gone because oil prices have dropped significantly, and the Saudis have blown through their vast cash reserves. Wages have fallen, government subsidies are disappearing, and the Saudi people need real jobs, especially since 70 percent of the population is under thirty years old. You probably know all this."

"Much of it," the Pope replied.

"All right, so we believe that the best help that Israel can provide to modernize Saudi Arabia is first a transfer of technology from the West and second enhanced education, which is starting to happen and is already moving the country forward. We can do this throughout the Middle East."

"I applaud your motives, but the Wahhabis have dominated Saudi religion for hundreds of years," Cardinal Marino replied. "You can't really believe that the promise of technology, education, and new jobs will change an ingrained, ultra-conservative religious doctrine and culture."

"Not overnight or with the flip of a switch, but eventually, yes, without a doubt," Galit said. "The Saudis now let women drive. They show Western movies. And the internet is opening up, so the youth of Saudi Arabia sees how the free world lives. At this point, the Saudis can't move backwards. This will take work, money, and time."

"It's not going to be as easy as you think," the Pope said.

"Your Holiness, given the history in the Middle East, everyone is skeptical, with good reason. But there is no other better option if we wish to change the dynamics in the Middle East. If we're right, it *will* change the world."

Cardinal Marino nodded and replied, "You might be right." The Israelis took this as a major concession.

Klein cut in. "Your Holiness, who better than the Church, the Templars and Israel to embrace the Muslim world in a ceremony that *will be* one of civilization's most historic events? Wouldn't your support for the MFP be consistent with today's Jubilee for Peace? You are already a global ambassador of peace."

The Pope laughed. "Mr. Klein, for someone who claims not to be a diplomat, it seems to me that your words are quite convincing." He paused, then added, "But I'm not sure I understand. Won't there be a Jewish religious service on the Temple Mount when you reunite the Ark and the Ten Commandments?"

"Good question. My thinking is if we are to be successful in bringing the cultures together, it can be an *interfaith* service among Judaism, Christianity, and Islam."

The Pope crossed his arms and contemplated Klein's remark. "Your people have waited 2000 years for the Ten Commandments and the Ark of the Covenant to be reunited. And probably no one ever thought this would happen. Don't you think your government might have something else in mind, considering the significance of this event?"

"Yes, I know. I don't speak for the government. I recognize there are political and other considerations involved."

"What Chaim didn't tell you is that the Prime Minister and the Rabbinate accept that he is the General of the Sons of Light," Beer said. "They will listen closely to Chaim when he returns to Israel with the Ten Commandments, especially now that he's met with you."

"And I report directly to the Prime Minister," Galit said.

"I didn't know that," Klein interrupted.

"Now you do," she said to Klein before turning back to the Pope. "Anyway, Mr. Zamir told me that the constant back and forth violence, rhetoric, and threats between Israel and Muslim countries simply cannot continue. We know the region is so volatile that *anything* could lead to a total meltdown. Most Arab states don't even recognize Israel's right to exist. So our hope is that the combination of supporting the MFP and reaching out to the entire Islamic world community on the Temple Mount will be our most viable chance to begin healing the deep wounds between the Muslim and Jewish worlds. Chaim bringing home the Tablets is a game changer."

"And the Knights Templar support all of this, Your Holiness," Baroness Collins said. "We believe this was all meant to be. None of this is a coincidence."

Klein rubbed his neck for a few seconds. "Your Holiness, I admitted earlier I tried stealing from you, so I don't want to lie to you now." He paused and exhaled hard. "The concept of the service just came to me now. Honestly, I wasn't sure I'd find the tablets. I certainly never expected to meet you and have this talk. And I never actually considered what would happen next if I found the tablets. But what I said is what I believe, including that the Vatican should participate in this peace initiative. Christianity needs to be part of the solution and make its own peace with Islam."

Pope John rose and walked over to Klein, reaching for his hands, which he held. "Thank you, Mr. Klein. You didn't *wing* what you said to me. Those words came from the heart. And I agree with them and hope the theme of the ceremony will be about peace."

"Peace and forgiveness," said Klein. "There can be no peace without forgiveness."

Pope John addressed the room. "My papal name honors Pope John the twenty-third. He served God and the people from 1958 through 1963. During World War Two, he worked secretly to save many thousands of Jews from the Germans." The Pope looked down, shook his head and continued, "The Jewish people and Israel deserve better than what history has given them. You have been victimized back to the days of the Pharaohs and virtually ever since. Unfortunately, this Church is responsible for its share of conduct that was detrimental against both the Jewish and Islamic people. Normally, I would consult with Cardinal Marino and others about your proposal but hearing what you have said and seeing the miracles today make it obvious to me. You even showed up on my doorstep on the day that I hold a Jubilee for Peace, so maybe Baroness Collins is right...this was meant to be. Certainly Mr. Klein, you are right about the state of this world. It is a dangerous place, and it needs to change."

The Pope extended his hand to the baroness. "The mere existence of the Knights Templar will be almost as big a news story as finding the Ark of the Covenant and the Ten Commandments and this quest for peace. You have been right in the middle of all this. You are to be commended."

"This is all for the common good. Holy Father, we came to the Vatican to get the Ten Commandments, which is something we need. But I also happen to have something you want."

"I don't know what that could be. We want for nothing."

The baroness pulled out a bubble-wrapped package from her shoulder bag and handed it to the Pope. "I brought this with me, if necessary, to negotiate a trade with you for the tablets. But now I give it to you as a gift."

The Pope unwrapped the package and Cardinal Marino's eyes instantly opened wide. "Is that what I think it is?"

Clutching the item with both hands, the Pope stared at the white ceramic goblet. It had a faded blue Star of David painted in the middle.

"Did the Templars also find this when they dug at the Temple Mount?"

"No, but Chaim and I traded the chalice for the sword when he first visited Westminster Abbey."

The Pope looked at Klein. "So how did you get the cup?"

"When I found the Ark, it was inside."

"Really? Jesus's cup from the Last Supper was inside the Ark of the Covenant?"

"Technically, it was a seder," Klein answered with a smile.

Cardinal Marino picked up the cup and held it out for all to see. "The Christian world has long believed the cup was either fictional or disappeared into history. Michelangelo created artwork that exists around the world and in this building that depicts this very cup. That's how I knew what it was! Mr. Klein, this cup is further proof that it is time for the world to change. The cup is a key to the Holy Grail."

The Pope exclaimed, "Yes, of course! It symbolizes the teachings of Jesus. Brotherhood. Loving one's fellow man. And peace." The pontiff then took Klein by the arm and walked him to the polished wooden box in the front of the room. "As I recall, 'Chaim' means life."

"Yes, Your Holiness."

"It is fitting that the General of the Sons of Light is filled with and cherishes life." He knelt down, opened the box, and removed two thin, foot-long, rectangular pinkish granite tablets, upon which was perfectly engraved Hebrew. "Mr. Klein, these are yours. We look forward to working with you, your government, and appropriate representatives of Islam on this most righteous endeavor. May you go in peace."

Ten minutes later, the Israelis were standing at St. Anne's Gate with Cardinal Marino, Commandant Pagano and his two Swiss Guards, waiting for Ezana Meroe to return with the Mercedes. The street was still packed with worshippers milling about who attended the Jubilee for Peace service. Klein was holding the box containing his sword and Beer held the box with the Ten Commandments.

"Chaim, you should be very proud of what you accomplished today," the baroness said. "It's possible you could have just helped change the world."

"That's a big statement, but let's see. I'd like to be optimistic. But the reality is, I didn't do much. Every one of us had a role and we came together as a team. And Baroness, I could make a good argument that none of this would have happened if not for you."

"You are too kind, Chaim," the baroness said as she leaned in to give him a light kiss on the cheek.

None of Klein's group was paying attention to the civilians as a young, unassuming priest with a scraggly beard casually approached them. When the priest was about forty feet away, he pulled a small, short-barreled machine gun from his cloak and opened fire on Klein's group and the civilians. For seven long seconds, bullets sprayed everywhere until finally, with a single shot, Pagano's own weapon caught the gun-toting priest square in the head, killing him.

Klein looked left and right and saw blood and bodies everywhere. Although the roar of the bullets stopped, the screaming and chaos began. Both of the Swiss Guards accompanying Pagano and the Israelis lay dead. Numerous civilians were down, either motionless or groaning.

Looking to his left, Klein saw that Beer was grimacing and had blood flowing from his shoulder. Through a hoarse whisper he exhaled, "Quick, take the box," but before Klein could reach him, Beer fell to his knees and the Ten Commandments tumbled onto the ground. Klein dropped the sword box and scooped up the tablets.

He then noticed Galit's left arm was bleeding and he called out her name, but she seemed almost unconcerned.

"Flesh wound. I'll be fine," Galit said. She pointed behind Klein, wearing a frantic expression.

He turned to see Danzig lying on his back, his face white, his breathing labored by blood gurgling from his mouth and pouring out of his neck.

Kneeling next to him on all fours was Baroness Collins. "He jumped in front of me! He took my bullets!" She dropped her head on his chest and moaned, "Oh my dear man!"

Audible only to her, Danzig whispered, "You must finish this." His head tilted slightly and then his blank open eyes fixed on the skies. Galit broke into tears as she saw her mentor die.

Sirens wailed from all directions. Klein stared at Beer, then at Danzig, and then Klein put the Ten Commandments back in the box. He dropped to his knees, covered his face for almost a minute, and when he removed his hands, his eyes were red and wet. He rose and focused on all the dead and wounded in the vicinity, then slowly walked over to the attacker's corpse.

After studying it a few seconds, he said to Galit, "This is Eyad Hamoud. He is the Hamas operative who photographed everyone at Ori Levin's funeral. He's friends with the younger brother of Mahmoud Kassem, the suicide bomber who perpetrated the attack at the Wall."

Untouched by the bullets and scanning the surrounding carnage, Cardinal Marino said, "It seems to me, Mr. Klein, that there are already people out there who wish to stop you."

25

Jerusalem

"That which the world long has thought was a historical, religious fact, or perhaps mythology or fable, has turned out to be real and stunning, especially for the nearly four billion Muslims, Christians, and Jews whose religious beliefs are founded, at least in part, on the Old Testament. Eighteen days ago, it was revealed that the long-lost Ark of the Covenant and Ten Commandments were separately found by an Israeli soldier and validated as authentic. There are two other almost equally astonishing related news matters. The first is an agreement between the Palestinian Authority and the Muslims for Peace to participate with Israel and the Vatican in a joint inter-faith service being held in Jerusalem today. The second is that the Knights Templar, long thought to be disbanded seven hundred years ago, played a major role in making this remarkable event come to fruition. From this day forward, the Ark of the Covenant and the Ten Commandments will be permanently placed on the Foundation

Stone within the Dome of the Rock, which will be open to all people as a place of worship, regardless of their religious beliefs. Nearly two thousand political, civic, and clergy leaders from all corners of the globe have traveled to Jerusalem to attend the Ceremony of Peace. From the Temple Mount in Jerusalem, this is Carl Wilhoit reporting for IND News."

Sitting on a stained green couch, Omar Rafsani grunted and turned off the television. Khaled leaned forward in a wooden chair, staring blankly at the dirty brown tile floor. "Khaled, you welcome death today, right?" Rafsani asked.

Khaled stayed silent, so Rafsani continued, "Many shahid can't wait to die in battle and be greeted in heaven by their seventy-two virgins and Allah. Maybe the virgins exist or maybe not, but today is our turn, so we'll find out. Allah has blessed us, Khaled. Our timing could not have been better. We were going to destroy the Old City anyway, and now he has brought all these infidel leaders here for this blasphemous service today. So all of them, along with hundreds of thousands of other infidels around the world, *will* die today. Who could ask for more than that?"

Khaled looked up. His eyes moved from the rust-colored paint peeling off the walls, to the buzzing fluorescent light that dominated the tiny one-room apartment, to Rafsani's stare. "Omar, I'm thinking about my brother, Mahmoud, who died close to here only two years ago. The next day the Jews bulldozed my family's home. I vowed that day to get my revenge, and today I will. And thanks to you, I understand the bigger picture of what we will accomplish. So I am at peace with dying today. But you know I don't like destroying the Dome of the Rock. It is one of our holiest shrines. Allah himself may not even like that."

Rafsani exploded, "Allah is blessing us this very moment for stopping this blasphemous Ceremony of Peace service today! The Jews, Christians, and this ridiculous Muslims for Peace cannot stand together on Haram al-Sharif and speak of unity and peace. If we must destroy the Dome of the Rock today, so be it. Tomorrow, when our people again control Jerusalem, it will be rebuilt."

Khaled rubbed his chin for a moment. "What about killing the Director General of the Waqf and the Grand Mufti of Jerusalem? They are not the enemy. The Israelis, the Americans, the Europeans—they're the enemy."

Rafsani was unmoved. "No, they are traitors, and we are obligated to execute them. And later today, their ceremony will not proceed, and we will devastate the cities of the infidel Americans and Europeans. It will be Islam's greatest victory since Saladin vanquished the Crusaders by pushing them out of Jerusalem in a bloody battle."

Khaled reflected and nodded. "Okay, then it is time for me to send out the final instruction to our cells." He grabbed his backpack, pulled out his laptop, and quickly hacked into someone's local Wi-Fi. He accessed Tor and in a few keystrokes was on the Kill the Infidels website.

"Omar, are you sure you don't want me to instruct the cells to all begin their attacks at three p.m., as Hosnu suggested?"

"No, send the message I gave you. I care more about *us* initiating the first attack over everyone proceeding at a precise time, which is probably not manageable anyway."

"Okay." After logging in and reaching the website's message board, Khaled typed, *Upon seeing fire on top of Jerusalem, you shall Kill the Infidels Today.* He announced, "Now our cells cannot be stopped, and our attacks will hit fifty-four cities worldwide!"

Glancing at his watch, he added, "It's almost three o'clock. The first part of the ceremony at the Church of the Holy Sepulcher begins in about forty-five minutes. Let's finish getting ready." Using his Swiss Army knife, Khaled took apart the laptop, removed the hard drive, and repeatedly smashed it with the heel of his boot until it broke into pieces.

The mid-afternoon start time for the Ceremony of Peace was selected to maximize viewership for its live worldwide broadcast. It was expected to be the most-watched television event ever. The Far East, with its 1.8 billion heavily moderate Sunni Muslim population, was five to seven hours ahead of Jerusalem. Africa and most of Western Europe were an hour or two time zones behind. In the Western Hemisphere, everyone's day was just getting started. That meant about 85 percent of the world's population could watch the broadcast live.

Security had never been tighter in the Old City. Only the Damascus Gate into the Muslim Quarter and the Jaffa Gate at the Armenian Quarter were open, for they provided the closest routes to the Church of the Holy Sepulcher, where the ceremony was to begin. Residents could leave the Old City at any time but would not be allowed back in until the next day. Weapons were strictly prohibited, even for bodyguards of the VIPs. The Israelis and the Palestinian Authority provided all security, since nobody knew the Old City better than them.

Rafsani pointed at a small aluminum table a few feet away, covered with clothing and weapons. "Eyad's younger brother Ismael collected all this? It's impressive, given the circumstances."

"When Ismael learned that his brother Eyad died a shahid for us in Rome, he wanted to help in some way. He was always a very industrious guy. I'm not sure where he got the uniforms, but the suicide vests and guns came from Hamas. You'll see, he'll continue to help our cause."

Rafsani and Khaled believed that disguising themselves as Israeli Defense Forces was their best option for slipping into the ceremony, because it was the only possible way to get weapons past security. The men helped each other tie on their suicide vests, which were then hidden under olive green IDF shirts. A silver pin with wings on both sides of a fleur-de-lis was clipped above the right pocket, signifying Unit 269, Sayaret Matkal, Israel's elite, notorious anti-terrorist special forces unit. White military rank epaulets sewn onto the right shoulders of their uniforms established Rafsani as a colonel and Khaled as a lieutenant colonel. Their bright green berets bearing a half-green, half-white Star of David and a fleur de lis patch, were tilted to the left.

Fake ID cards matched the fake Hebrew names stitched above their left pockets. Strapped onto their hips were Israeli issue Glock 9mm pistols. Secreted into pockets were knives and extra clips. Short haircuts and clean beards completed their disguise as IDF officers.

Standing face to face, their palms facing up, they recited the Shahada, the Declaration of Faith, praising God, which they recited a minimum of seventeen times daily. They concluded by telling each other, "May we die as shahid, and may Allah have mercy on our souls."

They walked outside the small apartment into a junk-filled, graffiti-covered courtyard emanating the smell of rotting garbage. They dropped their backpacks into a garbage can, and Khaled tossed the laptop behind a rusted refrigerator. Dozens of small, boxy beige limestone homes rose at different levels above them on the Muslim Quarter hill. Flimsy balconies and rooftops were peppered with satellite dishes, bicycles, clotheslines, drooping electrical lines, water tanks, and an occasional air-conditioning unit. Over 32,000 Muslims were stuffed into the seventy-acre Muslim Quarter, making it the most densely populated Jerusalem neighborhood.

Rafsani and Khaled had spent the past three days memorizing the Old City by walking its streets, disguised as old men by wearing worn clothes, makeup, and wigs. They headed to El Wad Road, the heart of the Arab Market. Normally, the colorful and noisy market would be packed with tourists and locals at cafés, with tiny stalls and stores selling everything imaginable. But the market was nearly empty today; the Old City was closed to the public. Twenty yards onto El Wad, they passed a handful of Muslim women sitting in the cobblestone walkway, chatting away, their straw baskets filled with fruits and vegetables. Khaled tossed his destroyed laptop hard drive into a nearby garbage can.

They passed the first part of the Via Dolorosa near St. Stephens Gate, across from the Mount of Olives. They then turned right off El Wad onto the main section of the Via Dolorosa. The passageway featured the last nine Stations of the Cross and led into the Church of the Holy Sepulcher. In order to avoid any unnecessary interaction, the two men walked with authority and spoke casually between themselves.

"After we succeed here today and our cells launch their attacks, the West will come at what's left of us with everything they've got," Khaled said. "We've lost Iraq and Syria. We're almost out of money because the Americans froze our bank accounts and burned our warehouse of cash. And with al-Bagdadi being killed by the Americans, I don't know how ISIS survives."

Rafsani shook his head and grunted. "Khaled, I've told you this before: the infidels can beat our armies, but they will never beat our soldiers. We always knew that we'd be outgunned on the battlefields. And you should understand that al-Baghdadi was destined to die as a martyr. Abu al-Qurashi has already replaced him. Could be you next. You're ready."

"That's interesting. You really think so?"

"Absolutely. Khaled, always think about the big picture. In Syria and Iraq, we gained the hearts of our brothers worldwide by how we put up the fight. Even if we lost territory, we won that war. And now, with the United States' president selling out the Kurds to Turkey, it has already opened the door for ISIS to reemerge in Syria. Even so, you know we have already moved to smaller bombings, assassinations, sidewalk-truck attacks, and child bombings. It's impossible to stop one of us from renting a truck and running down civilians on sidewalks!"

"I understand all that. But we're broke!"

ISIS had been provided unquantifiable funding from sympathetic state sponsors, and it collected billions by seizing the Baiji Refinery in Iraq and stealing about $500 million from banks. It had also levied heavy taxes, along with extorting Iraqi and Syrian civilians under threat of death, for another $200 million. Those sums enabled ISIS to cause astronomical damage in Iraq and Syria, but now its operations had dwindled to next to nothing.

"Khaled, don't worry about money. ISIS is an important force among Islamic freedom fighters. Going forward, our websites will be our best weapons. They have already produced more recruits. Just one shahid suicide bomber can do more damage than one hundred soldiers on a battlefield. These new shahid pledge allegiance to us and even form their own cells, but they cost us nothing because they fund their own operations. Allah has blessed the internet."

"Well, I agree our recruits love our training and execution videos, especially the beheadings. They've helped us establish cells in India, the Philippines, Australia, and Africa," Khaled replied. "But remember that rogue group who carried our flag and blew up the Sufi mosque in Egypt and killed three hundred worshippers as they ran outside?"

"Yes, that was brilliant. They recruited twenty-five to thirty soldiers and were self-funded."

"But they shouldn't have killed fellow Muslims and all those children. They aren't the enemy."

Rafsani's head jerked around. "What's with you today, Khaled?"

"Nothing. I'm here with you to die a shahid," Khaled replied. "But since Afghanistan, I've objected to killing fellow Muslims, especially children."

"You're wrong, Khaled. Those who don't practice Islam like us are heretics, and it's better to kill their children now, before they can populate further. Just like these disgusting moderate Muslims who now think they speak for Islam. They are the enemy and need to die. You'll see. In ten years, our view of Islam will control even Indonesia, and the MFP will become extinct."

They next turned left up Suo Khan ez-Zeit and hit congestion with Ceremony of Peace participants moving en masse toward the event. They passed the Ninth Station of the Cross, where Jesus fell for the third time, and entered the courtyard of the Church of the Holy Sepulcher, consecrated in 335 by Helena, mother of Constantinople. The noisy courtyard was already nearly filled with an exclusive crowd of world and civic leaders. Rafsani wove his way through the crowd to the steps opposite the church's entrance for a clear view of everyone and everything.

ONLY EIGHTY FEET AWAY, just inside the church's entrance, Klein and Galit found their own perfect spot to watch the VIPs pass by after touring the church. French President Michel Jagor had just sauntered by, speaking softly to German Chancellor Stefan Vinwud, with Canadian Prime Minister James Paige following them.

Galit realized that she'd never seen Klein so cleaned up, with a fresh haircut and his beard scruff perfectly trimmed. She said, "For whatever it's worth, Chaim, your new General uniform makes you look very distinguished."

He rolled his eyes and replied scornfully, "I didn't earn the rank of General through years of service and proving myself in the military."

"But Chaim, you're the General of the Sons of Light. You can't wear a Lieutenant uniform anymore. Besides, you've more than proven yourself in other ways."

Klein liked that Galit wasn't shy about challenging him. "I don't even like the uniform and, frankly, I feel stupid wearing this sword. I'll bet Napoleon was the last soldier to wear a sword. Nobody wears swords anymore."

"Do you really want to bet on that?" Galit asked. "Prince Charles is here somewhere. He'll be wearing a sword as part of his dress uniform. And besides, the Chief Rabbi insisted you wear your sword. So please, of all days, don't whine. Today you're a General. You not only look the part, but you've earned it. This entire event has come about because of you."

Klein looked straight into Galit's eyes and said, "Well, not entirely. None of this would have happened if Debra hadn't been killed. My breakdown over her murder led me to finding the Ark. And here we are today. I still think about her a lot."

It struck Klein for the first time how beautiful Galit looked— today she was wearing a sleek black pantsuit and white blouse, her long hair pulled back, with just enough makeup to highlight her features. He was about to compliment her, then suddenly thought, *Why, of all times, am I thinking about this now? Not here, not now. And I'm not mixing women with work.* But then he looked back at Galit and thought, *Well, maybe when this is over. She is pretty special.*

As if Galit was reading his mind, she playfully said, "You don't like girls, do you?"

"I do. You know I've had girlfriends," he replied defensively. "I just don't do well with them. Remember, one shot me."

"You don't like me?" She batted her expressive brown eyes, which she knew how to manipulate for any situation.

He paused to measure his words before speaking. "Not when we're working together. I can't afford the distraction."

"Well, I'm glad that at least I'm a distraction." She touched his hand. "Chaim, I think you're amazing, and not because of the Ark and Ten Commandments, but because of how you handle yourself and your moral code. I still get a shiver up my spine when thinking about your conversation with Pope John."

Before Klein could respond, Baroness Collins and Dan Beer joined them. The baroness exclaimed, "With all the dignitaries here, I cannot believe Pope John invited us to tour the church with him. It was wonderful. You really should have come."

"I'm trying to stay low key while I can," said Klein. "Besides, I've been in this church countless times. I've actually lead a tour myself." Klein knew that the moment the Ceremony of Peace ended and his role in bringing it about was revealed to the public, his privacy would be gone forever.

"And I wasn't going to leave Chaim to stand here all by himself," Galit said.

Beer exuberantly interjected, "Pope John introduced us to everyone as his *friends* who were responsible for today's events. The Emperor of Japan bowed and called me Beer-San."

"Well, Pope John is right," said Klein. "Today's ceremony resulted from everything we did together—going back to that terrorist attack at the Wall. How many times after that were we nearly killed? Ethiopia, London, Rome. Enjoy the moment and the credit. You earned it. You all did. This wasn't just me."

Beer raised his index finger and said softly, "Let's not forget Ori and Danzig."

The group reflected stoically for a few moments, until Klein said to the baroness, "Great outfit, especially the cape."

She beamed and proudly said, "I am the first Grand Master to wear a formal Knights Templar uniform in public in over 700 years." The flowing knee-length white cape, marked by a red Templar cross over her heart, assured that Baroness Collins would stand out in the crowd. The cape covered a black pantsuit and a white tuxedo shirt with a red-ribboned Knights Templar Grand Master gold medallion neckpiece.

"Has anyone asked you about it?"

"Actually, only Prince William did!"

"What did you say?" Klein asked.

"The truth. That it's been in my wardrobe for a long time."

"Was he wearing a sword?" Galit asked, knowing the answer.

"Of course," the baroness replied. "In fact, look at this!" She opened her cape to reveal a twenty-inch sword, secured in an ornately jeweled and sterling silver sheath. "This has been passed down from one Grand Master to the next, almost from the beginning of the Order."

"Wow, that's a sword, isn't it?" Galit said mischievously.

"It's not Chaim's sword, but yes, of course!"

For a couple of seconds, Klein stared straight ahead, then he burst out laughing. "Do you want to trade?"

"Absolutely not, unless yours will do for me what it does for you."

He smirked. "It hasn't before, but you can try again, if you want."

The baroness closed her cape and nodded to the right. "How about that? That's the Saudi Crown Prince next to the Stone of Anointing. It's amazing the Saudis would even attend the service today, much less send their Crown Prince and King!"

"The Saudis finally realize there are benefits to being friends with Israel," Klein replied.

"Well, everyone knows about the technology and defense arrangements between Israel and Saudi Arabia," the baroness said.

"That's right, but did you know that after Iran planted the Shamoon virus in Aramco's computers that shut down 85 percent of its oil production, the Saudis couldn't figure out how to fix them, but we could. That helped build the relationship between our two countries."

Baroness Collins's eyes opened wide. "The Saudis needed Israel to get their computers working? Why would Israel help them with that?"

"As the expression goes, 'The enemy of my enemy is my friend.' Iran is their enemy and our enemy. The Shiites wish to dominate the region and they already have a significant presence in Iraq, Syria, Lebanon, and elsewhere. Iran is on a collision course with the Saudis, who are Sunni. So we can help each other on defense. The Saudis need us for tech, and we need them for oil. Think about this…Israel is suddenly so important to the Saudis that the Crown Prince not only said the Iranian Supreme Leader is the new Hitler of the Middle East, but also, that Israel has a right to exist."

"Yes, Chaim, but Saudi Arabia funded as much terrorist activity over the years as anyone. Like bin Laden," replied the baroness. "What's really going on?"

Klein crossed his arms. "What do you know about the Muslim World Foundation?"

"I understand that it's a Saudi-funded, charitable organization that spreads the word of Wahhabism by building mosques. They claim to reject terrorism although over the years they've been tied to Hamas, al-Qaeda, and other terrorist groups. Wasn't the foundation run by the sheik you kidnapped in London?"

"It's more than that, Baroness. Without government approval, its Secretary General, Sheik al-Talib, went rogue and convened a group of terrorists in Mecca during the Hajj, where they agreed to fund a massive terrorist plot to attack the West and Israel."

"Massive? Meaning what?"

"His group built a coordinated terrorist network to execute a simultaneous attack against numerous major cities across the globe, mostly in the West."

"That sounds terrifying," said the baroness. "How do you know this, Chaim?"

"I learned it after I kidnapped al-Talib from Harrods. But before that, we knew he was funneling money to terrorists everywhere, including to Sheik Sawalha at the Finsbury Mosque."

The baroness studied Klein. "I don't understand. What am I missing?"

Klein focused on the baroness's eyes. "When Dan and I kidnapped al-Talib, we got lucky and recovered his laptop. Mossad cracked it, and between their review of the computer and questioning of al-Talib, we learned about his nefarious terrorist scheme. Ultimately, Prime Minister Zamir confronted the Saudis as to what al-Talib planned to do with their funds. They were remarkably grateful for the intel. It seems 9/11 was enough for them. They don't want another major terrorist attack on their backs."

"Baroness, here's what we're dealing with," Beer said. "The terrorist who opened fire on us at the Vatican was Eyad Hamoud. His best friend was Khaled Kassem. It was Kassem's brother, Mahmoud, who was the suicide bomber at the Wall two years ago. Right after that, Hamas recruited Khaled, who hooked up with Omar Rafsani, formerly head of Saddam Hussein's secret police and now a senior ISIS leader who has strong ties to al-Qaeda."

Galit cut in, "To give this some context, Khaled Kassem's mother is probably the best-known correspondent for Al-Haqq, and his grandfather is *the* Ghassan Kassem."

"I met Ghassan with the Pope only about twenty minutes ago, although of course, I had heard about him for years." Baroness Collins bit her bottom lip while processing it all. "Presumably, both Kassem boys were viewed by the radicals as symbolic propaganda puppets because of their family name."

"That's our assumption," Klein replied.

"So what does all this have to do with today?" Baroness Collins asked.

"I'm getting there," Klein said. "Rafsani was literally at the table in the café in London with Khaled Kassem when I killed Sheik Sawalha. Obviously, al-Talib was in London to assist Rafsani. All we know is that their terrorist network has a large-scale attack planned but we don't know when and where. For obvious reasons, we think any terrorist would want to stage an attack here today."

"Good God! You brought all these world leaders here in the face of a major terrorist attack?" The baroness looked shocked.

"We have no information to conclude where or when an attack could occur," Klein said. "But we advised *every* country here about the risk and what we know. And every country responded that they assumed this ceremony would be a logical location for an attack, yet no one canceled due to the threat. We've had full cooperation on all security issues, especially from the Saudis."

A moment later, Klein discreetly pointed to an elderly man in the audience. "What a coincidence! That's Ghassan Kassem and his family." He didn't mention that Kassem was accompanied by his long-time friend and former CIA Station Chief, Norman Richards.

A moment later an IDF soldier approached them, advising that the ceremony was about to begin. They were escorted to a spot just opposite a flight of steep steps leading up to the Greek Treasury, located next to the Calvary where Jesus was crucified. By now, about 400 people had packed into the courtyard. Every guest was provided transmitters tuned to different frequencies to hear real-time translations of the day's speeches.

The Kassems—father, son, and twin teenaged grandsons—were positioned close to the Pope at the bottom of the steps. "I'm proud to be your son today," Amir Ghassan whispered into his father's ear. "You worked all your life for peace with Israel and a Palestinian state. And now it looks like it's finally here."

"Yes, but at a painful price," Ghassan said. "We will never get past losing Mahmoud at the Wall. And for all we know, Khaled is dead or in prison. Thankfully, praise Allah, even Suha has come to realize the violence and hate must stop." He smiled at his teenage grandsons standing next to him. "Today gives me hope that the twins will have a better life."

Only one hundred feet away, Rafsani and Khaled hadn't moved from their perch scanning the courtyard crowd, picking out world leaders and whispering to each other about today's intended victim list. When Khaled unexpectedly spotted his father, two brothers, and grandfather through the thick crowd, his heart skipped a beat; he had given no thought to the prospect that his family would be here. But then he told himself that their presence was irrelevant. Nothing would interfere with this mission's success. There was no point even mentioning it to Omar.

Instead, he turned toward Rafsani and said quietly, "Remember, these uniforms are our credentials. When we go through security at the Jewish Quarter, I'll go first to handle any discussion. Then you just walk through and nod at the IDF soldier like you're all business. You're a colonel. No one should challenge you. If someone speaks to you in Hebrew, what do you do?"

"I shake my head to show frustration, then point at my watch and say, 'Please not now.'"

"Say it in Hebrew."

"*Selichah lo achshav.*"

"Good. And if we get stopped, then it's Allahu Akbar, right?"

"Yes, Khaled, but we will get through. It is Allah's will."

THE PIPED-IN ORCHESTRAL MUSIC stopped, and Pope John stepped out from the Greek Treasury door to a microphone set on a platform overlooking the courtyard. He stood about forty feet from the spot of the crucifixion of Jesus inside the church. Deafening cheers and applause exploded, continuing for two minutes, despite the Pope's efforts to quiet the crowd.

When there was finally silence, Pope John extended his arms to the audience. "Welcome to this historic event, the Ceremony of Peace. Representatives of the world's nations and religions have come here to the city of Jerusalem—a city of God, a city of war, and now today a city of peace—to herald a new dawn of mutual respect, cooperation, and brotherhood among the religions of Judaism, Christianity, and Islam.

"Most would have never dreamed this possible, for the divisions among these three great religions have existed for millennia, and a river of blood has been shed among us all, in this city alone. But the unimaginable circumstance of finding both the long-lost Ark of the Covenant and the Ten Commandments tablets has caused us all to look inside our hearts so that we can and must all imagine a new era of peace. Today we will begin to heal deep wounds. The Ark of the Covenant is the manifestation of God on Earth, and the Ten Commandments are His most basic laws. All three religions observe the Old Testament and respect these commandments. We may view differently the words of many holy books and God's demands on us, but one thing is certain: there are not three Gods. There is only one God, and He is God for all people. And we are all children of Abraham.

"Each religion is strongly connected to this city. King David made Jerusalem the Jewish capital 3,100 years ago, and two great temples were built on the Temple Mount. Judaism has had a presence in this city and a claim as its capital since David. Christianity was born here. Jesus walked down the Mount of Olives onto the Temple Mount. Indeed, only forty feet from where I stand, Jesus was crucified. Islam has had a strong presence here since the days of the Prophet

Mohammad. Al-Aqsa, situated on Haram al-Sharif, is one of Islam's most sacred mosques. The beautiful Dome of the Rock sits over the Foundation Stone, which is where Mohammad rode his horse Buraq in his Night Journey to heaven. That rock is also where the Ark of the Covenant was kept until it disappeared, and where it shall be restored today.

"As Israel and the Palestinian community move forward to a brighter future, let us focus on their present positive successes. For instance, how many of you know about the partnership among the Augusta Victoria Hospital in East Jerusalem and the Israeli Peres Center for Peace, or the Hadassah University Hospital in Jerusalem, which recently has opened a pediatric oncology unit for Palestinian children? What about the Israeli national soccer team and Maccabi Haifa soccer team, the best in Israel, with both a Jewish and Palestinian makeup, and whose fans dress in green and white, but carry a flag bearing the Star of David? Or the solar panel initiative which draws water from deep underground to irrigate fields in the town of Auja in the West Bank—financed by both Muslims and Jews in the United States, and with both Jews and Palestinians on its technical team? There is the also Yad b'Yad or Hand in Hand preschool in Jaffa, which teaches young Arab and Jewish children about coexistence. Each class has an Arabic and Hebrew-speaking teacher. The children are taught both languages, and the school respects all Jewish, Muslim, and Christian holidays. And let's not forget the internationally acclaimed Seeds of Peace, which since 1983 has taught and empowered thousands of young men and women to advance coexistence and reconciliation between Israel and the Palestinian people.

"There are so many more examples that prove respect and cooperation already exist between Israel and the Palestinians. All of these are foundational to attaining peace here. It will take work. It will take time. It will take forgiveness."

The Pope looked over the crowd. In an emotional voice, he continued, "And because forgiveness must occur, it is clear that the

Crusades, first instigated by Popes one thousand years ago, caused pain and distrust between Islam and Christianity, which continues to this day. On behalf of my church, I apologize to all Muslims for those acts of aggression, and on behalf of the Church I humbly ask for your forgiveness. I now share the Lord's Prayer: 'Our father who art in heaven, hallowed be thy name. Thy kingdom come, thy will be done, on earth as it is in heaven. Give us this day our daily bread and forgive us our trespasses, as we forgive those who trespass against us. And lead us not into temptation but deliver us from evil. For thine is the kingdom and the power and the glory forever and ever. Amen.'"

Pope John paused to allow the crowd to reflect upon The Lord's Prayer. "I ask now that all of you please join me as we walk together in our Solidarity March of Peace to the Western Wall Plaza, where the Ceremony of Peace service will continue."

More than 200 yards away, right outside the busy Jaffa Gate, Ismael Hamoud, cleaned up and dressed in a suit to avoid scrutiny, walked right up to the gate. With his finger already on the detonation button so he could not be stopped, he yelled, "Allahu akbar."

The next second, a deafening explosion reverberated through the Old City.

26

The courtyard at the Church of the Holy Sepulcher fell quiet, no one doubting that what had just happened was a terrorist attack. Slowly, rising chatter turned into a nearly panicked roar. The Pope had not left his lectern and repeatedly waved his arms and shouted into the microphone, trying to hush the crowd. When there was finally quiet, Pope John pleaded, "Obviously something tragic has happened close by, but please, my friends, we cannot panic. Look around. None of us here is injured. We are all safe, and I ask that each of us take a moment for silent prayer for the well-being of everyone who may be at the explosion site."

The Pope looked down and closed his eyes, as did everyone in the courtyard. He then broke the silence by gesturing at the crowd and demanding, "We must continue our Ceremony of Peace! We cannot live in fear! We cannot back down! We must show those who live by hate that they will not prevail! Whoever just committed that atrocity did so intending to stop us from doing that which must be done. I am going to begin *our* Solidarity March of Peace to the Jewish Quarter right now, without hesitation or fear. I urge you to join me!"

At first, as the Pope walked down the steps from the Greek Treasury where Swiss Guard Commandant Pagano was waiting, a few people applauded the Pope. The applause quickly became unanimous, followed by rousing cheers, drowning out the wail of approaching sirens. A path cleared for the Pope to lead the way, and the world leaders quickly lined up behind him to continue. Most were on their cell phones trying to get details about what had just happened. Still standing on the short steps in the back of the plaza, Khaled turned to Rafsani. "So now, Ismael Hamoud knows whether or not Allah has greeted him with seventy-two virgins."

"So that's what you meant when you said he'd be helpful. That was well done. And now we will finish the job," Rafsani replied confidently.

"We can do it right now. If we walk into the middle of that crowd and detonate, we will kill almost every European leader and the president of the United States."

"Patience. It will be far more dramatic when we do it at the Temple Mount."

As participants in the ceremony, Chaim Klein and Ghassan Kassem walked closely behind Pope John. Because the Pope stopped to greet all those in his path, it took ten minutes to inch their way to the back of the plaza.

The Kassem family reached the back steps near the plaza exit and Ahmad, one of the twins, glanced to the right. His eyes locked onto an Israeli soldier who was staring at him from the top of the short steps.

Ghassan gently pushed the boy forward, but after only a few feet, Ahmad stopped and spun around to look back again at the soldier. This time, once Ahmad caught his gaze, the startled soldier jerked his head the other way. Ahmad grabbed the arm of his brother, Bashar, and whispered into his ear. Bashar then turned to look at the soldier. He saw what he needed to.

Klein finally reached Dudi Bareket on his cell phone. After that, he and Galit left the march, excusing themselves for aggressively pushing through the crowd. As they broke free of the people, they ran toward the nearby Jaffa Gate. They reached it at the same time that Bareket pulled up on a small Honda motorcycle.

Bareket understood Klein's bewildered look. "It's a fifteen-minute walk from the Wall to anywhere in the Old City, but because this is quick and mobile, it's only two to three minutes. We have ten of them spread out over the Old City today. You can use one of them."

"You mean *two*," Klein replied, glancing at Galit. "Right?"

She planted her hands on her hips. "Seriously? I've been riding motorcycles as long as you."

Bareket made a phone call to get them immediately sent over.

"What do you know?" Klein impatiently asked him.

"Nothing, except that there are a lot of casualties right outside the gate. Also, we think that Rafsani and the Kassem kid are in the Old City right now."

"Meaning they're responsible for the bombing?"

"Probably. That makes sense, but it might be worse than that."

"Worse? What could be worse?" Klein asked.

"Chaim, remember how after you recovered al-Talib's laptop we learned about Professor Hosnu, who was working with Rafsani?"

"Yes."

"He was found floating in the Bosphorus about a month ago," Bareket said. "One shot to the head."

"No honor among terrorists, huh?" Klein said dryly.

"That's the consensus," Bareket replied.

"And he set up the dark net Kill the Infidels website that we've been monitoring?" Klein said.

"Right. About ninety minutes ago, a new message popped up on the website." Bareket pulled a small slip of paper from his shirt pocket and read from it. "Upon seeing fire on top of Jerusalem, you shall Kill the Infidels Today."

Galit frowned. "Dudi, are you saying that the attack just activated Hosnu's network of cells?"

"Not sure, but quite possibly. The message was very specific, by referencing both fire *on top of Jerusalem* and *today.*"

"You think the message means an explosion *on top* of the Temple Mount?" Galit asked. "The real attack is next?"

"That's more likely, when the whole world will be watching the ceremony. We think that what happened out there is a decoy for us to divert critical resources, instead of having them at the Wall and Temple Mount. More importantly, Rafsani would want to kill the Western VIPs and disrupt the service while it's being broadcast live. Numerous other posts on Rafsani's website over the last two weeks have focused specifically on the Temple Mount. It's unfortunate we have victims out there, but they're not the world leaders the terrorists want to kill, and it wasn't on television."

Klein replied, "I think you're right. Rafsani's cells were just activated. And only Rafsani, with his experience, could improvise enough to even dare try to pull off any meaningful attack here with only eighteen days' notice. If they're talking about a fire on top of Jerusalem, which would be the Temple Mount, it means Rafsani and Kassem are here. That's their target."

"That's pretty much it." Bareket grimaced.

"But Dudi, what about the cells?" Galit asked. "Didn't you shut them down?"

"We believe so, but honestly, we don't know for sure," Bareket said. "Mossad's dark net specialists planted a unique virus in an attachment on the Kill the Infidels website. It supposedly infected and wiped the hard drives of everyone who opened the attachment. Then, after that, every time Hosnu or Rafsani posted something on the site, *we* responded, so they'd think they were communicating with the cells."

"I get it," Galit said. "Rafsani and Kassem likely believe they are still in communication with the cells and that their plan is on track—proven by the fact they sent that message today."

"Correct," Bareket said. "And so, you know, right after Dan and Chaim recovered al-Talib's laptop, we found files that enabled us to trace all the money sent by the Muslim World Foundation to the cells. Although it took a lot of work, we drained every cell's bank account down to zero." Klein exchanged fist bumps with Bareket. "That money was the blood that keeps the terrorists' heart pumping." Bareket continued, "Without cash, there's a decent chance that some, most, or all of the cells disbanded. These jihadists believe in their cause, but they need money for their operation and living expenses."

"Yes, but let's not be naïve," Klein said. "While we hope that the cells do not proceed with their attacks today, we don't really have any way to know for sure. Because we must always be extra vigilant about terrorism, we have to work on the assumption that the cells still exist and are operational. Unfortunately, we also know from experience that since terrorists are typically both industrious and motivated to cause death and destruction, they can and do act on their own. Complicating this further is that although we know the target cities where the cells are located because we traced and took their money, we don't know who the cell members are or if they are willing or capable of executing a plan and acting on their own."

"Agreed," added Bareket. "So right now, we must assume Rafsani and Kassem are in the Old City with the worst of weapons, and we probably have less than an hour to find them. We must absolutely, positively stop anything else from happening."

"Guys, you realize that this is a make-or-break moment for Israel," Galit said. "If they are out there, and they pull off an attack on our soil at this event, and any VIP dies, world public opinion will bury our country."

Klein and Bareket looked at each other and remained silent. Their mutual nod was recognition that Galit was right.

"Assuming we can find them, we'll stop them," Klein said. "But first, I want to take a quick look out there."

Klein marched the twenty yards to outside the Jaffa Gate, and Bareket and Galit followed. It was immediately clear to Klein that the suicide bomber had used a special vest loaded with extra shrapnel and special packets of a napalm-like substance that created flying fireballs. The victims lying within thirty yards of the homicide bomber were sliced up or burned—or both. The range of damage covered seventy yards, leaving at least 120 dead and 200 wounded, some of them dignitaries. Pandemonium was everywhere.

Tears welled up in Klein's eyes. He flashbacked to the explosion at the Wall when his cousin Debra died in his arms. He hated that whenever he was confronted with death from terrorist violence, the final moment of Debra saying "Don't worry, cousin. Everything will be okay," popped into his mind. This attack was worse than the one at the Wall. Much worse.

Bareket walked over to a black limousine with a German diplomatic license plate. The car's engine was running, even as its driver was slumped over the steering wheel. The back door was open, and a black-suited man hung motionless over it, half his face missing.

Fifteen feet away, Galit stood over a young Orthodox woman lying dead, face-up on the ground, with her young son lying in a pool of blood. A baby wailed away unharmed in a carriage that sat next to them. Nearby, a little girl sat on her knees, pounding her dead mother's chest, screaming, "Mommy!" Galit broke into tears and cried out in anguish.

The many death scenes pushed Klein's button into the cold, intense mindset of a battlefield soldier whose job was simple: kill the enemy. Galit ran toward him and fell into his arms, sobbing. Klein blankly stared ahead, his chest pounding with anger and hurt. He had no words of comfort for her. Not now.

A moment later, Bareket approached with his phone to his ear. "I think we have them," he said. "We have drones covering the Old City. One of our tech specialists just found video of two Matkal officers walking through the Muslim Quarter. It's troubling because they walked out of a building in a courtyard near the Damascus Gate where they shouldn't even be, then threw two backpacks into the garbage and a laptop behind a refrigerator. We can't see their faces."

"That's them, no doubt about it," Klein said. He told the distraught Galit, "What happened here is unspeakable. I have to stop them and I want your help, but I need you to tell me that you can forget about the atrocities that happened here—for now. If you can't, you're a liability."

Her eyes narrowed and without hesitation, she replied, "I'm fine. I'm with you."

"Good. Then let's go find Rafsani and Kassem and end this."

FOUR HUNDRED YARDS AWAY, the Kassem family and Norman Richards were walking up the Street of the Chain in the Solidarity March of Peace, only yards behind Pope John. The somber crowd was respectfully quiet, contemplating the terrorist attack that already stained this Ceremony of Peace.

Amir Kassem tapped Ghassan on the shoulder. "Father, Norman, I was just told something very disturbing from Ahmad and Bashar. You need to hear this."

Ghassan barely turned his head.

"They saw Khaled at the Church. He was wearing an Israeli soldier's uniform."

"Obviously, they were wrong. They are young boys with vivid imaginations."

Amir grabbed his father's bicep. "No, they were certain it was him. This could be serious."

Richards stopped and turned, causing Ghassan to do so as well. "I want to hear what the boys have to say," said Richards. "Ghassan, what's the harm?"

The Kassems and Richards stepped out of the Solidarity March of Peace line to let others pass by. Both boys described what they had seen to the adults. Richards followed up with a gentle interrogation, then told the Kassems, "The boys are convinced it's him. From my experience, I would never rule out anything until I have confirmation one way or the other. If it's Khaled and he's behind us, he should be here shortly, and we can see for ourselves. And if it is him, we should be very concerned about why he's wearing an IDF uniform."

"I agree," replied Ghassan, running his fingers through his hair.

A few minutes later, Ahmad pointed at two IDF soldiers walking toward them and yelled, "Look, there's Khaled!" He and Bashar sprinted toward their brother, then collectively hugged him tight, one on each side.

With a hand on each boy's shoulder, Khaled—with Rafsani next to him—walked up to Ghassan, Amir, and Richards. He smiled warmly and said, "Father, Grandfather, Norman, I was hoping to see you here today. I've missed you all so much." He looked down at his younger brothers and said, "You guys have no idea how much I missed you!" He tousled their hair, then added, "This is my friend Uri Gross. We work together."

Rafsani pleasantly nodded and said "Shalom," the only Hebrew word he knew. He immediately saw that none of the men bought Khaled's ploy.

Wasting no time, Amir demanded, "Why are you wearing an Israeli uniform?"

"I've been working undercover in an anti-terrorism unit with the IDF for two years now. I've been prohibited from contacting anyone. It's to protect you. Uri is my commanding officer. And I was also really hoping to see mother."

"Maybe if you phoned her, she might have come," Amir brusquely replied.

In perfect Arabic, Richards said to Rafsani, "I've known General Gilad Herzog for twenty years, but haven't seen him in a while. How is he doing?"

"He's great. It's amazing how he still works as hard as ever."

There was no General Herzog. Rafsani's answer confirmed that which Richards almost instantly knew: he was standing opposite Omar Rafsani. To fuel the fire, he next asked him in Hebrew, "What unit did you start out in?"

Rafsani's silence and the narrowing of his eyes told Richards that he had just pushed Rafsani's hot button. Rafsani also knew all about Norman Richards, going back to when Richards interrupted the plans of Carlos the Jackal and Saddam Hussein to kill the U.S. president.

"Khaled, I want the truth," Amir said firmly. "Why are you here today?"

"To prove that the Palestinians and Jews can work together cooperatively. I wish I could have told you and mother about my work." Khaled knew his answer wasn't even a good lie.

Ghassan especially did not want an encounter with Khaled and Rafsani to become a public scene, so he pointed to a nearby alley so they could move out of the way. As they walked the twenty yards, Richards said to Khaled, "I assume you know about the incredible honor bestowed on your grandfather by the world community today for his contributions to the peace process. This is monumental and he's worked his whole life to get to the point where there would actually be peace between Israel and the Palestinians."

The moment they turned the corner and were out of sight, Richards's bear-sized hands grabbed Khaled's forearms, locking him in place. "Khaled, I've known you since the day you were born. Remember, you used to call me Uncle Norman. So listen. I beg you—it is not too late to stop this!" He pulled Khaled in for a hug, then backed away and stared hard at him. "You're wearing a shahid bomber's vest. Didn't you already do enough damage today? Look at your brothers. Think of your mother. Do you really want to fucking die?"

While Richards focused on Khaled, Rafsani stepped toward Richards and jammed a knife into the middle of his back. Richards gasped and bolted erect. Rafsani yanked out the knife, spun Richards around, and thrust it into his stomach. Rafsani yanked the blade upwards, sucking the air out of Richards and saying with a sneer, "This is for my brothers-in-arms, Ahmed and Khalil al-Sharif, who are dead because of you." Richards fell back against the wall, blood pouring from his stomach. He collapsed to the ground, dead. Rafsani looked around to assure that no one had witnessed the murder.

Ahmad and Bashar were already crying. "In the name of Allah," Amir cried out, and he fell to his knees leaning over Richards.

Despite his advanced age and lack of weapons, Ghassan took a threatening step toward Rafsani, who raised his bloody knife and sliced the air with it back and forth near Ghassan's face. "One more step old man and you're next. You will all die today anyway, so I would be happy to finish you off right now and watch you choke on your own blood like that dead pig."

Amir rose and in a trembling voice screamed, "What happened to you, Khaled? Norman was family to us! You know violence doesn't solve problems. It doesn't fix the issues our people face."

"Norman Richards was an American spy pig infidel who deserved to die," Khaled replied in a monotone.

"You are wrong! You've studied the Koran. Allah would not condone this."

Khaled returned a cold, blank stare. "Mother would approve of me dying a shahid, just as she did for Mahmoud. She was proud of him. She will be even prouder of me."

"You are wrong! Totally wrong," Amir yelled back. "Yes, right after Mahmoud's sacrifice your mother *thought* she was proud of him. And the day the Israelis bulldozed our house she was absolutely furious. But then you left. You don't know how your mother still cries for Mahmoud. And how much she cries for you as well, not knowing what's happened to you, but believing you were following in Mahmoud's footsteps. Do you know why she's not here with us right now?"

"Because she is disgusted with the thought of this Ceremony of Peace and is boycotting it by staying at home," Khaled replied.

"No, Khaled!" Amir retorted. "She practically begged Al-Haqq to be the lead correspondent today. She wants peace now. She supports this Ceremony of Peace. She believes it can provide the opportunity for better lives for our people. She doesn't even fight with me or your grandfather about these issues anymore."

Tears running down his face, Ahmad tugged at Khaled's pant leg and with his eyes wide open, he asked softly, "Are you going to kill me, Khaled? Are we all going to die? I don't want to die. I don't want you to die." He grabbed Khaled's leg, hanging on tightly and wailing.

Khaled stayed silent and stone-faced.

Ghassan looked down at his long-time dear friend lying dead in the street. He shook his head and swallowed hard. Wagging his finger at Khaled, he said, "Leave your brothers here. Let them live. Do one right thing today, Khaled."

In a flash, Rafsani pushed Ghassan against the wall, then pressed the edge of the blade against his neck. "I've sliced a lot of throats, so listen closely. We are all walking together to the Western Wall and the boys will walk with me. If you say or do anything to attract attention, I will kill them both wherever we are standing. But if you cooperate, once we pass through security, I will let them go. But not you, old man. You're my hostage and a traitor to our people. I look forward to killing you. Now let's move."

"Do what he says," Khaled said with a distressed look at his brothers.

BACK NEAR THE JAFFA Gate at the Citadel, Bareket was clipping button-sized cameras and audio communicators to the clothes worn by Klein and Galit, who were already sitting on their motorcycles. Bareket pointed at the long line of guests in the Solidarity March of Peace, walking toward the Street of the Chain and into the Jewish Quarter. "Take the loop around onto Bate Mahse because you'll never get through that crowd."

They nodded, opened their throttles, keeping their thumb on the horn as they aggressively zipped around pedestrians. Taking a quick right, they accelerated past the Citadel into an empty 300-yard stretch. The road ended into a hard left, and they leaned into the turn to keep their balance. Thirty seconds later, they were on Bate Mahse, which took them up to the Dung Gate entrance to the Western Wall.

Bareket had called ahead so the heavy steel security gate for cars and trucks was already open for them. After being waved through, they coasted slowly for the 150 yards to the far edge of the Western Wall Plaza. They parked their bikes in front of the Visitor Center opposite the Western Wall and adjacent to the steps that led up to the security gate off the Street of the Chain. To accommodate the media, a temporary press box had been constructed on top of a scaffold, flush with the Visitor Center.

Klein and Galit were mesmerized by the specially constructed eighty-foot-long platform built in front of the Wall, filled with chairs, a podium, and the flags of Israel, Palestine, and the United Nations. Hung from the top of the Wall behind the platform, were the flags of the many nations participating in the Ceremony of Peace. The divider between the men's and women's prayer section was removed for the day in order to accommodate the guests.

A soldier approached them. "Mr. Klein, Ms. Kevetch, please follow me. Prime Minister Zamir is waiting for you." They walked through a stone-arched entrance marked by a sign that read: The Western Wall Tunnels and were greeted by Zamir, who looked upset. He led them into the next room, which contained a model of the Temple Mount.

Waiting for them were Pope John; Commandant Pagano, Cardinal Marino, Chief Rabbi Schteinhardt, Jerusalem Grand Mufti Sheik Mustafa Busa, Salan Barghouti, the new President of the Palestinian National Authority, and Cherif Bassiouni, the United Nations Secretary General.

Pope John got right to it. "I understand you visited the scene of the explosion. How bad is it?"

"About 120 dead and 200 wounded," Klein said as Bareket entered the room.

"Has anyone claimed responsibility?" asked Bassiouni.

"No, but we're pretty sure the perpetrator is tied to two ISIS terrorists. We think they are still in the Old City right now, ready to wreak havoc during the ceremony. One of them is Khaled Kassem, Ghassan's grandson."

"Then the ceremony is on hold. How can we proceed if 120 people already have died here today?" Secretary General Bassiouni said authoritatively. "We will not put anyone else at risk. We must assure everyone's safety."

President Barghouti added, "I agree. If more people die today, especially at the hands of terrorists, *all* Muslims will be blamed. The world will never forgive us."

Grand Mufti Busa exclaimed, "What a catastrophe! Our entire peace plan hangs by a thread. And poor Ghassan. To have this happen to him again, and he is supposed to speak today!"

Pope John shook his head and said softly, "If we continue, we disrespect the souls of those who passed."

An uncomfortable silence filled the room until Klein spoke. "Everything you said is accurate, but I must respectfully disagree. Give me a little bit more time. We know who the terrorists are, what they look like, and what they're wearing."

"Mr. Klein, your story is extraordinary. The world owes you a debt of gratitude that can never be repaid," said the Secretary General. "But these deaths are terrible. Putting us in the position of even holding this ceremony is beyond comprehension. It is inexcusable. And what if you don't stop them? Then what? Total disaster!"

"That's right. Go look in the plaza, Mr. Klein. It is already filling up," added Grand Mufti Busa. "The terrorists could already be down there, mixed in with the guests."

"Perhaps you are right. But if they are already in the crowd, then we have a totally unfixable problem because that is right where they want to be," Klein replied. "That's where they can do their damage."

"They haven't yet passed through security," Bareket quickly said. "Gentlemen, please, think about this…the terrorists' goal must be to mount an attack in front of the television cameras, either down here at the Wall or up on the Temple Mount. There is only one way into the plaza today, and it's through the security booth that's right outside here at the top of the steps. They will pass through security there shortly. When they do, we will stop them. That allows us to protect the people in line. We're looking for them right now on the Street of the Chain. We have drones covering every inch of the Old City and cameras on almost every street, and it all goes through facial recognition software. They are *not* getting through."

"I understand everyone's security concerns," Klein said. "But every second I spend here is a second wasted in protecting everyone. Would you please excuse me so I can get back to work?"

"Chaim, with all the security specialists we have here today, why are you putting yourself in jeopardy?" asked Zamir.

"My son, don't you have a greater purpose, for today and the future?" added Pope John.

"No!" Chief Rabbi Schteinhardt shouted. "We are here because of Chaim. It is not for us to tell him what to do. If he wishes to find and fight the terrorists, then that is what he must do."

"You would sacrifice Chaim?" the Pope asked.

"The General of the Sons of Light chooses his own destiny."

A few seconds of silence followed until Klein said, "I came here today not expecting I'd have to deal with terrorists, but they are the enemy. If we don't kill them, they will kill us. I am going to deal with them. It is what I have always done, and today of all days, this is *my* responsibility. I'm leaving."

"Chaim, keep your com link on, so you'll know what's happening in real time," Bareket said.

Klein turned and addressed the others. "It is incredible to think that we are here today for this Ceremony of Peace. This day might never have come, but it has. I don't want to disrespect the dead, but if we don't proceed today, there probably is no tomorrow. If you believe in Pope John's comments at the church that we cannot live in fear and that those who live by hate cannot prevail, then at this moment, you must decide how you wish to lead. Will you stand up to evil or let those who live by it prevail? We will start late, but we will hold this ceremony today. So please excuse me. Galit and I are going to deal with them."

As Klein turned, Pope John exclaimed, "Mr. Klein, I want my words to have meaning. And from what I've seen from you, I put my faith in you. Please make sure this ceremony goes forward."

"Thank you, Your Holiness," Klein said, then he and Galit left.

Bareket turned to address the group. "We have already moved everyone who is near the Wall to the back prayer rooms inside the Temple Mount. We have buses moving into the plaza right now. We're parking them end-to-end to serve as a blast zone buffer in front of the Wall. We are also evacuating everyone who may live in homes in the immediate vicinity."

Bareket stopped to accept a phone call. A moment later, he announced, "Rafsani and Kassem are approaching the security checkpoint. We are safe here, and the Western Wall Plaza is secure."

MINUTES LATER, RAFSANI, KHALED, and the Kassem family reached the security checkpoint. Khaled turned to Rafsani. "We need to let my family go, now. We will be shahid regardless. Do this for me, Omar. They don't need to die to prove our point."

Rafsani glared at Khaled, then reached down and squeezed Bashar's shoulder so hard that he yelped. "Your family serves as leverage to get us through security if these uniforms don't work. They are expendable. I would say the same if it was my family. In Allah's name, you're a soldier, a shahid! Act like one!"

Ghassan reached out, grabbed Khaled's arm, and said, "Khaled, the vast majority of our people want peace. They have lived with violence and hatred and poverty too long. Today provides a real chance for a new beginning. Why would you want to destroy that?"

"You don't understand. This is the will of Allah. I have—"

"You're right. I don't understand," Amir interrupted. "The Koran does not support killing innocent people in Allah's name. Who are more innocent than your brothers? You were taught that for many more years than the nonsense you've heard from this murderer!"

"Enough!" declared Rafsani. "One more word from either of you infidels and I will kill the boys right here. Then I will still have you as hostages to get us through security."

With Khaled leading the way, they passed through security without a suspicious word or glance, entering the Western Wall Plaza exactly as planned.

The top steps provided them with a full clear view of the Wall. Rafsani frowned upon the scene before him. The Ceremony of Peace platform was empty. There were no guests either in seats or standing around chatting. The people who had entered right before them were being ushered away by IDF soldiers. Busses were lined up across the outer edge of the prayer section, at least one hundred feet in front of the Wall.

Rafsani's adrenaline jumped, and he took the lead, slowly walking the Kassem group down the steps while processing what was happening.

When Rafsani and the others were halfway down the steps, Klein and Galit walked out from behind the Visitor Center, standing at the bottom of the steps.

Klein raised his arms above his head, and shouted, "Omar Rafsani and Khaled Kassem, we've been waiting for you. Let me guess that you didn't know that Sayaret Matkal soldiers almost *never* wear their uniforms. They wear street clothes to protect their identities even for special events, and that includes colonels and lieutenant colonels. So between your disguises and the drones we have flying over Jerusalem today, you made it very easy for us to find you. Too bad you didn't wear a nice business suit like most of the guests. That would have made it a lot tougher on us. You'd have blended right in with all these world leaders." Klein started walking up the steps, with Galit right behind him.

Rafsani pulled Bashar into him; the tip of his knife pressed against the boy's throat. "Take one more step. Do it! I *will* kill him." Rafsani moved his hand off Bashar's shoulder and ripped open his shirt, displaying his suicide vest. "Take two steps and I'll disintegrate you all right now."

"Then at least your mission in stopping today's events will have failed. Regardless, the Ceremony of Peace *is* proceeding, and nothing you do can stop it." Klein couldn't help himself from smiling. "Rafsani, look behind you. No people. They're safe up on the Street of the Chain. Look behind me. See the buses. When you blow yourself up, they'll insulate everything by the Wall from the blast, so you'll kill only us. Exactly eight people."

A woman's voice from behind Klein announced, "No, nine."

Minutes earlier, Bareket told Suha Kassem of the events involving her son. She climbed down from the press box yards away and now stood behind Klein and Galit.

Khaled's shoulders slumped, his eyes opening wide with sadness. "You shouldn't have come, Mother."

"You've left me no choice. If you're going to kill yourself, your father, your brothers, and grandfather, I wish to die as well. I will have nothing left, so push your button and kill me too."

Khaled's head dropped and he was speechless.

Rafsani's demeanor remained defiant. He said mockingly, "None of you have any idea what's planned for the world today. You are all meaningless specks of sand. Millions of infidels will die."

"Really?" Klein taunted. "You think Professor Hosnu's cells are going on their missions today? Listen to this, Rafsani." Klein pulled a piece of paper from his shirt pocket and read, "'Upon seeing fire on top of Jerusalem, you shall Kill the Infidels Today.' See Rafsani, many months ago, we hijacked your website and inserted a virus that wiped the computers of everyone who signed on, and when you thought you were talking to them, you were talking to us! We also traced and impounded all of your cells' money that came from the Muslim World Foundation so none of the cells could execute their plans. Some of that money is actually being used to pay for today's ceremony. Thank you for that. So right now, all you've got today are you and Khaled. That's it. Not what you planned, huh?" He smiled.

The fury in Rafsani's eyes showed that he believed Klein, but he calmly said, "Whether what you say is true or not, now you will die, as will I, but with honor as a shahid."

"Whatever," Klein said, taking small, slow steps toward Rafsani. "But how about if you and I first go at it together? You can keep your vest on. You want me for a lot of reasons, don't you? I'm a Jew. I kidnapped your friend al-Talib. I killed Sheik Sawalha. I stole your money. I destroyed your big plan. And I can't wait to kill both of you. So let's settle this between us. Two on one. If you don't like how the fight is going, you can always push the button at any time."

"I don't need to fight you. I just need to kill you. It doesn't matter how you die. Allah will be pleased."

"No Rafsani, there is only one God for *all* of us and he won't be pleased with you, and I can prove it. Let me show you the real power of God." Klein pulled his sword from its sheath, held it erect in front of him, and instantly it glowed and hummed. As Klein swung the sword, it sang as never before, and from thirty feet away, Rafsani and Khaled could feel the gusts of wind it emitted with each slash through the air. Klein stopped, pointed the sword at his foes, and declared, "This is the Sword of the Righteous! The Sword of David!"

Rafsani and Khaled remained silent, but Rafsani's wide-open eyes told Klein that even the hardened terrorist was stunned. Khaled extended his hands and prayed.

"Now watch this." Klein dropped to one knee and gently placed the sword on the ground. It began to change form, with its silver glistening blade quickly turning to its greyish cement state.

Rafsani let go of Bashar, stepped backwards, then looked to the skies. As he moved his hand toward his vest's igniter button, three shots simultaneously reverberated through the plaza. Rafsani fell dead, with half his head missing and both arms blown off.

Before anyone could even react, Klein yelled, "Khaled, there are three snipers on the Temple Mount focused on you. Raise your arms above your head. Drop to your knees or you're dead as well."

"Khaled! Please! I beg you! We all love you! Do as he says!" screamed his mother, followed by pleas from his father, grandfather and younger brothers. Khaled stood motionless for a few seconds, then slowly complied.

Suha rushed up the stairs and the Kassem family knelt in a circle around Khaled. They all shed tears, even Khaled. An Israeli bomb squad waiting inside the tunnel's entrance slipped between the family members and disengaged Khaled's suicide vest.

At the same time, Rafsani's remains were picked up by a team of soldiers and his spilled blood was washed away. After a few minutes with his family, Khaled was led away in handcuffs. The buses left the Western Wall Plaza. The guests that were held back on the Street of the Chain were quickly cleared through security.

27

The Western Wall Plaza quickly filled with all 2,000 guests—the largest such gathering of global senior political, civic, and religious leaders ever. The crowd silenced itself when Johann Pachelbel's Canon in D Major was piped into the plaza, starting the second phase of the Ceremony of Peace. Israeli Prime Minister Eli Zamir and Palestinian Authority President Salan Barghouti marched together in measured steps onto the platform, where they stood side by side, facing the crowd. Close behind were Chief Rabbi Schteinhardt, Grand Mufti Busa, and between them, Pope John. They were followed by Chaim Klein, Baroness Collins, and Hassan Tamimi of the Muslims for Peace. Finally, Secretary General Bassiouni led a delegation of the United Nations Security Council. Once everyone had taken their places and the music stopped, Prime Minister Zamir strode to the podium and those on the platform took their seats.

"My friends, welcome to Jerusalem to celebrate this historic day. It is no coincidence that the Hebrew word for peace is *shalom* and the Arabic word for peace is *salaam*. *Shalom* also means harmony, prosperity, welfare, and tranquility. In Genesis 43:27 and Exodus 4:18, *shalom* is used in reference to action taken for the well-being of others, which is, of course, fundamental to the concept of peace. Today, three great religions have set aside longstanding complicated differences and now recognize the similarities among our people and our religions. Today marks the dawn of a new era of friendship and peace among Jews, Muslims, and Christians. Whether you adhere to those or any other faith, a common thread among us all is that we want better lives, especially for our children. In the past, our children have suffered, and hate has been passed down through the generations. Today we move forward collectively, to assure that us and our children will have better lives in a better world. Today marks *Shalom.*" With his arms outstretched to the audience, through a large smile, Zamir cried out, "Shalom!" and the crowd joyously replied, "Shalom." Zamir yelled, "Salaam!" and that too was returned to him, along with happy applause.

Zamir continued, "Eighteen days ago, a monumental discovery was revealed to the world. The finding of the Ark of the Covenant and the actual Ten Commandments tablets, with the rule of law visibly etched into stone by the finger of God, was a miracle. Eighteen is a symbolic number to Judaism. It ties to the word *Chai,* which means life. And so today, we also celebrate life.

"Earlier this afternoon, Pope John spoke of certain existing social and economic endeavors of cooperation between Israel and the Palestinian Authority. Today, to improve the lives of Israeli and Palestinian citizens, we take the next step forward. Israel will devote substantial resources to bring new infrastructure to Gaza and the West Bank, such as desalinization and water projects, new schools, new hospitals, and technological improvements, all of which will create jobs—and jobs create hope and prosperity. Indeed, we are thrilled to announce that a comprehensive Peace Agreement between Israel and the Palestinian Authority was executed only hours ago. Tomorrow morning, the United Nations will vote to recognize and welcome the new State of Palestine to the UN. So today we honor *shalom* and *chai,* peace and life."

The crowd erupted into a roar of approval. When Barghouti moved next to Zamir and they held hands, raising them high, the crowd's boisterous response increased even further. After about three minutes, Barghouti returned to his chair and Zamir continued.

"We note that the United States previously moved its embassy from Tel Aviv to Jerusalem, recognizing this city as the capital of Israel. Indeed, Jerusalem has been our capital back to the days of King David over 3,000 years ago. However, the Palestinian people also have lived on this land for over a millennium and Islam has had a strong historic presence here since Mohammad's night journey to heaven, making Jerusalem one of Islam's most holy cities. Given these unique circumstances, if we are to have peace, we need to coexist, especially in Jerusalem. Thus, the Palestinian Authority and Israel agree that Jerusalem shall be considered Israel's capital, but it will also be the capital of Palestine, which will set up its government in East Jerusalem. We believe the proximity will enhance communications going forward, strengthening the relationship between our two nations. And finally, we appreciate the near unanimity of the United Nations countries supporting the peace announced here today, and their restated recognition of Israel's right to exist. As-salaam-alaikum, peace upon you."

President Barghouti walked up to Zamir and extended his open arms to him as the men embraced. They then held each other at arms-length and spoke for a full minute before moving in for a second hug, causing the crowd to again erupt in cheers. Both leaders wiped tears from their eyes. As Zamir walked to his chair, the other world leaders on the platform lined up to shake his hand.

Barghouti stood at the podium for a few seconds, composing himself before speaking in a strong voice and sincere tone. "Shalom! Salaam! My friend Prime Minister Zamir speaks the truth. The Jewish and Palestinian people are cousins, but for too long we have acted like a broken family fighting over everything. From this day forward, pointing fingers about who did what to the other no longer matters.

Today we move forward together, united in not just the hope, but the firm belief that our two nations, our families, will now not only coexist, but will thrive together. And the more we succeed, the more positive the momentum for peace will take hold. Anything and everything are now possible. With this cloud of hate and distrust lifted, beginning today, our lives and those of our children will improve.

"It is undeniable. Throughout history, the Jewish people have been victimized both by unfair stereotypes and because they celebrate God differently than others do. Israel has been a constant target of prejudice, hatred, and attacks since its founding in 1948." Barghouti pointed his index finger at the audience and yelled, "That stops now! The Palestinian Authority recognizes Israel's right to exist, and to be respected as an equal, indeed as a leader, in the world community. We state our great respect for all that Israel and its citizens have accomplished in building a prosperous, modern, beautiful nation out of sand, despite its size and the many battles it has had to fight. And equally importantly, we fully renounce terrorism. As of this moment, we will consider an act of terror against Israel or Judaism or Christianity to be an act of aggression against the best interests of Palestine. Hamas, Hezbollah, al-Qaeda, ISIS...accept this peace and lay down your arms or be treated as criminals.

"We are here for another historic reason besides our treasured peace. Two thousand years ago, the Ark of the Covenant and the Ten Commandments sat upon the Foundation Stone inside the Jewish Second Temple. Since the seventh century, that spot has housed the Dome of the Rock, Islam's revered shrine. Respect for peace must equate to respect for each other's religions. That rock is holy to Judaism, Christianity, and Islam. The Old Testament is foundational to all three religions. Accordingly, the Waqf and Palestinian Authority have agreed that the Ark and the tablets of God shall again sit upon the Foundation Stone. And the Dome of the Rock shall now be open to all people of this world to visit, regardless of religious belief. Come view and pray at the Ark of the Covenant!"

Barghouti's invitation was interrupted by exultant applause. "In closing, thank you to Pope John for recognizing the origin of the difficulties between Christianity and Islam. Peace between our religions also begins today. Moreover, thank you to the Pope and the Church for your instrumental role in making today a successful reality."

Barghouti walked over to Pope John. They briefly conversed through smiles with hands locked together, then sat down. Ghassan Kassem, Hassan Tamimi, and Baroness Collins approached the podium.

Standing in the middle, Tamimi, wearing his first new suit in years, slightly adjusted his white *kufi* skull cap. Leaning into the microphone and sounding a bit nervous, he announced, "I am Hassan Tamimi, Imam of the Grand Mosque of Paris. I am also President of the French branch of the Muslims for Peace. I am honored to participate in this historic celebration. A day in which Jews, Muslims, and Christians come together to commence a new era of communication, cooperation, and friendship.

"I have been asked to spend a few moments describing the MFP's mission. First, it is to educate fellow Muslims about tolerance for others. We reject those intolerant radical Islamists who commit terrorist acts and subvert the Koran. *Allahu akbar* means 'God is great.' It is not a battle cry. It is heresy to shout God's name when committing a crime. *Allahu akbar* is said in prayers thanking God for something that you would have been incapable of attaining but for his benevolence. For many years, Western nations have battled radical Islamists, often through military occupation in Muslim countries. That action has supported the Islamists' argument that the West was trying to kill Muslims. To my fellow Muslims: going forward, we must participate and take responsibility for solving this problem. Only Muslims can educate each other. We can no longer allow fanatics to distort our religion with violence, hatred, and distortion of the Koran. We are peace-loving people who would like the world to be a better place. The MFP strongly supports this peace initiative, which we join in part by recognizing the State of Israel and denouncing terrorism of any kind toward any people."

Tamimi paused to sip water. "Second, the MFP is a charitable organization that already has been blessed to receive over eight billion dollars in contributions. This money will be used worldwide, but much of it will go to Gaza and the West Bank to build infrastructure.

The MFP will do its part to assure this peace is permanent. Allahu akbar for granting us this peace."

Next up was Baroness Collins. She knew it was impossible to keep the Knights Templar's existence and role in today's events secret. The entire story about how this day came about was just too big. So, after consulting with the Templar's High Council, they unanimously concluded it was better to go public, in order to control the message as much as possible.

"Good afternoon to all of you. I am Baroness Jillian Collins, a member of Great Britain's House of Lords." She paused to draw everyone's attention before continuing. "However, I appear before you today in a capacity that most people will say could not be true. But it is, and the incredible events leading up to today have made it necessary to disclose that…I serve as the Grand Master of the Knights Templar."

As she expected, a murmur flowed through the audience. "Since 1307, our group allowed the world to believe we disbanded. In those dark ages, this became necessary for our own safety. History books correctly report that we amassed a great fortune and with no wars to fight, we became businessmen and investors. Today we operate much like an international corporation." Then, adding through a smile with exaggerated intonation, "And yes, our many companies, some of which you have heard of, pay taxes. But the Knights Templar story cannot overshadow today's Ceremony of Peace. We see a bright future for the world; we already have donated five hundred million dollars to the MFP. Given today's events, the Knights Templar is pledging another two billion dollars to the MFP. Thank you."

As the baroness stepped back from the podium, Ghassan Kassem quickly grabbed her hand and pulled her back. Leaning into the microphone, he announced, "Baroness Collins is far too modest. I have heard the story of how today came about. The truth is, we would not be here without her and the Knights Templar's significant involvement, which includes locating the Ten Commandments." He dropped her hand and started clapping, inducing the audience to join in. Pope John walked up to her, applauding and confirming to the world her significant contribution to today's peace. She repeatedly mouthed, "Thank you," clasping her hands together and touching her chest.

Just as Ghassan Kassem was about to address the audience, he slipped his written speech back into his suit jacket and smiled. "I've been dreaming for a lifetime that peace would happen. It is amazing that even those most potentially unattainable dreams can come true, especially when you least expect it."

Kassem stopped speaking for a moment, then with misty eyes, he whispered, "Peace," then said it again louder. He continued in a strong voice, "There was so much negative history over the years that prevented today from happening sooner. For too long, the Jewish and Palestinian people were both locked in a standoff, disliking and mistrusting each other, engaged in circular violence. No one could budge or see what good would come if both sides made a leap of faith. But finally, it has happened and brought us together."

Kassem's smile turned to a frown. "Even today, a suicide bomber killed dozens outside the walls of this Old City. May Allah have mercy on all their souls. An hour ago, my longtime friend from America, Norman Richards, the hero who saved President Tate a few years ago, was brutally murdered right in front of me. And then thirty minutes ago, my grandson was arrested for trying to disrupt this wonderful ceremony. But somehow, I am here. We are here. This day of peace was meant to be. As an old man, I'll tell you this: please everyone, never stop believing and dreaming and working to assure that this peace lasts until the end of time. This dreamer quotes one of history's great poets: this world will be a better place if everyone can just… give peace a chance."

After vigorous applause, he continued, "I am also pleased and honored to announce that I have been named Chairman of the MFP. Starting tomorrow, I will form an international advisory board of political and civic leaders, businessmen, and others to both raise funds for the MFP and to assure that all funds are put to the best possible use. In closing, shalom and salaam to everyone here, in Israel, in Palestine, and across the globe."

Kassem walked back to his chair, but the resounding cheers didn't stop until the baroness coaxed him back to the podium to thank the crowd.

Chief Rabbi Schteinhardt stepped up next. "Ladies and Gentlemen, this portion of the Ceremony of Peace has concluded. We ask that you please proceed to the Mughrabi Bridge walkway on your right, up to the Temple Mount. For those of you who will not fit inside the Dome of the Rock, large, high-definition video screens with a speaker system will assure that everyone has a clear view of the Ten Commandments being reunited with the Ark of the Covenant. To commemorate this solemn event, we ask that starting now and through the conclusion of today's service, you observe silent meditation. And please, no photography."

The Chief Rabbi, the Grand Mufti, and the Pope led the processional down an aisle leading off the platform. Directly behind them, Klein, Baroness Collins, Beer, and Galit walked together followed by Zamir, Barghouti, and Tamimi, and then in no particular order, the world's top political and civic leaders. They entered the Mughrabi Bridge, a public walkway leading directly from the Dung Gate security station up to the Temple Mount. In eighteen days, the Israelis and Waqf had built an insert into the bridge that led from the Western Wall Plaza in order to provide speedy access for the procession up to Haram al-Sharif.

In silence, the procession quickly moved onto the Temple Mount with the Al-Aqsa Mosque a stone's throw away on the thirty-six-acre, Muslim-controlled platform. Turning left, the participants walked down a perfectly manicured marble-tiled plaza, lined with five-story-tall cypress trees. They continued up an easy flight of wide steps and through a twenty-five-foot-tall, quadruple-columned arched "scale," so named because on Islam's Judgment Day, the souls of the dead hang from them to be tried.

The Dome of the Rock stood in front of them with its intricately blue-tiled, impressively beautiful golden dome, gleaming in the cloudless azure-blue sky.

The most select group of world and religious leaders were allowed down to the small circular bottom level surrounding the Foundation Stone. About another 200 leaders of UN countries stood in the Dome's plaza level, looking down on the rock. Two remote-controlled television cameras were mounted on each level, filming live footage for the rest of the guests and the estimated 3.5 billion worldwide television viewing audience.

Prime Minister Zamir and President Barghouti stood on opposite sides of a red velvet curtain. They pulled it open, displaying the Ark of the Covenant sitting on the Foundation Stone for the first time in modern history. Everyone stared at the gold-covered, ornately designed box, which was completely consistent with its description in Exodus 25:10. Two golden winged angels, the Cherubim, sat on the lid facing each other, their wings nearly touching. Acacia wooden poles covered in gold were attached to each side of the Ark.

Klein, Cardinal Marino, Commandant Pagano, and Ghassan Kassem lined up next to the Ark. In unison they bent over, grabbed its poles, and in slow, measured steps, led by Chief Rabbi Schteinhardt, the Grand Mufti, and Pope John, they carried it to a pre-marked flat portion of the Foundation Stone.

The Rabbi stood over the Ark and recited a prayer in Hebrew. Klein and Beer lifted the lid off the Ark and placed it to the side as

Galit, Beer, and the baroness walked onto the rock together. Galit carried the polished mahogany box containing the Ten Commandments and placed it next to the Ark.

Standing behind the Ark, the Chief Rabbi reached for the hands of the Pope and the Grand Mufti. Together they recited a prayer written by Martin Buber: "'The purpose of creation is not division, nor separation. The purpose of the human race is not a struggle to the death between classes, between nations. Humanity is meant to become a single body. Our purpose is the great upbuilding of unity and peace. And when all nations are bound together in one association living in justice and righteousness, they atone for each other.' This day and the days that follow will be known as the Age of Enlightenment."

Following the prayer, Secretary General Bassiouni and representatives of the United Nations Security Council walked onto the Foundation Stone. Holding a candle in a silver bowl, the Pope knelt, placing the candle in front of the Ark. Rising to his feet, he announced, "This is the light of peace. From this day forward, at sunrise, a fresh candle shall be lit here to symbolize the dawn of a new day of peace, for every day will have to stand on its own."

The Grand Mufti stepped forward and announced the Muslim Prayer for Peace, based on the Koran, 49:13, 8:61. "In the name of Allah, the beneficent, the merciful. Praise be to the Lord of the Universe who has created us and made us into tribes and nations, that we may know each other, not that we may despise each other. If the enemy incline towards peace, do thou also incline towards peace, and trust in God, for the Lord is the one that heareth and knoweth all things. And the servants of God, most gracious are those who walk on the Earth in humility, and when we address them, we say, 'Peace.'"

Together, the UN Security Council leaders read, "Grant peace to the world: goodness and blessing, grace, love, and compassion to all peoples. Bless us, our creator, united as one in the light of your countenance. By that light, Our God, You gave us a guide to life:

the love of kindness, righteousness, blessing, compassion, life, and peace. May You bless all people at every season and at all times with Your gift of peace."

Chief Rabbi Schteinhardt then said, "May God bless and protect us all."

Pope John added, "May God's countenance shine upon you and grant you kindness."

The Grand Mufti concluded, "May God's countenance be lifted toward you and grant you peace."

The Chief Rabbi announced, "I now introduce General Chaim Klein, who found the Ark of the Holy Covenant, as well as the Ten Commandments. He will reunite them."

Klein took a deep breath, stepped forward, and walked onto the Foundation Stone. He looked down into the Ark to see Moses's manna pot and Aaron's staff inside it, just as when he'd first found the Ark. He moved two steps to the mahogany box and removed the Ten Commandments. Grasping one tablet in each hand, he balanced them against his chest, then slowly walked the perimeter of the Rock, for all to see these sacred objects. He returned to the Ark, dropped to one knee, and placed the tablets inside. Bowing his head, he whispered, "Please God, forgive my sins and those of all people who celebrate and wish to honor the peace made here this day before you. Allow us all the opportunity to make this dream a reality." He rose, standing erect, his head held high.

The Chief Rabbi, the Pope, and the Grand Mufti approached the Ark. The Grand Mufti turned to Klein with his hand outstretched. He said softly, but loud enough for the microphones to pick up, "This ring belonged to the prophet Mohammad."

"I understand," Klein said as he placed the ring into the Ark.

Pope John reached into his vestment, retrieved a small dark blue velvet bag, and removed the small white goblet with a blue Star of David painted on it. He nodded to Baroness Collins, then held it out so the cameras would zoom in on it before giving it to Klein. He softly said, "Chaim, when you found the Ark, I have to believe this was in there for a reason."

Klein nodded and replied, "I know you are right, Your Holiness."

The Pope turned, knelt, and placed the cup of Jesus back in the Ark.

Klein, the Chief Rabbi, the Pope, and the Grand Mufti then lifted the gleaming lid and carefully placed it on top of the Ark. Intense yellow and blue electrical sparks shot between the cherubim. Everyone was in wonder as the temperature of the interior of the Dome of the Rock dropped twenty degrees and a powerful whooshing wind materialized, enveloping the building. No one present except Klein had any reason to expect the Ark would come alive. But those present and watching on television were stunned in awe to see the presence of God.

After several minutes to allow everyone personal reflection, with great emotion, the three religious leaders stood before the Ark. In one unified voice, they recited Ecclesiastes 3:

> *"There is a time for everything, and a season for every activity*
> *under the heavens.*
> *a time to be born and a time to die,*
> *a time to plant and a time to uproot,*
> *a time to kill and a time to heal,*
> *a time to tear down and a time to build,*
> *a time to weep and a time to laugh,*
> *a time to mourn and a time to dance,*
> *a time to search and a time to give up,*
> *a time to tear and a time to mend,*
> *a time to be silent and a time to speak,*
> *a time to love and a time to hate,*
> *a time for war and a time for peace."*

The other speakers walked off the Foundation Stone, leaving Klein standing alone, lost in thought, oblivious to the fact that the world television audience was focused only on him. He finally looked up and walked over to a nearby crevice in the rock. He pulled his sword from its sheath and raised it high above his head, revealing its full glory with the blade glistening, humming, and singing.

Suddenly, he spun around and in one quick movement, he sliced downwards, thrusting the blade deep into the crevice. He froze in that position for a moment, staring at the blade. As he removed his hands, a thunderclap erupted and a lightning bolt shot through the dome straight into the sword, which began transforming into its former concrete-like state. Klein's eyes remained locked on the sword as he slowly backed away from it and the Ark.

After he moved off the Foundation Stone to Galit's side, she leaned into him. "I can't believe you did that!"

"I can't either. It felt like that's what I was supposed to do. At the same time, I know the sword will remain there for me if I need it, or maybe for anyone else who can pull it out of the rock."

"Well, maybe it won't be needed."

Klein turned his head and looked at Galit, then asked her, "You don't think that just because of what's happened here today, and with all of these speeches and prayers, that we're going to wake up tomorrow and there's going to be world peace? Do you believe, for instance, that ISIS or Hezbollah will just lay down their arms?"

"No, of course not, but today is a start. And a great one," she replied.

"That it is. And *great* is an understatement. But somehow I think the battle against the Sons of Darkness might just be getting started."

AUTHOR'S NOTE

The conflict between the Jewish and Arab peoples dates back to biblical times. In the eleventh century, the Crusades, instigated by the Catholic Church and some of the European kings, resulted in an East versus West chasm, with violence and political clashes that continue to this day. The early twentieth century gave rise to Islamic fundamentalism when Haj Amin al-Husseini, the Grand Mufti of Jerusalem, instigated riots in Palestine in 1921 that killed forty-seven Jews. By 1944, the Grand Mufti was working in Berlin with the Nazis, trying to get Himmler to create an Arab-Islamic army to help Germany invade Jewish-controlled Palestine. On May 14, 1948, the day the State of Israel was founded, Tel Aviv was bombed by Egypt, and Israel staved off an invasion across all borders shared with Arab countries. Israel was attacked again in 1956, 1967, and 1973. I started learning about Israel's history as a boy, mostly taught by my parents, given that hundreds of our Hungarian Jewish family members were murdered at Auschwitz.

I started studying terrorism immediately following the 1972 Summer Olympics in Munich, where eight members of the Palestinian Black September terrorist organization snuck into the Olympic Village and kidnapped and killed eleven athletes and coaches. By that time, Ilich Ramirez Sanchez, otherwise known as Carlos the Jackal, had become a household name given the astonishing scope of his terrorist acts, which later included his 1975 kidnapping of OPEC

ministers and staff, flying them to Tripoli, and then escaping. Paren-
thetically, Carlos agreed to grant me his first-ever interview after he
was arrested in Sudan and thrown into a Paris prison. Unfortunately,
the Attorney General of France obtained an injunction prohibiting
the interview on the basis of "state secrets."

Carlos was the antagonist in my first novel, *The Last Inauguration*,
which he reviewed in a letter he wrote to me: "I have just finished
reading *The Last Inauguration*, and I must admit that although I am
depicted as a rogue mercenary mass murderer, I did have a few good
laughs seeing myself in the most unseemly situations, some of which
could have happened in real life."

Modern international terrorism began in the 1960s with actions
of the Popular Front for the Liberation of Palestine (PFLP) and the
Palestine Liberation Organization (PLO), controlled by Yasser Arafat
from 1969 until his death. In 1979, the Iranian-Islamic revolution
overthrew the Shah of Iran, leading to the growth of violent Shia
Islam, which surfaced in Afghanistan, Yemen, North Africa, China,
and elsewhere. Four years later, in 1983, Hezbollah was founded, and
it was supported by the governments of Iran and Syria. The terrorists
began the use of suicide bombers and large-scale attacks, including the
bombings of Pan Am Flight 103 and the U.S. Embassy in Beirut, killing 241 Marines. Then came Osama bin Laden and al-Qaeda, which
created the infamous day of tragedy we call 9/11. By the twenty-first
century, ISIS and countless other terrorist groups had surfaced. Today,
al-Qaeda is as strong as it has ever been and ISIS is thriving, even with
its losses in Syria and Iraq.

I have come to learn that Islamist extremists do not speak for the
majority of Muslims worldwide, who I believe are largely peaceful
and reject the notion that every non-Muslim should die. Given my
research, I have come to the conclusion that the West cannot fix the
extremist problem—only other Muslims can.

Indeed, the world is a more dangerous place now than ever before.
Globally, all eyes remain focused on the Middle East as the world's

principal hot spot, as if it could explode at any time. Israel and its people are surrounded by enemies on all borders who are constantly threatening to push the nation into the sea. Still, there is new hope: in 2020, peace treaties were entered into among Israel, the United Arab Emirates, Oman, and Sudan, and now even Saudi Arabia does significant business with Israel. But there is still a long way to go.

With this historical background in mind, I conceived *The Sword of David* as a story of hope. Hope that perhaps, under the most unusual change of circumstances, the world's diverse religions and people could come together and universally accept all people regardless of their beliefs.

Investigating the locales I wrote about while researching and writing this book were fascinating and great fun. I hope that you find *The Sword of David* entertaining, educational, and thought-provoking. What if....?

Although this is a work of fiction, it is known that numerous tunnels and rooms do, in fact, exist under the Temple Mount, although neither the Israeli government nor the Waqf, which controls the Temple Mount, has confirmed what remains hidden from public view. For over 1,000 years, historians have reported that the Knights Templar spent years digging on the Temple Mount until they found something extraordinary, which they brought to the Pope and which made them rich, famous, and powerful. It has long been rumored the Templars found the Ark of the Covenant and/or the Ten Commandments, but there is no known record of what they actually found. But then, practically overnight, the Knights Templar, along with their vast fortune and powerful army, seemed to have virtually vanished forever. Or do they continue to exist?

The St. Mary of Zion Church in Ethiopia is a very real place, where its priests have sworn since the time of King Solomon that Menelik, son of Solomon and the Queen of Sheba, stole the Ark and brought it to Ethiopia, where it has been hidden ever since. The War Scroll, which depicts the Battle of the Sons of Light led by its general against the Sons of Darkness, is an actual Dead Sea Scroll. The locations within Parliament and Westminster Abbey exist as I described them, including the effigy of Sir Bernard Brocas with his sword. And there actually is a library and keeper of Muniments at Westminster Abbey, but the secret room located there really is secret. I once read there is a catacomb under the Palais de Justice in Paris that was built on top of the Knights Templar compound and controlled by the Louvre, but I have never been able to confirm that as fact. With its various historical, religious, and astrological windows and other beautiful artifacts, Chartres Cathedral exists as I described it.

Given the Vatican's vast wealth and inventory of priceless artifacts, it doesn't reveal exactly where they keep certain of their irreplaceable items. But the Chinon Parchment with the Pope's pardon of the Knights Templar is real.

So, if one puts everything above together, who can say where certain incredible historical artifacts might really be located? And what might happen with them? Stay tuned!

ACKNOWLEDGMENTS

Of utmost importance is that *The Sword of David* would not have reached you but for the help provided to me by others. A heartfelt huge thanks to my agent and editor, Tom Miller. Luckily, I ended up being just smart enough to allow Tom's strong will to overcome my strong will on making appropriate editing changes, which led to *The Sword of David* manuscript being "right" and getting published. Thanks also to Dana Isaacson, whom I met through Tom, and who helped me get the book down to its final version. And then Tom found me the perfect publisher, Post Hill Press/Bombardier Books. I am so grateful to David Bernstein and Michael Wilson for taking a chance on me and this novel, and for all of their hard work in getting the book to market. I also thank my longtime friend and publicist David Hahn of Media Connect, who did incredible work making my first novel, *The Last Inauguration,* a success and in setting up a great marketing plan for *The Sword of David.*

Many other people helped me on research matters that make my story as real as possible. My longtime Israeli friend Ron Beer taught me more about behind-the-scenes history of the Temple Mount and Israel than I could ever read up on. Thanks also to some anonymous people at the Western Wall tunnels who showed and told me things about the Temple Mount that the general public doesn't see or know, which were immensely helpful.

Tremendous thanks to the best hostess ever and my longtime friend, Baroness Jill Knight of Collingtree, England. Jill gave me a private tour of the entire Houses of Parliament and Westminster Abbey, showing me rooms, hallways, and locations that the general public never sees, which appear in critical chapters. My dear friend and mentor, Bob Danzig, is no longer with us, but he pushed, pulled, and prodded me for over twenty years in every way possible, and he truly believed in this story. Thanks also to two of my law partners, Laz Schneider and Robert Barron, who were very helpful sources of information on history, Christianity, Islam, and Judaism. Also, while I only met the legendary antiquities dealer Kaider Baidun and his son Alan in the Arab Quarter of Jerusalem for one long afternoon, our conversation about attaining Middle East peace was one of the most inspirational discussions I've ever had; it gave me hope for the future which continues to this day. I am honored that we have now become long-distance pen pal friends.

Finally, and most importantly, my unending love goes to Gayle, Brooke, and Jordan with their long-term, nonstop support and love over the ridiculously long period of time it took for me to complete writing *The Sword of David*. I love the three of you more than anything, and I would be nothing without you.

ABOUT THE AUTHOR

Chuck Lichtman is an expert in Middle East affairs and issues regarding terrorism. He lives in South Florida where he is working on his next novel. He has twice been recognized as "Lawyer of the Year," founded a national voter protection program, and is an avid photographer and pianist. Chuck can be found at chucklichtman.com.